DOUBLE OR DIE

CHARLIE HIGSON

PUFFIN

PUFFIN BOOKS

UK | USA | Canada | Ireland | Australia | India | New Zealand | South Africa
Puffin Books is part of the Penguin Random House group of companies
whose addresses can be found at global.penguinrandomhouse.com.
www.penguin.co.uk   www.puffin.co.uk   www.ladybird.co.uk

Penguin
Random House
UK

First published 2007
This edition published 2018
001

Copyright © Ian Fleming Publications Ltd, 2007
Young Bond and Double or Die are trademarks of Danjaq, LLC, used under licence by Ian Fleming Publications Ltd

The Ian Fleming logo is a trademark owned by the Ian Fleming Estate,
used under licence by Ian Fleming Publications Limited
All rights reserved

The moral right of the author has been asserted

Set in Monotype Bembo by Palimpsest Book Production Limited, Falkirk, Stirlingshire
Printed in Great Britain by Clays Ltd, St Ives plc

British Library Cataloguing in Publication Data
A CIP catalogue record for this book is available from the British Library

ISBN: 978–0–241–36484–0

All correspondence to:
Puffin Books
Penguin Random House Children's
80 Strand, London WC2R 0RL

PUFFIN BOOKS

DOUBLE OR DIE

James Bond is the most famous spy the world has ever known. His life in the shadowy world of the British Secret Services was brilliantly documented in fourteen classic books by Ian Fleming, from *Casino Royale* to *Octopussy*. But until the release of *SilverFin*, we'd only been allowed fragmentary glimpses of James Bond's formative years.

Charlie Higson revealed the real young Bond for the first time in *SilverFin*. Read on to discover the James Bond hero no one had seen before – the boy who became the hero.

Ian Fleming first wrote about James Bond over fifty years ago. He was uniquely placed to chronicle Bond's secret-service career – he was himself involved at a high level in intelligence-gathering operations in the Second World War.

Charlie Higson is a well-known writer of screenplays and adult thriller novels, as well as a performer and co-creator of *The Fast Show*. Both his Young Bond and The Enemy series are global bestsellers.

'This is writing for children of the highest order' – *Spectator*

youngbond.com

Books by Charlie Higson

SILVERFIN
BLOOD FEVER
DOUBLE OR DIE
HURRICANE GOLD
BY ROYAL COMMAND

DANGER SOCIETY: YOUNG BOND DOSSIER

MONSTROSO (POCKET MONEY PUFFINS)

SILVERFIN: THE GRAPHIC NOVEL

THE ENEMY
THE DEAD
THE FEAR

Praise for Young Bond

'Good, gritty and funny . . . Very clever, Bond, very clever indeed' – *Daily Mail*

'Why didn't someone think of this years ago?' – *Time Out*

'Double-oh so good' – *Sunday Times*

'Charlie Higson's Young Bond books get an A★' – *GQ*

'Perfect for fans of the Alex Rider books' – *Evening Standard*

'An instant hit' – *Daily Mirror*

For my dad

Acknowledgements

My thanks to Sandy Balfour and John Halpern for guiding me through the world of cryptic crosswords and helping with clues. And to Simon Chaplin at the Royal College of Surgeons.

Contents

Part Three: SUNDAY

The Hungry Machine

The human brain is a remarkable object. It contains a hundred billion neurons, all talking to each other via tiny electrical sparks, like a never-ending fireworks display inside your skull.

Your brain weighs three pounds. It makes up only one-fiftieth of your body, yet it uses up over a fifth of your blood supply and oxygen.

The brain is a hungry machine. It never shuts down. Even while you are asleep *it* is awake, keeping your lungs breathing, your heart beating, the blood flowing through your veins. Without your brain you can do nothing. It allows you to ride a bike, read a book, laugh at a joke. It can store a whole lifetime of memories.

But it is very fragile.

Alexis Fairburn was painfully aware of this, because there was a pistol pointing at his head, and he knew that if that pistol were fired, all those precious memories, that he had been storing up for the last thirty-two years, would be blasted into oblivion. Then his lungs would fall still. His heart would stop pumping. The blood would freeze in his veins and Alexis Fairburn would cease to be.

The pistol was a six-shot revolver with a short, stubby barrel. Not very accurate at long range, but deadly enough close up. What made it more deadly was its grip, which doubled as a knuckleduster. The fingers of the man holding it were curled through big brass rings. One punch would shatter a man's jaw.

Fairburn knew that this type of gun was called an Apache, after the vicious street thugs who had carried them in Paris at the end of the last century. Their weapons had also carried blades that swung out and could be used like bayonets.

He sometimes thought he knew too much.

And even as he stared at the nasty black hole in the gun's nose he heard a click, followed by a metallic scraping sound, and a four-inch-long, spring-loaded stiletto blade slid out from beneath the barrel and snapped into place.

Sometimes Fairburn wished that he could be happy and stupid, blissfully unaware of everything that was going on in the world around him. Sometimes he wished that, instead of spending half his life expanding his brain and filling it with facts and figures, he had devoted some of that time to his body. In moments like this he wished that he had big muscles and quick reflexes. If only he had learnt how to disarm a man he might now be able to grab his attacker's wrist and wrestle the gun out of his hand, maybe even turn it on him. He had read about such things. He knew in theory that it could be done, but he also knew that it would be useless to try. He was weak and he was timid and he was clumsy.

Now that he thought about it, however, he realized that he wasn't scared.

That was interesting.

He would have assumed that he would be terrified. But, no, all he felt was disappointment. Regret that his remarkable brain was soon to be switched off.

'Don't try to run, or resist in any way,' said the gunman and, for the first time, Fairburn looked at him, rather than at his gun. He was tall and thin and stooped, with a huge, bony head that looked too heavy for his shoulders. His large black eyes were set in deep hollow sockets and the skin was pulled so tight on his head that it resembled a skull.

The gunman was not alone. He had an accomplice, a younger man with a pleasant, unremarkable face. He wouldn't have looked out of place behind the counter in a bank, or scribbling away at a ledger in an office. Fairburn found that it helped to think of him as a clerk rather than as a potential assassin. It made him less threatening.

'You know what will happen if he pulls that trigger?' said the clerk with a hint of menace.

The menace was unnecessary. Fairburn knew exactly what would happen. The hammer of the gun would snap forward and strike the percussion cap at the rear of the bullet casing. This would set off a small explosion which would propel the shell at twenty-five feet per second out of its casing and down the barrel, where a long spiral groove would cause it to spin, so that it would fly straighter. Finally, it would burst out of the gun, not six inches from Fairburn's forehead.

The bullet would be soft-nosed, designed to stop a man. As it hit bone it would flatten and widen like an opening fist and then it would tunnel through his head, sucking out any soft matter as it went.

A bird sang in a tree nearby. Fairburn knew from its song that it was a chaffinch. He glanced up and saw that it was sitting on the branch of a yew tree. It was a British custom to plant yews and cypresses in graveyards. A custom they had adopted from the Romans. It was also a Roman custom to put flowers on a grave.

Fairburn sighed. His brain was full of such a lot of useless information.

'What are you looking at?' said the clerk.

'I'm not looking at anything,' said Fairburn. 'I'm sorry. I was distracted.'

'I would advise you to pay attention.'

'Yes. I do apologize,' said Fairburn. 'But might I ask what exactly it is you want me to do?'

'We would like you to accompany us, Mister Fairburn,' said the gunman.

So they knew his name. This was not a random attack. They must have followed him here. But what did they want?

Fairburn thought hard, casting his mind back over the day. What had happened? Who had he met? What had he said that would cause these two men to be here in the middle of Highgate cemetery, with one holding an Apache to his head?

Up until now it had been a fairly ordinary Saturday. He had followed the same routine that he had been keeping

4

to for the last few weeks. He had driven up to London first thing from Windsor, visited the Reading Room at the British Museum, then had lunch at his favourite restaurant in Fitzrovia, and finally he had come here to the cemetery, where he had been making sketches and jotting down notes for a book he was planning to write on eminent Victorian scientists, several of whom were buried here.

The last thing he had done was to take a rubbing from a headstone with an interesting inscription. He had forgotten to bring any rubbing paper with him and had been forced to use the back of a letter from his friend Ivar Peterson. He still took a childlike delight in rubbing the wax over the paper and watching the writing form. He had just finished and was putting the neatly folded letter back into his coat pocket, when the men had appeared. They had walked briskly up the path, nodded a friendly greeting and the next thing he knew the ugly snout of the pistol was in his face.

Peterson. Of course. This must be to do with him. Or, more precisely, to do with what Peterson had written about in the letter.

This was to do with the Nemesis project.

He realized that he still had the letter in his hand, hidden inside his pocket. Perhaps he could drop it somewhere. It would be some small clue that he had been here, and, if anyone read it, they might be able to help him.

Idiot.

It would be meaningless to anyone else. Unless somehow he could direct the right person here, someone who could understand what it meant.

Good. His mind was working. He squeezed the paper more tightly into the palm of his hand.

'We are going to walk you to your motor car,' said the clerk. 'Calmly and casually, like old friends. Then you will drive my brother and I to our destination. We will advise you of the route along the way. The gun will be trained on you at all times, and if you do not follow our precise instructions, we will not hesitate to shoot you. Another colleague of ours will be following in our own motor car. Is that clear?'

'Perfectly,' said Fairburn, treading on one end of a shoelace and feeling it come undone. 'But I still don't know what you want of me.'

'For now you don't need to know,' said the gunman. 'Just walk.'

Fairburn took a step and then stopped. 'My lace,' he said, looking down at his shoe.

'Tie it,' said the young man.

'Thank you,' said Fairburn. He crouched down and carefully slipped the piece of folded paper up inside the bottom of his trouser leg. If he dropped it now it would be easily spotted, but this way he could delay it until the men were distracted again.

He straightened up.

'All set,' he said, as cheerily as he could manage.

He glanced around at the cemetery, taking a last look and imprinting the images on his brain. He looked at the statues and crosses, and at the gravestones, standing beneath the trees, many overgrown and neglected. Then he took his first step, brushing against some low winter foliage, and, as he did so, he shook his leg and felt the scrap of paper fall out. He didn't look down to check, but he prayed that it would be lying hidden by the side of the path.

It wasn't much to go on, but it was all he had. All the hope in the world.

His heartbeat skipped and he felt a tingling in his scalp.

He had lived a dull and secluded life with very little danger and nothing to disrupt the even flow of his days. He was experiencing a new emotion now, excitement. In a way, he was even enjoying it.

He still had his brain. He must use it somehow to escape from his predicament. He was confident that he would think of something. There wasn't a problem in the world that couldn't be solved with brainpower.

You just had to make sure that you kept your brain inside your head.

Part One: FRIDAY

Thoughts in a Bamford and Martin Tourer

James Bond was sitting in the passenger seat of his Bamford and Martin tourer wrapped in a heavy winter overcoat, his face masked with goggles and scarf.

His friend Perry Mandeville, similarly dressed, was at the wheel. It was too cramped and awkward to drive with the rain cover up, so they were completely exposed to the grisly December weather. They didn't care, though, they were on the open road and, despite the icy wind buffeting them, they felt reckless and free.

The car had belonged to James's uncle who had left it to James when he died. James kept it secretly at the school. Perry had always dreamt of taking it out on the road but James had never let him before today.

This was an emergency.

Perry drove well, but fast, and James had to constantly remind him to keep his speed down. There was very little traffic on the road, but they still had to be careful. They didn't want to risk being stopped by a police patrol or, worse still, crashing into a ditch.

Perry was older than James, but not yet seventeen, which was the minimum driving age. If anyone found out what they were up to they would at best be beaten soundly and chucked out of Eton, and at worst thrown into jail.

But James wasn't thinking about any of that. He was filled with a burning excitement. He needed the thrill of danger. It was only on an adventure like this that he came alive. His day-to-day life at school felt grey and dull, but now the boredom had lifted and all his senses were heightened.

That didn't mean that he could be careless, however. The goggles, hats and scarves were as much worn as disguises as to shield the two boys from the cutting wind.

They were speeding away from Eton towards Cambridge having left a pack of lies behind them. A pack of lies that could soon be snapping at their heels if they didn't watch out.

James thought back to when this had all begun.

It had been the end of the summer holidays, a few days before James was due to return to Eton. He had been helping out at the Duck Inn in Pett Bottom, the village where he lived with his Aunt Charmian. He earnt a bit of pocket money there, washing barrels and stacking crates of empty bottles behind the pub. He was rolling an empty barrel across the ground when he looked up from his work and saw a black car driving through the fields.

He straightened up and followed its progress.

There was a chill in the air and he shivered. The summer was nearly over.

The car slowed as it approached the pub and stopped. The window was wound down. James recognized the familiar face of his classical tutor, Mr Merriot, the man responsible for his education at Eton. With him was Claude Elliot, the new Head Master. They both looked rather serious.

'Climb aboard,' said Merriot, and he tried to force a friendly smile on to his face, his unlit pipe wobbling between his teeth.

James got in.

'Do you know why we are here, James?' asked Merriot kindly.

James nodded. 'I've been expecting a visit since I talked to you at Dover, sir.'

Earlier in the summer holidays James had gone on a school trip to Sardinia with two masters, one of whom had turned out to be a criminal. Both masters had been killed and James himself had nearly lost his life. When he came home, James had been met by Mr Merriot straight off the boat, and had told him everything that had happened. At the time Merriot had asked James not to breathe a word about it to anyone else. Now it looked like the Head Master had come to make sure that the secrets would remain buried.

James sat in the back of the car between the two men feeling hot and stuffy.

'We have been talking about what happened in Sardinia,' said the Head, a tall man with round, wire-framed spectacles whose hair was receding at the temples, leaving only a thin strip down the centre of his high forehead. 'And we think it is for the best if you never speak about these things,' he went on, 'not at home, not at school, not anywhere. We would prefer it not to get out that one of our masters was a bad sort.'

James sat in silence. He just wanted to forget about the whole episode and be a normal schoolboy again.

'We shall stick to the story that the locals have given out,' said Mr Merriot.

'What story is that, sir?' said James.

Merriot sucked his pipe. 'The official line is that there was an accident,' he said. 'A dam burst and both Mister Cooper-ffrench and Mister Haight died in the flood that followed.' He paused before adding, 'They both died a hero's death.'

James smiled a brief, bitter smile before nodding.

'The truth must never come to light,' said the Head.

'I understand,' said James, although he thought it was terribly unfair that an evil man should be remembered as a hero. But, if it meant that he wouldn't have to deal with endless questions from curious boys, and newspaper reporters, and people pointing at him in the street, he would go along with the lie.

'I won't tell anyone,' he said.

'This is the end of it, then,' said the Head, his face brightening. 'None of us will ever talk of this again. And, James?'

'Yes, sir?'

'From now on you must live a quiet life. Will you promise me that you will stay out of danger? Keep away from excitement and adventure.'

'Yes, sir.'

'Good.' The Head slapped him heartily on the knee. 'Thank you, James, I hope that it will be some time before our paths cross again.'

'Yes, sir, so do I, sir,' said James.

'Now. Perhaps we could get you an ice cream, or something?'

'That's all right, thank you, sir,' said James. 'I need to get back.'

'Of course, of course . . .'

James laughed when he remembered that day. He'd stayed out of danger all right. He'd avoided excitement of any kind as the long weeks of the Michaelmas half had played themselves out. The days had plodded past, growing shorter and darker, and as winter crept in, it brought with it fog and rain and chilly air. James had struggled through endless dreary Latin lessons, and science demonstrations, and maths tests. The only thing he'd had to look forward to was Christmas with its promise of roast goose and carol singers and presents underneath the tree.

He'd managed to be a model, if unenthusiastic, pupil all that time, and the effort had nearly killed him, because, despite what he had said to the Head Master, he knew that he could never keep out of trouble.

And now, at last, he was cut loose. Now he was doing what he loved best. He was facing danger. He was taking risks.

He was alive again.

Just four days ago, everything had changed and his life at Eton had once more been turned upside down.

He had been in his room at Eton playing cards with two friends, Teddy Mackereth and Steven Costock-Ellis, and his Chinese messmate, Tommy Chong.

15

Tommy, as usual, was winning. He was passionate about cards and claimed that the Chinese were the best card players in the world. 'After all,' he was fond of saying, 'the Chinese invented playing cards.'

It was very cold in the room. The boys were each allowed only one big lump of coal every other day, and today it was James's turn to have a fire. The tiny fireplace didn't throw out much heat and the boys were wearing fingerless gloves.

Outside the room a group of boys were playing a very noisy game of passage football and they could hear their thumps and shouts as they charged up and down the corridor using someone's hat as a 'ball'.

It was a new year at Eton, and James and his friends were no longer among the youngest boys in the school. They felt quite grown-up and couldn't quite believe that they had once been as scared and helpless-looking as the timid fourth formers they saw wandering about the place.

There were changes in the House. Last year's senior boys had moved on and a new group had taken their place. This new bunch seemed keen to push their weight around and show the younger boys who was in charge. They had carried out a record number of beatings and had not made themselves at all popular.

But James and his friends felt safe now, tucked away in this little room, playing cards and chatting.

'I'll trounce you one day, Tommy,' said James, throwing his cards down on to the tabletop and looking across at Tommy, who was eagerly scooping up a small pile of coins.

'You must be cheating,' said Teddy Mackereth sourly.

'No,' said Tommy. 'I'm just better than you saps.'

'One more hand?' said Costock-Ellis. 'You've got to give us the chance to win some of our money back.'

'That's fine with me,' said Tommy.

'Give it up, James,' said a fifth boy, who was lounging on James's bed filling in a crossword puzzle from that morning's *Times* newspaper. He was James's other messmate, Pritpal Nandra, the son of an Indian maharaja.

'I'm not the type to give up,' said James. 'I'll keep chipping away at him until something gives.'

'I fear you will be an old man with a long white beard before that happens,' said Pritpal.

'You want to join us, Prit?' asked Tommy, shuffling the cards expertly.

'No, thank you. I will stick to my crossword,' said Pritpal.

'I don't know what you see in those things,' said James.

'It is a challenge,' said Pritpal. 'I am pitting my wits against the person who set the puzzle. But I am afraid I am stuck.'

'Here. Let me have a look.' Costock-Ellis snatched the newspaper from Pritpal and peered at it, wrinkling his nose.

'This doesn't make any sense at all,' he said.

'You're all useless,' said James, reaching across and plucking the paper from the other boy's hands. 'I'll show you how it's done.'

He looked at the crossword. Pritpal had neatly filled in half the answers in the grid and crossed out the clues he had completed.

'Three down,' said James. '"Top-secret monkey" – four

letters, first letter "A".' He stopped and frowned. 'I don't even understand the clue,' he said. 'So how am I supposed to work out the answer? Anyone here heard of a top-secret monkey?'

'King Kong,' said Tommy. 'He was a secret until they found him on Skull Island.'

'It is a cryptic crossword,' said Pritpal, taking the paper back. 'It is like a code that you have to unlock. A secret message.'

'A top-secret message,' said Teddy Mackereth.

'Well, it's beyond me,' said James. 'I can't do anything more complicated than "Small flying mammal, three letters". Second letter "A", third letter "T".'

'Rat,' said Tommy, dealing a fresh hand.

'A rat can't fly,' said James.

'It can if you throw it out of the window,' said Tommy and he laughed.

'Ha, ha, very funny,' said James.

'Or a cat,' said Teddy. 'If it was chasing the rat.'

'I'll throw you lot out of the window if you don't stop making feeble jokes,' said James, picking up his cards. He had always been a good card player, but at Eton his skills had improved enormously, mostly due to the experience he'd gained playing, and regularly losing, against Tommy.

So far this evening they'd played pontoon, poker, Black Maria, a Chinese game called Big Two and another Chinese game that Tommy had given a rude English name to.

They were currently playing rummy, at sixpence a hand.

'Rummy is stolen from the Chinese game, mah-jong, you know?' said Tommy, leaning back in his chair.

'No, it's not,' snorted Costock-Ellis. 'What proof do you have?'

'Don't bother arguing,' said James. 'According to Tommy, the Chinese invented everything.'

'It's true,' said Tommy. 'We have always been hundreds of years ahead of you Westerners. Paper money, gunpowder, playing cards, kites. You name it. We invented it.'

'Cricket,' said Teddy Mackereth.

'Nobody but the English could have invented a game as strange and as pointless as cricket,' said Tommy.

'Well, if this game's Chinese, no wonder you keep winning,' said Teddy Mackereth, dropping his cards on to the little square table. 'Let's play something else.'

'OK,' said Tommy, collecting up the pack. 'I'll show you a casino game. It's like pontoon. It's called baccarat, or chemin de fer.'

'That's French for railway,' said Pritpal, without looking up from his newspaper.

'Go back to your crossword,' said Costock-Ellis.

'Are you in, Steven?' asked Tommy.

'Afraid not,' said Costock-Ellis. 'You've cleaned me out. I'll tell you what, why don't we share all the money out and start again?'

'That sounds like communist talk,' said Tommy.

'I bet you don't even know what a communist is,' said Costock-Ellis.

'I've been reading up on the Russian Revolution,' said

Tommy. 'I know all about how the peasants were poor and badly treated by the tsar so they rose up and threw him out. No more bosses! Everybody equal! Share out all the money so that there are no more poor people and no more rich people.' Tommy laughed. 'It could never happen in China.'

As soon as Tommy stopped speaking the noise from the game of passage football also stopped and there was an ominous silence outside, which could only mean one thing.

'Codrose!' said James and the boys snapped into action.

Codrose was their House Master, and while he couldn't stop the boys from playing cards, he didn't allow gambling.

Teddy had made a false top for the table in the Woodwork School. It fitted neatly over the real top and had just enough depth beneath it to hide all the cards and money.

In a second the top was in place and the boys assumed expressions of sweet innocence.

Presently there was a knock and a familiar face appeared round the door.

Cecil Codrose was one of the most unpopular House Masters at Eton. He was small and tough with a pale face and a wiry beard. His suspicious, flinty eyes were ringed with blue skin and his heavy brows had a permanent frown.

He peered at each boy in turn and then moved slowly into the room.

James realized there was someone with him. It was the Head Master, Claude Elliot.

Pritpal slithered off the bed as the other boys jumped to their feet and they all stood awkwardly in the small room.

Codrose looked slowly from Teddy Mackereth to Costock–Ellis to Tommy.

'You may leave us,' he said and the three of them gratefully hurried out, mumbling their goodbyes and nodding to the two men.

James wasn't sure whether to stay or go. He was in an awkward position as this was his room, and although he was curious to know what this was all about, he also wanted to get away. He shuffled towards the door.

'Stay please, Bond,' said the Head. 'This concerns you.'

'Oh,' said James and he stood there, feeling uncomfortable.

'A letter has arrived for you, Nandra,' said Codrose, his voice dry and dusty.

'I see, sir,' said Pritpal, who was plainly confused.

Codrose held out a slim white envelope towards Pritpal. 'We took the liberty of opening it,' he said, 'for reasons that will soon become apparent.'

Pritpal studied the envelope. His name was on it, but there was no stamp or address.

'It arrived this afternoon, inside a letter addressed to myself,' the Head Master explained. 'It is from Alexis Fairburn.'

'Oh,' said Pritpal, taken aback.

'You may have noticed,' said the Head Master, 'that Mister Fairburn has not been at the school for the past few weeks.'

'I know he wasn't there for my last two mathematics classes,' said Pritpal. 'Bloody Bill took us instead.' Pritpal stopped suddenly and looked panicked. 'I mean Mister Marsden, sir. I'm sorry.'

Codrose cleared his throat but said nothing.

'Also, sir,' said Pritpal, trying to fill the lengthening silence, 'he wasn't at our last Crossword Society meeting. I gather he has not been well.'

The Head Master sniffed and looked intently at a picture of the king on James's wall. 'That is the version of events that we have been encouraging,' he said, 'but the truth of the matter is that Mister Fairburn has left the school.'

'Oh,' said Pritpal with a puzzled expression on his round face.

'You run the Crossword Society, do you not?' said the Head Master.

'Yes, sir, I do, sir,' said Pritpal. 'Though, really, it is Mister Fairburn who's in charge, without him we would never have . . .'

'It is in your capacity as head of the Crossword Society that Fairburn has written to you,' the Head Master interrupted.

'Really, sir?' said Pritpal.

'Yes. In his letter to me he gave instructions that I should pass this note on to you.'

'I'm not sure I understand, sir,' said Pritpal.

'I'm not sure *we* do either,' said the Head Master and he smiled, trying to put Pritpal at ease. 'The letter we received today is the first we have heard from Mister Fairburn since he left,' he said. 'It is a letter of resignation.

22

It is highly irregular and most awkward. He has not given us any notice and left us short-staffed. He claims that he is unable to continue at the school and has been offered a better post in London, but his letter to me is brief and rather vague. We were hoping that his letter to you might throw some light on the matter, which is why we opened it, but it has left us mystified.'

'We should like you to read it aloud,' said Codrose. 'And then tell us if it has any meaning for you?'

Stevens and Oliver

Pritpal took the letter out from its envelope and unfolded it. 'There's no return address, or anything,' he said. 'It just starts *Alexis Fairburn, London*, and the date . . . *seventh of December, 1934* . . . Oh, he's put that wrong. It's not yet *1934*.'

'The man always was absent-minded,' said Codrose dismissively. 'His head was permanently in the clouds. He was always forgetting what day it was.' Codrose said this in such a way as to imply that this was not something he himself would ever do in a million years.

'Carry on,' said the Head Master.

Pritpal swallowed and began to read. '*My dear Pritpal,*' he said, his voice shaky and self-conscious, '*it's not every Tuesday one comes across seven boys with a love of crosswords. Don't feel down! The mighty Crossword Society will easily solve puzzles by themselves, now that I am gone. As I am sure the almighty Elliot will have explained . . .*' Pritpal stopped and blinked at the Head Master, embarrassed.

'Go on,' said the Head Master.

'*As I'm sure Mister Elliot will have explained,*' said Pritpal, '*I have had to leave Eton. In fact I am leaving the country. My next crossword will be my last, as I will be gone before my next deadline.'*

'What does he mean by that?' said Codrose.

'Mister Fairburn sets puzzles for *The Times*, sir.'

'Does he now?' said Codrose. 'Never knew that. Don't do them myself. Too busy.'

'Shall I carry on?' said Pritpal.

'If you would,' said the Head.

'*Please pass on my apologies to the other six members of the Crossword Society, Felix Dunkeswell, Percy Odcombe, Luc Oliver, Stephen Devere, little Speccy Stevens and, of course, Iain Cummings.'* Pritpal paused and frowned, then carried on reading. '*I will leave behind many happy memories. As you know, I was a boy at Eton myself. How well I remember scoring the winning try in the Field Game against the Duffers, and coxing the* Callisto *in the parade of boats on June the Fourth. Yes, there are many things I shall miss about the old place. Apart from you lads in the Crossword Society (of course) I will miss Latin lessons most of all. I love all those old stories of ancient Rome, like Nero's great love affair with Cleopatra. You should try to visit the great necropolis in Porta Alta one day and see the marvellous statue of him gazing across towards her obelisks.'*

'Obelisks!' snorted Codrose. 'The man is rambling. He always was an odd sort.'

'Read on,' said the Head, ignoring Codrose's outburst.

'*Eton is a place like no other,*' said Pritpal, '*with its own marvellous traditions. I shall really miss watching the Wall Game, but perhaps every time I read the famous poem, "The Wall Game", by David Balfour, it will all come back to me, as vividly as if I was still standing there . . .*

Come on, we cry, ignore the pain!
Tingling with excitement in the rain,
Knuckling, pressing, panting, now they're stuck,
Nigh twenty minutes in a heaving ruck,
All muddy in a mighty scuffle,
Mishaps galore, but what a battle!
Atop the wall we curse the other side,
Villains! They have won the ball,
A shout goes up as some brave chap
Eludes the pack and throws for goal.

In closing, then, whatever you do, don't give up on crosswords. I know not everyone enjoys crosswords like you do. For instance, your messmate, the runner –' Pritpal stopped and looked at James. 'I suppose he means you,' he said.

'Did you talk to Mister Fairburn about Bond, then?' asked the Head.

'I suppose I must have mentioned him,' said Pritpal, 'but I don't ever remember saying that James didn't like crosswords.'

'We've never really talked about them before tonight,' said James.

'Read to the end, please,' said the Head.

'Erm . . . *For instance, your messmate, the runner,'* said Pritpal, *'must accept what he is and begin to mature. Yours, AF.'*

Pritpal looked up from the letter and for a minute there was silence in the small, cramped room.

'What an odd letter,' said Pritpal after a while.

'Decidedly,' said the Head Master.

'I fear the man may be unwell,' sniffed Codrose.

'It would explain his actions,' said the Head Master. 'We must assume he has had some sort of brainstorm.'

'He *is* the type,' said Codrose darkly, taking the letter back off Pritpal. 'And with that in mind, I think it best if I keep this.' He looked at the handwriting, mouthing the words and raising one eyebrow quizzically. 'Most peculiar,' he said after a pause, and put the letter in his pocket.

'I would ask you boys not to speak to anyone about this,' said the Head Master, throwing a quick look at James.

'Of course,' said Pritpal.

'Does anything in the letter hold any particular significance for you?' asked Codrose.

'Not that I can think of at the moment, sir,' said Pritpal. 'There's a lot about sport. I've never been much of a sportsman myself.'

'Nor is Fairburn,' said Codrose.

'If you think of anything,' said the Head, 'you must come and tell me. In the meantime – goodnight to you both.'

'What did you make of that, then?' asked Pritpal when the two men had gone.

'I'd certainly agree,' said James, 'that it was a very odd letter. Do you think he's lost his marbles like Codrose said?'

'I do not know,' said Pritpal, sitting on James's bed. 'The more I think about it, the less sure I am.'

'Oh, come on,' said James. 'You said yourself when you

finished that it was odd. I'll tell you what it reminded me of.'

'What?' said Pritpal.

'That crossword you were doing.'

'That's it,' said Pritpal, jumping up and pacing the room. 'I knew there was something. You are absolutely right.'

'When I looked at your crossword puzzle earlier,' said James, 'the sentences all appeared to be normal, but they were strange, slightly nonsensical. Making sense but not making sense, all at the same time. That's exactly what the letter was like. Everything's wrong about it. Even the date.'

'I agree,' said Pritpal. 'And that was only the smallest of the errors.'

'What was the biggest?' said James.

'The names of the boys from the Crossword Society,' said Pritpal. 'Codrose and the Head weren't to know. In fact I am probably the only person who *would* know. We don't keep a membership list, after all.'

'Know what?' said James.

'About Luc Oliver and Speccy Stevens.'

'What about them?' said James, who was growing more and more impatient.

'Neither of them is *in* the Crossword Society,' said Pritpal. 'In fact I would bet you good money that they do not even exist.'

James stared at Pritpal.

'Go on,' he said. 'This is getting interesting.'

'I believe the letter is a cipher,' said Pritpal.

'What's a cipher?'

'A coded message,' said Pritpal. 'A puzzle. To an outsider it might appear quite straightforward, but anyone here at Eton would pretty soon spot that it was full of mistakes. Though I think they are not mistakes at all. I think they are clues.'

'It's a pretty elaborate puzzle,' said James. 'A whole letter.'

'It is exactly the sort of thing Fairburn would do,' said Pritpal. 'He always did have a somewhat odd sense of humour.'

'Would he go so far as to pretend to quit?' said James. 'Because if it *is* a joke, then he hasn't let the Head Master or Codrose in on it.'

'He doesn't play by the same rules as everyone else,' said Pritpal. 'I wouldn't put it past him to write this letter as a sort of test. Maybe he even set it for us boys to solve. "The mystery of the disappearing master".'

James smiled. 'Do you really think he'd do a thing like that?' he said.

'I do.' Pritpal nodded. 'As I said, Fairburn is a very eccentric man. He loves codes and puzzles and mathematical problems.'

'All right,' said James, crossing his legs and pulling one ankle up on to his thigh. 'Supposing it *is* some sort of a puzzle, where do we start?'

'With Luc Oliver and Speccy Stevens, obviously,' said Pritpal. 'They are the most glaring false notes, the first thing I would be expected to notice. So we must first work out what they might mean.'

James stared at him blankly. 'How?' he said.

29

Pritpal grinned at James, his eyes gleaming with excitement.

'Sit down,' he said. 'And I will show you . . .'

Pritpal settled himself at the table and wrote out the two names on a piece of paper.

'They stand out in the letter like a pair of sore thumbs,' he said. 'Fairburn must have known they would be the first thing I spotted. They are the most obvious mistakes, so perhaps they are the most obvious type of clue.'

'And what's that?' said James. 'You must remember I'm new to this.'

'The easiest and most obvious clues are anagrams,' said Pritpal. 'You know what an anagram is, I presume.'

'I'm not a complete idiot,' said James. 'An anagram is when you muddle letters up and change their order to make a new meaning. Like "Same Hatred" is an anagram of Head Master.'

'Or "Death Smear",' said Pritpal and the two of them laughed.

James stared at the letters in front of him.

LUC OLIVER SPECCY STEVENS

He tried jumbling them up and rearranging them in his head, but he was getting nowhere. The possibilities seemed endless.

'Do you jab demons?' said Pritpal after a while.

'What are you talking about?' said James.

'It's an anagram of James Bond.'

'Very clever,' said James, 'but it's not helping solve this puzzle. I haven't a clue where to start.'

'Aha!' said Pritpal. 'You've got it.'

'I have?'

'Yes. The first thing you must do with any code, or puzzle, is establish a context,' said Pritpal.

'You're going to have to explain,' said James. 'Maybe I *am* a complete idiot after all.'

'Well, let's say, for example, I gave you the letters P–R–O–U–E–E,' said Pritpal. 'And said they were an anagram. You'd fiddle around, trying to rearrange them, and eventually, after a lot of head scratching, you would probably stumble across the answer.'

'Don't count on it,' said James, trying to make a word from the letters.

'But supposing I told you it was an anagram of a continent,' Pritpal went on. 'Then you'd get it straight away.'

'Europe,' said James.

'Exactly,' said Pritpal. 'You have a context, you see? As another example, let us imagine that there is a war on, and our army intercepts a secret coded message from the enemy. They know it is from an airfield, so they assume that the message will be about aeroplanes and suchlike. There will be technical terms in it – makes of plane, numbers of planes, weather conditions, and words like *fog* or *cloud*. The code breakers will make up a list of likely words and then look through the message for coded words that might match the words they are looking for. And they will look for patterns and repeated words, until they find one word that fits. And once you solve one word, the rest will easily follow. You see, when you know what a message is about, you know where to start looking for clues. So what is this message from Fairburn about?'

'We don't know yet,' said James.

'Yes we do,' said Pritpal. 'It is a cipher, a puzzle. So what are we looking for?'

'We're looking for clues,' said James, feeling like he was saying something stupid.

'Exactly.' Pritpal grinned at him. 'So look at the letters again and tell me if you can see any clues.'

James looked again, but still saw nothing.

LUC OLIVER SPECCY STEVENS

'Look at the name "Luc",' said Pritpal. 'Does it not seem odd to you? Why did Fairburn choose that particular name? Those particular letters?'

'I don't know,' said James crossly. 'What am I looking for?'

'A clue.' Pritpal jabbed his finger down on the paper. 'Look!'

'Where . . .?' said James, and then he saw it and laughed. 'Rearrange "Luc" and you get "clu". Add an "e" and you have your "clue". It's obvious once you see it,' he said.

'And what do you do with a clue?' said Pritpal.

'You try to solve it,' said James and even as he said it he saw the word *solve*, using the 'S' from 'Speccy' and some of the letters from 'Oliver'.

He showed Pritpal who nodded enthusiastically.

'Already we have two possible words,' he said, crossing

clues".'

James looked at what they were left with.

I R P C C Y S T E V E N

'We have fewer letters,' said Pritpal, tapping his teeth with his pencil. 'But it is harder; there are no obvious words to go with the two we already have.'

'What about "seven"?' said James. '"Solve seven clues"?'

'You are learning fast,' said Pritpal. 'That feels right. But what would it leave us with?'

'I-R-P-C-C-Y-T,' said James and he sighed. 'We need to think again. There's no word you can make out of those letters.'

'You don't think so?' said Pritpal, scribbling something down on the paper. He turned it round so that James could read it.

SOLVE SEVEN CRYPTIC CLUES

James whistled and sat back in his chair. 'That's surely no coincidence,' he said. 'It *is* a puzzle.' He grinned at Pritpal. 'One clue solved and six to go. Do you suppose there's a prize?'

'I don't know,' said Pritpal. 'With Fairburn, the fun is always in solving the puzzle. The solution is its own reward.'

'But surely this is something bigger,' said James. 'Why would he go to all the trouble of actually disappearing off the scene?'

'I don't know,' said Pritpal, jumping up and rubbing

33

his hands together. 'We must get to work and solve the rest of the clues.'

'There's only one small problem,' said James.

'What is that?'

'Codrose has the letter.'

'Ah. That is tricky,' said Pritpal and he sank on to James's bed, deflated. 'I don't suppose he would give it back to me.'

'Fat chance,' said James. 'They're worried about Fairburn. They think he's gone crackers. No. Codrose will have locked that letter safely away in his study somewhere.'

'Then we will just have to get it back,' said Pritpal.

'You're not normally this bold,' said James.

'Ah, but this is a puzzle,' said Pritpal. 'I love puzzles. Can you get the letter out for me?'

James looked at his friend. He couldn't stop a smile from spreading across his face. A familiar feeling of excitement had already gripped his heart, making it beat faster. He felt like someone waking up after a long sleep.

He leant back in his chair and stretched, his joints cracking.

'Leave it to me,' he said.

The Raid on Codrose's

The following afternoon at three o'clock James was hiding in the dark, cramped space beneath a sideboard in the House dining room. He had been waiting there since lunchtime, surrounded by the smell of floor polish and dust. He looked at his pocket watch. It was time. If all had gone to plan the other members of the Danger Society should be in position.

The Danger Society had been founded by Perry Mandeville and was a club made up of boys like himself who wanted a bit of extra excitement in their lives. The society had been quiet lately. The damp, cold weather didn't inspire the boys to be doing anything more adventurous than huddling round a fire trying to keep warm.

But not today.

James's friend Andrew Carlton was on the roof. Just before lunch Carlton had come over from his own House and James had shown him his secret route to get up on to the top of the building, using a crawl space beneath the bathroom floor that led to a disused storeroom with a skylight. It was a route that James used if he ever needed to get out of the House after lock-up. Carlton was a couple of years older than James and, although a keen member of the Danger Society, he had a level head and could be relied on not to panic or get carried away.

He was crouching by a large glass dome that looked down into Codrose's study, flattened against the sloping side of the roof, and keeping perfectly still. He had a clear view of Codrose sitting at his desk, reading a letter. Carlton could see right down on to the top of his head where there was a perfectly circular bald patch about as large as a penny.

Ten minutes earlier, as arranged, Pritpal had asked Codrose if he had heard anything more from Mr Fairburn and then talked about a couple of passages from the letter. Afterwards, as hoped, Codrose had come straight up to his study, removed a key from inside a hinged wooden globe that opened out into two halves, unlocked a drawer in his desk, and taken a letter out.

Carlton had watched the whole thing. He was as sure as he could ever be that it was the letter from Fairburn.

He heard a whistle that meant that Perry and Gordon Latimer were in place below, and he gave his answering signal by flicking a small pebble over the top of the roof. It clattered down the other side into the gutter.

Everything was set and ready to go.

Perry and Latimer heard the rattle of the pebble. They looked both ways along Judy's Passage to double-check that there was no one coming, then Perry lifted his hat to reveal a half-brick carefully balanced on top of his head.

'Here goes,' he said, weighing it in his hand, and then he hefted it as hard as he could at a ground-floor window.

There was a loud, satisfying smash, and the two boys started up a terrible racket, shouting and yelling.

'There he goes!'

'Did you see him?'

'He went that way.'

'Catch him, somebody!'

There was movement within the building, boys were coming to the windows and peering out to see what was happening.

Presently the Dame appeared.

'What on earth is going on?' she said, and Perry and Latimer started jabbering away at her, both at the same time.

'It was a boy.'

'We saw him.'

'A local boy.'

'From the town.'

'He ran up and threw a brick through the window.'

'We tried to catch him.'

'He looked a terrible ruffian.'

The Dame bustled back inside, tutting and clucking.

The next person to see her was Carlton, up on the roof. He watched as she came into Codrose's study and told him what had happened.

In a moment, Codrose was up. He hastily returned the letter to the drawer, locked it and put the key back inside the globe before folding it shut.

As soon as he had left the room, Carlton flicked another pebble over the roof and hastily started scribbling on a large piece of paper he had brought with him.

From his hiding place beneath the sideboard James heard footsteps and in a moment he saw Codrose's feet as they marched across the wooden floor closely followed by the Dame's. As soon as he was quite sure that they had gone he slid out and ran over to the door that led into Codrose's private quarters.

If he was caught here James would surely be beaten, but he wasn't thinking about that now. He just had to get on and do the job as quickly and efficiently as possible.

He had been summoned to Codrose's study on a few occasions so he knew the way well enough, and he ran up the carpeted stairs all the way to the top floor and pushed open the study door.

He glanced up at the dome in the ceiling where Carlton was holding the piece of paper against the glass for him to see.

Written on the paper in thick charcoal were the words:

KEY IN GLOBE - LETTER IN DESK - TOP RIGHT DRAWER

James soon had the drawer open and the letter out.

He had with him a camera, the very latest Leica mark III. It was the prize possession of Gordon Latimer, who was a member of the Eton Camera Club, and he had been very reluctant to let James borrow it.

There was daylight coming from the windows and the dome, but James switched on the ceiling light and a desk lamp to get as much illumination on to the letter as possible.

He hoped it would be enough.

He steadied his elbows on the back of a chair and held the camera as still as he could, focusing on the letter. Latimer had given him a crash course in photography that morning, showing James all the dials on the camera and explaining what they meant. Luckily James was a fast learner and had a good head for mechanical things.

The Leica had a slow shutter speed, which was vital in this low indoor light, and James fired off five pictures with slightly different exposures.

He flipped the letter over and took five more pictures of the back.

He was done.

The letter went back into the drawer. The key went back into the globe.

Then he switched off the lights and gave the thumbs up to Carlton who scurried away across the roof to make his escape.

James left the room, closing the door behind him.

The whole thing had taken less than two minutes.

He ran down the stairs three at a time and was soon back in the dining room, from where he cautiously peered out into the hallway.

Pritpal was waiting there for him, looking nervous and jumpy. He nodded that it was all clear. James crossed the hallway and passed the camera to Pritpal.

As casually as he could manage, Pritpal sauntered outside. Codrose and the Dame were still there, along with most of the senior boys from the House.

When they saw Pritpal come out into the alleyway,

Perry and Latimer knew that James had got away safely and they could allow Codrose to go.

It had taken them all their ingenuity to keep him there. Perry had had to go so far as to say that the mysterious local hooligan had attacked him. He had made a big song and dance about showing Codrose the bruise, pulling up his shirt and vest and showing him some marks on his side.

Codrose wasn't to know that Perry had got the marks playing the Field Game the day before.

At last the crowd began to disperse and Codrose went back inside after sending a younger boy off to fetch the caretaker to mend the broken window. Pritpal secretly handed the camera to Gordon Latimer and watched with some relief as the boy followed Perry back down Judy's Passage.

It was over. Pritpal let out his breath and dried his sweaty palms on his trouser legs.

He hadn't enjoyed the last half an hour one little bit. He wasn't cut out for this kind of life. Solving puzzles was one thing, but break-ins, lying and vandalism were something else. In future he would leave this sort of escapade to James and his reckless friends.

That evening, just before six o'clock, Latimer delivered two decent prints, one of each side of the letter, which clearly showed Fairburn's handwriting.

James hid the 35mm film behind a loose skirting board and sat down with his messmates to copy everything out in larger letters on to a big piece of card. When they had finished James stashed the two prints in the hiding place with the film.

They stuck the card to the back of a map of the world that James had hanging on his wall. Now they could all study the clues together and when they were done they could simply turn the map the right way round again and the cipher would be safely hidden from view.

'Where do we start, then?' said James, staring at the words on the card.

'We know there are seven clues hidden here,' said Pritpal, picking up a pencil and walking over to the wall. 'And we have already solved one.'

He carefully circled the list of names from the Crossword Society, then underlined the two fake ones – Luc Oliver and Speccy Stevens.

'The next logical step,' he went on, 'would be to assume that there are seven distinct parts to the letter, each one giving us a different clue.'

James read the letter aloud.

'*Alexis Fairburn, London, seventh of December, 1934. My dear Pritpal, it's not every Tuesday one comes across seven boys with a love of crosswords. Don't feel down! The mighty Crossword Society will easily solve puzzles by themselves, now that I am gone.*

'*As I am sure the almighty Elliot will have explained, I have had to leave Eton. In fact I am leaving the country. My next crossword will be my last, as I will be gone before my next deadline.*

'The next part we've done,' said James, and jumped ahead. '*I will leave behind many happy memories. As you know,*

41

I was a boy at Eton myself. How well I remember scoring the winning try in the Field Game against the Duffers, and coxing the Callisto *in the parade of boats on June the Fourth.*

'*Yes, there are many things I shall miss about the old place. Apart from you lads in the Crossword Society (of course) I will miss Latin lessons most of all. I love all those old stories of ancient Rome, like Nero's great love affair with Cleopatra. You should try to visit the great necropolis in Porta Alta one day and see the marvellous statue of him gazing across towards her obelisks.*

'*Eton is a place like no other, with its own marvellous traditions. I shall really miss watching the Wall Game, but perhaps every time I read the famous poem, "The Wall Game", by David Balfour, it will all come back to me, as vividly as if I was still standing there . . . Come on, we cry, ignore the pain! Tingling with excitement in the rain . . .*'

'You can skip the poem,' said Tommy. 'Go on to the last bit.'

'*In closing, then,*' James continued, '*whatever you do, don't give up on crosswords. I know not everyone enjoys crosswords like you do. For instance, your messmate, the runner, must accept what he is and begin to mature. Yours, AF.*'

'Right,' said Tommy. 'We're looking for seven sections. Well, there's the first bit, about the Crossword Society and leaving the school. Then there's the bit you've already solved, with the false names. Then there's the bit about the Field Game and the parade of boats. That's three.'

'Then there's the odd stuff about Nero and Cleopatra,' said James. 'That makes four.'

'Nero was never in love with Cleopatra, was he?' said Tommy.

'No,' said Pritpal, 'that was Mark Antony and Julius Caesar. Nero came a lot later.'

'Then there's the rotten poem about the Wall Game,' said James. 'That's five. And finally, the bit about me not liking crosswords.'

'That's only six,' said Tommy. 'What have we missed?'

'The date!' said Pritpal excitedly, circling the false date at the top of the letter.

'What could it mean, though?' said James. 'The seventh of December, nineteen thirty-four.'

'It could be a number code,' said Pritpal. 'Mister Fairburn is a brilliant mathematician. He is in love with numbers.'

'Seven, twelve, nineteen, thirty-four,' said Tommy. 'Are the numbers significant?'

'Not in any obvious way,' said Pritpal, slipping a finger under his turban and scratching his head. 'They don't appear to be in any kind of sequence. I cannot see any relationship between them.'

'Maybe it's not that complicated,' said James. 'Maybe they just correspond to letters in the alphabet, or something. You know, like A is one, B is two, and so on.'

'That is possible,' said Pritpal.

'Seven?' said Tommy, thinking aloud and counting on his fingers. 'The seventh letter of the alphabet is G.'

'Then twelve gives us L,' said Pritpal, who was ahead of him. 'And then . . .'

'One thousand nine hundred and thirty-four,' said James, sourly. 'That's no good.'

'Perhaps one, nine, three, four?' said Tommy. 'A, I, C, D?'

'"Glaicd"?' said James. 'What kind of a word is that?'

'No,' said Pritpal. 'We are barking up the wrong tree.'

'What if each number somehow gave us a word, then?' said James. 'Instead of a letter.'

'I'm not sure I understand you,' said Pritpal.

James stood up and walked over to the card.

'What if we count the words?' he said. 'From the top of the letter, ignoring the date? We've got seven, twelve and nineteen–thirty-four. So we count seven along, then one, then two, then one again, then nine, three, four . . .'

James went through the letter, underlining the words as he came to them.

'*My dear Pritpal, it's not every <u>Tuesday</u> <u>one</u> comes <u>across</u> <u>seven</u> boys with a love of crosswords. Don't feel <u>down</u>! The mighty <u>Crossword</u> Society will easily <u>solve</u> puzzles by themselves, now that I am gone.*'

'Tuesday, one across, seven down, crossword, solve,' said Tommy. 'Clear as mud!'

'They are crossword clues,' cried Pritpal. 'He's telling us to solve two clues in a crossword puzzle on Tuesday – one across and seven down.'

'Today is Tuesday,' said James. 'But which puzzle?'

'*The Times*,' said Pritpal, slapping his forehead. 'Fairburn's puzzle appears in *The Times* every Tuesday.'

'Do you have it?' said James.

'Of course,' said Pritpal, hurrying out of the room. 'But in all the excitement today I haven't even looked at it yet.'

Ape X

'This is ridiculous,' said Tommy. 'Why has this crazy beak gone to so much trouble?'

'He obviously doesn't want any of the masters to know what's going on,' said James. 'It's like a game. Us versus Them. We have to keep it secret from Codrose. It's for our eyes only.'

'It had better be worth all this brain ache,' said Tommy.

'Anything that gets one over on the beaks is a good thing in my book,' said James, smiling.

Presently Pritpal bustled back in, waving the newspaper.

'I have it,' he said, and he put the paper on the table and opened it at the crossword page.

'You're going to have to show us how to do these cryptic crosswords,' said James. 'What was that clue last night? Something about a top-secret monkey.'

'The answer was "apex",' said Pritpal.

'I still don't get it,' said James.

'What is an apex?' said Pritpal.

'It's the top of something,' said Tommy.

'Yes.' Pritpal grinned. 'That's the first bit of the clue, the word "top". To be really fair the setter will put a normal crossword clue in. In this case, top, meaning apex. Then the rest of the clue will be a sort of code, a set of cryptic instructions to give you the letters.'

'What do you mean?' said James. 'How do the words "secret monkey" give us the letters A-P-E-X?'

'Ape means monkey,' said Pritpal.

'Yes,' said James. 'But why ape X?'

'What code name would you give to a secret agent?' asked Pritpal.

'I don't know,' said James. 'Maybe a number?'

'How about Agent X? Or, if he was a monkey, Ape X?'

The boys laughed.

'That's too tricky for me,' said James.

'Don't give up hope,' said Pritpal. 'It just takes a bit of practice. Think of it as a secret code that needs to be cracked. Now, let us look at today's clues, one across and seven down. Here we are, one across – "Spinning tornado, King Alexander's problem". And seven down is "Three-part sporting achievement's smothered in it".'

'Three-part sporting achievement?' said James. 'Could that be anything to do with the Triple Cup here at Eton last Easter?'

'Don't be bamboozled,' said Pritpal. 'Don't try and look for a direct meaning in the words; remember it is a code. The first clue will have nothing to do with a spinning tornado, and the second clue is probably not about a three-part sporting achievement. In the same way that "top-secret monkey" was not about a monkey.'

'So what *are* they about, then?' said Tommy.

'Let us break the clues down,' said Pritpal. 'We'll look

at the first one. The answer is two words, of seven letters and four letters.'

'"Spinning tornado, King Alexander's problem" . . .' said James slowly, hoping that by reading the words they would somehow reveal their meaning.

'The word "spinning",' said Pritpal, 'might mean that we have to spin some of the letters.'

'You mean it might be another anagram?' said James.

'Very possibly.'

'There are the right number of letters in the words "tornado king" to give us seven and four,' said Tommy.

'Good,' said Pritpal. 'So we need an anagram of "tornado king" that would somehow mean Alexander's problem.'

'Alexander who?' said Tommy.

'Who is the most famous Alexander in history?' said Pritpal.

'Alexander the Great?' said James.

'Yes,' said Pritpal. 'And what do you know about him?'

'That he ruled half the world,' said James, 'and he had a horse called Bucephalus.'

'And what problem did he have?' asked Pritpal.

'I should imagine he had lots,' said James.

'No. Come on. Do you not know the story of the Gordian knot?'

'Vaguely,' said James, searching his brain for the information. 'Didn't some Persian king tie a knot that was supposed to be impossible to undo?'

'That's right,' said Pritpal, 'and he said that whoever could undo it would rule his kingdom.'

'And Alexander didn't waste any time, did he?' said James. 'He just cut the thing in half with his sword.' He smiled. 'That's exactly what I would have done.'

'I know,' said Pritpal. 'You are a man of action, James. A blunt object.'

'Not the right sort of man to be solving crossword puzzles,' said James. 'I wish I had a sword that could cut through the knots in Fairburn's cipher.'

'I still don't get it,' said Tommy.

'"Gordian knot" is an anagram of "tornado king",' said Pritpal.

'So that's the answer, then?' said Tommy. 'Gordian knot?'

'Exactly,' said Pritpal. 'Alexander's problem.'

'But how does that help us?' said James. 'We've solved the crossword clue, but what is Fairburn trying to tell us?'

'We will have to solve the other clue to find out, I fear,' said Pritpal. '"Three-part sporting achievement's smothered in it". One word, seven letters.'

But, try as they might, the boys couldn't solve the clue. Pritpal thought that the answer might be something to do with threes, and they played with every variation of words beginning 'tri' that they could think of – trio and triplet and tricycle and triathlon . . .

In the end it was something of a relief when they heard a long-drawn-out shout of 'B-o-o-o-o-o-o-o-oy!' from the upper boys' corridor.

They all three leapt to their feet. One of the senior boys, a member of Library, needed something done – his boots polished, his tea cooked, or an errand run – and it was up to one of the lower boys to do it for him.

Tommy and Pritpal ran out. James hastily turned the map back round and followed them. Whichever boy arrived last at the Library would have to run the errand.

As James sprinted down the corridor, easily passing slower boys along the way, he was fruitlessly turning the clues over in his head.

James couldn't sleep that night. The clues were still running around his brain, teasing him, taunting him. Odd bits of Fairburn's cipher swam in and out of focus . . . *Luc Oliver . . . Speccy Stevens . . . how well I remember scoring the winning try in the Field Game against the Duffers . . . I love all those old stories of ancient Rome, like Nero's great love affair with Cleopatra . . . Eton is a place like no other . . . 'The Wall Game', by David Balfour . . . Come on, we cry, ignore the pain . . . Three-part sporting achievement's smothered in it . . .*

The words and phrases stayed with him all through lessons on Wednesday morning, and when he trudged out on to Dutchman's playing field that afternoon to play the Field Game he was at first distracted and found it hard to concentrate on play.

A muddy ball in the face soon brought him to his senses, however, and after that he threw himself into the game with his usual blood and guts.

James was tall for his age, a fast runner and utterly fearless, so he had been selected to play for his House on the lower boys' team. This match was against another House, and Codrose and Mr Merriot were umpiring.

The Field Game was unique to Eton and was only

played in the Michaelmas half. It wasn't exactly rugger and it wasn't exactly football. James had been told that it was similar to American football, but it felt like a weird mixture of sports and he was struggling to learn the rules. This was made doubly hard by the fact that the rules seemed to change from year to year and were constantly being noisily argued over by both teams.

After half an hour he was covered in mud and bruises. He had been running non-stop. It was raining and there was very little grass left on Dutchman's. His boots were so clogged with soil that they felt like lead.

A shout went up from the opposing team.

'Cornering! Sneaking! That's not allowed, sir!'

'I'll give it. Sneaking it is.'

Mr Merriot blew his whistle and play stopped. The two teams rested for a moment and regrouped.

James bent forward, his hands on his knees, and took a great lungful of air. He hadn't noticed it while he was playing, but now that there was a pause he realized just how exhausted he was.

It was fatal to stop running, because his brain was soon filling up with words – trident, triangle, triplet. He shook his head.

Stop it!

Play resumed and James was soon involved in a bully. He linked arms with six players on his own side; they got their heads down and then locked with the other team. Spread out behind him were the rest of the Codrose players, four Behinds, Flying Man, Short, Long and Goal.

The ball was passed in to the bully and the boys started

trying to grab it with their feet. The Codrose bully surged forward and James found that he had the ball between his boots. He dribbled it along the ground. It was a little smaller than a football and quite heavy. Suddenly the bully broke apart and James found he still had possession. He powered ahead, controlling the ball with his feet. It was absolutely forbidden to pick it up: not even the two boys defending the goals were allowed to touch it with their hands.

He suddenly noticed that he had an open space in front of him and a clear run to the Timbralls' line. All he had to do now was cross over and touch the ball down, scoring a try.

No. Not a try, he reminded himself, *that was rugby, in the Field Game it was called a* rouge.

James's mind wandered again. What had Fairburn said in his letter? *How well I remember scoring the winning try in the Field Game against the Duffers . . .* That must be significant. Why had he put *try* instead of *rouge . . .?*

A barrage of screams from the Codrose supporters dragged him back into the game. He was inches away from the Timbralls' line. What were they shouting?

Oh, yes. He wasn't allowed to kick the ball directly over the line.

Hell. These rules were so complicated. It was just like doing a cryptic crossword puzzle. You couldn't take the most obvious route. You couldn't just run down the field and put the ball straight over the line. You had to go round the houses. Without rules there was no game, he supposed. It was just a free-for-all. James didn't much care for rules. He knew how Alexander had felt when he sliced through that knot with his sword.

The only way he could score was if the ball was last touched by a defender before crossing the line.

Well, that could be achieved.

He turned sharp right just before the line, then ran straight at a defender, who was bearing down on him at great speed. At the last moment James kicked the ball at him with all his strength. It got him in the stomach, knocking the wind out of him. The boy's body absorbed most of the impact and the ball dropped a couple of feet over the touchline. James fell on it and the cheers from the spectators told him that he had managed to score the precious *rouge*.

His team ran over and congratulated him.

Now, to gain extra points, they would try to ram the ball.

A defender from Timbralls took up the position of Post, standing a yard in front of the goal with the ball between his feet. The rest of the defenders dug in to try and protect him and the ball. The Post was a stocky lad, and he would need all his strength because the attackers were going to try and force him over the line.

James and the three biggest members of the Codrose team grabbed hold of each other by the waist and charged forward. There was a loud thud as the leader's head battered into the enemy defenders.

Instantly there was chaos as both teams pushed and shoved. Someone jammed a knuckle into James's ear and a flailing boot caught his shins. He was crushed from both sides and couldn't breathe. He was smothered – surrounded by the other boys – but he hardly noticed. His brain was working again. Those damned clues were swarming around him like flies.

Rouge . . . *Try* . . . *Three-part sporting achievement* . . . *Trio* . . . *Triplet* . . .

Try . . .

A try was a sporting achievement.

Three-part sporting achievement's smothered in it.

What if the word *try* smothered the words *in* and *it*?

Suddenly something gave, the defenders fell, the ram collapsed and everyone was tumbling to the ground.

As the various bodies picked themselves up and the area was cleared, they discovered that the ball had just got over the line.

Another cheer went up and Mr Merriot blew his whistle for half-time.

As his teammates slapped him on the back, James limped off the field. His ear was ringing and his face was a mask of mud, but he had only one thought in his mind.

Pritpal had been watching the match with the other Codrose supporters on the touchline. James went straight over to him and, before Pritpal could say anything, James grabbed him by the shoulders.

'Trinity,' he said.

'What?' said Pritpal.

'It's the answer to the clue,' said James. '"Three-part sporting achievement's smothered in it" – trinity.'

Gordius

The following morning, after early school and breakfast, James was wandering along Keate's Lane with a noisy mob of boys on their way to chapel, when he saw Pritpal nosing his way through the crowd towards him.

'James,' he called out, waving a piece of paper. 'I've been looking for you all morning.'

'What's the matter?' said James.

'I think I have worked out the significance of the Gordian knot,' Pritpal explained.

'I knew you'd figure it out in the end,' said James. 'You're much cleverer at this than I am.'

'Not at all,' said Pritpal. 'I haven't done anything more clever than open this letter.'

'Who's it from?' asked James. 'Not from your Mister Fairburn, surely?'

'No, no,' said Pritpal, 'it is from a friend of his, reminding me that he is coming to Eton this evening to address the Crossword Society.'

They arrived at the chapel and began to file inside. There were two chapels at Eton. Henry VI's original chapel, known as College Chapel, and a newer one, Lower Chapel, which had been built at the end of the nineteenth century when the school had got so large that not all the boys could fit into College Chapel.

As younger boys, James and Pritpal used Lower Chapel, a simple stone building decorated with tapestries commemorating the Great War of 1914–18. They found an empty pew near the back and sat down.

'Mister Fairburn once told us that he had studied mathematics at Cambridge,' said Pritpal, 'and that a great friend of his from those days was now a professor there, and a fellow crossword compiler.'

'And that's the man who sent the letter?' said James.

'Yes,' said Pritpal. 'It all fell into place this morning when I looked at today's crossword in *The Times*.'

'Go on,' said James.

A hush fell over the chapel as the Lower Master approached the pulpit and Pritpal slipped a torn piece of *The Times* out of his pocket.

'Look at the name above the puzzle,' he whispered.

James looked. The crossword had been set by someone called *Gordius*.

The two boys couldn't talk any more and James had to wait impatiently for the service to end before he could carry on their conversation.

Twenty minutes later, as everyone shuffled back out again, Pritpal was at last able to explain about the name.

'It is a tradition that the men who set crosswords give themselves an alias,' he said.

'Like a code name?' said James.

'Exactly,' said Pritpal. 'Just as if they were spies. If you had looked yesterday you would have seen that Mister Fairburn signs himself *Deadlock*.'

'And today's puzzle was set by someone calling themselves *Gordius*?' said James, handing the newspaper page back to Pritpal.

'Gordius was the Persian emperor who tied the famous knot,' said Pritpal. 'The *Gordian* knot. Very appropriate for someone who writes crosswords, don't you think?'

'Don't tell me,' said James. 'Fairburn's friend is *Gordius*.'

'Yes. I don't know his real name,' said Pritpal. 'The letter was just signed *Gordius*.'

'And he's coming here to Eton tonight?'

'Yes,' said Pritpal. 'Although I have absolutely no memory of Fairburn ever telling us about it. That doesn't mean anything, however, as he was always very absent-minded.'

'It can't be a coincidence,' said James.

'I know,' said Pritpal. 'It must be part of the game.'

'If it *is* a game,' said James.

'What do you mean?'

'I don't know, Prit,' said James. 'I've got a funny feeling about all this. It's all so odd and complicated. Maybe this is something more serious.'

Pritpal laughed. 'It is just a puzzle,' he said. 'That is all.'

'Maybe,' said James. 'But I'm going to come along tonight to your meeting and see this Gordius chap for myself, just to make sure.'

The Crossword Society met every Thursday evening in a small back room at Spottiswoode's bookshop on the

High Street. The boys sat around on an assortment of mismatched chairs among shelves collapsing under the weight of dusty, forgotten books. A bare bulb hung from the ceiling and very little light made it through the small, grimy window. James found the room cold, cramped, dingy and uncomfortable, but the other boys were obviously so wrapped up in the world of crosswords that they didn't seem to notice.

James got there early to make sure he was settled in by the time their special guest arrived, but he needn't have worried because Gordius was late.

When he eventually turned up he made a big show of being polite and chatty with the boys.

'I know all about boys,' he said, flopping down into the largest chair in the room. 'After all, I used to be one.'

He looked around and the boys smiled politely back at him.

'I'm sorry,' he said. 'You've probably heard that joke a hundred times. And it was never much of a joke in the first place.'

He laughed and rubbed his eyes with nicotine-stained fingers. James took the opportunity to study him. He had a narrow moustache and longish hair swept back from his forehead. He was wearing an expensive, well-cut dark suit but it was crumpled. He had the look of a man who hadn't been to bed for a couple of days and hadn't changed his clothes in that time.

He muttered something to himself.

James could smell alcohol on his breath. His eyes drooped sleepily and seemed unfocused and watery, the skin around them puffy. He had obviously once been quite handsome, but he was losing his looks. His skin was pale and greyish, as if he rarely went out into the sunlight. One side of his face seemed to sag – the left side – and James saw that his left hand had a slight tremor, so that it constantly shook. He had an ivory-topped cane with him, and he had limped slightly when he came in.

'Now then?' he said, looking round at the boys. 'You all know that *I* am Gordius. Let's find out who you all are.' He turned to Pritpal. 'You must be Pritpal Nandra, who Alex has told me so much about.'

'That's right,' said Pritpal.

'And what about you others?' said Gordius, looking around. 'No, don't tell me. Let me guess.' His gaze settled on a tall, impossibly thin boy with a very long neck and a drooping nose that made him look something like a flamingo. He was wearing a twelve-foot-long scarf, considered fashionable among some of the boys. It was wrapped once around his neck and the two ends were tied behind his back.

'You look like a Felix Dunkeswell to me,' said Gordius.

'Spot on,' said the boy. 'Right first time.'

He guessed a couple more of the boys, getting one right and one wrong, and then turned to James, who was sitting out of the way in a dark corner.

'And you . . . ?' he said, peering blearily into the gloom. 'Skulking back there in the shadows. I would hazard a guess at Luc Oliver. Am I right?'

'That's very good,' said James. 'I wish I knew your secret.'

Pritpal started to say something, but James warned him with a quick glance to keep quiet. The other boys played along, enjoying the game and fooling this adult.

'It's simple detective work,' said Gordius. 'Based on observation. I understand people. I can read them like books. I can tell everything there is to know about someone in a single glance.' He clicked his fingers. 'Like that!'

'That's a very useful trick,' said James. 'What gave it away with me?'

'You look different,' said Gordius. 'Not like the other boys, and, with a name like Luc Oliver, I'm guessing you've some foreign blood in you.'

'Scottish father, Swiss mother,' said James, without needing to lie.

'Yes, well,' said Gordius and he seemed to lose interest. He gazed around the room and stroked his moustache, a distant look on his face. Then he came back to his senses, blinked and slapped his hands down suddenly on the arms of his chair. 'Now then,' he barked, 'it was Alexis who invited me along to meet you lot tonight. I must say I am surprised to find that he's not actually here.'

'Do you not know, sir?' said Pritpal.

'Know what?'

'He has left the school,' said Pritpal. 'I thought he might have written to let you know.'

'No,' said Gordius. 'I've heard nothing from him these last few weeks. He used to write to me regularly and tell me all about you boys and what you got up to in these meetings of yours.'

'Then you'll know we like to come up with clues and

test each other,' said Pritpal. 'I wonder, do you have a favourite clue, sir, or a real brain-teaser to try us on?'

Gordius stared at Pritpal as if he was seeing him for the first time. He held the stare for ages, saying nothing. 'What did you say?' he asked at last.

'A clue, sir? Do you have a favourite clue?'

Gordius waved a hand distractedly. 'I'm sure you swots would be much too clever for me,' he mumbled.

'Go on, Gordius,' said Felix Dunkeswell. 'What's your favourite clue?'

'I'm not sure I have one,' said Gordius impatiently. 'But, tell me. Have you really heard nothing from Alex since he left?'

'You must have a favourite?' said Pritpal.

'I don't have one!' Gordius snapped. 'So *do* please stop going on about it. It's very irritating. *You* are very irritating.'

'I'm sorry,' said Pritpal and he shifted nervously in his seat.

James realized that Gordius was one of those adults who doesn't really like children. In which case he wondered why he had agreed to come and talk to a group of schoolboys. Maybe he was just here because of his friendship with Fairburn.

Or maybe there was another reason.

There was an awkward silence in the room, which was at last broken by Pritpal.

'I did get a letter from Mister Fairburn,' he said.

'But he never read it,' James interrupted quickly, with another look to Pritpal. 'It was confiscated by our House Master, Mister Codrose. He has it under lock and key in his study.'

'Why would he do that?' said Gordius.

'He didn't want Pritpal to see the letter,' said James. 'It was a bit odd apparently.'

'Alex is an odd chap,' said Gordius.

'Mister Fairburn would set us puzzles,' said Percy Odcombe, a small, serious boy wearing spectacles. 'I mean, at these meetings.'

'Well, I am not Mister Fairburn, am I?' said Gordius.

'Well, what *are* we going to do?' said Dunkeswell with some amusement in his voice.

Gordius shrugged.

James didn't trust him. He was up to something. He had come here for a purpose, and it wasn't to talk about crosswords. James wondered if he was even who he said he was and, if so, why he wasn't going to more trouble to keep up the illusion.

And then it dawned on him. The man had underestimated the boys.

'Perhaps we could talk about your puzzle in *The Times* this morning,' said James.

'Must we?' said Gordius, without much enthusiasm.

'You don't seem very keen on crosswords,' said James.

'Keen on them?' said Gordius sarcastically. 'How could I not be keen on them? I dote on them. I dream them. They are meat and drink to me. Ah, crosswords! Mankind's greatest creation. What would we do without them?'

He stopped and ran a hand through his hair. The boys looked at each other, embarrassed, not quite sure how to take his outburst. But James wasn't going to let it lie. He picked up a copy of *The Times* from the table. Some of the boys had been looking at it earlier and discussing the clues. He picked one at random.

'I'm rather stuck on one of the answers,' he said. 'Perhaps you could explain it for me.'

'Why not?' said Gordius wearily. 'That should be tremendous fun.'

'Six down,' said James, ignoring the man's sarcasm. 'The clue is just four letters. You'll remember – "GSGE", and the answer's two words, nine and four.'

James looked at Gordius and Gordius looked back. Neither of them wanting to be the one to look away first. James studied the man's face to see if there was any reaction. There wasn't.

'I'm surprised you haven't got that one,' said Gordius, taking the newspaper and looking at the crossword. 'It's an easy one.'

'Can you give me some hints?' said James.

'Well,' said Gordius. 'It's obviously the initials for something, isn't it? And if I said any more I'd be giving you the answer on a plate.'

'All right,' said James. 'What about eight across –'

'Never mind all that,' Gordius interrupted, throwing the paper away across the room. 'Alex told me that you lot don't always just solve crosswords in these meetings of yours, you play all sorts of games.'

'We did once play chess,' said Percy Odcombe, but Gordius wasn't listening.

'Let's have a bit of a card game while we chat, eh?' he said. 'I'm sure some of you lads must enjoy card games.'

There were murmurs and shrugs from the boys.

'I play a little,' said James.

'Splendid! There's one, then,' said Gordius. 'Oliver's in. Any other takers?'

'I'll play,' said Dunkeswell, and Percy Odcombe agreed to make up a fourth.

Gordius took a pack of well-thumbed cards out of his pocket and shuffled them expertly. James saw that there was a fresh light in the man's eyes now. He seemed eager and excited in a way he had not been when talking about crosswords.

'Do you all know how to play hearts?' he said. 'That's a nice simple game.'

James and Felix Dunkeswell nodded, but Odcombe seemed less sure.

'It's quite straightforward,' said Gordius. 'You deal out all the cards and then play tricks as in any standard whist game.'

Odcombe looked slightly blank.

Gordius rolled his eyes. 'Highest card wins,' he said.

'Someone lays down a card,' said Felix Dunkeswell kindly, 'and if you have a card of the same suit you have to play it. So, for instance, if I played the five of Clubs, you'd have to play a Club if you had one. The highest Club played wins the trick.'

'And what if I don't have any Clubs?' said Odcombe.

'Then you can play any card you like,' said James. 'But you can't win the trick.'

'Then the winner starts off the next trick by laying down any card from their hand,' Felix explained.

'So I want to win as many tricks as I can, then?' said Odcombe.

'In a normal game of whist, yes,' said Felix. 'But hearts is a little different. In hearts you have to avoid winning any tricks containing Hearts, or, God forbid, the queen of Spades. Hearts count for one point against you, and the queen is an unlucky thirteen. There are a few more rules, but you'll pick them up as we go along.'

'But how do you win, then?' said Odcombe.

'The game's over when someone reaches a hundred and fifty,' said Gordius. 'Then whoever has the lowest score wins.' He turned to Pritpal. 'Do you have something we can use as a score pad, old sport?' he asked. Pritpal handed over his notebook. He didn't look too happy about it. He had been hoping to fill it with tips and clues from the great Gordius, but now it was going to be used to keep the score of a card game.

Gordius put the pad by his side and began to deal out the deck to the four players. 'One more rule,' he said, expertly flicking the cards around the tabletop. 'Before we start, we all pass any three cards that we don't want to the player on our left. On the second hand we pass to the right, on the third we pass opposite, and there's no passing on the fourth.'

James looked at his cards. He had only two Diamonds, the king and a ten. He picked them out. He was also holding the ace of Spades so he picked that out as well, so as not to risk winning the queen if somebody led Spades.

James had Felix to his left, Odcombe to his right and Gordius opposite. He slid his discarded cards to Felix and took three from Odcombe.

Odcombe may have been inexperienced, but he was bright enough to realize that it probably wasn't wise to hang on to the queen of Spades, and he'd passed it on to James, along with the ace of Hearts. He'd also passed on the jack of Diamonds. James tried hard not to react in any way. Playing cards was as much about knowing what the other players were thinking as having the best hand.

He would have to get rid of that queen at the earliest opportunity.

'The player with the two of Clubs leads,' said Gordius, whose face was completely blank. He had hidden all his excitement and was obviously a serious card player. He was sitting completely still, apart from the tiny tremor in his hand.

Felix had the two of Clubs and laid it down. Gordius played a cautious six on it and Odcombe played a ten. There were no Hearts on the table so it was safe for James to win the trick. He played the king of Clubs.

It was his turn to lead now.

Odcombe had passed him the jack of Diamonds. It was the only Diamond in his hand. He wanted to get rid of it, so risked playing it. It was a high card and could easily win the trick, but at this early stage the odds were that all the other players would still be holding Diamonds, and besides, nobody could dump the queen of Spades on him because he was holding that himself.

He played the jack and everyone followed suit. Again the trick was his. This time he put down a low card, the three of Clubs, and Odcombe won the trick with a nine. James was relieved to see him lead a Diamond. The eight.

As James had got rid of all his Diamonds he was free to play any card he liked. He didn't like to do it to the inexperienced boy, but couldn't risk hanging on to the queen of Spades. He laid it down and heard Odcombe say 'Oh' quietly.

Felix and Gordius played a six and a two and Odcombe was left with the queen. Four tricks in and he was already thirteen points down. He didn't do much better for the rest of the hand, and ended up with most of the Hearts as well. James was landed with two and Felix took four. Gordius managed not to pick up any penalty points at all.

The game continued like this for several hands. James noticed that Gordius was cautious to start with, testing the boys' skill and getting to know how they played. But as the game continued he became bolder and took more risks, until he was playing quite aggressively. He was also playing tactically, trying to knock back any other player who posed a threat, and frequently letting Odcombe, as the weakest player, off the hook. Instead he began to concentrate his attack on James, who was the most experienced player among the boys. In trick after trick Gordius tried to land him with penalty cards, so James had to concentrate hard.

With the cards in his hands Gordius had become a completely different man, animated and cheerful, where before he had been bored and listless. He hadn't mentioned crosswords since they'd started playing. He did, though, talk freely about cards and gambling and told a long and complicated story about how he had once won several thousand pounds in one night's play at the casino in Royale-les-Eaux in France.

He kept a tight control on his emotions, trying not to let them show. James knew that gamblers called this ability to look blank and not give anything away a poker face, and Gordius was good, but not good enough. You had to read more than just the face to understand someone. You had to study the whole body and see the little things that gave them away. James had noticed that Gordius rubbed his hands together, not when he was happy, but when he was excited. He did something different when he was happy. When he had dumped the queen of Spades on someone, for instance, or avoided a nasty trick, he made a tiny movement with his fingers. He flicked the edges of his cards with a fingernail. He probably didn't even know he was doing it.

But James saw it. James saw everything.

He saw that when Gordius was annoyed – for instance, if a trick didn't go his way, or if someone passed him a nasty set of cards – he sniffed.

In these little ways James could tell what the man was really thinking.

And it wasn't pretty.

Gordius was enjoying beating these boys.

As the game had progressed the other boys had drifted off back to their Houses in ones and twos until there were just the four card players and Pritpal left.

The game now stood at Odcombe on 142 points, Felix on 105, James on 71 and Gordius on 46.

It was James's turn to deal and he went around the table until all the cards were out.

'It looks likely that our friend Percy Oddbod's not going to last another round,' said Gordius, looking at his hand and giving it a triumphant little flick with his fingernail. 'It looks like it's between you and me, Luc.'

'You may be right,' said James. 'But I could still catch you.'

He was glad that Gordius didn't know his real name. It was like a disguise, a spy's cloak. Gordius thought he could read him like a book, but James was keeping most of himself hidden from the man.

'I know you're some way behind,' said Gordius. 'But how'd you like to make this a little more interesting? Hmm?'

'You mean gamble?' said James.

'Might be fun,' said Gordius.

'For you, maybe,' muttered Dunkeswell. 'You're just about to win.'

'Well, I don't think I could show my face in London if I lost to a schoolboy.'

'In that case, I'll definitely take the bet,' said James. 'I've got a reputation to keep up as well.'

'Five pounds I win the game this hand,' said Gordius.

'That's a lot of money,' said James. 'I am, after all, only a schoolboy.'

'Come now. You're an Eton boy. You're all rich.'

'Not me, I'm afraid,' said James.

'So you won't take the bet?'

'I didn't say that,' said James. 'I just said it's a lot of money.'

'Scared?' said Gordius, smiling at James.

James shook his head and smiled back at him. 'Five pounds it is,' he said.

Shoot the Moon

James had been disappointed in his hand at first; it had contained a lot of high Hearts and Spades, but then he'd remembered another rule of the game and calculated his odds of success. It was a narrow chance, but he was pretty sure he could pull it off as long as Gordius didn't realize what he was up to until it was too late.

It was an all-or-nothing plan. If it went wrong, in even one trick, he would be left looking very stupid indeed. But with a bit of luck he could do it. He looked over his cards again. He had all the high cards he needed, except for the jack of Hearts and the queen of Spades.

He was fairly sure he knew who had her, though.

He had noticed Gordius's little flick when he'd looked at his cards, which meant that he probably had the queen of Spades and was looking forward to passing her across to James. If Gordius decided to hang on to her, though, the game would be very hard to win.

James passed his only two Diamonds to Gordius together with the ace of Spades. Passing the ace was a big gamble, but he risked it in order to throw up a smokescreen. He had seen enough of Gordius's play to know how he would be likely to react and he hoped he would stay true to form.

Gordius passed the queen, with a straight face. James fought back the urge to grin madly, and instead looked at the card and showed disappointment, knowing that Gordius would be watching. Now everything was in place, he just had to stick to his plan and hope that Gordius didn't spot his tactic too soon.

Play started and the first few tricks had no penalties. James managed to offload some low cards and then won a couple of tricks containing Hearts. To his delight Percy Odcombe dumped the jack on him. This was just what he had been hoping for. It was the only Heart he had been scared of. Now, if he had calculated right, he could pull off his scheme, just so long as he could make Gordius dump the ace of Spades.

He took another trick with a Heart in it and made a sour face. He had now won three Hearts and was the only player to have taken any penalties.

'Do you have the five pounds on you, or will you have to borrow it?' gloated Gordius.

James sighed and made a big show of looking at his cards and scratching his head. He had to make Gordius play that ace of Spades.

He didn't have to pretend to be nervous now. He was on a knife-edge. But not for the reason Gordius thought.

James led the three of Spades. Felix played a seven. Gordius knew that James had the queen. He had passed it to him himself, after all. Now that he knew that there was no danger of winning the queen back, Gordius was safe to play the ace. There was a small threat that Percy might play a Heart, but for Gordius it was a risk worth taking. A Heart was only one penalty point. The queen was thirteen.

The risk to James was much bigger. If Percy *did* play a Heart then James was sunk.

But James had been paying attention and counting the cards and was almost certain that Percy had no more Hearts in his hand.

Almost, but not *absolutely* sure.

Gordius was thinking hard. Would he risk the trick?

He had to.

James felt a warm flush of triumph as Gordius put down the ace.

He hadn't spotted what James was up to.

But the danger wasn't over yet. What if James hadn't paid enough attention? What if Percy played a Heart now?

He didn't.

He played a harmless Diamond and Gordius took the trick.

James was still the only player to have won any Hearts.

He was home and dry. The rest was plain sailing.

Gordius played it safe and led with the two of Hearts.

James won the trick, pretending that it hurt, and took the next one as well, winning more Hearts off Felix and Gordius.

As he scooped up the cards Gordius suddenly understood what James was up to. He sniffed, and, for the first time in the game, his face showed emotion; the tremor in his hand grew more noticeable, his eyebrows scrunched together into a frown and he glared at his cards.

He had finally twigged.

But it was too late.

His eyes darted left and right, hoping to spot something he had missed. Then he calculated what cards had been played, what tricks James had already won and what was left to him. Fat beads of sweat sprang up on his forehead. He took out a handkerchief and wiped his face.

'You underhand swine,' he said finally. 'You're trying to shoot the moon!'

'What does that mean?' said Odcombe.

Gordius grabbed the score pad and quickly ran through the sums in his head.

Felix laughed. He was hugely enjoying the situation, even if it meant that James was going to soundly beat him.

'If you win every single penalty card in one hand,' he explained to Odcombe, 'including the queen of Spades, instead of taking the penalty, you add twenty-six points to everyone else's score.'

'Ah . . .' said Percy, weighing this up. He glanced at the score pad then round at James. 'So you'd win the game, then?'

'There's always the danger, though,' said Felix, 'that if you don't quite pull it off and somebody else wins even just one Heart, then you're left with an awful lot of penalty points at the end of the hand.'

James looked across the table at Gordius, trying to keep a straight face. 'Do you have the five pounds on you?' he said. 'Or will you have to borrow it?'

'There's no need to be cheeky,' said Gordius angrily and James could hold back a smile no longer.

They carried on, but there were no surprises. James won all the Hearts, and then he was left with the king and queen of Spades. Just to rub it in, he didn't play the queen until the very last card.

Nobody could beat it.

He took the trick.

He had shot the moon.

'That's twenty-six points each to the three of you,' he said.

Pritpal did a quick addition and read out the scores.

'The game is over,' he said. 'Percy is on one hundred and sixty-eight. Felix is on one hundred and thirty-one. Gordius is on seventy-two, and Ja–Luc is the winner with seventy-one.'

Gordius had pulled himself together and wore a calm and unruffled expression now. He even managed a smile.

He slid a £5 note from his pocket book and passed it over the table to James.

'You had a lucky hand there,' he said. 'Perhaps I shouldn't have gone so easy on you. I wasn't really playing to win. But thanks for the game. Most amusing.'

'It was my pleasure,' said James. 'And thank you for coming to talk to us. We've really learnt a lot about crosswords.'

James held Gordius's stare and the man tried to read the boy. Was James mocking him? Was this a deliberate challenge? After all, Gordius had said virtually nothing about crosswords in all the time he had been here.

He sniffed and stood up to leave.

'So long,' he said. 'We must do it again sometime.'

He picked up his cane, and as he walked to the door James called after him.

'Wait a minute – Gordius?'

'Yes?'

'You haven't told us your real name, sir. We're all dying to know.'

'My real name is, well, ah, ha . . .' Gordius paused, rubbing his hands together. He seemed to be wondering what to say. At last he sniffed again and spoke. 'My real name is Peterson. Professor Ivar Peterson.'

By the time the four boys left Spottiswoode's it had grown dark and the air was damp and chilly. James carefully turned up the collar of his overcoat. One of the more obscure rules at Eton was that it was forbidden for lower boys to wear their collars down. It was also forbidden for them to walk on the west side of the High Street. So they crossed over and walked up the east side until they came to the school buildings on Long Walk, where James and Pritpal stopped to say goodbye to Felix and Percy who were carrying on towards their House.

James and Pritpal had to cross back over the road to get to Codrose's. It looked all clear, but they were halfway across when a big black Daimler Double 6 roared up and nearly ran them down. They jumped out of the way and the car sped past, far closer than was comfortable, sending up a fine spray of water that soaked them.

James got a good look at the driver, who was sitting

up front, out in the open, separate from the enclosed passenger compartment behind him. He was a tall man with a huge head like a skull, his lips pulled back into a grimace away from rotting brown teeth.

'That idiot is driving far too fast,' said Pritpal.

'It's almost as if he was trying to knock us down,' said James.

'If he'd really wanted to he could have done,' said Pritpal.

'Perhaps.'

They carried on walking. Pritpal had been dying to ask James something since they'd left Spottiswoode's, but Felix had been chattering away, reliving the drama of the card game, and he hadn't had the chance. Now, as they trudged along Judy's Passage towards Codrose's, he could hold it in no longer.

'Why on earth did you pretend that you were Luc Oliver?' he said. 'What was that all about?'

'Lucky the real Luc Oliver wasn't there to give me away,' said James.

'Don't play the fool,' said Pritpal. 'You know as well as I do that Luc Oliver does not exist. He was made up by Mister Fairburn in order to create an anagram for his puzzle.'

'So how did Gordius know the name?' said James.

'Well, he . . .' Realization at last struck Pritpal and he stopped dead. 'Why did I not spot that?' he said, batting a brown hand against his forehead. 'You are right. The only way that Gordius could know the name Luc Oliver was if he had read Fairburn's letter.'

'A letter that he pretended to know nothing about,' said James.

'But if he is a friend of Fairburn,' said Pritpal, 'maybe he is in on the game.'

'I'm not so sure any more that it is a game,' said James. 'Gordius didn't seem to be very interested in crosswords and puzzles, did he?'

'No,' said Pritpal. 'I'm afraid not.'

'And when I asked him about that clue it was obvious he didn't know the answer,' said James. '"GSGE". I don't claim to fully understand cryptic crosswords, but they don't just put four letters in as the initials for something, do they?'

'No,' said Pritpal. 'I don't know what the answer is, but I'm sure it has nothing to do with initials.'

'All he cared about was playing cards,' said James.

'Not at all,' said Pritpal. 'He asked a lot of questions about Mister Fairburn.'

'I didn't trust him from the start,' said James. 'That's why I lied about you not having read it. Whoever that man was, I'm pretty sure he wasn't Professor Ivar Peterson of Cambridge University.'

'What is going on, James?' said Pritpal. 'Why would someone impersonate Gordius?'

'I don't know,' said James. 'Maybe the best way to find out would be to go to Cambridge and talk to the real Professor Peterson.'

'How would we find him, though?' said Pritpal.

'We go to his college.'

'Which one? There are so many.'

'The crossword clue,' said James. 'Isn't it obvious? Fairburn has already given us all the answers.'

'I'm not following you, James.'

'Trinity,' said James. '"Try smothered in it". *Trinity*. It's a college in Cambridge. And I'd be more than happy to bet you the five pounds I won off so-called Gordius that it's where we'll find Professor Peterson.'

That night James couldn't sleep. He lay in bed, staring at the ceiling, the tip of his nose icy cold. He had promised the Head Master that he would stay out of trouble, but he had got the scent of danger at the Crossword Society and his blood was running hot in his veins.

Somehow he had to get away from Eton and up to Cambridge, but he could think of no way to do it. He decided that he needed help. Pritpal was no good. He was too timid, and besides, he wasn't sure he should lead his friend too deeply into troubled waters. At the first opportunity tomorrow he would find Perry Mandeville and ask his advice.

He spotted Perry in chapel the next morning and signalled to him that he needed to talk. Outside on Keate's Lane Perry ambled over. He was a big, gangling lad who was always in a state of fidgety excitement. He talked very fast, his mouth running ahead of his brain, so that his words tumbled over each other and fell out in a stammer.

'Filthy day,' he said. 'Roll on Christmas, God rest ye m-merry gentlem-men and all that, I've had enough of school for one year, all this studying is m-making m-my brain ache. What did you want to talk to m-me about?'

'The letter,' said James. 'The one we photographed in Codrose's study.'

77

'What about it?'

As they walked up the lane James filled Perry in on everything that had happened since Tuesday.

'I'm stumped, though,' said James, once Perry was up to date. 'I can't think of any way of getting to Cambridge before the Christmas holidays.'

'I could m-maybe look into it for you,' said Perry.

'How?' asked James.

'I've m-managed to wangle m-myself some long leave this weekend,' Perry explained. 'It's m-my father's birthday, he's having a big beano and I'm going up to our place in London.'

'That'll be fun,' said James.

'It should be,' said Perry. 'Particularly as m-my father won't be there.'

'What?' said James. 'I thought you just said he was having a party.'

'He is,' said Perry and he laughed. 'At our country place in Buckinghamshire! He didn't see fit to invite m-me, but the school doesn't need to know that, seemed like a good excuse to trot off and enjoy m-myself in London while the folks are out of the way, if you'd let m-me borrow the m-motor, I could leave for Cambridge straight after lunch and be up there by teatime, then I could make it back down to London in time for a late supper.'

James sighed. 'I don't know, Perry,' he said. 'If you were caught you'd be in serious trouble, and so would I for lending it to you. I'd feel rotten.'

'Well, come with m-me then,' said Perry, as if it was

the easiest thing in the world. 'You drive. You take all the blame. I'll forge a letter from m–my pa saying he'd like to invite you down.'

'Codrose would never go for it,' said James. 'It's too short notice. Couldn't you just take the train up to Cambridge from London on Saturday?'

'No fear,' said Perry. 'I have a full weekend planned, if you won't let m–me have the m–motor, then it looks like you'll just have to wait until the holidays. Think it over, James. If you change your m–mind I'm going to Upton at lunchtime before I set off for London. You'll find m–me at the King's Head near St Lawrence's.'

James watched Perry walking away and cursed. He knew Perry was only trying to get hold of the car for the weekend, but James couldn't risk it. He'd just have to think of something else.

James paid little attention in his lessons that morning. In science he got the measurements completely wrong in an experiment and only narrowly avoided blowing up the lab. In history he gave the wrong answer to an easy question about the Napoleonic wars and was jeered at by the whole division. To cap a rotten morning, Mr Merriot hit him with a ruler and accused him of daydreaming in Private Business.

He wasn't daydreaming, though, he was thinking, and thinking hard – trying to devise a plan that would get him away from Eton. It was frustrating being stuck here, freezing to death in dark, unheated classrooms when all he wanted was to be out solving Fairburn's mystery.

Try as he might, though, he could think of no solution to his problem.

His plans became wilder and more improbable as the day wore on. He even considered setting fire to Codrose's, but as it turned out, someone beat him to it and his means of escape came from an unexpected quarter.

When he arrived back at the House for lunch he found the place in total confusion. There was a burning smell and smoke hung in the air.

Lower boys were running around excitedly. The senior boys from Library were standing in Judy's Passage trying to look important and useful. There were two policemen with them.

James tried to go in but was turned away by one of the policemen as a group of firemen clattered past wearing helmets and big boots.

James found Pritpal and asked him what was going on.

'There has been a break-in,' Pritpal explained. 'Codrose's study has been ransacked. The intruders made a terrible mess, apparently, and started a fire. The general idea is that it is connected somehow to the incident the other day.'

'What incident?' asked James.

'You remember,' said Pritpal, with a knowing wink. 'When that local boy threw a brick through the window and ran off.'

'Ah, yes, of course,' said James loudly. '*That* incident.' And then he lowered his voice and added, 'Let's hope the police don't look too closely into that, and find out it was all down to me and Perry.'

'I'd keep out of the way, if I was you,' said Pritpal quietly.

'Was anything stolen?' said James as a third policeman came out to talk to his colleagues.

'They don't know yet, it is chaos in there. Codrose is in a foul mood. His study is a ruin and he hasn't been able to go up there and see for himself. The firemen are still checking to see if the building is safe. The fire wasn't very serious, I don't think; the thieves probably started it to cover their tracks and create a diversion, but the building has been damaged and there is smoke in all the rooms. We're all to be sent home tonight so that the workmen can come in and make their repairs.'

'It seems my prayers have been answered,' said James, smiling broadly.

Just then Tommy Chong hurried over.

'I've been talking to the Dame,' he said, excitedly. 'Any boy who can't make arrangements in time is going to be packed off to the Eton Mission in London.'

'What's the Eton Mission?' asked James.

'It is a charitable organization that was set up by the school in Hackney,' said Pritpal. 'So that Eton could do something for the poor. And the East End of London is very poor indeed.'

'As it's nearing Christmas, they thought that we might go down and help out,' said Tommy.

'Did you find out anything more about the fire?' James asked.

'The only person who saw anything was the maid, Katey,' said Tommy. 'She's half barmy with fright, apparently. It happened during chapel and there was no one else here. A man knocked her over in one of the corridors. She didn't see a lot because the place was full of smoke.'

'She must have seen something,' said James, looking up at the windows in Codrose's study where smoke was still drifting out into the cold air.

'She says it was the devil that attacked her,' said Tommy, laughing. 'Spring-heeled Jack. All sorts of crazy ideas.'

'What did he look like, then, this devil?'

'She says he looked like death himself,' said Tommy, with a theatrical leer.

'Death?' said James. 'You mean a skeleton?'

'I suppose so,' said Tommy. 'Though I hardly think that it really *was* a skeleton that attacked her.'

James frowned. An image came into his mind of a man driving a Daimler. A skeletal man with a face like a skull.

'So what do you think?' said Pritpal. 'Will your aunt be able to take you this weekend, James, or will you go down to the mission?'

'Perry said he could forge me a letter,' said James. 'From his father. In all this confusion we might be able to get away with it. If I hurry I might just catch him. Wish me luck. I'll see you later.'

So saying, James turned and sprinted off down Judy's Passage, images of a skull-faced man drifting through his mind like a ghost.

A Lovely Wreck

St Lawrence's Church in Upton was the other side of the playing fields, on the edge of Slough. As long as he kept the pace up, James could be there in ten minutes. He raced across Agar's Plough, the cold air cutting into his lungs. A damp, yellow fog hung over the school grounds and he could see barely twenty feet in front of him.

He knew his way across the fields well enough, but once he came to the town on the other side he was less sure of where he was going. He soon spotted the spire of the church, though, and as he pounded down the Datchett road he saw the unmistakable form of Perry Mandeville, sauntering along the pavement, using a piece of broken branch as a makeshift walking stick.

James called out to him and Perry stopped and turned round.

'James!' he cried. 'You changed your mind! I knew you would.'

James caught up and for a moment was too out of breath to speak.

'I'm glad you came,' said Perry, taking him by the arm. 'I have something to show you.'

Before James could protest Perry dragged him across the road and round the back of the King's Head pub into a small, scruffy yard.

Resting on cinder blocks in the middle of the yard was a once-magnificent $4^1/_2$ litre Bentley 'Blower', the powerful, long-nosed two-seater motor car that was the favourite of British racing drivers.

But this model had evidently seen better days.

It had no wheels, the leather seats had been eaten away and the racing-green paintwork was badly scratched and worn.

'What do you think?' said Perry. 'Isn't she a lovely wreck?'

'It's a brutal machine,' said James, running his hand along the big, imposing bonnet. 'My aunt has one just like it. Although hers is in slightly better condition. What happened to this one?'

'She was racing at Brookfield,' boomed out a deep voice and James turned to see a man in a tweed overcoat coming out of the back door of the pub. 'Her first time out,' he went on. 'And she threw a wheel.'

The man approached the car and lovingly patted her radiator. 'She came off the track,' he said. 'Had quite a nasty smash. That was January. By May they'd put her back together and she was ready to race again. Halfway round the track, on her first lap, the engine caught fire. The driver was nearly killed. She was abandoned, poor thing, no one would take her, they thought she was unlucky. I picked her up in the summer for a song. I've been tinkering with her, trying to get her back on the road, but I'm no mechanic. Now my Beverley has said I've got to choose between her and the Bentley.' He sighed. 'Sadly, she has to go.'

'Who?' said Perry. 'Your wife?'

'It was a hard choice,' said the man with a smile. 'But I'm not selling the wife.'

'What do you think?' said Perry, clapping James on the shoulder. 'M-Mister Hanson's offering to sell her for two hundred and fifty pounds.'

'Wait a minute,' said James. 'You're not suggesting we buy her?'

'I m-most certainly am,' said Perry. 'We'll never find another m-motor like this for that sort of m-money.'

'But we don't have that sort of money,' said James. 'At least *I* don't. Do you?'

Perry dragged James out of earshot of Mr Hanson.

'Not so loud,' he said. 'I've hinted that we have the m-money.'

'Well, *do* you?'

'Of course I don't,' hissed Perry. 'But we can work on it. I'm sure we can come up with the cash from somewhere, hard graft and toil, armed robbery if we m-must. Just look at her, James. Between us we could put her back into shape and she'd be really something. The pride and joy of the Danger Society.'

'We already have a car,' said James.

'That's yours,' said Perry. 'And you won't ever let anyone take her out for a blast. M-my plan is for everyone in the society to club together so that it can belong to us all. That'd be something, wouldn't it? Wouldn't it, though, just?'

'I don't know, Perry,' said James. 'It's madness.'

'Life would be empty without m-madness,' said Perry.

'I can't think about this now,' said James. 'I need to talk to you.'

'Doesn't it break your heart, James?' said Perry. 'Seeing her sat there like that?'

'Perry,' James snapped. 'I'm serious.'

'Very well,' said Perry and he arranged to come back and see Mr Hanson at a later date.

Once they were out of earshot and heading back towards Eton, James told Perry about the fire. Perry thought it was the best thing to happen at the school for a long time.

'So, shall we drive down to London together in style?' he asked.

'You have a one-track mind,' said James. 'For the last time, we are not taking the car.'

'Do you have no sense of urgency?' said Perry. 'Who knows what's happened to your M-Mister Fairburn.'

'If we could only work out the rest of the clues,' said James, 'I could answer that question. We got off to a good start, but the cipher's gone cold on us. We've only managed to solve two clues out of seven so far. The anagram of the boys' names and the crossword clues that pointed us towards Professor Peterson in Cambridge.'

'Remind m-me what the other ones are,' said Perry.

'There's one about scoring in the Field Game and captaining a boat on the Fourth of June.'

'Right.'

'There's one about Nero and Cleopatra. There's one

about me not liking crosswords. Oh, yes, and there's that awful poem about the Wall Game.'

'You have no idea why he put the poem in the letter?'

'None at all,' said James. 'Pritpal has looked for it in every poetry collection he can get his hands on, but he can't find any mention of it, or the man who wrote it, David Balfour.'

'Like in the story?' said Perry.

'What story?' said James.

'Oh, come along, James,' said Perry, 'you must have read it. Everyone I know has read it.'

'Read what?'

'The book by Robert Louis Stevenson!' Perry exclaimed, throwing up his hands. 'David Balfour must be just about one of the m–most famous fictional characters around.'

James stopped walking and clutched his head in his hands.

'Don't tell me,' he said. 'I know I've read it. Now you say it, the name sounds so familiar . . .'

And then it hit him and everything changed.

'My God, Perry,' he said. 'You've solved the next clue.'

'Have I?'

'Yes,' said James. 'I know the book now, it's *Kidnapped*, isn't it?'

'It is,' said Perry.

James grabbed him by the shoulders, a wild look in his eyes. 'Perry,' he said, 'we're going to Cambridge.'

'In the m–motor?' said Perry, grinning.

'It'll be the quickest way,' said James. 'I *knew* this was

more than a game. Fairburn's been kidnapped and we've got to find him before it's too late.'

It had been almost too easy arranging things with Codrose. The House was in chaos, with parents, policemen, boys and workmen coming and going. Codrose barely looked at the forged letter and seemed glad to be getting rid of James. It was one less thing for him to worry about.

And now it was an hour later and James and Perry were skirting round London in the Bamford and Martin, disguised in their goggles, hats and overcoats.

'Let's hope you're right about all this,' Perry bellowed into the wind.

'I don't know whether I'd rather be right or wrong,' shouted James. 'If I'm wrong, and this is all just part of a damned silly game, then we're risking a hell of a lot for nothing, but if I'm right, then it could get pretty serious.'

Perry slowed as they came to a village and the drumming of the wind quietened down.

'Are you sure we shouldn't just tell someone and let the police deal with it?' he said, keeping his eyes fixed on the road ahead.

'No, of course I'm not sure,' said James. 'Which is why I want to check it all out myself before I go blabbing to any grown-ups. What if it came out that we'd broken into Codrose's study and stolen that letter? Especially as I promised the Head that I'd keep out of trouble. And now look at us. On top of everything else we're driving a motor car.'

'Best not to think about that,' said Perry, accelerating as they left the village.

'We'll talk to Professor Peterson,' James shouted. 'He'll know what to do.'

'It's pretty thrilling, though, isn't it?' Perry yelled at the top of his voice, skilfully manoeuvring the car around a lumbering farm lorry packed with sheep. 'To think that we could be solving a m-major crime.'

'We're not going to solve anything,' James shouted. 'If we find out for certain that Fairburn has been kidnapped then Peterson will probably go straight to the police and we'll just have to face the consequences.'

Two hours after leaving Windsor they were driving into the outskirts of Cambridge. They didn't want to risk being spotted on the busy streets so they parked the car in a quiet side road south of the town around the corner from a cafe whose brightly lit windows were fogged with condensation.

They climbed out of the car, their cold, stiff limbs complaining.

James removed his goggles. 'We need to hurry,' he said.

'Listen, James,' said Perry, hanging back. 'I don't think we should both go.'

'What?' said James. 'Why?'

'Just to be on the safe side,' said Perry. 'What if this Professor Peterson is m-mixed up in this somehow? What if the m-man who came to the Crossword Society meeting was him after all? We don't know what Fairburn's letter m-meant, he could have been trying to warn us. I'll stay here and look after the car, then if anything happens I'll be able to help you.'

'You're probably right,' said James. 'Maybe we shouldn't both go blundering in there.'

'I'll m–meet you in that cafe we passed,' said Perry. 'Good luck.'

James thanked him and walked off towards the centre of Cambridge.

All the light had gone from the sky. The streets were lit by flickering orange street lamps and an enticing glow that spilt from the windows and doors of the shops. There were already some Christmas decorations up and James spotted a model shop that he would normally have stopped to have a look round.

The route was well signposted and James soon found the right way to Trinity. There was a lively, busy atmosphere in the town. Students on bicycles, wearing long scarves, clogged the roads, ringing their bells and calling out to friends. Mothers and nannies with small children strolled on the pavements, looking in the shop windows. A group of music students stood on a corner opposite King's College, singing carols, accompanied by a four-piece brass band.

In the same way that Eton was a town entirely dominated by a school, Cambridge was a town entirely dominated by a university. The huge rectangular chapel of King's, with a pointed spire at each corner, reminded James of the chapel at Eton, and he vaguely recalled that it had been built at the same time. The king who had founded this college was the same king who had founded Eton, Henry VI, and the idea was that boys educated at Eton would come to study here when they left school.

James walked on a little further and found the Trinity gatehouse; again he was struck by a resemblance to a building in Eton, this time the tall, red-brick Lupton's Tower in School Yard. The gatehouse was squatter, though, and looked something like a miniature Tudor castle. An ancient and rather pathetic statue of Henry VIII stood above the entrance clutching a chair leg where his sceptre should have been, probably put there by a drunken student.

Inside the gatehouse he found the porter's lodge where a porter, wearing a dark-blue suit and bowler hat, was sitting drinking a cup of tea. James told him that he was running an errand for someone and had to deliver a message to Professor Peterson.

'He's popular this evening,' said the porter, cheerily. 'You're his third visitor. Hang on a mo.'

The porter strode out into the courtyard and gave a shrill whistle, then waved to someone and shouted something. Presently he returned with a tall, slightly scruffy young man.

'This gentleman can show you the way,' he explained. 'He's a regular visitor – aren't you, Mister Turing? He was just on his way to the professor's rooms himself.'

James signed in, at the last minute deciding to use a false name. He chose 'John Bryce', thinking that if he kept the same initials as his own name it would be easier to remember. Then he followed the young man into the college.

'Are you a professor here?' James asked.

'Me? Good lord, no.' The young man laughed. 'Not yet, at least. I'm not even at this college. My name's Alan by the way, Alan Turing. I'm working on a research project with the professor. He's a very brilliant mathematician.'

'I'll take your word for it,' said James. 'I'm afraid mathematics is not my strong point. Not that I know what my strong point *is* exactly,' he added.

The courtyard they were crossing was huge, with more Tudor buildings around the sides and an elaborate stone fountain in the middle. It was like School Yard, only on a much larger and grander scale.

As they walked the college clock began to chime.

'Do you know,' said Turing, 'in nineteen twenty-seven one of the students, Lord Burghley, ran all the way around the square in the time it takes the clock to strike twelve? That's less than thirty seconds. Never been done before or since.'

It turned out that Turing was a keen runner and they fell into a relaxed conversation about athletics. As they talked, they passed through a long, Gothic building and into a second courtyard and then a third, much smaller one.

'Here we are,' said Turing, as he led James inside and up a noisy, wooden staircase. At the top was a door of black oak, studded with iron nails.

Alan smiled at James and knocked. They heard what sounded like someone moving about on the other side of the door, but there was no answer.

Turing knocked again but there was still no reply.

'I'm sure I heard someone,' said James and he looked down to see a sliver of light shining from under the door.

'Must have imagined it,' said Turing. 'Or else it was

coming from one of the other rooms. Very hard to tell in these old buildings. It's odd, though,' he added, scratching his untidy hair. 'He was expecting me.'

'Is he often late?' asked James.

'Never,' said Turing. 'He's one of the most organized men I know.'

James felt disappointed and frustrated. He had been expecting Peterson to answer all his questions and now he was faced with the possibility of not meeting him at all. A possibility he had not even considered. Maybe Turing could help, though. There was certainly one point he could clear up for him.

'What does the professor look like?' James asked.

'What does he look like?' Turing rubbed his chin with his hand, thinking hard. 'I'm not sure I could say for certain. He doesn't look like much, really. Just ordinary, I suppose. Yes – just perfectly ordinary.'

'He doesn't have a moustache?'

'Not so as you'd notice.'

'Well, he either does or he doesn't!' said James, trying not to laugh.

'Doesn't,' said Turing.

'Is he tall? Short?'

Turing chuckled. 'I'm not much use to you, am I?' he said. 'As I say, I've not really noticed. He's about my height, I suppose. I mean, don't think me a fool, if I was to see him on the street I'd obviously recognize him. "There's Professor Peterson!" I'd say. But visual things aren't really *my* strength, you see. If you asked me to draw him for you I'd be all at sea. He's got the usual complement of arms and legs, one nose, two eyes, all that sort of thing.' He stopped and looked at his watch, unsure of what to do.

James knocked again. As hard and as loud as he could, but there was nothing but silence from the other side of the door. Turing sighed.

'I think I'm going to come back later,' he said. 'Maybe I got the days muddled. I'm not as organized as the professor. Will you wait? Or shall I show you out?'

'I'll hang on a minute longer, I think,' said James. 'Thank you for your help.'

'Help?' said Turing. 'I don't think I was much help. Good luck.'

James listened to his footsteps clattering down the stairs, and once it was all quiet he carefully tried the door to see if it was locked. If Peterson wasn't there, maybe James could at least find some clues in the room.

He grinned as the handle turned and the door clicked open. It led directly into a cosy, well-lit sitting room. A fire burnt in the grate. There were books around the walls, some battered old furniture, and a mug of coffee sitting on a low table by the fireplace. The smell of cigarette smoke hung in the air.

'Professor Peterson?' James called out softly. 'Gordius?'

Apart from the crackle of the fire there was no sound.

James knew he should get out of there quickly. If he was caught it would take all his cunning to think of an excuse, but his curiosity got the better of him and he walked over to the fireplace.

Above the mantelpiece was a cork noticeboard, with notes, letters, bills and photographs neatly pinned to it.

James looked at the photographs. They were nearly all of the same person, from different times in his life. This must be Professor Peterson, but it was very definitely *not* the man who had introduced himself as such to the Crossword Society.

Turing had been right. Peterson looked completely ordinary. These were photographs of an ordinary life. Here was a young boy in a sailor suit holding a flag. Here an older boy, looking very serious, with his mother and father. There was a more recent photograph of him looking slightly uncomfortable in academic robes, wearing an elaborate hat. And there were several which must have been taken in his student days. They showed a happy, open-faced young man. One picture caught James's eye. Peterson was posing with two friends in fancy dress. Peterson wore an eighteenth-century costume with a long curly wig, the person next to him wore a suit of armour complete with closed helmet, and the third person was dressed as a cowboy.

There was a speech bubble, as in a cartoon, coming from the cowboy's mouth and someone had written inside it with a scratchy pen:

Happy days. Happy memories. Good luck in everything you do. Alex.

Alex?

James realized with a shock that the cowboy in the photograph was Alexis Fairburn. The picture must have been taken when he was at university with Peterson.

Fairburn had more distinctive features than his friend, with a large nose and ears, and wild, curly hair pushed up to one side like a breaking wave.

James continued searching the room and found a small door behind a curtain that must have been hung there to keep the draught out. He carefully opened it and went through.

He found himself in a study. There were even more books in here, shelf after shelf of them, and orderly piles of papers resting on every available surface, but James paid no attention to any of this.

There was a man at a desk by the window, sitting very still and staring at James, his hands resting on the desktop, a pen stopped halfway through writing a sentence. A cigarette was smouldering in an ashtray, filling the room with smoke.

It was Peterson.

'Sorry,' James muttered. 'There was no reply . . . I knocked . . . I didn't mean to . . .'

James ran out of steam under the man's icy stare.

A three-bar electric fire stood in one corner, pumping out heat, but the room suddenly seemed very cold, the walls pressing in.

James stepped closer. There was something wrong. The man was *too* still, *too* icy, and, as James moved, the eyes didn't follow; instead they remained fixed, staring blindly at the doorway.

See Cambridge and Die

Peterson was as unmoving as a statue and James knew for sure that he was dead.

This ordinary man, whom James had seen growing up in the photographs next door, was dead.

And death had made him extraordinary.

There was no breath coming out of the body. There was no rise and fall of the chest. No faint tick of a pulse at his temples. The eyes were dull, drying up. A spark had gone out, a light switched off.

There is a difference between a living person and a dead one, something indescribable. A dead person is somehow no longer a person. He is a lump of flesh. The only part of Peterson that was still alive was the bacteria in his stomach. They would thrive and grow and the gases would build up until the stomach burst and the bacteria would spread through the rest of the body.

Already it was beginning to rot and decay.

James gingerly held out a hand. There was still some warmth in the skin, which meant that he wasn't long dead, but how had he died? James could see no signs of violence, no mark on him of any kind. Perhaps he had had a heart attack?

No. There was no evidence of pain. No grimace. His face looked bland, almost calm. Whatever had happened, had happened fast.

James was mystified, but as he looked at Peterson, a tiny drop of blood welled in the corner of his right eye then trickled slowly down his face, like a scarlet tear.

There was a small soft *pat* as the drop fell from Peterson's chin on to the desk.

James looked down. Peterson had been writing a letter.

Dear John, it started.

James looked back at Peterson's face and saw a small, puckered, puncture hole in the tear duct of his eye, about the size of one of the Os in the letter.

He swallowed. His throat was very dry. He had crossed a line; from the ordinary world of carol singers and bicycles and model shops, into this bizarre world where a dead man sat calmly at his desk, forever frozen in the act of writing a letter.

His mind was struggling to make sense of it all. It was almost like another weird puzzle in Fairburn's game.

He shivered, even though he was sweating inside his heavy overcoat. He was paralysed. As rooted to the spot as Peterson.

Then there was another *pat* as a fresh drop of blood fell on to the letter, and James felt a movement in the air. With the change of air came a smell. A smell of lavender and blocked drains. And then a series of thoughts crashed into his head all on top of each other.

Peterson was still warm.

Peterson had only just been killed.

Someone had killed him.

Someone had pierced him through that tiny hole in his eye, and it had been done so quickly and so neatly that he had died instantly and seized up at his desk.

James and Turing had been outside for several minutes. They had seen no one go in or come out, but there had been that noise when they had first arrived, as if someone were moving around inside Peterson's rooms.

The porter had said that James was the third visitor that evening.

Turing was the second.

The killer must have been the first. And they must have surprised him moments after he had murdered the professor.

That meant that when James had come in, the killer was still here.

And he was still here now.

James was suddenly alert. His senses screaming. The focus of his vision, which had been narrowed down on to the body at the desk, now snapped wide and took in the whole room in an instant. There was a second door. And his ears picked up a tiny sound. The rustle of a sleeve perhaps.

There was someone behind it.

James knew it. As surely as he knew that Peterson was dead and that whoever was on the other side of that door had killed him.

As surely as he knew that if he didn't get out of here, he, too, would be killed.

Almost without thinking James grabbed a chair and

99

jammed it under the door handle, then he snatched the letter from under Peterson's hand, and as he dragged it away, the stiffly held pen drew a neat line across it.

Peterson sat there unchanged, the pen now resting on a piece of paper that had been underneath the letter. Written on it was what looked like code. Rows and rows of minute ones and zeros.

James grabbed this as well, and in a second he was out of the room and running. Back through the sitting room and out on to the landing. Then he stopped, made a quick decision, and ran back. He plucked the photograph of Peterson and Fairburn from the noticeboard, stuffed it in his pocket and bolted out again. He raced down the stairs and out into the cold night air.

Past a row of parked cars he could see another exit from the college. He sprinted towards it and into a side road that ran between high brick walls. He came out on to Trinity Street and got his bearings. King's College was to the right. That was the way he had come. He set off at a fast jog.

The road was full of students on bicycles and families bundled up against the cold. James had escaped the strange world behind the college walls and the lifeless man sat forever writing at his desk in that stuffy room. He could be gone from here, he could disappear back into the ordinary world and not be mixed up in all this.

The body would soon be discovered, after all . . .

No. He must tell someone.

He stopped and was just about to turn back when he spotted a familiar figure.

It was Alan Turing, looking into a bookshop window.

James ran over to him and tugged at his sleeve.

'Bryce!' said Turing, surprised to see James. 'Did he turn up?'

'No . . . well, yes . . . well . . .' James didn't know what to say and blurted out the first thing that came into his mind. A question that had been nagging away at him.

'What were you and the professor working on?' he asked, trying to appear calm.

'Ah . . .' said Turing, pulling a scarf from his pocket and wrapping it around his neck. 'We were seeing if we couldn't improve on Babbage's work and build a new sort of Difference Engine. I say *build*, but it's all theoretical, really . . .' Turing stopped and looked properly at James for the first time. 'I say, are you all right?' he said. 'You look quite agitated.'

If Turing had only known it, this was the understatement of the year.

James hadn't really been listening to Turing, because he had just spotted someone over the student's shoulder.

A man was walking slowly up the street, tall and stooped, wearing a long black coat and top hat. His huge head like a skull.

It was unmistakably the man James had seen driving the Daimler that night in Eton after the Crossword Society meeting, when it had almost run him down.

James knew that it was no coincidence that he was here now, walking purposefully towards him.

Death – that's how Katey, the maid at Eton, had described him – as the figure of death. And she hadn't been far wrong.

'Don't go back there,' James blurted out. 'To the professor's rooms. Don't go back alone. Go to the police. Take them there. And do it now.'

'I say,' said Turing. 'Whatever are you talking about? What's all this about the police?'

The skull-faced man locked eyes with James and grinned. That sealed it. James would never forget those two jagged rows of brown, rotting teeth.

And even from a distance of more than fifteen feet, James could smell him. The smell of bad breath poorly disguised with lavender water.

'Please,' he said, moving away from Turing. 'Just do it.'

'I don't understand, Bryce,' said Turing. 'What's this all about?'

'I shouldn't be here,' said James and he shuffled backwards a few paces. 'But it wasn't me. You have to believe me.'

At last he turned and ran, shouting over his shoulder to the confused Turing: 'Tell them it was Peterson's first visitor. All right? It wasn't me!'

James didn't check to see if the skull-faced man was following. He prayed that he would be fast enough to get away from him on the still-crowded streets.

He barged through a knot of people, leaving a trail of curses and protests behind him as he ran across the road. A cyclist swerved to avoid him, losing control and crashing into another student on a bike. There was a clash of metal and a stream of shouted abuse, but James didn't stop or look back. He rushed madly down the pavement until he came to a well-lit pub and pushed in through the front doors. Even at this hour the place was busy with students and locals. It was a Friday night before Christmas, and people were in a party mood.

He squirmed his way between the damp bodies of the men and found a back door that led out into a quiet back alley. He pounded along it and, as he reached the end, he risked a backwards glance.

There was no one there. For the moment he had lost his pursuer, but, as he turned back to run on, he collided with a young man who was strolling along whistling a snatch of Mozart. The two of them sprawled against the wall and held on to each other for support.

'Watch where you're going,' said the young man with a smile. 'You nearly had us both over.' He looked like a sober law student or a clerk. James muttered an apology and walked briskly on.

He may be safe for now, but he knew he mustn't relax. He needed to find Perry and get well away from Cambridge before deciding what to do next.

Using back alleys and side streets he worked his way towards the cafe they had arranged to meet at. It had started to drizzle, and the drizzle turned to sleet. The streets began to empty, which wouldn't help him as he would stand out more. Also, the pavements were getting slippery, and he had to slow down.

He stumbled on, getting soaked to the skin, until he at last saw the cafe up ahead. He speeded up the final few feet and hurried in through the door.

The cafe was filled with a fug of smoke and steam. There was a puddle of slush in the doorway and a smell of boiled potatoes and sticky cakes. A giant tea urn bubbled and hissed behind the counter.

James looked over the pink, shiny faces of the customers, searching desperately for Perry. The place was packed. People were obviously using it as much for shelter as refreshment.

'Can I help you, dearie?' said a large woman, bustling over and wiping her hands on her apron.

'I was just looking for someone,' said James. 'A boy. He's bigger than me, a little older. He was by himself.'

'I know who you mean,' said the waitress. 'A stutterer, poor lad.'

'That's him.'

'He left about ten minutes ago, I think.'

'Thank you,' said James. 'Maybe I'll wait for him. Could you bring me a cup of black coffee?'

'Course I can, love,' said the woman and she waddled over to the counter.

James found an empty table and sat down. He put a hand into his coat pocket to check his money and felt the letter he'd taken from Peterson's study.

He suddenly felt scared again. As if everyone was watching him. Why had he taken the letter? It was stupid and reckless.

He knew why. If *he* hadn't taken it then the killer would have. It might be a clue to what was going on. As might the piece of paper with the code on it.

The photograph of Peterson and his college friends was in his other coat pocket. He slipped it out and studied it in his lap, hidden below the edge of the table.

Seeing Peterson's smiling face he felt desperately sad. The young man in the picture had been so full of life, without a care in the world, and now he was dead.

James turned the photograph over. There was something written on the back in a flamboyant scrawl.

Ivar. I thought you might like this picture of the three of us from the May Ball. The terrible trio! Peterson, Charnage and Fairburn. Or should I say, Sir Isaac Newton, Sir Lancelot and Hopalong Cassidy! I have kept a copy for myself. It will be a fine way to remember you and John. I hope, though, that we shall always be friends.
Alexis

John?

James put the photograph away and slipped the letter out of his pocket. It was addressed to John. Could it be the same John from the photograph?

He glanced up to see an old woman staring at him. He smiled at her, then quickly read what Peterson had written before he'd died.

Dear John,
I have heard nothing from either you or Alexis since I came to see you in Berkeley Square the other day.
I know you told me not to panic. I know you assured me that Alexis would be all right and that we needn't

involve the police, but I am very worried about him. I
think the time has come to . . .

The next few words were obscured by blood, and there
was nothing after that.

James put the letter back in his pocket and took out
the piece of paper with the code on it. It was written by
hand, but in the smallest, neatest handwriting James had
ever seen. Row after row of ones and zeros in blocks,
separated by little black dots.

He kicked off one of his shoes. There was a secret
compartment in the heel, which came in useful when he
needed to hide things, and which always held a small
penknife. Under cover of the table he carefully folded the
coded paper and squeezed it into the hollow heel, before
putting the shoe back on.

He knew he couldn't fit anything else in, so he took
one last look at the letter to memorize it and put it back
in his pocket with the photograph.

He felt safer now and when the waitress brought over
his coffee he sipped it gratefully. Its bitter taste shocked
him into alertness and its heat soaked into him. He drank
it slowly, hoping that Perry would return, but by the time
he had finished there was still no sign of his friend. So
he paid and went back out into the night.

The brief warmth of the cafe had only served to point
up how cold and wet it was outside. Praying that Perry
had gone back to the car, James headed towards where
they'd parked, turning his collar up against the sleet. When
he got there, though, he could find no sign of his friend

and the car was standing, bedraggled, in a big puddle, the seats soaked.

He looked in all directions and called out Perry's name, but the sound was swallowed up by the tall buildings and the sleet-filled air.

Now what?

Maybe Perry had gone to Trinity to look for him?

James badly needed someone to talk to. He didn't know what to do next. He was utterly alone. The sleet was falling on him. He was shivering. He was cold and wet and miserable and frightened.

He kicked the front wheel of the Bamford and Martin and swore.

He wiped away tears of frustration and, as his vision cleared, he saw the young man he had bumped into earlier approaching cautiously in a slight crouch, his arms spread wide in front of him.

Then James heard the soft ticking of an engine and the street was flooded with white light from a car's headlamps. The young man shielded his eyes from the glare. James twisted round. It was the Daimler.

What a fool he'd been.

The skull-faced man wasn't working alone.

There were two of them.

James didn't think twice. He sprang over the side of his car, pressed the electric starter and wrenched it into reverse gear. As the engine exploded into life the young man stopped briefly, then broke into a run.

James released the handbrake and the car leapt backwards, seeming to tear at the ground in its eagerness to be off. He pressed his foot down on the accelerator and headed straight for the young man, who jumped aside, slipping and sliding into the gutter.

James stamped on the brake and the car slid to a halt. Quick as he could he pressed the clutch and jostled the gear lever into first. The young man was back on his feet, though, and he made a grab for the car, just managing to get a grip on the top of the doorframe with his fingertips.

James accelerated and as the car pulled forward the man yelped and let go.

James didn't stay to watch. He careered down the street and pulled left on to the main road, the back of the car slewing round into a skid. He steered into it and goosed the accelerator just enough to regain control. Once he had straightened up he changed gear and roared off, a line of startled cyclists pulling over to the side to let him pass, the rasping scream of his engine echoing off the shop fronts.

He headed south, hoping to get away from Cambridge and hide out somewhere until it was safe to return and look for Perry.

He was soon on the outskirts of town and was feeling quite pleased with himself when he saw the dark bulk of a car pulling up alongside. He turned his head quickly.

It was the Daimler, with the skull-faced man at the wheel, and the younger man at his side.

Hell. It wasn't over yet . . .

9

The Smith Brothers

James dropped into a lower gear and stamped the pedal right down to the floorboards. The engine complained but the Bamford and Martin speeded up. After a second, with the revs almost off the dial, he changed up, then up again. The car was flat out now, going more than sixty miles an hour. He overtook two cars then pulled back over to the left of the road, spraying muddy water over a line of people who were waiting at a bus stop.

He kept his speed up, but was blinded by the sleet that was slamming into him. He wiped his face and saw that the buildings had dropped away and he was in open countryside. Out of town there were no streetlights and all he could see clearly was the small patch of brightness that his headlamps carved out in front of him.

James was gripped by a mixture of panic, fear and excitement. He had never driven this fast before. He could feel the body of the car shaking and rattling. Every tiny bump in the road felt like he was hitting a great boulder. His face was frozen, his lips forced back from his aching teeth. He fought to keep the car under control as it bounced over the road, but his hands were numb on the slippery wheel.

He didn't know if he could outrun the Daimler. It was larger and heavier than the Bamford and Martin, but it was more powerful and its driver more experienced. Plus, the skull-faced man had the advantage of being able to follow James's rear lights. James had nothing.

He was on the point of looking round to see how far behind the Daimler was when he felt a mighty jolt and heard a bang.

They had rammed him. He swerved across the road and narrowly avoided a car going the other way, shrouded in a cocoon of spray. He fought the Bamford and Martin back under control and coaxed a little more speed out of her. She was still handling all right, so the collision hadn't caused any serious damage, but if they rammed him again he might not be so lucky.

There were lights up ahead and they thundered into a village. James was aware of a brief blur of buildings and a howling racket and then darkness again.

This was fenland, flat and featureless for miles around. There was nowhere to hide out here. It was totally exposed. The wind cut across it, flat and hard. James wasn't sure how long he could keep this up. He was driving on instinct, the thinking part of his brain was shut down. His eyes were stinging, and no matter how often he blinked them he could barely see anything. Then he remembered that his goggles were in the glovebox. He leant over and fumbled for them, steering with one hand. His fingers closed around the strap and he yanked them out. He tried to pull them over his face. For a moment he was completely blinded, but then they were on. Almost immediately they were plastered with sleet and he had to wipe them clean, but it was still a small improvement.

Once again the Daimler rammed him and his head jerked painfully back. If they kept up this crazy chase they would eventually either run out of road or crash. Either way, James was done for.

In the next village they came to, James suddenly took a right fork and left the London road. Then he took a series of wild turns and switchbacks in an effort to shake off the Daimler, at one point even crashing through a hedge and crossing someone's garden to reach a road on the other side. But at every turn the Daimler kept up with him. Twice it pulled alongside and tried to nudge him off the road and it was only by wrenching the wheel and manoeuvring the car with all his strength that James held the tarmac.

At last, in the small town of Fulford, he saw his chance.

The road was blocked by a broken-down lorry.

There was a gap just wide enough to squeeze the Bamford and Martin through, but there was no way the Daimler could follow.

Barely slowing down, James threw the car into the opening. There was a hideous scraping and screeching as he ground against the lorry. Sparks flew up into the air. Then he was out the other side like a cork from a bottle. He glanced back. The lorry driver was chasing after him, waving his fist, but there was no sign of the Daimler. He shouted in triumph and slowed down to a sensible speed.

He'd made it.

Just.

He was exhausted, completely drenched and cold to his very core. He was driving in a daze now, not sure where he was going or what he should do. The shock of finding the dead man and then driving at full speed for all that time had drained him. He struggled to keep his eyes open and focused. When he thought about what he'd just done he didn't know whether to laugh or cry. He had been too close to death. If anything had gone wrong he would have been smashed to pieces . . .

He wiped his goggles for the hundredth time and the blood turned to ice in his veins.

He would recognize the pattern of those twin beams anywhere. They were burnt into his brain. It was the Daimler. It was stopped in the middle of the road, blocking the way. Somehow they had got round him and ahead. Maybe on a faster road. They probably had the benefit of a road map.

Now James definitely felt like weeping. This wasn't fair after all he'd been through.

Well, damn them. Damn them to hell. He wasn't done yet.

He pushed the accelerator down as far as it would go and aimed straight for them.

He wasn't thinking about anything, he was just staring at the lights as they got bigger and bigger. He would drive straight between them if necessary. Drive straight through and carry on going.

He cackled.

It had finally happened. He'd gone crazy.

Just so long as *they* thought the same.

The gap narrowed, the Daimler got closer, its big bonnet glistening.

He saw the panicked faces of the two men.

'Come on,' said James, through clenched teeth. 'Are you going to get out of the way, or are you going to die?'

At the last moment the skull-faced man decided that he was going to get out of the way.

In a mad scramble he shunted the engine into first, released the clutch, twisted the wheel round and juddered off the road into a ditch. James shot past him, whooping in triumph, but then his eyes stretched wide in horror. The Daimler had been blocking his view of the road ahead. There was a dip and a huge puddle of half-frozen water. The Bamford and Martin ploughed into it and the wheels lost contact with the road. A great spray of water exploded and he was skimming across the surface like a boat. On the other side of the puddle the road curved slightly and climbed up to a narrow bridge with thick stone walls. The front of the car crunched as it bottomed into the slope and James was thrown forward, smashing his face against the steering wheel. The car hurtled on. It clipped one wall of the bridge, bounced across to the other side and crashed through the stonework.

Still holding the wheel, James was flying through space. The nose of the car dropped and it performed a lazy somersault. He was aware of the ground rushing up and flipping over, then he was thrown clear, not knowing which way was up or down. He soon found out, though, as he thudded into a bed of weeds at the river's edge.

He was jarred and winded and for a split second he blacked out. But then he felt a great thump as the car hit the ground some twenty feet further on.

He struggled woozily to his feet and hauled himself up the bank, his feet sinking into the thick wet sludge. The car had gouged out a long muddy furrow and was resting upside down. Befuddled and confused, James staggered towards it, with the hazy idea of somehow righting it and driving away. He had not gone three steps, however, when he was flung backwards as the petrol in the car's tank exploded.

He was unconscious before he hit the icy water of the river.

Their names were Wolfgang and Ludwig Smith, and they were brothers. Ludwig was the older of the two and all his life he had looked like a skeleton. He was so pale and thin when he was born, and his skin clung so tightly to his bones, that the midwife had gasped in horror, fearing that his mother had given birth to a corpse.

'Don't worry,' his father had said, 'he'll soon fill out.' But he never did. No matter how much he ate, he stayed gaunt and skeletal. His giant head had almost killed his mother when he was born, and his back was bent out of shape by its great weight. He was plagued by headaches that made him irritable and bad-tempered. In contrast, Wolfgang had always looked perfectly normal. Boringly normal, in fact, so that people often questioned whether the two of them were really brothers at all.

Their parents had been musicians who played largely

in the music halls. The father a violinist, the mother a pianist. They had named the two boys after their favourite composers, Ludwig van Beethoven and Wolfgang Amadeus Mozart, in the hope that they would follow in their footsteps.

They hadn't. They had followed a very different path from their parents.

Maybe it was because of their names. Growing up in Hackney, in the East End of London, was tough for any kid. It was a hundred times tougher if your parents had given you a funny name. Particularly if your names sounded German and your country decided to go to war against Germany.

It was always a source of great amusement to other boys that someone with such an exotic name as Wolfgang should look so ordinary, and Wolfgang had learnt very early in his life that the best way to stop people from laughing at you was with your fists.

Skull-faced Ludwig was picked on for his name *and* his looks, but he was as quick with his fists as his brother.

They gradually gained a reputation for being the toughest kids in the area, and the names Ludwig and Wolfgang Smith, instead of inspiring laughter, inspired fear. They found that their reputations made it easy for them to get money and favours from weaker boys.

Their parents tried to discipline them, but they were rarely around. They mostly worked at night and were often away for days on end playing in far-flung concert halls and theatres.

Neither brother was in any way musical, and even if

they had been, they had no desire to follow their parents into a life of hard work and near poverty. They turned instead to crime, with its promise of quick, easy money.

They joined London's most feared and powerful gang, the Sabinis, under their boss Darby Sabini, where they very soon established themselves as ruthless and heartless thugs. After killing two men in a street brawl, however, they had to flee to Paris to hide out. They stayed in France for two years, living the same life they had lived in London. It was while they were there that Ludwig heard about the infamous Apache gangs from the turn of the century. Fascinated by their evil and ingenious weapon of choice, he had had two of them made for himself.

When it was safe the brothers returned to England where they found themselves in great demand. If anyone wanted a rival bumped off they would call on the Smith brothers. If there was a dead body to be disposed of, a wealthy shopkeeper to be threatened, a building to be torched, or a loose mouth to be silenced, then the Smith brothers were the men for the job.

Up until tonight they had been enjoying their new job immensely, but it was no longer going according to plan. Each blamed the other and they had been arguing about it all the way from Cambridge.

Like all brothers they argued constantly.

They were arguing now as they stood in the rain on the edge of the ruined bridge and stared across to where the Bamford and Martin lay blazing in the field.

'He's dead, Wolfgang,' said Ludwig, picking one of his rotten teeth with a long, dirty fingernail.

'We should check,' said Wolfgang. 'You don't know he's dead for certain.'

'How could he not be dead?' said Ludwig scornfully. 'Look at that bonfire.'

'We should check,' said Wolfgang.

'We'll get muddy,' said Ludwig. 'I don't fancy getting muddy. I'm wet already. To add mud into the mix would be adding insult to injury.'

'But we need to make sure,' said Wolfgang.

'Well, why don't you go and look, then?' said Ludwig. '*You* get muddy, Wolfgang. I'm wearing my best shoes.'

'We should both go,' said Wolfgang. 'What if he's got away? What if he's hiding? What if we have to give chase?'

Ludwig passed a baleful eye over the flat, open countryside. 'Where would he hide?' he said.

'I'm going to look,' said Wolfgang. 'And you're coming with me, Ludwig. Otherwise I shall tell the boss that you couldn't be bothered, because you were scared of getting mud on your best shoes.'

'You *would* tell him, as well, wouldn't you, you little sneak?' said Ludwig. 'You always were a sneak. Why's it so important I come with you?'

'Because if I'm going to get muddy, so are you,' said Wolfgang. 'You always make me do the dirty work.'

'That's because you're the youngest,' said Ludwig, his skull face splitting into a nasty grin.

'It's not fair.'

'It's not fair that I should get muddy,' said Ludwig. 'It's not fair that I should get rained on. It's not fair that I should be out on a dog of a night like this looking for some little brat. Life isn't fair, little brother. Get used to it.'

'I'm serious,' said Wolfgang. 'If you don't come with me, I shall tell the boss.'

'All right, all right, I'm coming,' sighed Ludwig and they set off across the bridge. 'You're just scared, aren't you?' he said, thrusting his hands deep in his pockets. 'You want me to hold your hand.'

'Oh, shut up,' said Wolfgang and they trudged into the field. 'You're giving me a right pain in the gut.'

They followed the long furrow that the car had dug, but couldn't get very close to the burning vehicle as the heat was so intense.

'We need to hurry,' said Ludwig. 'This fire will attract people from miles around.'

'We can't go before we've properly checked.'

'Nobody could survive that,' said Ludwig, waving a hand at the inferno. 'If the fall didn't kill him the explosion would have, for sure.'

'Look for footprints,' said Wolfgang. 'If he walked away from the car we'll see some evidence.'

They circled the burning wreck, scouring the wet earth for any signs of disturbance. They searched as far as the riverbank, but there was nothing to show that anybody had survived.

'I think we've done our duty,' said Ludwig. 'Now, let's get out of here before someone turns up.'

'Let's take one more look at the car,' said Wolfgang. 'See if there's a body in there.'

'You look,' said Ludwig. 'I'm going back to the Daimler.'

118

Wolfgang cursed under his breath and walked back over to the fire, shielding his face from the heat. He tried to make out any recognizable shapes, but what the crash hadn't buckled and ripped and twisted the fire had finished off.

He spat, hearing his spittle hiss as it boiled away, and, at almost the same moment, the heat inside the engine caused a cylinder to rupture, burst open by the expanding gas inside it. With a noise like a gunshot, the sparking plug in the end was blasted out, and it tore through the heat-crazed air like a bullet.

Wolfgang saw it coming and instinctively jerked his head to one side, but he heard a crunching sound by his right ear, and he felt a blow, almost as if he had been slapped.

He felt a stinging in the side of his head, but when he put his hand up to feel if his ear was all right, he found that it was gone.

The spark plug had vaporized it.

Under the bridge, James heard a long agonized howl and then Wolfgang started calling for his brother. Presently there were hurrying footsteps above him on the road and then there was the groan of an engine starting and the Daimler swished away into the distance so that all that remained was the sound of the rain and the gurgling of the river.

The shock of hitting the cold water had woken him and he had found himself entangled in the frame of an abandoned bicycle under the bridge, where the river had washed him.

He had hauled himself out on to the bank and sat huddled and shivering in the darkness, listening to the two men bickering above him and then watching as they searched the field.

Now his thoughts were not so very different from theirs. He wanted to get away from here. Soon people would be arriving and they would be asking questions. Whose car was it? Who had been driving it? Maybe they would believe his story of being chased by two killers, but he doubted it. He would be taken to a police station and it could be days before the whole mess was untangled, and by then anything could have happened to Fairburn.

What had Fairburn said in the letter?

That he was leaving the country, that this week's crossword would be his last, and he would be gone before he could send his next one in.

His puzzle appeared in *The Times* every Tuesday. When would he send it in? On the Monday? The Sunday? Saturday?

There was so little time. He had to hurry.

Hurry . . .

Don't think about crosswords now. Just get away.

He crawled out from his hiding place and set off across the fields running as fast as he could. Which was not very fast at all. He was dazed and confused. There was blood pouring down his face from a cut on his forehead where he had hit the steering wheel. The world seemed to spin around him and he had no clear idea of where he was going. The clouded sky showed no moon or stars and he fell over repeatedly in the darkness. He had lost his coat and his watch in the river and had no idea what time it was, but he forced himself to keep plodding on.

Every now and then, he would close his eyes and stumble forward, more asleep than awake, his head heavy as a boulder. He was cold and wet and exhausted. There was a tingling up his arms and legs, like pins and needles, and as he walked he started to lose the feeling in his hands and feet.

Time seemed to jump about, skipping backwards and forwards, so that one moment he was in a field, surrounded by black-and-white cows, and the next he was walking along the middle of a road. Then he was fighting his way out of a hedge. Then he was among trees. One moment it was sleeting and the next it had stopped. Then he was lying face first in the mud with one of the cows staring curiously down at him.

He closed his eyes and felt the comforting blanket of sleep wrap itself around him. He dreamt he was walking again. He dreamt of a road. And voices came to him, but he couldn't understand them.

His whole body was numb now. He had lost all feeling. He felt calm and peaceful. He wondered if this was how it felt to die. And then the numbness spread to his brain and he sensed it shutting down, bit by bit, like doors closing in a house and the rooms falling silent.

Part Two: SATURDAY

The Big Smoke

James opened his eyes. He was warm. He was dry. And he appeared to be lying in a bed. He raised himself up and looked around, his head throbbing.

Pale-green walls. A row of iron beds. A clock ticking.

A word came to him but wouldn't form. A word that would make sense of all this. He fought to remember what it was, but his brain wasn't working properly.

There was a bandage around his head and he was wearing someone else's pyjamas. There was a strong smell of disinfectant.

What was the word?

He lay back down and closed his eyes.

Hospital.

That was it.

He felt a glow of satisfaction and triumph. His brain was working fine.

Hospital. He was in a hospital.

Soon he was asleep again.

After some time voices came to him. He stayed still and listened. His eyes closed.

'What time was he brought in?' This was a man's voice. Used to giving orders, bossy and cold.

'Just before midnight.' This was a woman's voice. Irish. A young woman. Kinder than the man. 'A travelling salesman found him wandering in the road and drove him here.'

'Do we know anything about him?'

'Not a thing. He had no identification on him. He must have been in an accident of some sort. We'll find out more when he wakes.'

'Has he been out like this since he arrived?'

'He was just conscious when he was brought in, but delirious. We couldn't understand anything he said. We cleaned him, dressed the wound, gave him an analgesic, and he's been sleeping since.'

'Have you notified the police?'

'Yes. They're coming first thing in the morning to talk to him.'

'No clues at all?'

'Nothing. We searched all his clothes. All he had on him was a few coins.'

'Where are his clothes now?'

'They're being dried.'

'Hang on to them. The police will want to see them.'

'Yes, doctor, of course.'

Footsteps receding. Voices murmuring quietly. A rustle and a moan from one of the other beds. Then silence.

James opened one eye a crack. At the far end of the ward he could see the nurse and the doctor standing by another bed. They stayed there for a while, talking, then walked out of view.

James shifted his head a fraction until he could see the clock. It was nearly five.

They'd brought him in just before twelve. That meant he'd been here five hours. Five hours' sleep. That was enough. He certainly felt wide awake now. Talk of the police had focused his mind magnificently. He wasn't going to wait around here until the morning, of that he was sure. The last place he wanted to be these next few days was in a police station.

Carefully, squinting through his eyelashes, he made a sweep of the area. Once he was certain there was nobody else around – at least nobody else who was awake – he rolled out of bed.

He would need some clothes.

As he straightened up, a wave of nausea and dizziness passed over him, but he rode it out until his head cleared, and then checked the small cabinet by his bed. All he found were his damp shoes. Someone had stuffed them with newspaper to help them dry.

He padded along the row of beds, looking in all the other cabinets. A few of them were as empty as his, but a couple contained piles of neatly folded clothes. When he came to a man who was about his own size – a little old fellow of about fifty, with a wheezing chest – he opened his cabinet and found a pair of dark suit trousers sitting neatly on top of a folded jacket.

He pulled the suit on over his pyjamas. He didn't have time for socks and his pyjama top would have to stand in for a shirt.

He went back to his own bed, took the newspaper out

of his shoes and slipped them on. He was about to leave when he heard voices and jumped under his covers, pulling them up to his chin.

Through slitted eyes he watched the nurse come back along the ward with a sister. They stopped by one of the other beds, exchanged a few words, and then carried on.

He let out his breath in a long sigh and waited a few minutes before getting out of bed again. It was a real struggle this time. The bed felt warm and cosy and safe. A little voice in the back of his mind was telling him to stay, to go back to sleep, to let someone else sort out his problems.

No.

He shoved his pillows under his sheets in the rough shape of a sleeping body, crept down to the end of the ward and peeped around the corner. There was a lighted nurses' station where the young Irish girl sat drinking a cup of tea and reading a magazine. Beyond was another ward.

The sister reappeared and James flattened himself against the wall. He realized he was next to a coat stand with a couple of coats and hats on it and he tried to lose himself among the folds of heavy material.

He needn't have bothered, neither the nurse nor the sister looked his way, and after a while the sister walked briskly off again.

James carefully removed one of the coats and slipped it on. Then he grabbed a hat and pulled it down over the bandage on his head.

He backed into the ward and looked around for another

way out. There was no chance of getting past the Irish nurse.

In one wall was a large casement window, opened slightly to let in fresh air for the patients. He tiptoed over to it, forced it up and looked out. He was three floors above the street, but there was a narrow ledge running around the building towards an iron fire escape. He slithered out and crawled on to the ledge. It was just wide enough for him to fit, and, holding on to the window for support, he carefully eased himself upright until he was standing with his back pressed against the rain-slick wall.

A fine drizzle filled the misty air and it was still dark, but he could see enough from up here to tell that he was in a city. There were large buildings all around and the streets below were well lit and had traffic, even at this time of night. The most likely conclusion was that he was in London – the Big Smoke. Though exactly whereabouts in London he had no idea.

And if he was in London, then he could get to Perry's house. Whether or not Perry would be there was not something James wanted to think about right now.

He took one step and his shoe slipped. He just managed to keep his balance but told himself to go steady. Some fifty feet below was a wall with a set of lethal-looking spiked iron railings along the top of it. It wouldn't do to fall.

He crabbed slowly along the ledge, feeling his way with his feet, until he reached the safety of the fire escape and climbed gratefully on to it.

Getting down the fire escape was easy and he was soon

at the bottom in a dingy side alley that was packed with stinking dustbins.

A large mouse scurried from behind a bin and was pounced on by a mangy old black cat with one ear. The cat pinned the mouse down with one paw and looked up at James with a blank expression.

'Don't mind me,' said James and he was just about to walk on when he realized that there was somebody staring at him with wide, shining eyes.

It was a tramp, crouched among the bins, wearing a tattered coat. He had sunken cheeks and only one tooth, and pinned to his chest was a row of medals from the war.

James backed away as the tramp struggled to get up, reaching out a shaking hand towards him. James had nothing to give the man and shook his head. The tramp hopped out of the shadows and James saw that he was missing a leg.

'Don't mind me,' James repeated and walked quickly to the end of the alley.

He turned right when he reached the main road, away from the hospital, and kept walking, his collar turned up and the brim of his hat pulled down.

Once again he had got away safely. He'd had a series of lucky escapes in the last few hours, and he hoped that his luck would hold out.

He laughed.

What was he thinking of?

Here he was in the middle of God knows where, a bandage round his head, no money in his pockets, trudging along in the rain with no socks on, wearing a stolen suit.

What was lucky about that?

What was lucky about finding a dead body, being chased by two killers, crashing his car and watching it burn?

It was how you looked at it, he supposed.

At least he was better off than the one-legged war veteran, sharing his alley with a mangy cat.

If you looked at it another way it looked better.

He had escaped from the killers and survived a car crash.

Why, it almost made you want to whistle a happy tune.

He passed a well-dressed drunk in black tie and tails, who swerved out of his way and swore at him for no reason.

'And a very good morning to you, too,' said James, and he started to laugh, slightly hysterically.

A little further along he came to a group of four hungry-looking men who were standing in a shop doorway for shelter, smoking cigarettes. They were unshaven and lifeless, their suits shabby, their boots worn. They all stared at James with the same expression as the cat – cold and slightly hostile.

James felt a little like the mouse and hurried past.

He had no idea there were so many people out and about at this time of the night. He supposed that things were different in London. If, indeed, that was where he was.

He looked around for any signs but could see no landmarks, and the street names meant nothing to him. All he knew for sure was that he was in a poor and run-down part of town. And then he saw a workshop with big gold letters over the window of its shop front: THE LONDON BOX COMPANY.

His guess was right, then. He supposed that if the travelling salesman who had picked him up had come in on the Cambridge road and stopped at the first hospital he came to, then this must be somewhere in the north-east of London.

Perry's house was in Regent's Park. James knew the name of the road and the number but had no idea how to get there.

The wet shoes were cutting into his bare feet and as his senses returned he realized he was sore and aching all over. He wondered whether to take shelter somewhere, like the group of men, and wait until daybreak, when perhaps he could take a bus. And then he remembered that he had no money. He searched the pockets of his stolen suit but they were empty.

He was in the same position as the tramp. Penniless on the streets of London. Maybe he'd have to start begging.

He stopped walking and leant against a lamp post, watching the drops of rain as they caught the light.

Which way was his luck going to run now?

He looked back the way he had come and saw the four men from the doorway, advancing slowly down the street with their hands in their pockets, staring at him from beneath the brims of their caps.

James swore softly, but viciously.

The night wasn't over yet.

The men walked slowly towards him. It was impossible to tell what they wanted. Their faces, when the streetlights caught them, were blank. The only thing that James knew for sure was that at this time of night any civilized person was safely tucked up in his bed. Normally, he would have just turned and walked briskly away, but he was tired. Dog-tired. Tired of running. Tired of danger. Tired of being scared. And, besides, where would he go?

The man in front took his cigarette from his mouth, tossed it to the ground and stamped the life out of it, all the while keeping his eyes fixed on James.

James heard an engine sound and looked down the street. There, chugging along through the rain, was a taxi. Without thinking, he jumped into the road, waved both of his arms in the air and yelled, 'Taxi!'

The taxi had no option but to stop. It was either that or run James down. The driver was a fat, red-faced man with a big nose.

'You're out late,' he said, winding down his window. 'Or are you up early like me? You're my first passenger of the day. Hop in.' He stretched an arm out to open the back door and James gratefully climbed aboard.

'Where to, mate?' said the cabbie, as he pulled out and moved off.

'Regent's Park,' said James, twisting round in his seat to look back. The men had stopped on the pavement and were sullenly watching the taxi drive away.

'A bit young to be out at this time of night, aren't you?' said the cabbie, glancing in his mirror.

James didn't have the energy to face any awkward questions and wondered whether he should get out of the cab the next time it stopped at a junction. But it was warm and dry in here and he had had enough of the streets. He said nothing, and pulled the stolen coat around his thin body, tipping his head forward to shade his face.

'It's none of my business,' the cabbie went on. 'But if you're in any kind of trouble –'

'You're right,' said James, interrupting. 'It isn't any of your business.'

'No need for that,' said the man. 'I was only going to say that maybe I can help. I know times are hard at the moment. There's all sorts of people out on the streets. Have you got somewhere to stay?'

'I've come to London to visit a friend,' said James. 'In Regent's Park.'

'You're a bit out of the way, aren't you?'

'I got lost. I'll be fine once I get there.'

But would he be? What if Perry wasn't home? James had no money and there was nowhere else to go.

'I know this city well,' said the cabbie. 'London town. You'd be amazed the things I've seen. The stories I could tell. The passengers I've carried. You've a story. I know that much. Maybe you want to tell it to me, maybe you don't. And I suppose you're right. It *is* no business of mine. I'll drop you off in Regent's Park and probably never see you again. You'll just be one more lost soul in a city of lost souls.'

James certainly felt like a lost soul. He stared out of the window at the endless passing streets of London. He couldn't begin to imagine how many people there were living in the city. There was house after house, in long grey rows. One or two had Christmas wreaths on the doors and decorations in the windows. He was swallowed up in a black shadow of sadness. Christmas hadn't been the same since his parents had died. He always enjoyed Christmas Day in his Aunt Charmian's little cottage in Kent, but it wasn't the same. In a sense he knew that he would always be alone in the world.

Perhaps he'd got involved in this crazy adventure to take his mind off the emptiness he always felt at this time of year, when the dark days deepened his sense of loss.

He shook himself and wiped his face.

Don't ever stop and think, James, just keep moving.

'Nearly there, son,' said the cabbie and James looked back out of the window.

They were passing a row of dreary, faceless buildings with names like 'Transco Trading', 'Alliance Holdings', 'The Minimax Fire Extinguisher Company' and 'Universal Export', then they turned off the busy main road and the commercial buildings were replaced by trees.

They were in Regent's Park.

It had stopped raining and there was the faintest glimmer of light in the sky, but the day was still flat and grey and lifeless. The park was ringed by elegant, cream-coloured terraces in a classical Greek style. Many had grand porches held up by pillars.

James had always known that Perry's family was rich, but he had never really thought before about the difference between the two of them. James was perfectly happy living in the little cottage in Kent and couldn't imagine what it would be like to live in such a large, imposing house. He was not sure that he would like it.

135

They found Perry's address – a house on Cumberland Terrace, overlooking the green expanse of the park.

The cabbie pulled up to the front steps.

'I shall have to borrow some money from my friend,' James explained. 'It was further than I imagined.'

'Don't try running off cos I'll come after you,' said the cabbie, though in an almost friendly way. 'I may not look very nimble, but believe you me, I've had plenty of practice chasing fare dodgers.'

'I won't run off,' said James, although he had been planning on doing just that if Perry wasn't home.

He went up the steps to the huge, black front door and pulled the bell.

Nothing happened. James heard no ring in the house and there were no signs of life. In fact, it was quiet as the grave. He pulled the bell again and waited, his heart thumping.

Again nothing.

He turned round. The taxi driver was watching him, the smile on his face slowly dying.

James gave him a reassuring wave and wondered just how fast the man could run.

Scrambled Eggs

James was just about to sprint off down the street when the door swung inwards and there stood a bleary-eyed servant, who had obviously dragged on his uniform in a hurry. He peered at James, who was all too aware what he must look like: a boy in a too-large overcoat, wearing no socks and with a hat pulled down over a fresh bandage on his forehead.

'Good morning, can I help you?' said the man, straining to appear civil.

'Good morning,' said James, as politely as he could. 'I'm a friend of Perry's.'

The man sighed and rubbed his face. 'I rather thought you might be.'

'Is he at home?' said James.

'He's asleep,' said the servant, who had dropped any attempt at politeness now.

'He sleeps no m-more!' came a cry from inside the house and Perry appeared in dressing gown and slippers. 'Strike m-me pink,' he said when he saw James. 'What the devil happened to you?'

'I'll explain in a minute,' said James. 'But I need to pay the taxi driver and I have no money.'

'Braeburn,' Perry said, clapping the servant on the shoulder, 'be a good chap and pay the m-man, would you?'

Braeburn muttered and grumbled as he shuffled down the steps, pulling a purse from his jacket. Perry took James inside.

'Come with m-me,' he said. 'You look like a fellow sorely in need of some breakfast.'

Perry led James through a vast entrance hall with a marble floor and a wide staircase curving upward. There were family portraits on the walls, but the few pieces of furniture were covered by dustsheets and the place felt chilly and unlived-in. James remembered that Perry's family was away, so the house must have been shut down for the winter.

'We'll fill your tank,' said Perry, taking James down a servants' staircase. 'Then you can tell m-me just exactly why you abandoned m-me in the city of dreaming spires.'

'Actually,' said James, wearily, 'I think you'll find that's Oxford.'

'What is?'

'The city of dreaming spires.'

'Well, I saw a fair few spires in Cambridge,' said Perry, 'and they looked pretty dreamy to m-me, but that's not the point. The point is – what the hell happened? I waited for you and when you hadn't shown up I toddled off to Trinity. When I arrived, there was some sort of commotion going on at the porter's lodge, a young m-man was there with a police-m-man.'

'We must have missed each other,' said James. 'I didn't exactly come back by a direct route.'

They had arrived in a large kitchen at the front of the house below street level. There was a range here, big enough to cook for a whole football team, and it warmed the room deliciously.

'When I got back the m–motor had gone,' said Perry indignantly. 'And the woman in the cafe told me you'd been asking after m–me, nice of you to dump m–me like that, I m–must say, I had to get the train home.' Perry stopped and looked at James. He frowned and sighed. 'Where have you been, James?' he said kindly. 'I've been worried sick.'

'It's a long story,' said James, sitting down by the range. He pulled off his shoes and pressed his feet against one of its warm metal doors. 'And I need some food inside me and a cup of strong coffee before I can start it.'

'I propose scrambled eggs,' said Perry. 'Not least because it's the only thing I can cook.'

Perry put a jug of coffee on to heat up, placed two slices of bread under a grill, then found some eggs and began to noisily whisk them in a bowl.

James watched hungrily as Perry tossed the eggs in a pan with some melted butter and stirred them till they were ready. A sudden thought struck him and he began to laugh.

'What's so amusing?' said Perry.

'Scrambled eggs,' said James.

'What about them?'

'It's the answer to a crossword clue.'

'What do you m–mean?' said Perry. 'What was the clue?'

'The one I asked the fake Gordius to solve at the Crossword Society meeting,' said James. 'It was simply the letters "GSGE". It's a sort of riddle and I've just worked out the answer. It's "scrambled eggs".'

'I don't get it,' said Perry.

'It's the word "eggs" all scrambled up,' said James.

'It's all beyond m-me,' said Perry as he put the toasted bread on a plate and scraped the eggs on to it.

James sat at the table and ate slowly and steadily until every last scrap of food was gone from his plate. At last he sat back with a great sigh and wiped his lips. 'That was the best meal I have ever eaten,' he said.

Perry smiled and passed James a mug of coffee. 'Now, your side of the bargain,' he said. 'I can wait no longer.'

And so James told his story, from finding Peterson dead in his study, through the car chase across Cambridgeshire, to waking up in the hospital. For once Perry was silent, listening intently. It was only when James finished, with his arrival on Perry's doorstep, that he finally spoke up.

'If I didn't know you better, James,' he said, 'I'd suspect you of m-making it up. You have a terrible habit of attracting trouble. You are a m-magnet for danger. What are we going to do now?'

'God knows,' said James. 'I haven't a clear thought in my head. Maybe the coffee and eggs will help, but I've been terribly confused, Perry. I can't tell you how glad I am to see you.'

'And m-me you,' said Perry, sitting down opposite James and smiling at him.

'The whole thing's a mess,' said James.

'As I see it,' said Perry, 'we have two options. Either we go straight to the local police station and tell them everything, then face the m-music, or the other option, which I m-must say is m-my favourite, we bury our heads in the sand like a couple of peacocks and let the police sort it out without our help.'

'Ostriches,' said James. 'Not peacocks.'

'You can be an ostrich if you like,' said Perry. 'I'd m-much rather be a peacock. All those feathers.'

James laughed. He was still feeling light-headed and slightly hysterical. 'Can't you ever take anything seriously?' he said.

'I try not to,' said Perry, and then his face dropped and he became thoughtful. 'I'm sorry,' he said. 'I wish I knew what to say. I can't take all this in, James. I really would prefer to go somewhere far away and hide till it was all over.'

'Is it right, though?' said James. 'Not telling anyone?'

'We need to think about saving our skins,' said Perry. 'They'll have found Peterson's body by now, m-maybe they can start piecing it all together themselves.'

'Except I took what might be the only clue,' said James.

'The letter,' said Perry. 'Do you still have it?'

'No,' said James, and he groaned. 'It was in my pocket with the photograph of Peterson and Fairburn. I lost it with my coat in the river.'

'You re-m-member what it said, though?'

James closed his eyes and thought hard. He imagined himself back in the cafe, reading the letter under the table. He pictured the words on the page and slowly they

141

formed in his mind. '*Dear John,*' he said. '*I have heard nothing from either you or Alexis since I came to see you in Berkeley Square the other day. I know you told me not to panic. I know you assured me that Alexis would be all right and that we needn't involve the police, but I am very worried about him . . .*' He stopped and opened his eyes. 'That's about all there was.'

'If we knew who this John chap was,' said Perry, 'we could go and visit him in Berkeley Square.'

'John Charnage,' said James.

'How do you know that?' asked Perry.

'The photograph,' said James. 'There were three friends in the photograph: Fairburn, Peterson and a third man called John Charnage. I'm sure he's the John the letter's written to.'

'The one in the suit of armour, Sir Lancelot?' said Perry.

'Yes,' said James.

'Now we're getting somewhere,' said Perry. 'Let's pour some m-more coffee inside you and see if you don't turn anything else up.' He refilled James's coffee cup, then sat back down at the table.

'Did you lose anything else in the river?' he asked.

'I don't think so,' said James.

'What about the other piece of paper?' said Perry. 'The one with the code on it? Do you still have that?'

'I hope so.' James picked up his shoe and opened the heel. There, tucked snugly inside, was the note. The outer layer was slightly damp, but the water hadn't penetrated far beyond it.

It was still legible.

James unfolded it and flattened it on the scrubbed surface of the kitchen table.

'What do you make of it?' he asked.

Perry studied the rows of ones and zeros. 'No idea,' he said. 'M-maths was never m-my strong point.'

'Nor me,' said James. 'The person we need to show this to is Pritpal. He's a genius with numbers.'

'We should go and visit him at the Eton M-Mission,' said Perry. 'We could be there in half an hour.'

'First we go to Berkeley Square,' said James, 'and find John Charnage. He obviously knows something about what's going on. He'll be able to help us.'

'You see,' said Perry. 'Now we have a plan and things don't seem so bleak. But you're not going out like that, you look like a scarecrow.'

James looked down at his shabby, ill-fitting clothes, and the pyjama jacket he was wearing as a shirt.

'You're right,' he said. 'I'm really not sure I could turn up in Mayfair looking like this.'

'I'll dig out some old clothes of m-mine,' said Perry. 'And I think you could do with a bath as well.'

They went by a back staircase up to the second floor where there was a large, unheated bathroom with a cast-iron bath in it, spotted with rust.

Ten minutes later James was lying on his back staring at the ceiling, which was cracked and stained with mould. He half-floated in the muddy-looking water and tried to empty his mind and think of nothing. He closed his eyes for a moment and felt sleep tugging at him. He tried to fight it but must have nodded off, because the next thing he knew he'd slipped under the water.

He woke with a start, coughing and spluttering, washed himself quickly and got out of the bath.

Perry had given him a three-button aertex shirt, a dark-blue worsted suit and some fresh underwear. He found that they fitted him rather well. Once dressed, he carefully removed the bandage from his forehead and inspected the damage in a mirror over the sink.

There was some bruising, but the cut wasn't as bad as he had feared. He pulled his hair forward with his fingers and arranged it over the wound. He was pleased with the result. The bandage had been too conspicuous. Now you could barely see anything.

He was ready.

It was nine o'clock by the time James and Perry pulled up in a taxi in Berkeley Square. The boys got out and Perry paid the driver.

The square was larger than James remembered. Tall houses stood on all sides and there was a garden in the middle, surrounded by iron railings. Several tall plane trees grew here, looking stark and gaunt without their foliage.

Thin, watery light filtered through the low clouds in the gunmetal-grey sky. The rain was still holding off, but Perry had taken the precaution of bringing an umbrella, which he swung about flamboyantly, its metal tip clacking on the pavement.

'Where do we start?' said James, who had no way of

knowing in which of the many houses John Charnage might live. 'To knock on every door would take all day.'

'I suppose we shall have to ask someone,' said Perry, who was utterly unembarrassed by this sort of thing.

The square was quiet at this time on a Saturday morning, but they spotted a grocery delivery cart, the horses standing tied to some railings. A grocer's boy was approaching the back of the cart carrying an empty basket. Perry strolled over and asked him if he perhaps made deliveries to a Mr John Charnage. The boy sniffed and looked blank.

Perry dug around in his pockets and fished out a handful of coins that he handed to the boy with a wink.

'John Charnage?' Perry repeated. 'Do you know him?'

The boy glanced around the square. There was nobody else about.

'We do all the deliveries round here,' he said proudly, then nodded down the street. 'Charnage's gaff is that one over there in the corner. Nice man, but doesn't always pay his bills on time.'

Perry thanked the boy and made his way with James towards an ugly grey-brick house. No light showed in any of the windows, some of which still had the curtains drawn.

Perry walked up to the front door and tried to peer in through the frosted-glass windows.

'Looks dead in there,' he said and then nearly fell over as the door swung open.

A butler whose immaculate uniform was straining to contain his bulky, muscular body stood there. He had a shaved head and the flattened nose of a boxer.

'Go away,' he said bluntly.

'Ah. Good morning,' said Perry confidently. 'Is this the house of M–Mister John Charnage?'

'*Sir* John Charnage,' said the butler with deliberate emphasis on the 'sir'.

'That's the m-man,' said Perry. 'Sir John. We rather need to see him.'

'I thought I told you to go away,' said the butler.

'It's very important that we see him,' said James. 'It's about his friend Alexis Fairburn.'

The butler looked at James, and wiped his nose with the back of his meaty hand.

'And who are you, exactly?' he said.

'He won't know us,' said James.

'He m–might know my family,' said Perry. 'Tell him that –'

James interrupted before Perry could say any more. 'We are Luc Oliver and Arthur Stevens,' said James. 'But the names won't mean anything to him. Just say we have important information concerning Alexis Fairburn and Professor Ivar Peterson.'

'Wait there,' said the butler and he closed the door on them.

'Sorry about that,' said Perry. 'I should be more careful. Which of us is which?'

'You're Stevens, I'm Oliver,' said James.

Presently the butler returned. He didn't look any friendlier but he let them into the house. 'Sir John will see you,' he said, reluctantly stepping aside.

The gloomy hallway had a stale, airless smell that

reminded James of full ashtrays and dead flowers, and something else, something he couldn't quite put his finger on. It was decorated with sporting prints that hung on green striped wallpaper. There was a coat stand near the door, laden with coats and hats, and next to it stood an elephant's-foot umbrella stand. Perry dropped his umbrella into it next to the others.

'Follow me, please,' said the butler and he took the boys into a library. It was dark and cold in here. There was an untidy writing desk and shelves of ancient leather-bound books. James had the feeling that nobody had read any of them in a good many years. The walls, where they were visible, were painted midnight blue and the small windows let in very little light. A mini grand piano was pushed into a corner, and looked as neglected as the books.

The only thing of any interest in the room was a cabinet of glass jars. They looked innocent enough but each one was neatly labelled with the name of a poison – Arsenic, Cyanide, Strychnine, Hemlock, Curare, Snake Venom, Gila Monster Venom, Black Widow Spider Venom, Scorpion Venom, Death Cap/Destroying Angel (Cyclopeptide Mushrooms), Blue-Green Algae, Aconite/Monkshood, Belladonna/Deadly Nightshade ... There were almost too many to count.

James stood in the chilly silence of the room, listening to the ticking of an ancient clock on the mantelpiece above the unlit fire and studying the jars.

'Beats a collection of porcelain figurines or toy soldiers, doesn't it?' said Perry.

'What sort of man collects poisons?' asked James.

147

Before Perry could say anything, James's question was answered.

The door creaked open on its hinges, and Sir John Charnage came in. He flicked a light switch. A small chandelier in the centre of the ceiling lit up and the room became a little more cheery.

James recognized Charnage instantly. He was the man who had turned up at the Crossword Society meeting pretending to be Gordius.

A Clarinet Sang in Berkeley Square

'Well, well, well,' said Charnage, smiling. 'We meet again. Shouldn't you be at school?'

'We're staying at the Eton Mission in Hackney,' said James.

'Doing good works for the poor,' said Perry.

'Bravo,' said Charnage, raising an eyebrow.

He was wearing a smoking jacket with a cravat loosely tied around his neck. He had a cigarette clamped between his teeth and held a glass of brandy in one hand. His other hand held his ivory-topped cane. He ran a finger along his thin moustache and looked at the boys with his sleepy brown eyes. He took a long, slow drag on his cigarette, then let the smoke out noisily from his nose. He slumped into an upright leather club chair with a sigh, as if the effort of smoking was too great for him. He crossed his legs, all the time staring at the two boys.

'So what's this all about then, eh?' he drawled, his voice as sleepy and lazy as his eyes. 'Why have you come knocking on my door, interrupting my weekend?'

'Why did you pretend to be Professor Peterson?' said James.

Charnage looked at him in silence for a long while, and then took a gulp of brandy.

'I believe I asked the first question,' said Charnage.

'We wanted to talk to you about Mister Fairburn,' said James. 'But I'm not sure now.'

Charnage's mouth slowly formed itself into the shape of a smile.

'I didn't mean to appear rude,' he said. 'Can I get you some refreshments? I don't know. What do boys like to drink these days? Fizzy lemonade? Soda water? Milk? It seems an awfully long time since I was a boy.'

'We're fine, thank you,' said James.

Charnage chuckled quietly. 'All right,' he said. 'I suppose I have some explaining to do. Alexis is a friend of mine. We were at Trinity together.' He chuckled again and tapped his temple with the hand holding the cigarette. Ash fell on to his sleeve and he casually brushed it away. 'Screw loose, you know. Eccentric is not the word to describe him. He always had his head in the clouds, turning over some problem in that great brain of his, and he was apt to wander off for days on end, but recently, as you know, he wandered off and never came back. I was worried sick about him, not sure who I could trust.'

'When Ivar Peterson came to you, you told him not to worry, though,' said James.

'You know about that, do you?' said Charnage.

'Yes,' said James.

'How?'

'I can't say right now,' said James. 'Like you, I don't know who to trust.'

'Very wise,' said Charnage and he took another drink. 'You're right, though, I did tell poor old Ivar not to panic. If something dangerous *was* going on, I didn't want him to get caught up in it. But he told me about the meeting of the Crossword Society and I thought it might be a good way to visit Eton and try to find out more. So I went in his place.' Charnage stopped and stared at James over the rim of his glass. His eyes may have been tired and bloodshot, but they were fiercely intelligent. 'We are the same, you and I, Luc,' he said and gave a little nod. 'We neither of us know who to trust. We are careful. We don't go blundering into things.'

'I'm trying to find out what's happened to Fairburn,' said James.

'And I think you know a lot more than you let on at the time,' said Charnage. 'You were obviously playing your cards very close to your chest. But now here you are. So, are you going to tell me what's going on, now? Have you spoken to Peterson?'

'Not exactly,' said James.

'Only, a boy fitting your description was seen at Trinity shortly before Ivar was found dead,' said Charnage quietly, looking into his glass. 'He is wanted in connection with the professor's murder.'

'We had nothing to do with that!' Perry blurted out and James cursed silently.

'My, my,' said Charnage and he tutted. 'You've been rather foolish, haven't you?'

James said nothing.

'You really should have gone straight to the police as

soon as you knew something was wrong,' said Charnage, dragging a hand through his hair.

'We were scared of getting into trouble,' said James.

'And consequently you have got yourself into much deeper trouble.' Charnage said this in such a way that James suddenly felt very small and stupid.

Someone shoved his head round the door, a beefy-faced man in a tweed suit. 'Come on, Johnnie,' he barked, 'get a shift on. The cards are getting cold.'

'I'll be with you in a minute, Baxter,' said Charnage without turning around. 'I'm just dealing with something.'

Baxter looked the two boys over with tiny bloodshot eyes and took a gulp from a tumbler of whisky. 'Kids,' he said dismissively.

'Go back upstairs, old man,' said Charnage. 'I'll join you when I'm done.'

Baxter muttered something and backed out of the room.

'Do you want to tell me what happened?' asked Charnage. 'Or should I just call the police?'

'If we tell you everything we know so far,' said Perry, 'could you keep us out of it?'

'Perhaps,' said Charnage. 'If you tell me the truth, and stop all this lying.'

'No,' said James. 'We're not telling you anything else.'

Charnage stuck his nose into his brandy glass, inhaled the fumes then drained the contents in one swallow. He sucked his teeth for a moment and stood up.

'Well, then, I might as well tell you that I had no intention of keeping you out of this,' he said. 'I am a respectable businessman. Are you seriously suggesting that

I lie to the police? Lie about something as important as murder? I don't know what sort of boys you are, but boys in my day had a stronger sense of right and wrong. We had respect for our elders, respect for the police. I sometimes despair about what is happening to this country. You are boys from a good school, as well. You are Etonians.'

'What are you going to do?' said Perry.

'I'll tell you what I'm going to do,' said Charnage. 'I'm going to telephone the police and I'm going to explain everything. I am also going to let them know that I have a couple of devious little snakes at my house who were witnesses to a murder. Witnesses? Or worse? I wonder.' He stubbed out his cigarette and went to the door.

'Stay here,' he said, turning in the doorway. 'Keep quiet and try not to dig yourselves any deeper into trouble than you are already.'

Charnage left the room, slamming the door, and, with a sinking feeling, James heard the key turning in the lock.

Perry turned to James. 'Well, that could have gone better,' he said.

'We've got to get out of here,' said James.

'Come off it,' said Perry. 'You heard what he said. We're already in hot water. If it gets any hotter we're going to end up as soup.'

'There's something not right about all this,' said James.

'Well, then, let's wait for the police,' said Perry.

'You stay if you like,' said James who was already at the window, seeing if it offered a chance of escape. It didn't. A sturdy iron grille barred it securely. The other window was the same.

153

'I suppose we could always climb up the chimney,' said Perry, craning his neck to look up inside the chimney breast.

'Concentrate, Perry,' said James. 'This is one occasion when you'll have to try and take things seriously. Is there another door?'

They quickly searched the room, but there appeared to be no other way out.

'Think,' said James.

'Please,' said Perry. 'Ask me to do anything else other than think.'

'Try,' said James.

Perry's face lit up. 'Some of these old libraries have hidden doors,' he said. 'Disguised as bookshelves.'

Almost before Perry had finished speaking, James spotted a section of shelving where the books were fake. The spines had been removed and pasted on to wood. From a distance it looked like part of the bookcase, but closer up James could see that it was clearly a door of some sort, though there was no obvious handle. He pressed against it and rattled it, but it wouldn't open. Perry nudged James as he spotted a small keyhole.

'We need to find the key,' said James.

He ran across the room to the writing desk and began to rifle through the drawers.

Then he froze.

'Look at this,' he said as Perry joined him.

'What?'

James pointed to a letter on the desktop. There were notes and scribbles written all over it.

'I knew it,' said James. 'It's Fairburn's cipher. And not a copy. It's the original letter.'

'The original?' said Perry. 'Are you sure?'

'I'd recognize it anywhere.'

'But how on earth did it get here?' said Perry.

'The break-in at Codrose's, when the place was set on fire. Charnage must have been behind it.' James snatched up the letter and shoved it into his jacket pocket. 'Are you convinced now?' he said.

'Yes,' said Perry. 'Let's get out of here.'

They could find no key so James grabbed a letter opener instead.

'This will have to do,' he said, jamming the long thin blade into the keyhole in the secret door. He jerked it hard and wrenched it round until he heard a crunch and felt something give. Then he forced the blade into the frame near the keyhole and levered the door open.

There was a narrow, winding staircase behind. It led up to another door on the floor above, mercifully unlocked, and also disguised as part of a bookcase. They pushed it open cautiously and went out on to the landing.

They tiptoed along, past pieces of dark, heavy furniture, more sporting prints and gloomy family portraits.

They could hear jazz music, presumably coming from a gramophone. A clarinettist was making his instrument sound like a human voice. It moaned and wailed like someone complaining of hard times. Then a woman began to sing wordlessly. It was obvious that *she* was trying to sound like a trumpet.

The music was coming from a half-open doorway

further along the landing. James inched forward and peered through the crack. The room was thick with smoke and the curtains were drawn, but he could see a group of men, including Baxter, sitting around a table. They had been drinking and playing cards, though they had stopped now and were looking at Charnage, who was standing with his back to the door.

There was a reek of tobacco and alcohol fumes drifting out of the room, together with a flowery scent that instead of disguising the other smells mixed with them horribly.

Charnage said something to the other men in the room and turned. James ducked away, quickly signalled to Perry to hide and flattened himself behind a rack of antique firearms.

Charnage limped out of the room, closed the door behind him and headed in the opposite direction from the hidden boys towards the main staircase. James and Perry waited a moment and then followed. They came to the banisters and looked down. The hallway appeared to be empty. The library door was still closed, with the key in the lock.

The boys crept down, the ancient wooden steps creaking beneath them. Halfway down they froze. They could hear someone talking and smell more cigarette smoke. James carefully leant over the handrail and saw a small room with glass doors under the stairs. Charnage was inside, talking on the telephone.

James indicated in dumb show what was going on and Perry nodded.

They could see the front door from here and a clear route to freedom.

They looked at each other.

Perry nodded again. James took a deep breath and they ran for it, leaping down the stairs. They hammered across the polished tiles, hardly believing that they had got away, but at the last moment a shadow fell across the frosted glass of the doorway. It was the butler. He had stepped out from a servant's door to one side of the hallway.

There was a shout from behind them.

'Stop them, Deighton!'

Charnage had come out of the telephone room.

They were trapped.

What happened next happened very fast, and James moved almost without thinking. Even before an idea had fully formed in his head, he had acted on it. He was working on instinct, not intellect. It was just like when he was playing the Field Game.

'Ram!' he yelled at Perry, who was just in front of him, and luckily Perry understood. He dropped into a crouch and James linked his arms around his waist. The two of them barrelled forward and slammed into the startled butler, who was thrown backwards against the front door, shattering the glass.

James wrenched the door open, crushing the butler against the wall. He then grabbed Perry by the back of his jacket and hauled him out on to the doorstep.

The grocer's boy was standing on the pavement outside, gawping, open-mouthed, at the house. He was carrying a full basket of food: cans and glass jars and bulging brown-paper parcels. James snatched the basket off him, and, just as Charnage came flying out of the front door, he tossed it at him with all his strength. Charnage yelled and fell heavily on to the step. The grocer's boy tried to catch hold of James, who shoved him out of the way and sprinted northward across the square with Perry hard on his heels. They ran down the middle of the road and a noisy Model Y Ford rattled round the corner towards them, its horn blaring. The two boys parted, swerved round either side of the car and carried on running. At the top of the square, as they turned into Davies Street, James glanced back. The butler was standing in the doorway, but Charnage was running after them, swinging his cane.

'He's after us,' James shouted. 'Don't stop.'

'I wasn't intending to,' gasped Perry.

They ran into Grosvenor Street then crossed over New Bond Street into Hanover Square, their feet slapping hard on the pavement, pedestrians scattering as they approached. James didn't risk looking back again. He was a fast runner, but had to be careful not to outstrip Perry and leave him behind.

They didn't stop running until they came to Oxford Street, which was busy with Saturday shoppers visiting the big department stores. They slowed down, lost in the crowds.

'You're going to have to tell m-me what's going on,' said Perry, trying to catch his breath. 'How does Charnage fit in with all this?'

'I'm not sure, yet,' said James. 'All I know is that he's

lied to us from the start. And I'm afraid I didn't buy any of that saintly guff about respecting your elders. Those men in that room had been playing cards all night. You could tell. The room stank of cigarette smoke and stale bodies. So, one minute Charnage is gambling and drinking with his cronies and the next he's had a terrible attack of the morals and he's up on his high horse ranting on about how boys these days don't know how to behave properly.'

Perry laughed. 'I think he was right on that count,' he said.

It was James's turn to laugh now. 'If we ever get caught, Perry, they're going to hang us.'

'Or give us a m-medal each,' said Perry. 'What do we do now?'

'We go and find Pritpal at the Eton Mission,' said James. 'And just hope he can decipher Peterson's coded message.'

Perry flagged down a taxi and the two boys were on the move again, this time going eastward, towards Hackney. The further they travelled, the poorer the people looked. Cars became less frequent. The houses became shabbier. The goods in the shop windows became cheaper and cheaper. By the time they reached Hackney Wick they were in a very different world to the one they had left. It was an area of low, cramped terraces, blackened by soot and smog. Big, ugly factories and workhouses dominated the streets like medieval castles.

Gainsborough Road, the street where the mission stood, was quiet, and as they arrived a group of children stared at them as if they had never seen a taxi before and were curious to see which rich aristocrats might be inside.

The mission itself was a cluster of odd buildings surrounding a Victorian red-brick church in the Gothic style with evil-looking gargoyles poking out from its tower.

'Do you want me to wait?' the taxi driver asked as Perry paid him.

'No, that's all right, thank you,' said James. 'We can make our own way back.'

'Suit yourselves,' said the cabbie, looking up and down the street dubiously before driving off.

'I must say this is a lovely part of town,' said Perry. 'Did you know that in the past they used to inoculate the boys before they came down here from Eton?'

They could hear singing from inside the church. Then the singing stopped and there was a minute's silence before the doors opened and boys started streaming out. James and Perry hung back, watching from a safe distance until they spotted Tommy Chong.

James hurried over and grabbed Tommy's elbow.

'Can you get away?' he said quickly.

'Think so,' said the startled-looking Tommy.

'Get hold of Pritpal and meet me round the corner in five minutes,' said James. 'We need his help.'

Breaking the Code

'It is binary code.'

The four boys were sitting on a low wall just along from the mission and Pritpal was studying the piece of paper James had taken from Professor Peterson's study.

'What's binary code?' asked James.

'It is a system of counting,' said Pritpal. 'We use a decimal system in which there are ten digits, from zero to nine. We make all our numbers from them, using multiples of ten as our building blocks. Binary code uses only two digits – one and zero.'

'How on earth does that work?' said Perry.

'Simple,' said Pritpal. 'In many ways it is the simplest form of counting. Zero is 0. Then, using only the digits 1 and 0, what is the next largest number you can make?'

'1,' said James.

'Good. So, 1 is 1,' said Pritpal. 'How would you make 2?'

'11?' said James.

'No. You would use 1 followed by 0. Two is 1-0. Three is 1-1. Then the next largest number you can make is 1-0-0, which is four. Then five is 1-0-1, six is 1-1-0, and so on.'

James thought for a moment. 'Seven must be 1-1-1,' he said, 'and then eight is 1-0-0-0.'

'Exactly,' said Pritpal.

James nodded at the paper in Pritpal's hand. 'So that's just a series of numbers?'

Pritpal looked at it again. 'Low numbers, mostly,' he said. 'Nothing higher than about thirty, I would say.'

'They could correspond to letters of the alphabet,' said Tommy, looking over Pritpal's shoulder. 'If A was 1, and B 1-0. What is the first block?'

Pritpal read it out. '100-101-1-10010. Or four, five, one, eighteen.'

Tommy counted on his fingers. 'D-E-A . . .' he said. 'Then we have a big number, 1-0-0-1-0, that makes, let me see, eighteen, which is . . .'

'R,' said James. 'The first word is "Dear". It's a letter. It must be. Make yourself useful, Pritpal, and decipher the rest of it for me, could you?'

'I beg your pardon,' said Pritpal. 'I have been very useful, thank you very much. Tommy and I have been working hard on Fairburn's cipher. While you two have been living the soft life in Regent's Park we have solved another of the clues.'

James was about to put Pritpal right when he heard an engine and looked round to see a police car pulling up.

'Make yourself scarce,' he hissed at Perry as two plainclothes policemen got out of the back. A third policeman, in uniform, stayed behind the wheel.

Perry thrust his hands into his pockets and sauntered off down the road without looking back.

James took a deep breath.

Now what?

The two police officers came over. They were wearing grey mackintoshes and brown trilby hats and had hard, world-weary faces. One of them had a broken nose. If James hadn't known they were policemen he would have had them down as criminals. He supposed that if they were local they were probably used to dealing with some pretty tough customers.

'You boys part of the mission here?' asked the officer with the broken nose, lighting a cigarette.

'Yes,' said Pritpal.

'You're Etonians, are you? From Eton school?'

'We are,' said Pritpal.

'Tell me,' said the policeman. 'We're looking for two boys. Luc Oliver and Arthur Stevens. You know them?'

Those names again. Which only meant one thing: Charnage had already reported James and Perry to the police.

Pritpal was about to say something when he caught James's eye. James was giving him a look that very clearly said keep your mouth shut.

'I do not know them, I'm afraid,' said Pritpal.

'What have they done?' asked Tommy.

'That needn't concern you, son,' said the second policeman. 'It's a police matter. Who's in charge here?'

'The Reverend Falwell, I suppose,' said Pritpal. 'Shall I take you to him?'

'Thanks.'

Pritpal took the two officers round behind the church

to the residential part of the mission. James held back a moment then followed, smiling. The policemen hadn't even noticed him. All they had seen were the other two. A Chinese boy and an Indian boy in their smart Eton half change suits. Add in Pritpal's turban as well and James had become invisible. That was why he had sent Perry away. If Charnage had given a description of James and Perry to the police then they didn't want to be seen together.

Once inside, James waited in a small porch as Pritpal showed the two policemen into a room further along a dark passageway. After a moment he came out and found James waiting.

'Where did you take them?' James whispered.

'To the Reverend Falwell's sitting room,' said Pritpal. 'Why? What is going on?'

'I'll tell you in a minute,' said James. 'You go back to the others. I need to try and listen.'

'It is two doors down on the right,' hissed Pritpal and he went outside.

James sneaked along the passageway. He passed a kitchen on his right and then came to the sitting-room door. He pressed his ear to it but could hear only muffled voices. He ducked back into the kitchen and picked up a glass he found drying on a rack, then hurried back and placed it carefully against the shiny painted wood of the door. He put his ear to it and instantly recognized the voice of the policeman with the broken nose.

'They claimed to be from Eton and said they were staying here.'

'What have they done? Is it serious?' This new voice presumably belonged to the Reverend Falwell.

'It's very serious, I'm afraid,' the policeman went on. 'They broke into the house of a gentleman in Berkeley Square. The gentleman returned unexpectedly and caught them trying to burgle the place. He locked them in a room and they told him their names and where they were from, but as he was telephoning his local police station they gave him the slip.'

'We're not quite sure we believe their story,' said a third voice, presumably the other policeman. 'It seems unlikely that two Eton boys would be breaking into people's homes, but they knew enough to say they were from here, and, well, stranger things have happened before.'

'It's possible they were local boys,' said the first policeman. 'Who knew about the mission and pretended to be from here.'

'We have to check these things out, you understand,' said the second policeman.

'Of course,' said Falwell. 'Two boys, you say? One of about sixteen, the other younger, with black hair and blue eyes?'

'That's right,' said the first policeman.

'Any number of boys could fit that description. What names did you say they used again?'

'Luc Oliver and Arthur Stevens,' said the first policeman.

'No,' said Falwell. 'I don't recognize the names. Besides, at the time you mentioned, all the boys were out with me. I really don't think it was anyone from here.'

'That's what we suspected,' said the second policeman. 'But if you *do* hear anything, please telephone us. In the

165

meantime we've put a call through to the station in Windsor. Officers from there will be speaking to somebody at the school. If these *are* Eton lads we'll find them sooner or later . . .'

'Professor Peterson obviously knew something about what was going on,' said James. 'And whoever solved the clues was supposed to go to him and find out.'

It was ten minutes later and the boys were sitting in the empty church, their breath making wispy clouds in the cold air.

'Unfortunately, though,' said Perry, 'someone else got there first.'

'Charnage,' said James.

'You don't know that for sure,' said Perry.

James pulled something out of his pocket and gave it to Pritpal.

'Fairburn's original letter,' he said. 'The last time we saw it, it was in Codrose's desk at Eton. Right?'

'Right,' said Perry.

'That was Tuesday,' said James. 'What happens next?'

'Charnage turns up at the Crossword Society pretending to be Ivar Peterson,' said Pritpal.

'Yes,' said James. 'He claims to know nothing about the letter when you mention it, but he's very interested. The next day there's a break-in at Codrose's and Katey the maid is frightened by a man with a face like a skull.'

'He was obviously there to steal the letter,' said Pritpal.

'That night we go to Cambridge,' said James, 'where I discover that Peterson has been killed.'

'By a m-man with a face like a skull,' said Perry.

'Exactly,' said James, 'and this morning we find the letter in Charnage's house. What more evidence do you need, Perry?'

'But he's a gentleman,' Perry protested. 'From a good family. With a respectable address. He's a knight, dammit!' Perry banged the pew with his fists.

'What do you mean?' said James. 'A knight?'

'He's Sir John Charnage, re-m-member? A knight of the realm. People like him don't go around m-murdering people.'

'So why did he lie to the police?' said James. 'Why didn't he tell them why we were really at his house? They obviously know nothing about Fairburn's disappearance.'

'You must go to the police,' said Pritpal. 'And tell them what is going on. You have done some wrong things, but it is better to be scolded by the police than to be murdered by these villains.'

'No,' said James and he jumped up and began pacing the aisle, too full of nervous excitement to sit. 'Think about it,' he said. 'Charnage called the police. OK?'

'OK,' said Pritpal.

'But he didn't tell them the truth,' James went on. 'He told them just enough to get them on our tail. And he made sure that if we *did* decide to go to them ourselves, as you suggest, we'd be in very hot water indeed.'

'I don't see what you're getting at,' said Perry.

'Let me finish.'

'Sorry.'

'Now, say the police found us and arrested us,' said James. 'What would happen?'

'We'd tell them the truth,' said Perry.

'And who would they believe? Us or Charnage?'

'Not us, that's for sure.'

'Exactly,' said James. 'It would be the word of two schoolboys against that of your precious knight of the realm.'

'At first, yes,' said Perry. 'But eventually they'd have to look into our story. It m-might take a few days, but sooner or later they'd find out that we were telling the truth.'

'Yes, and by then it would be too late,' said James.

'What do you m-mean?'

'Read me the start of the cipher, Prit,' said James. 'The bit where Fairburn talks about leaving Eton.'

'*As I am sure the almighty Elliot will have explained,*' Pritpal read, '*I have had to leave Eton. In fact I am leaving the country. My next crossword will be my last, as I will be gone before my next deadline.*'

'He's telling us,' said James, 'that he's been kidnapped and he's going to be taken out of the country. He sets a crossword every week, doesn't he? When's his deadline, Prit, do you know?'

'Yes,' said Pritpal. 'He sometimes liked to check the clues with us before he posted the puzzle to *The Times*.'

'When?' said James. 'When would his next deadline be?'

'Tomorrow,' said Pritpal. 'Sunday. He always put them in the post on Sunday evening.'

'That's why Charnage called the police,' said James. 'He was worried that he might not be able to track us down quickly enough by himself. He wants us out of the way.

If we're in a police cell we can't be out there solving the clues, can we? He's gambling that it would take a couple of days for the police to listen to us and by then he'll be gone – out of the country – and Fairburn with him. We've got to solve this thing ourselves and we've got to do it before tomorrow night. So, come on, Pritpal, what have you got?'

Pritpal flattened Fairburn's letter out on the shelf in front of him.

'We think we have solved a clue,' he said. 'Listen to this – *I love all those old stories of ancient Rome, like Nero's great love affair with Cleopatra. You should try to visit the great necropolis in Porta Alta one day and see the marvellous statue of him gazing across towards her obelisks.*'

'What does it m-mean?' said Perry.

'He obviously wants us to visit somewhere, and it must be somewhere not too far away,' said Pritpal. 'So it can't be Egypt or Rome. The mention of the obelisks made us think of Cleopatra's Needle on the Thames, but nothing else seemed to fit with that. So we looked at the Latin.'

'*Porta Alta?*' said Perry. 'Where is that?'

'It translates as "tall gate", or "high gate",' said Pritpal.

'Highgate?' said Perry. 'In North London?'

'We think so,' said Pritpal, 'because the rest fits.'

'What's Cleopatra got to do with Highgate?' said Perry. 'And what's a necropolis?'

'It's a city of the dead,' said James.

'Yes,' said Pritpal. 'And there is a big Victorian cemetery in Highgate.'

'Is there a statue of Nero there?' said James.

'I don't know,' said Pritpal. 'But there are some famous Egyptian tombs, complete with obelisks.'

'I've done it!' Tommy suddenly exclaimed.

While the others had been talking he had been slowly cracking the binary code and writing the translation out on to a fresh piece of paper. 'You were right, James, it *is* a letter. From Fairburn to Peterson. *Dear Ivar, forgive the code, but this is for your eyes only. I have come to a decision. It was not easy. I am afraid you will have to continue building Nemesis without me. I think I know who John is working for and cannot be a part of it. Do you remember how he laughed when I told him the story of Sir Amoras? Well, I believe that John has made his own pact with the devil. I left home, Ivar. I will never go back. I know the truth. I will not think badly of you, however, if you want to proceed. Best, Alexis.*'

'What does he mean when he says he left home?' said James.

'He is half Russian,' said Pritpal. 'His mother is from Manchester. He grew up in Russia, but he was sent over here to study when he was our age. He was born Alexei Fyodorov. Fairburn is his mother's maiden name.'

'What does the rest of it m—mean?' said Perry. 'What's Nemesis? And who is Sir Amoras?'

'I have no idea,' said Pritpal.

'There is a postscript,' said Tommy. '*P.S. It is strange to think that the cause of all this are those harmless-looking grey blobs sitting in Case Twenty-two, Room Five at the museum of the Royal College of Surgeons.*'

'Highgate cemetery and the Royal College of Surgeons?' said James. 'Which is nearer?'

'The Royal College of Surgeons,' said Perry. 'It's in Lincoln's Inn Fields.'

'Come on, then,' said James, heading for the door.

'Come on, where?' said Perry, hauling himself up from his seat.

'To the museum, of course,' said James. 'We have to find out what's in Room Five.'

Soft Tissue

The Royal College of Surgeons was an imposing, white building on the south side of the large square known as Lincoln's Inn Fields. The journey across London, by train and tube, had taken James and Perry ages. James realized what a huge place the city was, and how much of your time could be taken up just getting from one part of it to another.

This was an area of London where people came to work, mostly in the local law courts and lawyers' offices, and, it being the weekend, the streets were largely deserted. The boys had been worried that the college might be closed, but its front door was open. They walked up the steps through the row of tall pillars ranged across the front and went inside.

An old man in a uniform sat at a desk, he gave the boys a quick once-over.

'You here for the lecture?' he said.

'That's right,' said Perry boldly.

'It's already started,' said the guard and he passed the boys a clipboard with a piece of paper attached. 'You'll have to hurry. Sign in first.'

The two boys scribbled some illegible names on the list and then followed the sign up the stairs towards the lecture.

They found their way into an exhibition hall where several rows of chairs had been set out among the displays. The audience was a mixed bunch. There were a few nurses and people in Red Cross uniforms, a small group of eager-looking Boy Scouts, some young men and women who were probably medical students and some older, more serious-looking men with beards and spectacles.

A lecturer was standing at the front next to a screen on which a slide was being projected showing a group of soldiers posing stiffly for the camera.

'We'll wait in here for a while,' James whispered, finding a seat at the back. 'Then when we get an opportunity we'll slip away and have a look round.'

'All right,' said Perry and the two boys sat down.

James took in his surroundings. The walls of the room were lined with shelves and cabinets containing odd things in jars. He read some nearby labels with a mixture of fascination and horror: *Female monstrous foetus, found in the abdomen of Thomas Lane, a lad between fifteen and sixteen years of age, at Sherborne, in Dorsetshire, June 6th, 1814 . . . Imperfectly formed male foetus found in the abdomen of John Hare, an infant between nine and ten months old, born May 8th 1807 . . . Human female twin monster, the bodies of which are united crosswise, sacrum to sacrum . . . Intestines of Napoleon, showing the progress of the disease that carried him off . . . Embalmed body of the first wife of the late Martin Van Butchell . . .*

He hadn't really given much thought to what might be on display in the museum but realized now that it was full of medical curiosities. Perry nudged him and nodded towards the front. He had gone slightly pale and James wondered what could be worse than the things in the jars he had been looking at.

A new slide was being projected on to the screen showing a man's head. One side of it looked like it had been completely eaten away. The cheek was hollowed out, the eye missing, and large, crude staples held the pieces of flesh together. The wound was clean and the man had a bland, almost bored expression on his face.

The lecturer was speaking. 'During the war, we learnt a great deal about the effects and treatment of gunshot wounds and great advances were made in the field of plastic surgery. We gave help and hope to countless young men with horribly deformed and mutilated features. This next series of slides shows the step-by-step reconstruction of one such young man, Private Edwin Carter, who received a high-velocity, large-calibre bullet in the face at the battle of Passchendaele, in October 1917.'

James almost had to look away as the next slide came up. Again, the man looked calm and blank, despite the fact that his nose and upper jaw were missing and in their place was a dark hollow.

One of the Boy Scouts jumped up from his chair and ran out of the room, holding his mouth and nose, his skin green.

'This next slide clearly shows how cartilage from the

man's shoulder, and skin from his back and thigh were used to begin rebuilding the missing tissue . . .'

One of the Red Cross workers, a skinny young woman with bobbed hair, now followed the Boy Scout out of the room, looking equally sick.

James stood up.

'Now's my chance,' he said to Perry, who didn't look round, but merely nodded, his eyes transfixed by the awful pictures.

James headed towards the lavatories, where he could hear the Scout being sick, but didn't go in. Instead he peeled off and sneaked into the next gallery.

Dim working lights showed him an eerie scene. He was in a great hall, three storeys tall, with windows around the edge of the high, domed roof. The upper two levels consisted of book-lined walkways that circled the hall surrounded by iron railings on which were mounted the antlers and horns of numerous dead animals. Below them, the main floor of the hall was crowded with more wooden display cabinets and a variety of bizarre skeletons. There were dinosaurs and prehistoric beasts, but also more modern curiosities, like an elephant, an ostrich and a giraffe, as well as the remains of several humans. James saw one human skeleton that must have been nearly eight feet tall. He assumed it must be of a caveman or something, but when he went closer and read the label he found that it was the skeleton of Charles Byrne, an Irish giant who had died in 1783. Next to him was the tiny skeleton of a girl, less than two feet tall, Caroline Crachami, a Sicilian dwarf.

James wandered from display to display. The cabinets contained more jars. As well as the freaks and curiosities, there were countless examples of hideous diseases and accidents, and he couldn't help thinking about all the terrible ways in which a person could die.

He realized that he himself had been close enough to death in the last twenty-four hours to smell its foul breath. He hadn't thought about it before. He had kept moving and forced the memories to the back of his mind, but now the strain on his nerves was beginning to show and a dark mood was descending on him.

It was cold in here and his head ached. He was dog-tired. His body was stiff and he was suddenly aware of the bruises he'd got in the accident last night.

He looked at yet another skeleton and it looked back at him from its hollow eye sockets. He was all too aware that, no matter how handsome you looked, how full of life and energy you were, underneath your skin was a grinning skeleton. Sooner or later we all die. If violence didn't get you, disease would, and if somehow all the diseases in the world missed you, then there was only old age to look forward to and the slow decay of the body.

He shook his head and swore under his breath: 'Come on, James, this isn't helping. Get on with what you've come here to do.'

He hurried into the next room, past a display of surgical instruments. He was becoming used to seeing bizarre objects, so he barely stopped to look at a row of pickled lungs, a collection of hairballs removed from humans – one the size of a football – one of Robert the Bruce's ribs and the mummified hands of one of John of Gaunt's sons.

This was Room Five.

He saw a sign that read 'Series D. The evolution of the nervous system – of the brain and spinal cord.' There was a row of cases entirely covering one wall, showing brains of all shapes and sizes. From fish brains and tiny things belonging to rats, right up to massive elephant and whale brains. He scooted along the cases, reading the numbers, and then climbed to an upper gallery where there were more cases.

He came to the brains of apes – chimpanzees, orang-utans and gorillas – and then at last he found Case Twenty-two.

He peered in. More brains. But what was the significance? He read the labels: *Nos. D683 & D683a the brains of two microcephalic idiots.* No, surely that wasn't what he was looking for.

But what?

And then a name caught his eye: *No. D685 the brain of the famous mathematician, Charles Babbage, donated by the owner, 1857.*

Babbage? Where had he heard that name before?

Babbage . . . A mathematician.

Fairburn and Peterson had been mathematicians at Cambridge.

Cambridge. *Yes.* That was where he'd heard the name, from another mathematician. The student, Alan Turing. He'd said something about improving on Babbage's work.

James hadn't understood what Turing was talking about

177

and hadn't paid much attention at the time, but this *must* be what Fairburn had meant in his coded letter to Peterson.

He looked at the brain. It was in two neat halves, each in its own jar, like the two halves of a giant walnut. James peered at the knobbled, pale-grey lumps, swimming in clear liquid. It was hard to think that this had once been the brain of a great genius, that it had been crammed with lofty ideas, because now it was nothing. Empty and dead and useless.

When James got back to the lecture there was another man on the stage. He was wearing a rifleman's uniform and had a row of medals across his chest. He was obviously a gunshot survivor. Half of his face was shiny and mottled. The skin around one eye was pulled out of shape and his nose looked like a lump of rolled dough. A scraggly moustache below it barely concealed a scarred and twisted lip.

'Thank you, Bill,' said the surgeon and the soldier left the stage to applause from the audience.

'Now,' the surgeon went on, 'I would like to show you the effects of a bullet wound on soft tissue.'

An assistant brought up a preserved specimen and placed it on a table. It was the cross section of a human torso and you could clearly see where a bullet had gouged a jagged path through it.

James tugged Perry's arm.

'We can go,' he said quietly.

'Thank God for that,' said Perry, jumping up. 'I don't think I could take m-much m-more of this.'

As they left they could hear the surgeon carrying on, his voice matter-of-fact: 'As is very clear, the first priority with a gunshot wound is to disinfect it with a powerful antiseptic . . .'

Once they were outside, Perry gulped in lungfuls of fresh air. He didn't look at all well.

'I hope you found what you were looking for,' he said. 'Because I never want to go back into that chamber of horrors as long as I live.'

'I found it,' said James.

'What was it?'

James told Perry all about the brain.

'A bit ghoulish, don't you think?' said Perry. 'I'm not so sure that when I die I'd like m-my brain to be put on display in a m-museum.'

'I'm not sure any museum would want it,' said James.

'Ha, ha,' said Perry. 'And I suppose that every m-museum in the country will be fighting to get hold of your brain when you kick the bucket, great genius that you are.'

'I don't think I want to be remembered when I die, actually,' said James quietly. 'Ashes to ashes, dust to dust, and all that. It's living that's important. Doing things. Not getting bored and wasting your life. Before he died, my Uncle Max quoted a line from somewhere, "I shall not waste my days in trying to prolong them. I shall use my time."'

'So we've got your uncle to blame for all this, have we?' said Perry, and James laughed.

'Right,' said James. 'Time is ticking away. We need to get something to eat, we need to talk to Pritpal again and then we need to head for Highgate cemetery.'

They walked down to the Strand, where there was a big Lyons Corner House restaurant. It was full and noisy, and a small orchestra was playing at one end.

They found a cheap food counter and filled up on bread and soup, glad of the warmth and light and lively atmosphere. James soon felt restored and ready to carry on, and he had the strength to keep any black thoughts out of his mind.

There was a phone booth in the lobby and James put a call through to Pritpal at the mission.

'Who was Charles Babbage?' he asked Pritpal when he came on the line.

'He was a nineteenth-century inventor,' said Pritpal. 'And like Fairburn and Peterson, he studied mathematics at Cambridge. Why?'

'That's what was in the case at the museum, Babbage's brain.'

'Babbage spent his whole life trying to invent two machines,' said Pritpal, his voice made thin and distant by the telephone. 'They were supposed to be able to carry out mathematical calculations many times faster than any human. The first machine was called a Difference Engine. It would have changed the world if it had worked.'

'How do you know about all this?' said James. 'Did Fairburn talk to you about him?'

'Often,' said Pritpal. 'Like Babbage, Fairburn was obsessed with the idea of being able to turn all human thought into numbers. If you could express every thought as binary code, like on your piece of paper, then everything in the universe could be represented by ones and zeros.'

'I don't have a clue what you're talking about,' said James. 'You're making my head spin.'

'It's simple,' said Pritpal, which was what people usually said when they were about to explain something very complicated. 'If you can turn every idea into a series of numbers, then every problem in the universe could be solved by a calculating machine. Do you see?'

'Not really,' said James. 'But go on.'

'Maybe I am explaining it all wrong,' said Pritpal. 'What this is all about is the idea of trying to build a machine that works like a human brain, only a million times faster, like a sort of superbrain. You put in a mathematical problem at one end, and seconds later the answer comes out of the other end, like magic. Just think of the advances that could be made in science and mathematics. This was what Babbage was trying to do with his second machine, the Analytical Engine. It was much more complicated than his first machine, but unfortunately, as with the Difference Engine, he could never get it to work. The machinery available to him at the time was not good enough. It all came to nothing.'

'Do you suppose Charnage is trying to build one of these machines?' said James.

'I suppose it is possible,' said Pritpal.

'There's only one way to find out,' said James.

'What are you going to do?' Pritpal's voice sounded a million miles away.

'We're going to Highgate cemetery.'

'James, you must be careful,' said Pritpal.

'Don't worry. The cemetery's full of dead people, Prit,'

said James with a laugh. 'I'm hardly likely to come to any harm from *them*, am I?'

It was growing dark as they left the Lyons Corner House. The streetlights were coming on and London was washed in a sickly orange glow. They found a small hardware shop and bought a torch, then jumped in a taxi and set off for north London. On the way, James filled Perry in on his conversation with Pritpal.

'It sounds like we could do with one of these m-machines to help us solve the cipher,' said Perry.

James pulled Fairburn's letter out of his pocket. The original version that he had taken from Charnage's study. Charnage had written notes all over it. He had obviously been trying to solve the clues himself, probably to find out exactly what information the cipher contained. James was pleased to see that most of Charnage's ideas were way off course. He just had to hope that he could stay one jump ahead of him.

'We're getting there,' he said. 'We've solved four of the seven clues. We're over halfway.'

'What's left?'

'The poem,' James said, 'the bit about me not liking crosswords, and the sporting stuff.'

'Remind m-me what that bit was again,' said Perry.

'*How well I remember scoring the winning try in the Field Game against the Duffers,*' James read, '*and coxing the* Callisto *in the parade of boats on June the Fourth.*'

'Anyone would think the m-man had never been to Eton,' said Perry. 'There's m-more m-mistakes in that than in one of m-my Latin construes.'

'List them,' said James.

'Well, for one, you don't score a *try* in the Field Game, it's a *rouge*,' said Perry. 'Secondly, the Duffers are a *rowing* crew, m–made up of m–masters, not a *Field Game* team. Thirdly, there is no boat in the June the Fourth parade called the *Callisto*.'

'So, what's he trying to tell us?' said James. 'Is it something to do with boats, do you think?'

'M–maybe *rouge* is significant?' said Perry. 'A red boat, perhaps?'

'Any idea what *Callisto* is?' said James.

'It's a constellation,' said Perry. 'The Great Bear.'

'Of course,' said James. 'I knew I recognized the name.'

'So, we're looking for a red bear sailing a boat,' said Perry.

The boys looked at each other and grinned and for a moment James forgot all about his tiredness and his injuries and the cold knot of fear that sat in his stomach.

It's Your Funeral

'There you go,' said the cabbie as he took the fare money from Perry. 'You've the west cemetery to your left and the east cemetery to your right.'

The road they were on, near to Hampstead Heath, was dark and quiet and secluded, overhung by tall trees on either side.

'Which part has the Egyptian tombs?' asked James.

'You'll be wanting the older part,' said the cabbie, giving a handful of change back to Perry. 'The west. But I think you'll find it closes at dusk. Are you sure you don't want me to take you back to civilization?'

'No, thank you,' said James. 'We only want to take a quick look.'

'It's your funeral,' said the cabbie and he chuckled at his little joke before driving away.

The two boys waited for the taxi to disappear then went over to the cemetery to investigate. A substantial wall surrounded it and there was an ornate Gothic chapel guarding the entrance. Just as the cabbie had warned, it was locked shut.

Perry looked at James, who had a familiar, reckless look in his eyes.

'Don't tell m-me,' he said. 'We're going over the wall.'

'However did you guess?' said James. 'Come on, give me a leg up!'

James scooted up the wall, then lay down flat and hauled Perry up.

The heavy cloud cover, which had lain over London all day like a grey blanket, rolled aside for a moment, revealing a yellow moon whose light gave the boys a tantalizing glimpse of the cemetery. Then the gap in the clouds closed and they were plunged once more into darkness.

They jumped down and Perry switched on the torch. Its narrow beam picked out odd details: the statue of an angel, a granite funeral urn, an ancient, twisted tree choked with ivy. There was a wild and overgrown feel about the place and it was easy to imagine the spirits of the dead haunting it.

The cemetery was arranged on a wooded slope and the graves weren't laid out in neatly ordered rows, but were scattered, seemingly at random, among the trees and bushes between the winding, muddy paths.

A thin mist was trapped in the branches of the trees and it served to muffle all the sounds of the city. There was an eerie quiet. It was easy to forget that this was London.

'Where on earth do we start?' said Perry.

'I should imagine that the Egyptian tombs should be pretty easy to recognize,' said James.

They picked their way slowly uphill, moving deeper into

the cemetery. The graves nearer the path were for the most part well looked after, but the ones further away were being swallowed up by vegetation. Weeds and ferns and brambles scrambled among fallen headstones that were covered in moss. Many of the graves were marked with elaborate statues and carvings, some of which were unrecognizable beneath glistening shrouds of black ivy. As well as angels and crosses of all shapes and sizes, there were carvings of praying children and sleeping babies, open books and even dogs, faithfully watching over their dead masters.

James was shaking, but whether from fear or the cold he couldn't tell. His exhaustion was making his nerves jangle. This place would have given him the creeps in broad daylight, but at night, with the torchlight slicing a ghostly white beam through the misty air, it was easy to imagine all sorts of terrors lurking in the dark. He was beginning to wish he'd listened to Perry and they'd left it until the morning.

Don't be a fool, James, he told himself. *There's nothing to be afraid of.*

Only there was.

The past twenty-four hours had shown him that there was a lot to be afraid of. Not spectres and ghouls, perhaps . . .

The dark silhouettes of the statues looked like people hiding among the trees, and he expected someone to jump out from behind every grave they passed. He stayed close to Perry, wishing they'd bought two torches.

As well as the ordinary graves, there were huge stone mausoleums, standing like houses, their sides stained with green mould. The walls of some of them were collapsing and their roofs had fallen in. The Victorians must have thought that their last resting places would be looked after forever, but the cemetery was giving up, losing its fight with nature. Like the corpses beneath the ground, it was rotting and returning to chaos.

James and Perry were just about to give up hope when they rounded a corner and nearly bumped into two simple stone obelisks and they found themselves face to face with what looked like a ruined Egyptian temple. Perry played the torch beam over a high wall, built into the bank. Jungly creepers and vines spilt over the top and down great pillars, carved with lotus leaves, which stood on either side of a central archway. The archway led into a long, dark passageway lined with tombs.

'Good grief,' said Perry. 'I wasn't expecting this. We are well and truly in the city of the dead.'

There was an otherworldly atmosphere in this corner of the cemetery. James felt almost as if he had stepped out of time and been transported to some foreign place. But Perry quickly brought him back down to earth.

'OK,' he said. 'We've got obelisks, but where's Nero?'

'I don't know,' said James. 'Let's explore a bit more.'

They walked through the archway into the passage beyond. It sloped gently upward and had tombs along each side, whose metal doors had upside-down keyholes and were decorated with upside-down flaming torches. The roof of the passageway was open to the sky, and water dripped from overhanging vegetation and ran down the walls.

At the top of the passage they came out into a circular

sunken walkway, with walls at least twelve feet high. In the centre of the circle grew a vast cedar of Lebanon that loomed over them like a great black bat, making this the darkest part of the cemetery they had been to yet. Round the outside were more tombs, dug into the bank. They were even bigger and grander than the ones they had just passed. The names of the families inside were carved above the entrances, and several of the doors had small windows in them. By shining the torch in they could see stone coffins placed on shelves.

'I can't help thinking that the Victorians were overly interested in death,' said Perry. 'This whole place is a m–monument to death.' He stopped and pointed. 'Look there,' he said, 'one of the tombs is open.'

Sure enough, a little further around the circle the iron door to a tomb was standing ajar.

'Let's look inside,' said Perry.

'Be careful,' said James.

'You're not scared, are you?' said Perry.

'No, I'm not,' James protested, but the truth was that his heart was beating faster and, despite the cold, his palms were sweating. Before he could say anything else, though, Perry had marched forward and was peering round the open door into the tomb. James caught up with him just as he went in.

Inside was a medium-sized room, taller than it was wide, with damp stone walls and two wide marble shelves on either side. The air was chilly and musty and the tomb was entirely windowless. After all, the dead don't need a view. There was a sealed sarcophagus on the lower shelf to the left, but above it, on the higher shelf, was an open one, with the lid propped against the wall.

The two boys crept forward and Perry shone his torch into the open coffin.

There was a body inside, the body of a man, fully clothed in tattered rags, its face dark, as if varnished, its hair tangled and matted. It smelt awful. Sour and mouldy.

'I've never seen a dead body before,' Perry whispered.

'Leave it,' said James. 'Have some respect.'

'He's dead,' said Perry. 'What can he do now?'

James watched as Perry stretched out a hand towards the man's face. Just as his fingers touched his cheek, the dead man's eyes snapped open and suddenly the body was alive.

Perry screamed and let go of his torch. The tomb was instantly plunged into utter darkness.

James felt like a bucket of icy water had been emptied inside him. For a moment he stood frozen to the spot, unsure if what he had seen had really happened. But there were sounds of a scuffle and he heard Perry shout for help so he knew he had to do something.

He dropped to the floor and groped around for the fallen torch. There were horrible gasping and choking noises coming from Perry, and James got a nasty kick in the side from his flailing feet.

Then Perry fell still and James heard a man's voice, soft and menacing.

'And who would you be, eh?' he said. There was no reply from Perry, just a muffled grunt. 'And what would you be doing sneaking up on me like a thief in the nighty-night? Eh? Would you be a demon, sir? Would you be a rat? Or would you just be one of them boys who think it funny to hurt an old tramp when he's a-sleeping? What would you be? *Quid pro quo?*'

James's fingers at last found the smooth metal casing of the torch; he snatched it up, fumbled for the button, and switched it back on.

Perry was pinned to the wall by the man, who had one strong, brown hand around his throat. Perry was struggling for breath and his hands flapped feebly at the man's forearm.

'Stop it!' James yelled. 'We don't mean you any harm.'

The tramp's head flicked round and he glared at James, his eyes yellow in the darkness.

'There's two of 'em, eh?'

'Please,' said James, 'let him go.'

'Let him go, he says, as if it was as simple as that.'

'Honestly,' said James, 'I promise you. We thought you were dead.'

The tramp looked surprised. He released Perry and his whole body gave a long twitching shudder like a dog having a dream.

Perry slid down the wall until he was sitting on the floor, wheezing air into his lungs and rubbing his bruised throat.

'Dead?' said the tramp. 'Why would you think I was dead?'

'Well, m-mostly because you look like a corpse and you were lying in a tomb without m-moving,' said Perry crossly.

'I've lived among the dead too long,' said the tramp. 'The war was the worst. The trenches was full of corpses, all me mates. Many was the time I wished I could join them. Maybe now I have.' The tramp laughed with the sound of water gurgling down a plughole. 'You must have had quite a shock! Being strangled by a dead man!'

'We're really sorry to disturb you,' said James.

'*Dulce et decorum est, pro patria mori*,' said the tramp.

'Do you live here, then?' asked Perry, looking into the sarcophagus.

'I come in here in the winter,' said the tramp. 'To keep warm and dry. I pushes the door open and I makes myself comfortable. Seems a shame to let a good bed go to waste. But I have respect, sir. I know this is not my house. I won't do my business in here. I do my toilet elsewhere. Others don't have such respect. Others will drop their guts wheresoever it pleases 'em. Not I! *Omni fulcit temporens.* Oh, but I'm aching for a drink. My bones are like dust.'

'Do you know this cemetery well?' asked James.

'It's my world,' said the tramp.

'We were looking for something,' said James.

'I'm sure you were,' said the tramp.

'Maybe you can help us,' James went on. 'We were looking for Nero. Do you know of a statue of him? Or a grave with that name on it?'

'You're asking me if I know Nero?' said the tramp. 'Course I know whom Nero is. Everyone knows Nero. Nero's a lion. *Leo, leonis.*'

'Come on,' Perry muttered quietly. 'This is a waste of time. He's not all there.'

But James ignored him. The man might be slightly unhinged, but there was an intelligence behind his ravings. 'You're saying there's a lion here?' he asked. 'There's a lion in this cemetery?'

'Yes,' said the tramp. 'Though he don't roar none. Seeing as how he's made of stone.'

'It's a statue, then?'

'Course it's a statue! What did you think?' said the tramp. 'That there's wild beasts here? Prancing among the tombs? What do they teach you boys these days?'

He stopped and leant in closer to James. The stink coming off him was awful. It looked like he hadn't taken his greasy clothes off in years, let alone washed them.

James got a good look at his face. It was puffy and swollen, the skin bunched from old injuries, the nose broken and badly reset. His skin was black with ingrained dirt and from the effects of living outdoors for years on end.

'I don't know, though,' the tramp whispered. 'Some nights I do see things, when I've had myself some liquor. Then I swear old Nero gets up and runs around, chasing the pixies.'

'Why is there a ruddy statue of a lion here?' asked Perry.

'To mark the grave of old George Wombwell.'

'And who was he?' asked Perry.

'He had a travelling circus and a zoo,' said the tramp. 'Showing off his animals for anyone as would pay. He'd make poor Nero fight. Other wild beasts, dogs, whatever you liked. Oh, Nero was a popular attraction. But Nero and Wombwell both are long dead. *Ethday umscay ootay* us all.' The tramp crossed himself.

James realized that he was still shaking from the shock of seeing the 'dead' body come back to life and his heart was battering his ribs. Everything that had happened this evening had a sense of unreality about it. Now, it seemed, this tramp was going to solve their puzzle for them.

'Can you take us to the grave?' he asked.

'What? Now?' shouted the tramp. 'It's the middle of the flaming night.'

'It's not that late, actually,' said Perry.

'Who says?'

'Well, I only m-meant that —'

'Who are you to be saying how late it is, eh?' said the tramp, turning his battered, filthy head towards Perry. 'Who are you? Old Father Time? It's late for me, I'll tell you for nothing. I sleep when it's dark and I wake when it's light. *Caramba santifex, omnia mori.*'

'Please,' said Perry. 'We'll give you some m-money, eh? What about it? You can buy yourself a drink, a nice little *inkdray.*'

Perry dipped into his pockets and found some coins that he held out for the tramp. The tramp scratched his head and wiped his nose. 'It degrades a man to take money from a stranger,' he said. 'But I'll not refuse it.' He delicately plucked the money from Perry's palm. 'Come along, I'll take you to see Nero.'

As they walked back outside they felt a few drops of water and soon the heavens opened and threw down a barrage of heavy rain on to them. It stung their faces and drilled into the ground, churning it to sticky mud. Perry cursed. He had left his umbrella behind at Charnage's. They had nothing with which to protect themselves from the downpour.

The tramp didn't seem to notice. 'These are all my friends!' he shouted over the rain, like a proud homeowner showing friends round his house. 'The dead what lie sleeping here.'

'Any of them famous?' Perry yelled back at him.

'I'll say,' said the tramp. 'Greatorex, Wellbelow, Faraday, Petavel, Charlie Cruft and Tommy Sayers, why even old Karl Marx himself is buried here, the father of communism, the man who turned the Russian bear red! I'd like to be buried here myself, but no one will put up a gravestone with my name on it.'

'What *is* your name?' James yelled.

'You can call me Theo,' said the tramp. 'I had a longer name once, but it's no use to me now. It's gone. Along with all me teeth.'

He stopped and grinned at the boys, showing his purple and toothless gums. 'I have not a tooth in my head,' he said. '*Omnia dentistry fugit.*'

'His Latin's a little confused,' Perry whispered. 'What's he trying to say?'

'All his teeth have fled,' said James and Perry started to laugh. James couldn't help but join in, and as he laughed all the tension went out of him, washed into the dirt by the freezing rain.

They returned to the main part of the cemetery, Theo muttering and mumbling to himself as he led the way along the twisting paths. James saw that his feet were bare, the toenails grown long and claw-like.

After a while, Theo suddenly stopped.

'There he is,' he said and pointed to the life-size statue of a sleeping lion, resting on a grand stone plinth. James went in for a closer look. A plaque read *To the memory of George Wombwell (menagerist)*.

He turned to thank the tramp, but there was no sign of him. In the distance, though, was a jingling of coins.

'Charming fellow,' said Perry.

'Without him we'd have been stuck,' said James.

'We'd simply have had to come back in the daylight and ask a sane person to point us in the right direction,' said Perry. 'A groundsman, or a gravedigger, or something, this is utter m-madness poking around here in the dark, getting soaked to the skin and risking pneu-m-monia.'

'Less talk, more action,' said James. 'We need to find out why Fairburn wanted us to come here.'

James raked the area with the torch beam, slowly squaring the ground, his eyes alert for anything unusual, but as he didn't know quite what he was looking for, he was in the dark in more ways than one.

'This is hopeless,' said Perry. 'Why don't we come back in the m-morning?'

'Perry!' James snapped. 'We don't have time. Tomorrow is Sunday. They're taking Fairburn out of the country, and his machine too, for all we know. We *have* to do this. We'll stay here all night if necessary, but we have to find whatever it is Fairburn wants us to find.'

'Sorry,' said Perry. 'This place gives m-me the creeps.'

James said nothing, but got down on to his hands and knees and searched all round the base of the statue.

'There's got to be something here,' he said. 'We just have to find it.'

He pushed aside the brown, frostbitten fronds of a fern and there, on the ground, soggy and filthy, was a folded piece of paper.

He picked it up and was able to gently open it out without tearing it.

'What is it?' said Perry, crouching down next to James.

James showed him. On one side was the copy of an inscription, made by rubbing a wax crayon over the paper to reveal what was underneath: *In loving memory of Doctor Cornelius Shotbolt, F.R.S. and A.S.*

'Anything on the other side?'

James turned the paper over and gave a triumphant snort of laughter. It was a letter from Peterson to Fairburn.

'I'm sorry I ever doubted you,' said Perry. 'But can we go now? I'm cold and I'm wet and I want to be out of this ghastly cemetery. I feel if I stay here m-much longer they're going to have to bury m-me.'

'I'm sure that can be arranged,' came a voice from the darkness, shockingly close.

James wheeled his torch around.

Two men stood there.

Evidently Charnage had solved at least one of the clues in the cipher.

It was the two men who had tried to kill him last night.

Wolfgang and Ludwig Smith.

Carcass Row

Wolfgang had a bandage wrapped around his head with thick padding over where his right ear had been. His face was pale and his black-ringed eyes were shining feverishly. The rainwater pouring down his face made him look like he was crying.

He was holding a pistol and a torch. They were both shaking slightly.

Ludwig had his hands in his pockets. With his skull face he looked completely at home here in the cemetery. His top hat was keeping the worst of the rain off him.

'Well, this is a nice surprise,' said Ludwig, with no hint of emotion in his voice. 'Finding you here. An added bonus. Now, I think you've got what we was looking for. So, give us the piece of paper, boy.'

'Or what?' said James.

'Or whatever you like,' said Ludwig and he lifted his hands out of his pockets. He was holding two weird and sinister weapons – stubby revolvers, with very short muzzles, whose grips were knuckledusters.

Ludwig smiled. *His* hands were not shaking. They were rock solid. As he raised the guns towards the boys a narrow bayonet slid out of the end of each weapon with a metallic click and snapped into place. The blades were not much thicker than knitting needles and tapered to tiny stiletto points.

James swallowed hard and wiped his face. He had seen the wound in Peterson's eye. The last thing the professor would have seen was one of these blades as it slid into his skull.

'You should be careful with those things,' said James. 'You could do yourself an injury.'

'Very droll,' said Ludwig. 'Now, give us the piece of paper like a good little boy.'

James stuffed the paper into his jacket pocket.

'Watch him, Ludo,' said Wolfgang, his voice hoarse. 'He might be armed.'

'I *am* watching him,' said Ludwig irritably. 'What do you think I'm doing? I've got two bleeding guns pointed at his chest. If he pulls out anything more dangerous than a rabbit I'll put two holes through him and spit on his corpse.'

James remembered that he still had the other letter in his pocket, the one with the binary code on it.

He didn't need it any more. Tommy had made a copy. He crushed it into his palm.

'Here,' he said, stepping forward. As Ludwig put out his hand for the paper, though, James threw it as far as he could into the bushes. Ludwig sighed.

'Go and get that, Wolf,' he said.

'Why should I get it?' said Wolfgang. 'Make the boy go. He threw it there.'

'Oh, good idea,' said Ludwig sarcastically. 'What a very

good idea. Let the boy go traipsing off into the dark and get away from us. You've got the torch. Go and get it.'

Wolfgang grumbled as he picked his way into the undergrowth. Ludwig advanced on James, one of the thin, vicious blades pointing straight into his face.

'You really shouldn't have done that, boy,' he said. 'It's very annoying.'

'It was meant to be,' said James.

'James,' said Perry, quietly, 'I don't think you should annoy the m–man.'

'Shut your gob, you stuttering ape,' said Ludwig.

'I say. Don't you call me an ape,' Perry protested and Ludwig rounded on him just as Wolfgang called out.

'I can't find it, Ludo.'

Ludwig looked at the ground then yelled. 'Well, keep looking, you useless berk.'

Just then there was a terrific commotion in the bushes. Branches thrashed about. Wolfgang yelped in fright and there was the sound of a body crashing to the ground.

'Help me!' Wolfgang shouted, his torch beam zigzagging wildly in the air. 'There's some sort of animal. Help! Help!'

Ludwig turned away from the boys to try and see what was happening to his brother. It was all that James needed. He swung the torch with all his might and took Ludwig behind the ear. Ludwig grunted and stumbled forward, supporting himself on a gravestone. He was stunned but not unconscious.

When the torch had hit him, though, the lights had literally gone out. The glass had shattered and the end had flown off, spilling the batteries.

'Run for it,' James yelled. 'Get away, Perry!'

Perry didn't wait to be told twice; he hared off down the path without looking back, but, as James tried to follow, Wolfgang charged out of the bushes, like an elephant breaking cover, and collided with him. They both went down.

A moment later Theo appeared, roaring like a monster. Wolfgang rolled over and shone his torch directly into the tramp's tired face, blinding him. Then there was a double bang and a flash and Theo fell backwards with a small, pathetic cry.

Ludwig was standing there, his guns smoking.

James felt sick. Tears of rage sprang into his eyes and burnt like acid. Half-blind, hardly knowing what he was doing, he threw himself on Ludwig, knocking him to the ground.

As James rolled clear, Ludwig lashed out with one of his weapons. The tip of the blade sliced across James's chest, tearing his jacket but missing his flesh. James tumbled into the bushes and scrambled away on hands and knees.

'After him,' Ludwig yelled at his brother.

'Why me?'

'Because you've got the torch, you idiot.'

As James groped his way forward in the dark he felt a piece of marble half-buried in the mud, part of some broken monument. He got his fingers round it and pulled hard. It came free just as Wolfgang blundered up, and James let fly at his knee. Wolfgang howled and fell sideways like a felled tree. Then, as he tried to stand, James blindly swung again and this time hit him on the side of the face.

There was a hideous cracking noise, the marble broke, and James saw a spray of white fragments fly off through the air: bits of marble and broken teeth.

'*Omnia dentistry fugit*,' James muttered.

Wolfgang was out of the fight, and he'd dropped his torch somewhere. James felt a small glimmer of hope now. He might just get away.

He kept low and crawled deeper into the undergrowth, threading his way past graves and clumps of vegetation, getting soaked and filthy, the sound of the rain masking any noise he was making. He had no idea what direction he was going in, but knew that he needed to work his way downhill, so that he might be able to get back to the road and away to safety.

He risked standing up. He could see next to nothing in the dark under the trees and had to assume that it would be just as bad for Ludwig.

There was no movement except for the falling rain.

OK, he told himself, *it's now or never. You've got to run for it.*

He had hardly gone three paces, however, before he was caught by a branch, which threw him backwards and he fell awkwardly against a headstone. The blow jarred him and he felt dizzy, but he forced himself back on to his feet.

Ludwig was there, his skull face split in a brown-toothed grin. Somehow he had crept up on him. James backed away, feeling the bendy branch pressing into his back. A thought came to him and he kept moving, forcing the branch backwards, hoping that it was too dark for Ludwig to see what was happening. It took all James's muscle, but when he remembered what Ludwig had done to Theo, his anger gave him extra strength.

Ludwig chuckled.

'You won't get away from me again, boy,' he said. 'Squish, squish, I'll put out your baby blues for what you did to my little brother.'

James could feel the branch pushing hard against his back as it strained to return to its original position. He felt his feet slipping and he dug them in.

Ludwig stepped closer.

'You saw what I did to Peterson,' he said. 'He died without a sound. I pride myself on a clean death when it's necessary. My blade went straight into his brain. A little jiggle and a twist and it was goodnight, professor, sleep tight, don't let the bedbugs bite. But I'm going to do you nice and slow, boy. I'll start by sticking you in the parts where you've got no vitals. Then I'll work me way to something more juicy.'

'You talk too much,' said James and he flung himself to the ground. He felt a swish of wind as the branch whipped past him, and he heard the thud as it took Ludwig clean in the stomach and swatted him into the bushes.

James didn't stay to see if he was going to get up again. He dashed out from the bushes and on to the path. He didn't look back, but sprinted, taking great long strides on the wet mud of the path. Once he slipped and fell, grazing his knees, but he barely felt it, and in no time at all he was at the wall. Still he didn't stop, but climbed into a tree as quickly and efficiently as a cat, almost jumping from branch to branch. Then he was on top of the wall and he dropped down the other side on to the pavement.

Instantly he was back in the normal world. Standing on a quiet London street on a wet December night. A car hissed past and was gone before he thought of flagging it down.

He looked both ways.

The Daimler was there, parked next to the Gothic chapel and gatehouse.

A plan came to him.

He'd had enough of running from these men. It was time he stopped running and started fighting. He was damned if he was going to be the prey any longer, he was going to become the hunter. He ran past the Daimler and glanced through the iron gates into the cemetery. There was no sign of the brothers, or Perry, for that matter. Well, Perry had had more than enough time to get away; both brothers had chased James.

Perry Mandeville was big enough to look after himself.

James went to the back of the car and opened the boot, then took one last look around before climbing in.

The Smith brothers were going to take him to Fairburn.

He pulled off his shoe, twisted the heel, took out his penknife from the secret compartment and held it ready. If anyone opened the boot they were going to get a nasty surprise.

After a long while he heard voices outside and then a door opening. He felt the Daimler rock on its springs as someone fell heavily into the back. There was a groan and through the seat he heard the two brothers bickering. Then there came a long, pitiful moan and the door slammed shut. Soon afterwards there was more movement, presumably Ludwig getting into the driver's seat. Finally the engine started and they were moving forward. Wolfgang was sobbing and groaning continually now, and every time the car hit a bump there came an enraged whine of protest.

Wolfgang was obviously in some pain. James wasn't feeling too clever either. All the sensations that had been held at bay by his excitement were making themselves known. He was soaked to the skin and covered in mud. His jacket and trousers were ripped. His skinned knees were sore and one of them was sticking to his trouser leg where it was bleeding. When he added the bruises he had got in the car crash he was in a pretty sorry state indeed.

It was cold and noisy in the boot, but at least it was dry, and, even though he tried hard to fight it, tiredness was chewing away at him. He closed his eyes and fell into a fitful half-sleep, but he was quickly jogged awake by the car.

He had to do something to keep alert.

Then he remembered the piece of paper in his pocket that he had found hidden in the cemetery.

He fished it out and unfolded it, being careful not to tear it where it had got damp. There was just enough light spilling back into the boot from one of the Daimler's rear lights for him to be able to read it, although the writing had faded and the paper was eaten away in places.

Dear Alexis . . . it began, then there were a couple of lines of small talk before it got interesting. *I have started work on John's machine, using the plans you sketched out that evening in Berkeley Square. When it is finished it is going to be gigantic. It will almost fill a room. Whether it will work or not, I cannot say. I do so wish that you were helping me. I feel all at sea sometimes, but I understand your worries. John has not changed. He still holds the same beliefs he held at Trinity. I think you were right about who he is building the machine for . . .*

The next line was illegible and most of the bottom of the page was missing. The only other sentence James could make out read: *But what harm can a simple calculating machine do?*

James didn't know the answer to that question. But so far the machine had caused one man to be kidnapped and two more to be murdered.

He carefully folded the piece of paper and hid it in his shoe and concentrated on trying to work out where they were going.

They had left peaceful Highgate and come into a busier part of London. The Daimler stopped more frequently and James could hear traffic noise and voices, presumably people on the streets for a Saturday night out. After a while the traffic died away and the streets became quiet again. James reckoned that they must have crossed central London and come out the other side, but whether they had gone south or east he had no way of telling.

Then at last the car slowed down and came to a halt.

With much complaining and arguing the two brothers

got out. The doors slammed and footsteps disappeared into the distance.

James waited a long time, his ears straining to pick up any sounds. Once he was quite sure that it was quiet, he used his knife to pry the lid of the car boot open. He eased it upward and looked out.

It had stopped raining.

James climbed from the boot and closed it. He was in a gated yard of some sort, surrounded by high, soot-blackened walls topped with broken glass. It was utterly deserted and apart from dripping water it was very quiet.

The yard belonged to a big, ugly industrial building. It looked like a factory that had long since closed down. Some of the windows were broken and no smoke came from its tall chimney. It stood dark and lifeless.

Next to the main building, at the back of the yard, was a derelict outbuilding that might once have been a storehouse. The roof had fallen in and all the doors and windows had gone, but in one corner he found a pile of old calendars for the year 1930. They showed a painting of the factory in better days and James smiled when he read the name: *The Charnage Chemical Company.*

This was the final proof he needed.

Wolfgang and Ludwig definitely worked for Sir John Charnage.

He went back outside and tried the factory doors. They were locked. He wiped a layer of filth from a window and looked in, but could see nothing.

He searched for another door and found that the only other entrance was blocked by a pile of rubbish: rubble and rusted metal, old bottles and cans, a pile of oily rags and some rotted timber.

He heard a distant ship's horn and walked over to the gates. He wasn't surprised to find that they were chained and padlocked shut. He coughed and put a hand over his mouth. There was a stink in the air, which caught in his throat. He looked through the gates. There was a cobbled street outside, black and slick with rainwater. A single harsh lamp fixed to the side of a warehouse opposite shone on to a street sign, Carcass Row E1.

He was somewhere in the East End, then. The warehouse and the sounds from the river meant that he was probably near the docks.

The smell suddenly got worse as yellow smoke billowed around the end of the warehouse. He looked up and could just make out the dark shapes of two chimneys against the sky. From the smell of it, he thought it must be a glue factory, or possibly a tannery. The smell was animal carcasses being boiled down. That was probably the origin of the name of the street.

He wondered what to do next. Should he just hide in the outbuilding and wait here for the brothers to return? *No.*

He reminded himself that he was the hunter now.

He was going to find the brothers and he was going to pay them out for what they had done to him. Twice they had tried to kill him. They had wrecked his car. They had killed Theo the tramp.

James was going to take the fight to them now, and see how they liked it.

And see how Sir John Charnage liked it, too.

He went over to the Daimler and searched it thoroughly. In the back was a small flap that pulled down to reveal two decanters of spirits, some glasses and a little carousel of cigarettes. There was also a book of matches with a gaudy image showing two tumbling dice, some splayed playing cards and the name *The Paradice Club*.

He took the stopper out of one of the decanters and sniffed it. It smelt like brandy. Good. If it was heated up brandy burnt like petrol.

He grabbed both decanters and emptied their contents over the seat. Then he collected the rags from the rubbish pile and an armful of calendars from the outbuilding. He stuffed the rags underneath the seat and ripped out some pages from the calendars, which he crumpled into loose wads.

When he was ready he took another calendar, rolled it up and put a lighted match to its end. Once it was burning he lit the scattered pages in the Daimler. Soon flames were crawling among the rags, and oily black smoke filled the car.

James ran to the shelter of the outbuilding and hid himself where he could see both the car and the factory doors.

It was done now, there was no turning back. It was probably crazy but it felt good. His own car had burnt, now it was Charnage's turn.

He laughed silently.

Then there was a great *whump* as the Daimler became a raging ball of fire.

Paradice

The burning car lit up the whole yard, and James could see dancing, flickering lights reflected on the wall of the warehouse opposite. The fire hissed and crackled and popped and every now and then there came a louder bang as something exploded in its heart. Sparks flew off in every direction and a pillar of thick, blue-grey smoke rose up into the sky, rivalling the yellow smoke from the glue factory. There now came a tearing, roaring sound as flames burst out from under the bonnet and, with a terrific bang, the windscreen shattered. This was swiftly followed by a series of dull thuds and the Daimler settled on to the cobbles as the tyres burst.

Suddenly the doors to the factory flew open and three men rushed out. The first was a small Chinese man wearing a chef's outfit, the second was Charnage's butler, Deighton, and the third was Ludwig Smith.

James smiled. The rats were coming out of the woodwork.

But where was Wolfgang Smith?
There.

Limping and hopping along behind Ludwig, his leg

strapped up with a makeshift splint. He had a black eye and an ugly purple bruise down the side of his face, which was badly swollen where James had hit it with the piece of marble.

'Get some buckets,' yelled Ludwig. 'Get water, quick.'

'I can't carry anything in this state,' said Wolfgang, his voice slurred and muffled. 'And I'm not going anywhere near the car. Not after what happened last time.' He put a hand up to his bandage and touched the spot where his ear had been.

Deighton the butler ran back into the building. On the way he nearly collided with three more wizened old Chinese men in chefs' outfits. Ludwig shouted something at them and they shouted something back at him, and then they were shoved aside by an eighth man.

Charnage.

He waved his ivory-handled cane at the burning car and shouted for somebody to do something.

'Serves you right,' James whispered.

Soon there was a chain of men passing buckets and pans of water out from inside the building, but it was no good; even if they did manage to put the fire out, the car was already ruined. James remembered the Bentley up on blocks behind the pub in Slough. Her owner had spent months trying to restore her, but she was still a wreck.

Wolfgang found a hose and clumsily attached it to an outside tap. He fiddled and cursed but eventually got it working and aimed it at the flames, keeping a safe distance from the inferno.

The men stopped bringing water from inside and

instead stood in a group around Wolfgang, arguing and pointing at the burning Daimler. James saw his chance. He took a deep breath and moved in a crouch towards a gap in the outbuilding wall where a window had once been. He was hidden from the men here, so he quickly climbed out and edged his way around the wall until he could see the firefighters and the open doors.

He watched and waited, and as soon as he was sure that nobody would see him, he darted across to the factory and ducked inside.

He found himself in a long corridor with doors to right and left. He picked one at random and went through, closing it behind him.

He was once more in darkness, but he couldn't risk putting on the light; instead he lit another match. Its feeble glow showed him a large, empty workshop. There was not much in here except the remains of some machinery, a pile of broken shelving and a long workbench. A drill and a metal saw were fixed to one end of the bench, and on it were some thin brass rods. Boxes stacked next to it were filled with thousands of cogs of different shapes and sizes. Pinned to a nearby wall was a complicated blueprint for a machine, and as James was looking at it his match burnt down.

He waited in the dark.

It was freezing in here and he was painfully aware that his clothes were damp and tattered. He had to replace them somehow. He was far too conspicuous like this.

He heard footsteps and voices in the corridor. The men were coming in from outside. He listened until they had all passed by, then waited some more, counting slowly until he had reached a thousand.

He lit another match.

There was a door he hadn't spotted before, with a sign on it reading HAZARDOUS CHEMICALS – KEEP OUT.

He opened the door and looked inside. It was a small storeroom that had been almost completely emptied some time ago. There were a few dusty jars and canisters left, however. He read the labels – 'Caesium', 'Potassium', 'White Phosphorus', 'Magnesium', 'Lithium'.

He remembered lighting thin magnesium strips in a science class, how they had made a brilliant white light, and had carried on burning underwater. These other chemicals were all in their way highly unstable. Some ignited in air, some in water. An accident in this storeroom would cause a devastating explosion and a fire that would be hard to put out. Some of the bottles didn't look at all safe. They must have been here for years, and there was an unpleasant chemical odour seeping out of them.

James grabbed a bottle of potassium. He knew it was reckless, but, apart from his little penknife, he had no weapon. He looked at the contents of the jar. There were three silvery grey lumps of metal sitting in some cloudy liquid.

He slipped the bottle carefully into his pocket.

He went over to the main door and inched it open just enough to look out.

All quiet.

He moved into the corridor and headed deeper into

the factory. As he rounded the corner at the end he heard something: a distant hum and throb. He walked on towards the noise. He could make out a steady beat, now, as if there was music playing, and the buzz of voices.

Maybe the building wasn't deserted after all?

A big, rusted, steel door blocked the end of the corridor. The noise was coming from the other side. He put his ear to it and instantly jumped back as there was a harsh clank and a squeal.

Somebody was opening the door from the other side.

James flattened himself against the wall and mercifully the door opened towards him so that he was completely hidden by it. Deighton the butler came through and walked away down the corridor. He was dragging a man along, who was pleading feebly with him. The man was smartly dressed and had an aristocratic air about him.

'Please,' he said. 'I can pay. I promise you. I have the money. Please . . .'

Deighton bundled him round the corner out of sight.

There was a scream and a shout of 'No!' then James heard the sickening sound of a soft body being hit by a hard object. He didn't wait to hear any more and went through the door.

It was like stepping through the looking glass into another world.

This part of the factory had been utterly transformed. A plush carpet woven with a motif of playing cards and dice covered the floor. The walls were decorated with heavy flock wallpaper and hung with gilt-framed mirrors, ornate gold light fittings and paintings of plump nudes, lounging on beds, eating fruit. The music was unmistakable here, and the hum of voices had risen to a low roar.

There was nobody around and James took the opportunity to explore the area. The second door he tried opened into a changing room.

Christmas had come early for James.

This was better than stumbling into a sweet shop with pocketfuls of cash.

Men's clothes were hanging on pegs around the walls, and there was a rack of chefs' uniforms and waiters' aprons.

He wondered how many changes of clothing he would get through before this weekend was over. He had already lost his own clothes, which he had to abandon last night in the hospital, then the suit that he'd stolen from the patient. Now he was ditching the expensive outfit he'd borrowed from Perry, and was about to steal another one.

He searched the pegs until he found a jacket and trousers that looked like they might fit him. Then he undressed quickly and pulled them on, dumping his wet and torn clothes into a bin.

The suit was old and badly worn. It was shiny at the elbows and, although the legs and sleeves were roughly the right length, it was made for someone much fatter than James and was loose and baggy. It was a relief, though, to be out of the wet clothes and into something dry.

At the last moment he remembered the bottle of potassium and retrieved it from his old suit.

When he was ready, he moved on. The changing room led through into a huge kitchen that was bright and noisy and filled with busy Chinese cooks, who bustled about shouting at each other and noisily clattering pans on the banks of stoves. It was hot and humid in here and filled with delicious cooking smells.

James hurried through, trying not to be noticed. At the far end of the kitchen two doors were busily swinging backwards and forwards as waiters hurried in and out with dirty dishes or plates piled high with food.

James followed a waiter and found himself in the heart of the factory. Only it wasn't a factory any longer. All the machinery and factory fittings had been stripped out and replaced by tables and chairs. There was an open area in the middle and balconies around the sides. The balconies were filled with men and women who were eating and drinking and yelling at each other in order to be heard over the general racket.

It was a nightclub.

There was a stage at one end and a jazz band was playing wild dance music, but nobody was dancing, because where you would have expected the dance floor to be were gaming tables. Cards and dice and roulette. People, mostly men, crowded around the tables, throwing down money.

Apart from the central gaming area, which was flooded with light, the place was dim and shadowy. Tiny lamps on the dining tables were covered by scarlet shades and the waiters had to grope their way around in the gloom.

The air was thick with tobacco smoke and reeked of sweat and alcohol. The noise was overwhelming. A young black girl started singing a song about love, but nobody was listening. They were all intent on gambling.

There were all types here, from toffs in black tie, their

215

partners dripping with jewellery and furs, to gangs of drunken sailors in uniform. There were intense Chinese men from Limehouse, local criminals in loud suits, and here and there, standing or sitting alone, were quiet, desperate men with haunted looks on their faces.

A woman in a glittery red dress and too much make-up saw James and sauntered over, her wide hips swaying in time to the music.

'You're a bit young, aren't you, love?' she said. 'But you don't look very sweet and innocent. How'd you like to buy a lady a drink?'

'Some other time,' said James and he walked quickly away.

He noticed a few other young men there, boys of sixteen or seventeen, trying to look grown-up and cocky, but with slightly scared looks in their eyes.

James saw a bowl of matchbooks on one of the tables. He picked one up. It was the same as the one he'd found in the Daimler.

So this must be the Paradice Club.

James knew that gambling was supposed to be illegal in England, and although this casino was hidden inside a disused chemical factory, it was still big and noisy and obviously very popular. Hoping nobody would notice it was a little like hoping that nobody would notice an elephant in Oxford Street. That meant that nobody here had any fear of the police. Including the owner.

James decided he'd been here long enough. It was only a matter of time before somebody spotted him. He hadn't been expecting any of this. He wanted to get away and think things through.

He saw a door and headed towards it. It led into a smaller room, which, if anything, was even more packed and noisy than the first one. There was a makeshift boxing ring in the centre and two men were stripped to the waist having a bare-knuckle fight. Their faces were battered and gashed and they looked dead on their feet. The smartly dressed men and women in the front row were cheering loudly and laughing. Their clothing was spotted with blood.

James backed out and glimpsed another exit on the far side of the gaming floor. Two men stood guard, but they were checking the people coming in and ignoring anyone going out.

James pushed through the crowds.

A laughing sailor offered him a beer, which he refused. A woman in a fur stole and pearl necklace winked at him and ruffled his hair. But he kept moving, weaving between the tables.

Then a man grabbed him. A short man in a cheap suit and shabby grey shirt. He had an unhealthy look about him. His small baggy eyes were unfocused, his hair lank and greasy, his nose broken. He had a cigar clamped between his teeth and appeared to be as drunk as everyone else.

'Hey, kid,' he said in a thick American accent. 'I need some good luck. You got a lucky face. Help me out here.'

'I was just leaving, actually,' said James.

'Yeah?' said the man and he smiled. As James tried to walk on, however, the man grabbed him again and waved a yellow gambling chip in his face.

'Look at this!' he said. 'I'm down to my last chip. Five English pounds. You know how much I came in here

217

with? Five hundred.' He turned to a man at his side. A fat, pasty-faced fellow with receding hair. 'How much is that in real money, Abbadabba?' he said.

'Two thousand four hundred and thirty-five dollars.'

'You hear that?' said the American. 'Two thousand bucks down the swannee. Here . . .'

He pressed the yellow chip into James's palm.

'Put it on the table for me, kid. Turn my luck around.'

'No,' said James, but the man leant in close and tightened his grip on James's arm. He was surprisingly strong and his fingers dug painfully into James's flesh.

'Nobody says "no" to me,' he murmured with a hint of menace. 'Now put this chip on the table. If you win I'll give you a cut. If you lose . . .' He raised his eyebrows and nodded at James.

In a moment James found himself thrust through the crowd and staring at the roulette table in some confusion. It was covered with numbers and boxes and symbols that were littered with different-coloured chips. Tommy Chong had taught him the basics of roulette on a miniature set that his cousin had sent him. But they had only played a few times before Codrose had confiscated it. The betting system was complicated and James dredged his memory for the information about how it all worked. Slowly, it came back to him.

Alternate black and red numbers from one to thirty-six ringed the wheel, and there was a green zero. These matched up with the numbers on the table. You could bet on any number, and if it came up you'd win thirty-five times your original stake. The chances of your number coming up, though, were thirty-seven to one, which was close to being no chance at all.

There were other ways of betting, however. You could bet on either a red or a black number coming up, for which you would double your money if you guessed right. Or you could bet on odd or even numbers, or low or high numbers. There were also ways of dividing the table, so that you could bet on columns of numbers, rows or groups. By placing your chip on the corner of four numbers, for instance, you would be betting on any of them coming up, with odds of eight to one.

James didn't want to risk doing anything foolish, and he wanted to get out of here quickly before someone spotted him, so he played the safest bet he could think of and put the chip on red. There was a fifty-fifty chance of it coming up. Or at least there would have been if there hadn't been the zero on the wheel. If the ball landed on the zero, then, unless someone had bet on it, none of the other bets on the table would win. This gave the casino a slight advantage and made sure that whatever happened they would always come out on top at the end of the night.

The croupier, a hard-faced man with a thin moustache, spun the wheel in one direction and threw the ball on to it in the other. It clattered around, bouncing in and out of the slots, and at last settled on eighteen.

Red.

The American slapped James on the back, nearly knocking him over, and blew cigar smoke over him as he yelled, 'Well done, kid,' in his ear.

The croupier slid another yellow chip over to join the original one. The American's £5 had now become ten. It wasn't quite five hundred, but it was better than nothing.

With a feeling of huge relief, James turned to leave. But the American held him back.

'Where ya goin', kid?' he said. 'This ain't over yet. You're my lucky mascot. Play it again.'

'Really,' James protested. 'I've got to go . . .'

'What's the hurry?' said the American with all the menace back in his voice. 'Place another bet.'

There was nothing James could do. The man was drunk and looked like he could easily become violent.

James didn't want to draw attention to himself. He went back to the table.

'Well?' said the American. 'Whaddaya reckon?'

'Leave it where it is,' said James, miserably.

'On the red?'

'Yes.'

'You're the boss.'

Again the croupier spun the wheel, and this time the ball landed on thirty-four.

Another red.

James couldn't help smiling as the croupier pushed over two more yellow chips. He had won £15 for the man now.

The American was laughing. He put an arm around James's shoulder. 'You're all right, you know. What do they call you, kid?'

'Bond, James Bond,' said James without thinking, and

then instantly regretted it. He should have lied and used a fake name again, but he had got caught up in the excitement of winning.

'My name's Flegenheimer,' said the man. 'But you can call me Dutch.'

'Not so loud,' said the man's friend, Abbadabba.

'Cool it, Abbs,' said Dutch. 'Me and the kid are pals.'

Dutch sniffed and held James by the chin. 'We're goin' again, kid,' he said. 'Twenty pounds is peanuts. I came in here with five hundred and I ain't leaving till I've made my dough back.'

'No,' said James. 'I have to go.'

'Place your bets,' shouted the croupier.

'You heard the man,' said Dutch. 'Place your bet.'

James stared at the table. He had to get away from here. Well, he thought, the best way to get out was to finish it. If he could lose the man's money he wouldn't see him as a lucky charm any more. He recklessly pushed the pile of chips over towards the centre of the board, on to the number sixteen.

'Whoah,' said Dutch. 'You're putting it *all* on sixteen? That's a hell of a gamble, kid.'

'Do you trust in my luck or not?' said James.

The man stared into James's face. There was something cold and dead about his eyes, something inhuman. Here was a man who would kill you without a thought.

'Luck is a lady you got to treat real mean,' he said. 'If she smiles at you, you got to take her for all she's got. Yeah, I trust ya, kid. Half this dough should by rights be yours. But I warn you, I'm a very bad loser.'

Dutch turned away to say something to Abbadabba and the two men laughed.

James looked at the piles of chips on the table. It was a powerful feeling when you won, but to lose . . . what would that feel like?

The croupier prepared to spin the wheel and at the last moment James leant over and slid his chips along the table to number seven.

His own lucky number.

The wheel spun, the ball was rolled, it whizzed around the rim, dropping slowly, ever so slowly, then it caught the slots and bounced across, rattling and jumping in all directions. It seemed to rest for a moment in one slot only to jump out again a moment later and hop across the wheel to another.

James was sweating. He was aware of nothing else in the whole world except this one tiny object – the silver ball as it danced around the wheel.

He had no idea if the band was still playing, even if there was anyone else in the casino. It was just him and the roulette wheel.

He could bear it no more. He closed his eyes, just as the ball stopped making any sound. There was a brief hush then a cheer went up and James opened his eyes.

The ball was nestling snugly in the number seven slot.

James turned round. Dutch was staring at him with murder in his eyes. 'I warned you, kid, not to lose.'

'But I didn't,' said James. 'I changed the bet.'

'You did?'

'Yes. I put everything on seven.'

'What happened to the sixteen?' said Dutch, pushing past James and studying the table. 'Oh, Mamma, he done it! Keeyiyay, he done it! That'll get some money in that treasury. Quick, Abbadabba, what's thirty-five times twenty?'

'Seven hundred,' said Abbadabba without even stopping to think.

'Kid,' said Dutch, 'I like you. How'd you like to come and work for me?'

'Leave it,' said Abbadabba.

James was in a daze. Everyone around the table was clapping him on the back and congratulating him, and the croupier was raking over a big pile of chips with a sour look.

'Now,' said Dutch, rubbing his hands together, 'we're gonna go again. With a winning streak like this you can't just stop.'

'You've made your money back,' said James. 'Can't I go now?'

'You ain't going nowhere, kid,' said Dutch and at that moment James felt hands take hold of him by either elbow and he was pulled backwards.

'He's coming with us,' said a voice he recognized. It was Ludwig Smith, with Deighton the butler and another security guard.

They began to manhandle James through the crowd.

'Hey, kid,' Dutch yelled after him, 'where should I send your money?'

'Just send it to the Eton Mission,' said Ludwig with a nasty laugh. 'They can use it to pay for his funeral.'

What's Your Poison?

'You've been bad news right from the off, haven't you, Oliver, or Bryce? Or whatever you're called. What's your real name, I wonder?'

'Rumpelstiltskin,' said James, but nobody laughed.

He was in a room high above the casino floor. It must originally have been the factory manager's office. There were big square windows all along one wall looking out over the cavernous space below, so that the boss could look down on his workers and keep an eye on them.

It was decorated like any other rich man's office. There were boring landscape paintings on the walls, a telephone, brass lamps with green shades, shelves of books and files. The only odd note was a weird machine standing near the door. It consisted of a device like a typewriter connected to a metal frame filled with a complicated jumble of cogs, levers and gearwheels.

Sir John Charnage was sitting behind a big leather-topped desk. He was leaning forward, resting his chin in his hands. A cigarette smouldered in an ashtray next to a tumbler of whisky.

He was flanked by Wolfgang and Ludwig Smith, who

were standing at each shoulder. Deighton had left them to it and returned to his duties downstairs, but sitting in the shadows at the back of the room was a woman. With the desk lamp shining in his eyes James couldn't see her properly. She was sitting very still and very quiet, and her unexplained presence unnerved him.

'It's no matter,' said Charnage. 'We don't really need your name, old pal, because we've got *you*, haven't we, eh? And by the time we've finished with you, *you* won't need your name either. Except perhaps for your headstone. What do you think your epitaph should be? How about, "Here lies a boy who couldn't keep his nose out of other people's business"?'

James was determined not to let Charnage know just how scared he was.

'I prefer, "Here lies a man who lived to be a hundred and three",' he said.

Charnage chuckled and took a sip of whisky.

'How can you laugh, after what he done to your car?' said Ludwig.

'We've got him now, Ludo,' said Charnage casually, picking up his cigarette and taking a long drag. 'So everything's all right with the world, isn't it?' He let out a thin stream of smoke from between his lips. 'The only question *is*, now that we've got him, what are we going to do with the little pest?'

'Leave him to me,' mumbled Wolfgang through broken teeth, and he came out from behind the desk and advanced on James. 'I'll sort him out.'

'I wouldn't get too close to him if I were you, Wolfgang,'

drawled Charnage. 'Every other time you've met, you've lost part of your anatomy.' He laughed again and Wolfgang gave him a dirty look.

If anything, the look that Ludwig gave him was even dirtier.

'Shut your mouth,' he snapped. 'Don't you laugh at my brother.'

'Oh, don't be so pompous,' said Charnage. 'And don't forget who you're working for.'

'That still doesn't give you the right to laugh at Wolfgang,' said Ludwig.

'You must admit it *is* rather funny, though,' said Charnage. 'He's falling apart. First his ear, then his teeth. What next, I wonder? A kidney? His left leg? He's already hobbling about like a man who's trodden on a landmine.'

'There won't be a next time,' snarled Ludwig. 'Me and Wolfgang are going to string the brat up by his guts.'

'I appreciate your enthusiasm, Ludwig,' said Charnage. 'But we mustn't rush into things. We need to think carefully about this. We're not quite ready to move yet, and I don't want the police on my back before we are.'

'We can bury the body where no one will ever find it,' said Ludwig.

'I'm sure you can,' said Charnage. 'But it may be better if someone *did* find it.'

'How can that be better?'

'Because if they find him, Ludwig, they won't be looking for him, will they? Think about it. A young lad, discovered dead as the result of an unfortunate accident. Nobody's fault but his own. End of story.'

Charnage looked at James and smiled. The smile then changed to a theatrical expression of mock concern. 'Oh, how rude of me,' he said. 'I haven't offered you a drink. What would you like? I have whisky, brandy, gin . . . Russian vodka.'

'No, thank you,' said James.

'Oh, come along,' said Charnage, with a syrupy smile. 'You're among friends here. I won't tell anyone you've been touching the demon drink.'

'I won't drink anything you give me,' said James.

'Why ever not?' said Charnage. 'Oh, I know. You saw my little collection at home. You're worried I might slip you some poison.' He took a sip of his drink and licked his lips. 'Did you know,' he said, 'that in Renaissance Italy, that murderous, scheming family of cut-throats, the Borgias, were so in love with poison that they laid down rare bottles of the stuff in their cellars, just as if they were bottles of vintage wine? And one of the Borgias was the Pope!' He laughed at this and took another sip from his glass. 'I've always been an admirer of the Borgias,' he said, 'and have made something of a study of poison. Do you know how many different types of poisonous creature there are in our oceans for instance?'

'No,' said James. 'It's not something I ever think about.'

'Have a guess,' said Charnage.

'I don't know,' said James. 'A hundred?'

'Twelve hundred,' said Charnage. 'And that's just in the sea. On top of that we've got four hundred types of poisonous snake, two hundred spiders, seventy-five scorpions, sixty ticks . . . I could go on, but in short, it's a poisonous world out there. In fact *everything* is poisonous, if you swallow enough of it. Most medicines, after all, are simply poisons given in tiny doses. Too large a dose, and, instead of curing you, it'll kill you. Even water's poisonous. If you drink too much, your blood becomes so thin it's not really blood any more, and you drop dead of hyponatremia. So what I'm saying is that I don't need some fancy poison to polish you off, old pal. I don't need to dose your drink with arsenic while your back's turned, or hide a cyanide capsule inside my ring, or give you a secret shot of curare. All very colourful, I'm sure, but wholly unnecessary. What I have in mind is to kill you with an everyday substance, so that nobody is at all suspicious.'

'I'll drink to that,' said Ludwig and he sniggered.

Charnage drained his glass, which he instantly refilled, then he stood up and went over to a cabinet, which he opened, revealing a gleaming array of bottles.

'You and I are going to have a nice little drink,' he said. 'So, come along – what's your poison?'

Again Ludwig sniggered.

'I won't drink,' said James stubbornly.

'You will,' said Charnage. 'One way or another. Now, I think good old British gin. Let's be patriotic, eh? Let's drink to merry old England. Rule Britannia and all that rot. Let's drink to the British Empire. Let's drink to good old King George who sent millions of young men off to die in the war.'

'I won't drink,' James repeated.

'I really don't blame you,' said Charnage, filling a large

tumbler almost to the brim with gin. 'Alcohol is a positively lethal substance. Rots the liver, rots the guts, rots the brain, poisons the blood and clogs your arteries with fat. It turns a sane man mad and a clever man into a fool. I wonder why it is that most of man's greatest pleasures are things that kill him,' he added. 'Perhaps it's evidence of God's sense of humour. Now, then ... Who wants to be mother?'

He passed the glass to Ludwig and sat down on one corner of his desk.

Ludwig walked over to James and held the gin in front of his face. James smelt flowers and lemons and cleaning fluid, and the alcohol caught in the back of his throat.

'You going to take it?' asked Ludwig. 'Or am I going to have to make you?'

James defiantly took the glass. The gin looked so clear and so harmless, if it wasn't for the smell it could have been water.

Charnage raised his whisky. 'Chin–chin,' he said. 'What ho! Down the hatch!'

James hurled his glass with all his strength straight at his head. Charnage casually ducked out of its way and the tumbler smashed harmlessly against the wall behind him. The gin had gone everywhere and its stink filled the room.

'Oh, dear,' said Charnage, mopping at his desk with a silk handkerchief. 'The party just got boring.'

He opened a drawer and took out a pair of handcuffs.

'Use these,' he said, tossing them to Ludwig.

Ludwig caught them cleanly, but, while he was distracted, James leapt out of his chair and charged at him, slamming him back against the wall and winding him. Charnage grabbed James from behind and wrestled him back towards the chair, twisting his arms up behind his back. James lashed out with his heels, stabbing at his shins. Charnage cursed as James stamped down hard on his instep and he stumbled. He didn't let go, however, and jerked James's arms higher up his back.

Ludwig returned to the fight and got James in a headlock, but Wolfgang was keeping his distance.

It was quite a struggle; James didn't let up for a second. The men were stronger than him, though, and at last they got him sat down with his hands fastened to the chair behind him.

James saw with some satisfaction that Ludwig had a bloody nose and Charnage was limping worse than before. He hadn't held out any real hope of escaping and had simply wanted the satisfaction of not going down without a fight. The brief explosion of violence had also calmed his nerves, cleared his mind and released some of his anger.

'Right,' said Charnage, pouring more gin into a fresh tumbler. 'Let's try again, shall we?'

Without warning, Ludwig viciously pulled James's head back and clamped his nostrils shut so that he had no option but to part his lips or suffocate. Quickly Charnage tipped the gin into his open mouth, and James was forced to swallow or choke.

The gin was bitter and burnt his throat all the way down to his stomach, where it sat like a cold lump. Ludwig let him go and Charnage went over to the desk to refill the tumbler.

James sat there coughing and dribbling gin and saliva on to the carpet. He groaned. His body was already telling him that something was wrong. The stuff in his guts was bad and should be got rid of. But before he could do anything about it, Charnage jerked his head back again and emptied another glass of gin into his mouth. His throat tried to close up and he managed to spit half of the liquid out, but the other half went down.

'What I'm interested in,' said Charnage, staring into James's face and still holding his hair, 'is what exactly you hoped to achieve with your schoolboy heroics?'

'Find Fairburn,' James gasped. 'Free him, and stop you from doing whatever it is you're doing.'

'"Stop me from doing whatever it is I am doing"?' sneered Charnage, with heavy sarcasm in his voice. 'It's all rather vague, isn't it, old pal?' He picked up his own drink and gazed at James over the rim of his glass. There was a look of cruel amusement in his sleepy eyes. 'You don't really have a clue, do you?' he said, sitting down.

James was already feeling the effects of the alcohol. Everything looked woozy and distant. Part of him wanted to keep his mouth shut and say nothing, another part felt reckless and light-headed.

As ever the reckless side won.

'I know you're building a machine,' he said, his voice slurred.

Charnage sat back in his seat and raised his eyebrows in mild surprise.

'Go on,' he said.

231

'A machine that thinks like a person,' said James, 'only a thousand times faster.'

Charnage frowned and glanced back towards the woman who still sat motionless in the shadows.

James pointed to the machine near the door. 'Is that it, there?' he said.

'That thing?' Charnage laughed. 'That's just a toy.'

'You were working with Peterson, weren't you?' said James. 'I expect he built that one for you, didn't he? Maybe it's a prototype for the larger machine, I don't know.'

'Of course you don't know,' said Charnage wearily. 'You don't know anything, you're just a silly boy clutching at straws.'

'Peterson started work on the larger machine,' said James, 'but he couldn't do it by himself. You needed Fairburn, but he wouldn't help you, would he? Because he knew who you were making the machine for. He knew that you had done a deal with the devil.'

For the first time Charnage looked like he was taking this seriously.

'Who told you that?' he said.

'So you believe me now?' said James. 'It's sinking in that I *do* know what you're up to.'

'Who am I working for?' said Charnage coldly.

James said nothing.

The truth was that he had no idea. Three of Fairburn's clues remained unsolved.

Charnage nodded to Ludwig who stepped forward and forced more gin into James's mouth.

He gagged, his throat desperately trying to block the

poison. The gin bubbled and gurgled and some went down the wrong way into his lungs and spread fire through his chest.

Before James could recover, Ludwig tipped more in and his stomach gave a lurch. He retched and a gob of acid was released into the back of his mouth. He swallowed hard and retched again.

'It's deadly stuff,' said Charnage. 'It's no wonder the do-gooders got it banned in America. But you can't ban what men desire. The chief result of Prohibition was that criminal gangs sprang up everywhere, ready to supply the badly needed illegal liquor. I believe you met one of these American hoodlums downstairs, the charming Mister Schultz, beer baron of New York. He doesn't look much, does he? But this year I believe he made fourteen million dollars and killed God knows how many of his countrymen. What more do you know, boy?'

Charnage's voice sounded hollow and echoing. It hurt James's ears. A throb had started behind his eyes as if someone was hammering inside his skull, trying to smash their way out.

He looked around. The colours in the room were muddy and dull. Everything was reduced to sickly yellows and browns. He tried to latch on to something, but his vision couldn't get a grip and kept sliding. Finally his eyes came to rest on the woman.

The desk lamp must have shifted position, because he could see her clearly for the first time. She was dressed in a drab khaki outfit that clung tightly to her stocky frame. Her short hair was grey. She had a wide, flat face

233

that looked hard, as if it had been carved out of stone. If it wasn't for her eyes she would have looked like any middle-aged woman who had lived a tough, outdoors sort of a life. The kind of woman you saw on market stalls, or working in the fields. But her eyes were frightening. They were black and unspeakably ancient. They looked like they had seen everything and that nothing could ever surprise them. James knew that it would be pointless to appeal to these eyes for help.

The room began to spin, greasy and dizzying, as if James had been too long on a roundabout and made himself giddy. He closed his eyes and it was worse; he couldn't tell which way was up or down and felt horribly out of control.

'What more do you know, boy?' Charnage repeated. 'Who am I working for?'

Thoughts were sloshing about inside James's head like the evil liquid that filled his guts. They were confused and random, but a stray one kept fighting its way to the surface . . .

The tramp, Theo, had said something that had made a tiny connection in James's brain, so small he hadn't noticed it at the time, but that connection had made other connections. Bits and pieces of information were coming together in the churning soup of his drunken mind.

It was something about Karl Marx.

What had Theo said?

That Marx was buried in Highgate cemetery. *Yes.* But there was something else, a phrase he had used.

He was the man who turned the Russian bear red.

Russia was always represented as a bear, like the British bulldog or the American eagle.

And red was the colour of communism.

James remembered joking with Perry in the taxi outside the cemetery, that they were looking for a red bear sailing a boat.

Rouge Callisto. The red bear. Was that what Fairburn had been trying to tell them in his clue?

And Alexis Fairburn had been born Alexei Fyodorov.

James lifted his head and looked straight at Charnage, trying to get his eyes to focus.

'You're working for the Russians,' he said.

Charnage stood stock still, staring at James. The room had gone very quiet. It was as if time had stopped.

The spell was broken by the woman, sitting so silently at the back of the office. Now, for the first time, she spoke. One word.

'John.'

Charnage's eyes clouded for a moment. James realized he was scared of the woman. He wasn't the one in charge here. She was.

Charnage walked over to her and the two of them had a quick whispered conversation. James couldn't hear what they were saying. He was deafened by the blood roaring and whining in his ears. He closed his eyes and tried to cling on to sanity. It was no good. His whole body was shaking. The poison was spreading and there was nothing he could do about it.

There was no escaping it, no hiding from the fact that he was dying.

'Go on.' It was Charnage's voice. It sounded painfully close and impossibly distant at the same time.

James opened his eyes, but couldn't speak.

He tilted forward and his guts emptied in one great heave, showering the carpet and Charnage's trouser legs. Gasping like a landed fish, he tried to draw fresh oxygen into his lungs, but the alcohol fumes were coming back up his gullet and shrouding his face in a foul mist.

Charnage wiped James's face, but it wasn't an act of kindness, it was so that he wouldn't get dirty as he grabbed him again.

'No,' said James. 'Please . . .'

'What's the matter?' said Charnage. 'Does this offend your sense of fair play? Are you upset that it's not quite cricket?'

'Please,' said James. 'I –'

But his words were drowned by gin.

A Volatile Substance

Dust. Darkness. A howling noise. His brain was being crushed. Black shapes swirling across his vision. A rushing sound in his ears. The stink of vomit. Bare bricks. The clatter of feet on an iron staircase. Voices arguing. Echoing. Hands digging into his ankles and armpits.

'Watch out . . .'

A sudden flash of white light as his head hit a wall.

Laughter.

The creak of a door. Familiar wallpaper. A picture of a naked woman eating grapes. He had been here before. When was that . . .?

Fresh air. Cold air. Cutting like a knife. Waking him.

He was looking up at the sky. The Smith brothers had brought him out of the factory and into the yard. He sucked oxygen into his sore lungs. The clouds had gone. There were stars. They spun, a blur. He was disappearing down a giant plughole, spiralling round and round and round . . .

He passed out again.

He was dreaming. Confused thoughts swirled around in his head. Objects seemed to be rushing at him. He started to imagine that he was on Dutchman's field playing cricket. The bowler was hurling balls down at him and they were bouncing up and thudding into him, his face, his chest, his body, his legs. Every part of his body was aching.

He wanted to cry out that it wasn't fair, but he couldn't speak.

He tried to concentrate. He had to hold back the chaos. He had to focus his mind. All he could see were clues and impossible crossword puzzles. Binary code spooling away into infinity. Fairburn dressed as a cowboy, a speech bubble coming from his mouth, '*I know not everyone enjoys crosswords like you do. For instance, your messmate, the runner, must accept what he is and begin to mature.*'

'You're right,' James mumbled. 'I hate crosswords.'

Solve all seven cryptic clues.

'Solve them yourself . . .'

'What's he say?'

'He's rambling.'

He could hear the slap of water, and smell the rotting, fishy stench of the Thames.

He opened his eyes. The brothers were lowering him down a slippery ladder to a barge. He saw that they were in a large dock, choked with boats. A low yellow mist crawled across the water. Somewhere far off a ship's horn gave a long, wailing moan.

James flopped like a rag doll as they dumped him face down on to the deck of the barge. There was an inch of freezing water in the bottom. It revived him for a moment. He rolled on to his back. Wolfgang and Ludwig were looking down at him. Ludwig's skull face split into a grin.

'Awake, are you, boysie?' he said. 'Good. This wouldn't be no fun if you didn't know what was happening.'

'Get a move on,' said Wolfgang. 'You know I don't like boats.'

'It's not my fault you never learnt to swim,' said Ludwig.

'Let's just get this over with and get back to dry land.'

Wolfgang can't swim. He doesn't like boats.

It was like a tiny candle being lit in the back of James's mind. He stored the information away. Information was power. His uncle had told him that. Uncle Max, who had been a spy in the Great War. He had taught James that nobody could get the better of a Bond.

He had to fight. Fight to stay conscious. Fight the poison in his body. Fight these two killers.

He had to keep alive.

Ludwig knelt and pinched James's cheeks together with one hand. Then shook his head viciously from side to side, rattling his teeth.

'That's right. You stay awake, now,' he said. 'I want to hear you beg for mercy as we put you over the side.'

'Please,' said Wolfgang tetchily. 'Let's get going.'

'Cast off, then,' said Ludwig, standing up.

'Can't you do it? I might fall in.'

'You're useless, you are.'

'It's my knee, Ludo,' said Wolfgang. 'You know I'm unsteady on my knee, and carrying the brat hasn't helped none.'

'As usual,' said Ludwig, 'I have to do everything.'

In a moment James felt a throb and there was a chugging noise as the engine fired up. A cloud of diesel fumes filled the bottom of the barge and James felt a wave of nausea rising inside him. In a moment a gutful of stinging fluids punched up his gullet and hosed across the floor.

'Sort that out!' yelled Ludwig, and Wolfgang man-handled James to the side of the barge. Wolfgang quickly sat down again on the other side.

'Keep an eye on him,' said Ludwig. 'We don't want him going in here. We need to get out into Limehouse Reach where there's no chance of him swimming ashore.'

James held on to the side of the barge. Being sick had cleared his mind a little further, but he was hurting badly. He had drunk enough alcohol to kill him. It was in his blood, being taken round to all his major organs. His liver, his kidneys, his brain . . .

He knew that his body was struggling to survive. If they got him into the fast-flowing water of the Thames he wouldn't last a minute.

Keep your mind alert. Study your surroundings, James. Information is power.

He was on a motorized barge, made from rusted iron sections crudely riveted together. It was square-ended with high, flat sides. It wasn't built for comfort or speed. It was an industrial vessel, used to cart stuff up and down the Thames.

Ludwig stood at the stern, holding the wheel. James watched as he slowly manoeuvred the barge out past the other boats moored in the dock, ten to twenty deep. There were so many boats here you could walk from one side of the dock to the other across their decks. The dock was enclosed, with warehouses on all sides, but there were no signs of life. It must be the dead of night.

James could see two Ludwigs now as his eyes slipped out of focus. He struggled to refocus, but it was like he was inside someone else's body with no way of controlling it.

Concentrate, James. Think hard. Keep your mind alive.

If he ever got out of this alive he would still have to find Fairburn.

Solve all seven cryptic clues.

Your messmate, the runner, must accept what he is and begin to mature . . .

Why had Fairburn included him in his damned clues? How much simpler James's life would have been if he'd never got involved in this whole mess.

And why hadn't Fairburn used James's name in the clue? Why had he just called him '*your messmate, the runner*'?

His name must be part of the answer . . .

Of course.

Bond. The word *Bond* . . .

He must accept what he is and begin to mature . . .

He opened his eyes just in time to see that they were passing very close to another boat. He snatched his hand away from the side of the barge before it was smashed against the other vessel.

He smiled. His reflexes were still working. He had a strong will to live. He mustn't give up.

A vivid memory floated into his mind. Learning to sail with his father in the English Channel, their dinghy skipping over the choppy grey waters. He had enjoyed being with his father, who he never saw as much of as he would have liked. His father had been a very good

241

sailor, and James remembered how safe he had always felt with him.

Not like these two, not like Wolfgang and Ludwig. They weren't sailors. They were city men. Used to cobblestones and buildings and ground that didn't shift under your feet.

The front of the barge bumped into another boat and James was thrown forward on to the floor.

'Watch it,' said Wolfgang, and Ludwig swore at him.

Wolfgang was sitting on a narrow bench, gripping tightly to the side of the barge. He looked like he was holding on for dear life, even though they were only moving at a snail's pace and the barge was so sturdily built that there was no danger of being sunk by any of Ludwig's clumsy collisions.

James's head lolled on to his chest and a black veil came down.

He was in another place. A safer place. He was with his father again.

They were returning to Hythe. His mother was waiting on the quayside. But James had forgotten one of the rules of sailing and was holding on to the side of the boat. As they came alongside the harbour they hit a rope buffer and his fingers had been crushed. He had howled and his father had told him off for being an ass.

His mother had hugged him and kissed him and fussed over him as if he had received a mortal wound. He had resented her hugs, and felt that she was mothering him like a little baby.

He would have given anything to have her here now, though, and feel her arms around him.

Don't be a sap, James. She's dead. They're both dead. There's nobody to hold your hand now. You're going to have to get through this by yourself. You're on your own. So do something about it.

Accept what you are and begin to mature . . .

What was he?

Well, according to Fairburn's letter, he was a runner.

Begin to mature?

Cryptic clues were never about what they appeared to be about, Pritpal had told him that. This clue had nothing to do with Bond himself. It was just using the letters of his name to make a new word.

BOND.

So. What if he took the beginning of the word *mature*?

Begin to mature gave him – M.

Bond must accept what he is and begin to mature . . .

Yes. It was easy once you got the hang of it.

The word *bond* must accept the word *runner* and the letter *m*.

It was all making perfect sense.

All you had to do was put the letters R-U-N-N-E-R-M inside the letters B-O-N-D . . .

Brunnermond . . . borunnermnd . . . bonrunnermd . . .

Why had he ever thought he could solve it? Why had his useless drunken brain fooled him into thinking it knew what it was doing?

It was meaningless gibberish.

Another burst of nausea brought him back to reality. But his stomach was dry, and when his body heaved again there was nothing to throw up and he retched and gulped

243

painfully, his stomach contracting as if there was a fist inside it opening and closing.

When the contractions had passed he sat up and looked around. Up ahead, there was a narrow gap between a large steamship and a coal barge, and past that was a clear stretch of water leading to the exit from the dock into the Thames.

The noise of the diesel rose a pitch and the barge speeded up.

'Not too fast,' said Wolfgang.

'Oh, stop your moaning,' said Ludwig. 'I know what I'm doing.'

'It's dark, Ludo, and it's dangerous,' said Wolfgang. 'We shouldn't be out on the water at night. Look at this fog.'

Come on, James. You don't have much of a chance, but if you can't get your body working you've no chance at all.

He dropped on to his hands and knees. He was aware of the hard deck of the boat digging into him, but the pain sharpened his senses. He concentrated on it, it would keep him awake. If he could feel pain then he was still alive.

He began to crawl.

'Where does he think he's going?' said Ludwig, but Wolfgang didn't reply.

James inched painfully along the deck. A thin stream of sticky bile trickled from his mouth. He barely noticed it. He soon forgot where he was, or what he was doing, but he remembered enough to keep moving.

His head bumped into something. It was Ludwig's leg. He looked up.

'Get off,' snapped Ludwig and he kicked him away. James fell back against the side of the barge and blacked out.

He felt his mother's arms around him. She whispered something in his ear, which he couldn't hear.

No. She wasn't there. Don't be fooled. Open your eyes and wake up.

He tried, but his eyelids were made of lead. They weighed a ton each. He had to use his fingers to drag them up.

The big coal barge was just ahead of them. Once they were through this last narrow gap Ludwig could go full speed ahead and James would have lost any chance of escape.

He looked at Wolfgang. He was still in the same position and hadn't moved a muscle since he'd sat down. His back was rigid and hunched.

Ludwig was concentrating, staring ahead into the darkness, his mouth open, his tongue running along the broken ridge of his stubby brown teeth. He eased the throttle forward.

James toppled over and grabbed hold of Ludwig's legs again, and again Ludwig kicked him away. James didn't give up, though. He crawled back and this time Ludwig put his boot squarely in James's face.

'Keep it up, buster,' he said and giggled. 'This is fun.' He shoved hard. James was thrown several feet along the barge and he landed heavily on his side.

He felt something digging into him.

The jar. The jar of potassium he had taken from Charnage's storeroom.

He slipped his hand into his pocket and felt the cool, hard glass. His hand stung painfully. The jar was leaking and it had burnt his skin. He forced himself not to let go, using the pain to shock him awake.

As they came up alongside the steamship the noise of the engine intensified, bouncing back off its flat metal sides.

James got to his knees and faced Ludwig.

'Oh, look who it is,' said Ludwig. 'Young Sherlock Holmes!'

'Have this,' said James, and in one movement he took the bottle from his pocket and hurled it at the wheelhouse.

He wasn't sure what effect, if any, it would have, but he hoped it would be dramatic enough to cause a diversion.

As it turned out the effect was spectacular.

The potassium had been too long in the bottle and had grown unstable. The percussion as it hit the wheelhouse caused it to explode with a shocking bang and a blinding violet flash, sending shards of glass in every direction. Then, as the volatile contents of the jar hit the water in the bottom of the barge, they burst into flame, filling the air with a cloud of gas.

Ludwig yelled, and fell sideways, spinning the wheel.

The barge swerved, out of control, and broadsided the coal barge. Wolfgang screamed and threw himself out of his seat on to the floor, clutching his hand and shrieking in agony. The last thing James saw before he fell over the side was the ghastly mess the collision had made: all four fingers of Wolfgang's left hand had been severed at the root.

James was sinking. He could see nothing, and when he tried to swim to the surface his head bumped against something hard. He realized that he was under the barge. He frantically pulled himself to the side. His face broke the surface and he took in air. He couldn't feel anything now. His body was numb. He knew, though, that if he didn't get out of the water quickly he would die.

He could hear Ludwig.

'Shut up!' he shouted at his brother. 'Where's he gone?'

'Help me,' whimpered Wolfgang. 'Oh, God, help me.'

Ludwig killed the engine and the barge drifted.

'What the bloody hell's the matter with you?' he said.

'My fingers,' said Wolfgang. 'Oh, God, my fingers.'

'Show me . . . Oh, sweet Jesus . . .'

James pushed off from the barge and swam the few feet to where the steamship's anchor chain slanted down into the murky water. He took hold of it and held on, shivering, his mind reeling. Everything was dimming, as if he was looking down a long tunnel, the end of which was gradually receding.

He could still hear the brothers.

'Help me, Ludo.'

'I can't. This bloody stuff's burning everywhere. I can't put it out. And we've lost the brat. Where is he? Where's he gone?'

'Leave him,' sobbed Wolfgang. 'He fell in. That was the plan. He's drowned. Leave him and help me. I need a doctor. Help me, Ludo . . .'

Ludwig put the barge into reverse and backed away. Soon all James could see was an eerie violet glow in the mist and all he could hear were the wails and screams coming from Wolfgang.

He let go of the chain and swam on. Every couple of feet he dipped beneath the surface and he desperately tried not to swallow any water, but at last he got past the ship and clambered on to a wooden wharf. He flopped to the ground and lay there as if dead, meaningless words spinning in his head, lulling him to sleep . . .

Brunnermond . . . borunnermnd . . . bonrunnermd . . .

If he fell asleep he would never wake.

Get up.

He struggled to his feet and swayed for a moment, trying not to fall over. Then he did the hardest thing he had ever had to do in his life. He put one foot in front of the other and started walking.

The next few hours were a blur. He could only remember brief snatches.

His first memory was of trying to get out of the docks. But wherever he tried he was stopped. By gates or warehouses or high walls. In the end a dock policeman found him and took him to his hut. He sat him by a stove and went to make a phone call.

Somehow, while he was gone, James managed to climb out of a window.

After that there was a blank for a while. The next thing he knew he was walking. Walking, stumbling, falling, walking, stumbling, falling. And there was an irritating voice inside his head telling him not to stop.

If he could keep his body moving he would be able

to keep on fighting the poison. If he stopped he would die. It was as simple as that.

He remembered standing by a burning brazier with some tramps, warming himself. He remembered someone giving him a mug of hot tea, but had no idea who it was, or where it had happened.

He remembered stopping to be sick. Watching the tea drain away down a gutter.

He remembered Chinese faces. Chinese shop signs. A glimpse through a door of Chinese men sitting round a table smoking and shouting and playing a game with dried beans.

He remembered someone laughing at him.

He remembered sheltering in the porch of a church.

Somehow he acquired an overcoat, but couldn't remember where it had come from. It was too large for him and was ripped in places, one pocket was hanging loose, but at least it helped to keep him warm.

He remembered an argument of some sort, a fight, someone punching him, shouting. Afterwards, he had been left by the side of the road. He remembered crawling up against a wall where another policeman had found him. This one wasn't interested in where he had come from and moved him on, jabbing him with his truncheon to keep him walking.

Walking, walking, walking.

Where was he going? Who did he think was going to help him?

Rouge Callisto. Pritpal was going to be proud of him when he told his friend he'd solved one of the clues.

Could he find Pritpal? How far was Hackney Wick?
Too far.
The red bear . . .
Red.

Slowly a name came to him. A memory. A boy. Yes. He lived here somewhere. In the East End.

A friend.

He did have a friend.

That was something, wasn't it? Something to hold on to.

Red. Red Kelly. Did anyone know him?

Light was coming into the sky. People were beginning to move about the streets. Did anyone know Kelly? A boy. About sixteen.

Red Kelly . . .

'*Try this way . . . Try that way . . . Never heard of him . . . There's some Kellys live down Canning Town way . . . Have you tried Stepney, son? . . . Do you mean old Brendan Kelly? Try Cable Street . . . Try Shadwell . . . Is he Irish? The Irish are all in Wapping . . .*'

Thirsty. He remembered being thirsty. Drinking from a puddle. Lying on his belly like a dog. Sucking . . . Water . . .

And then nothing. Just a troubled sleep, with endless nightmares. A man screaming in his face, a never-ending scream. A man with four black stumps where his fingers should have been.

Part Three: SUNDAY

The Monstrous Regiment

'Who is he?'

'Search me.'

'Who is he, then?'

He could feel hands tugging at his clothing.

'What's he got? He must have something on him.'

'Nah. Look at his coat. He's a dosser.'

'It's a rotten suit he's got on.'

'Have you tried all his pockets?'

'Yeah. Just some soggy old bits of paper with Chinese writing on.'

'Is he a Chinkie, then? He don't look like a Chinkie.'

'He looks half dead.'

'Let's finish the job . . .'

James opened his eyes, blinking in the harsh winter light. Black and brown shapes swam across his vision. He tried to focus, to see past the floating shapes. He saw buildings. People. Children.

He was in a dingy yard behind a pub. Crates of empty bottles stood in piles. Soot-blackened houses loomed overhead. He was surrounded by a ragged group of girls. Some were tiny little urchins with pinched, wizened faces, some were much older with a hard, mean look about them. In the centre was the ringleader. A girl of about James's age. She had large brown eyes, set far apart in her broad, heart-shaped face, and a wide, full mouth that seemed stuck in a mocking smile. Her hair was deep, dark red, and it flopped untidily into her eyes.

She looked curiously at James and he looked back at her.

'What you looking at?' she said.

'You,' croaked James. His mouth was dry, his throat scalded.

'Who gave you permission?' said the girl.

'No one,' said James. 'Why? Do I need permission? Who are you? The queen, or something?'

'Don't be cheeky,' said the girl.

'Help me up,' said James.

'Why should I?'

'Suit yourself.' James tried to get up, but she pushed him back.

'Who are you?' she said.

'It doesn't matter,' said James. He felt as if a ring of iron was being slowly tightened around his head. His ears were singing and there was a stabbing pain in the small of his back.

'Let's do him,' said one of the girls, picking up a bottle. 'He's not from round here. He's a foreigner.'

'He sounds posh,' said one of the smaller kids. 'Who is he? What's he doin' 'ere? He's not a tramp. He's posh.'

'Let's do him,' repeated the girl with the bottle. 'And do him good.'

No matter how bad he felt — and he couldn't remember when he had ever felt worse — James wasn't going to lie here and be done over by a bunch of girls.

He struggled to his feet.

The girl prodded him with her bottle.

'Don't do that,' said James. 'I don't hit girls, but in your case I'm willing to make an exception.'

She jabbed him harder and James instinctively lashed out, slapping the bottle out of the girl's hand.

She calmly picked it up by the neck and smashed the end off it, then swung it at James who managed to duck out of the way before hooking her legs out from under her with his foot. She fell heavily and James tried to make a run for it, but his body felt sluggish and clumsy. He barged someone out of the way, but was grabbed, spun around and kicked. Another girl got hold of his hair and yanked his head back, pulling him over.

He was sent sprawling into a pile of crates, but he saw a length of wood, which he managed to pick up. He stood and kept the girls at bay with it, whirling it around in the air.

How long could he keep this up for? Not long. He felt weak and light-headed. There were too many of them, and a big part of him told him that he mustn't hurt girls.

'This is our turf,' said the ringleader. 'You shouldn't be here.'

'Oh, yes?' said James. 'And who are you exactly?'

'We're the Monstrous Regiment.'

'Well, I've got no argument with you,' said James.

'We're going to give you a hiding, anyway,' said the girl. 'It's what we do.'

'You can try,' said James, but even as he said it, someone snatched hold of his piece of wood and wrestled it off him. The next thing he knew he'd been pushed to the ground and he felt a boot in his side.

This was bad. He was down and defenceless. The state he was in, they might kick him to death. He put his arm around his head to protect it and curled into a tight ball.

'Get him,' spat the girl with the bottle. 'Mash him up good!'

Then a familiar voice rang out.

'Oi! What the bloody hell's going on here, then?'

'Why didn't you tell me you was James Bond? Why didn't you tell me you was Red's mate? We was halfway to kicking your lights out, you daft sod. Why didn't you say nothing? You're James Bond. You sorted out the bloke what killed Alfie? You're a hero, you are. Red don't ever stop talking about you. Why didn't you say something?'

James couldn't speak. The girl had him in a bear hug so tight she was in danger of cracking a rib.

'Let him breathe, Kel,' said Red Kelly, who was standing a little way off watching with an amused expression on his scrunched-up, bony face.

At last the girl let James go and he coughed feebly.

'You all right, mate?' said Red. 'You look like death.'

Red was a skinny boy of sixteen, with an explosion of bright carrot-coloured hair blossoming from the top of his head. James had met him at Easter on the sleeper train to Fort William. Red had been travelling to Scotland to try and find out what had happened to his cousin, Alfie, who had disappeared. James had helped him and the two of them had become firm friends despite their different backgrounds.

'It's not *my* fault,' said the girl. 'He was like that before we started on him.'

Red put an arm around the girl's shoulders.

'Allow me to introduce my darling little sister, Kelly,' he said.

'Doesn't she have a first name?' said James, rubbing his side where he had been kicked.

'That *is* her first name,' said Red. 'Me mum and dad christened her Kelly. Kelly Kelly. Kelly's an Irish name. Means warrior. They obviously thought it suited her.'

James looked at the girl. She wiped her nose and looked back at him, holding his gaze with her big, clear, brown eyes.

'We heard there was someone looking for Red,' she said. 'We didn't have any idea who it was. An outsider, was all we knew. We thought it was trouble.'

James gave a quick snort of laughter. 'It *is* trouble,' he said. 'Big trouble.'

'Wherever you go there's trouble,' said Red. 'Look at you. What the bloody hell happened this time?'

'It's a long story,' said James. 'And I'm sorry to say, I don't think it's over yet.'

James suddenly felt faint and he swayed on his feet. Red caught him, then wrinkled his small, pointed nose.

'Gordon Bennett,' he said. 'You don't half stink,

Jimmy-boy. You been on the booze? You look drunk as a fiddler's bitch. We better get you settled, mate. We don't want you to drop dead on us. We'll get you inside and cleaned up, find you some grub and you can tell us all about it.'

Red hammered on the back door of the pub until a bald, fat man in a stained vest opened it. They'd obviously woken him up and he had a thunderous look about him.

'Red?' he snarled when he saw who it was. 'What you doing here at this hour? Get lost.'

'Leave it out, Lou,' said Red. 'This is James Bond.'

'James Bond?' said Lou and his face lit up into a wide, gap-toothed smile. He gripped James's hand and pumped it up and down. 'James Bond. You're a hero round these parts, son.'

'So I've heard,' muttered James.

'Come in, come in,' said Lou, dragging him through the door. 'I'd be honoured to have you in my pub.' He stopped suddenly and bellowed, 'Maureen! Get your arse down here. We've got company.'

Pale winter sunlight was struggling to shine in through the grimy windows and failing. The pub was dark. It had a bare wooden floor scattered with sawdust. There was a battered assortment of ill-matched tables and chairs. The walls were greasy and the ceiling had been turned brown by tobacco smoke. A sour-sweet smell of alcohol, cigarettes and sweat hung in the air.

Lou cleared a space for James at a table whose legs had been heavily repaired over the years.

'What can I get you?' he asked. 'Beer? A fortified wine?

Spirits? How about a nice gin? Nothing's too good for James Bond.'

'No. Please,' said James as he was gripped by a spasm of nausea. The very mention of the word 'gin' had brought him out in a cold sweat. 'Just a glass of water would be fine.'

'Water?' said Lou. 'Never touch the stuff meself. But I'll get you some.'

'And get some nosh,' said Red. 'He looks like a feller who could do with some breakfast. Don't worry, we'll have a whip-round later.'

'No, no, no,' said Lou. 'This is on me. As I say, nothing's too good for James Bond.'

Lou disappeared behind the bar and James heard him shouting at someone in a back room.

Red sat down at the table.

'I told everyone,' he said, with a lop-sided grin. 'People round here are very close. You help one of us, you help all of us. You hurt one of us, you hurt all of us.'

James's eyes were sore and gritty, his head throbbing, his throat raw and dry. He was cold, sick and exhausted. But here was a friend. Someone who could help him. Since splitting up with Perry he had been alone. And this run-down pub felt like the safest, most pleasant place in London.

'I'm sorry we was going to kick your teeth out,' said Red's sister. 'You mustn't mind us. We ain't got the same manners as you posh folks.'

Manners? James remembered how Sir John Charnage had tried to poison him. People were pretty well the same the world over as far as he could tell. A man might try to kill you with a posh accent, or he might try to kill you with a cockney accent, or a German accent, or a Russian one, but it was all the same. Everyone was out to get you.

Lou brought a glass of water and James sipped it slowly. The cool, clean liquid tasted like the most marvellous thing he had ever drunk. It slipped down his throat, soothing the dryness and calming his churning stomach. He could feel it entering his blood and cleaning out the poisons. Washing around his body.

'So come on, then,' said Red. 'What's your story?'

James took a deep breath and started to talk.

'It all began,' he said, 'when we got a visit from the Head Master in my room at Eton . . .'

It took him a long time to tell them everything and when he finally finished, Red let out a long low whistle.

'Do you go looking for trouble, Jimmy-boy?' he said. 'Or does it just find you?'

'I don't know,' said James. 'But I don't seem to be able to avoid it.'

Lou's wife, Maureen, a short, round woman with a huge wart on her cheek, had brought in a chipped plate with a wedge of pork pie, two slices of hard, dry bread and a lump of stale cheese on it. James forced some down, though chewing was difficult and swallowing harder. The bread kept forming into a sticky ball in his mouth and he had to wash it down with more water.

'So do you know the Paradice Club?' he asked.

'Yeah, course,' said Kelly, leaning back in his seat and

scratching himself. 'It's down in Poplar. Everyone round here knows about it. Worst-kept secret in the East End.'

'And Sir John Charnage?'

'Always knew he was a wrong'un,' said Lou and he spat on to his floor.

'The Charnage Chemical Works has been there for at least fifty years, hasn't it, Lou?' said Red.

'Probably more like seventy,' said Lou. 'Bad place to work, it was. About the worst. All them poisons in there, and the fumes and the gas. Men was always dying there. There's a saying, when someone dies you say, "They've gone to work at Charnage's".'

'Why would anyone *want* to work there, then?' asked James.

'No choice,' said Lou. 'You only went to work for Charnage's if you couldn't work no place else. And still you'd see 'em queuing up at the gates of a morning. These are bad times, boy. There's no work around. Men will do anything to survive, to get a few coins to put bread in their babies' mouths. They knew it was killing them, the men who went there. The chemicals would burn your lungs, get into your brain, but men would figure out, maybe they'd get sick, but at least their families would live. At least their children would have grub.

'Old man Charnage, Sir John's dad, he was a terror. Wasn't a week went by without you'd hear of someone else falling sick, or getting blinded or just dropping dead. But Charnage claimed he was one of the best employers in the East End. And he had connections. He was a rich man. He paid people to turn a blind eye and look the other way. By the time the old man died and Sir John took over, it was too far gone, though. No one would work there any more. All Sir John could get was foreigners from the docks, fresh off the boats. It couldn't last. He closed down, and started to lose all his family's money. He was a gambler, and not a very good one. That's why he built his illegal gambling club, the Paradice, to try and make some money back.'

James had been concentrating so hard on the story he hadn't noticed that while they'd been talking the pub had filled up with people. And now, when the newcomers saw that the conversation was over, they started to approach the table in ones and twos. They all wanted to shake James's hand and buy him a drink, but he refused anything stronger than ginger beer.

James struggled to keep up with the endless parade.

'This is me Uncle Jack and me cousin Dave, these are me brothers Freddie and Dan, this is little Joe, this is big Joe, oh, look, it's me Auntie Claire, and there's Jerry . . .'

James sat on the bench with his back to the wall, drenched in sweat and shivering. The room seemed to be closing in on him from all sides, narrowing and darkening. The din of voices in the pub boomed and echoed. He wanted to crawl into a corner and curl up and not wake for a hundred years.

He felt a hand on his arm and turned to see the face of Red's sister, Kelly. She had a concerned look.

'You all right?' she said.

'Not really, no,' said James. 'I think I'm going to be sick.'

'I'm not surprised,' said Kelly. 'You drank enough to kill an 'orse last night. Come on, I'll get you out of here. When the Kellys get together, sooner or later there's always a fight.'

She pulled him up out of his seat and they left by the back door.

James was glad of the fresh air, but standing up had made him dizzy and his legs felt as if they were going to collapse under him. The bright light hurt his eyes.

He leant against a wall and breathed heavily.

Kelly put her hand on his shoulder. 'You gonna make it?'

'Not sure.'

She gave him a wry smile. 'Red said you was tough,' she said. 'You gonna let a little drink slow you down?'

James raised his head and smiled back at her. 'No,' he said. 'I'm not. What time is it?'

'One o'clock,' said Kelly. 'I just this minute heard St George's chime.'

'I need to go to Hackney Wick,' said James. 'I need to find my friends.'

'You ain't goin' nowhere looking like that, soldier,' said Kelly.

James looked down at his damp and ruined clothing.

'Come back to ours,' said Kelly. 'You can rest a minute, I'll find you some decent clobber and I'll get me mum to give you some proper nosh.'

James was too tired and weak to protest and he followed as Kelly led him through the streets. The area around the Eton Mission had been grim, but this was far worse. James had never seen anywhere so poor. The houses were small and crowded together. Tired women in heavy black dresses scrubbed their doorsteps or stood gossiping. Children with no socks and shoes ran, playing, in the gutter. There were hardly any shops, and those that they passed had only a few tatty things for sale in their windows. The sign outside a butcher's shop advertised the price of almost every part of an animal except its meat – tails, innards, hearts, head, feet, livers, kidneys and dripping.

People stared at James as he passed. For the most part they seemed friendly and cheerful, but groups of small, tough-looking men stood around on the street corners having serious conversations and smoking. It was impossible to tell how old anyone was. They all looked worn-out and ancient, battered by hard living and poor food.

As they passed another pub, two drunken women spilt out of the door, pulling each other's hair. They set to in the street, yelling, hammering and clawing at each other and attracting a noisy crowd.

'Typical Sunday lunchtime entertainment on Cable Street,' said Kelly.

Further on they passed a group of girls who had tied a length of rope to a lamp post and were spinning round it, screaming with laughter.

They turned into a side street and were soon lost in a maze of tiny alleyways and passages. After a while they came out in a street where the houses were slightly bigger. Halfway down Kelly stopped and opened a door that led straight off the pavement. Inside the front room was a tiny shop, selling cans of food and bottles of fizzy drink, Batey's Lemonade, Vimto, Tizer and Kooper's Kola.

A curtain separated the shop from the rest of the house, which was clean but cramped, and the family appeared to own almost nothing.

'Mum!' Kelly yelled. 'Look who's here. It's Jimmy Bond.'

A wiry, raw-boned woman appeared, wiping her hands on an apron.

'So this is him,' she said. 'Let's have a look at you.'

She held him at arm's length, staring into his face with coal-black eyes. She nodded.

'You'll do,' she said. 'But you've had some sadness in your life, haven't you, James?'

'Oh, leave him, Mum,' said Kelly. 'He's had some gin in his life, is all. He needs a lie down.'

'You can put him in Red's bed.'

Upstairs there was a tiny back room crammed with broken-down iron bedsteads.

James sat on the bed nearest the window. He wondered what Perry was up to, and if Pritpal had solved any more clues. Maybe he should telephone Pritpal at the mission.

But he was *so* tired . . .

'Don't let me fall asleep,' he murmured. 'There's so much to do. I have to stop Charnage –'

'Go on with you,' said Kelly Kelly. 'Five minutes' shut-eye won't kill you.'

But James was already snoring. Lying spreadeagled on his back, fully clothed and with his boots on.

The Knight Who Did a Deal With the Devil

'Are you sure we shouldn't have just gone straight to the police?'

'We'll stick to our plan. If he doesn't show his m-mug by this evening, we'll tell the police, and damn the consequences.'

Pritpal and Perry were on a train, rattling westward through the countryside towards Eton. It was a Sunday service that stopped at every tiny station along the way and the journey seemed to be taking forever.

'He could be in real trouble,' said Pritpal.

'Not our James,' said Perry. 'Something tells m-me he's all right. He's out there somewhere, three steps ahead of us, probably even now solving the last part of the puzzle.'

'I hope so,' Pritpal sighed. 'I sincerely hope so.'

'We need to give him m-more time,' said Perry. 'And, besides, if we can solve one m-more clue then we'll have something concrete to go to the police with, won't we?'

'I suppose so,' said Pritpal, though he looked miserable.

'James will be all right,' said Perry. 'He always bounces back.'

After the attack, Perry had hidden in a corner of Highgate cemetery. He'd spotted the Smith brothers leaving and watched them get into their car without James and drive off. He'd searched the grounds, but, finding no sign of his friend, he'd left and taken a taxi home. He'd waited up for James, but had finally given in to tiredness at half past one and gone to bed. When James still hadn't shown up in the morning, he'd called Pritpal at the mission to see if he'd heard anything from him.

Pritpal had also heard nothing, although a parcel had arrived for James that morning wrapped up in brown paper. Pritpal *had* had a breakthrough on another clue, however, but he told Perry that they would have to travel back to Eton to fully solve it.

In an act of uncommon boldness Pritpal had lied to the Reverend Falwell and told him that he was going to be spending the afternoon with Perry's parents. Instead, he had met him at Charing Cross station and they had boarded the train for Eton.

'So, are you sure we're on the right track?' said Perry.

'As sure as I can be,' said Pritpal. He had his notebook open on his knee and a copy of Fairburn's original letter. He had been showing Perry the poem about the Wall Game.

Come on, we cry, ignore the pain!
Tingling with excitement in the rain,
Knuckling, pressing, panting, now they're stuck,
Nigh twenty minutes in a heaving ruck,
All muddy in a mighty scuffle,
Mishaps galore, but what a battle!

Atop the wall we curse the other side,
Villains! They have won the ball,
A shout goes up as some brave chap
Eludes the pack and throws for goal.

'I tried every type of clue I could think of to crack it,' he explained. 'Container clues, anagrams, double definitions, but nothing would unlock it until I decided to try looking for hidden-word clues.'

'And what are they?'

'A hidden-word clue is simply a clue that contains the answer hidden among other words,' said Pritpal.

'Show m–me.'

'Well, your name, Mandeville, for example, would give us both *man* and *devil*. But a better example would be *super rye* where your name – Perry – is hidden across two words,' said Pritpal.

Perry smiled.

'And you're telling m–me this poem contains some hidden words?'

'Yes.'

Perry looked at the poem, to see if he could find any of the hidden words.

'There's *the*,' he said. 'Hidden inside *with excitement*. Don't suppose I'd get a prize for that, though?'

'Afraid not,' said Pritpal. 'Look at the ends of the lines.'

Perry looked at the first couplet:

Come on, we cry, ignore the pain!
Tingling with excitement in the rain,

'Aha,' he cried. 'I see what you m-mean, *pain tingling* gives us *paint*.'

'It gives us more than *paint*,' said Pritpal, 'it gives us *painting*. As soon as I spotted that I knew I was following the right scent. The clues are across the joins of each couplet.'

Perry read out the next couplet.

> Knuckling, pressing, panting, now they're stuck,
> Nigh twenty minutes in a heaving ruck,

He scratched his head. 'Can't make head or tail of that one,' he said.

'The clue is hidden across three words,' said Pritpal. '*Stuck*, *nigh* and *twenty*.'

'Knight!' said Perry. 'That was well hidden.'

The next couplet:

> All muddy in a mighty scuffle,
> Mishaps galore, but what a battle!

gave them *Flemish*. And the rest of the poem:

> Atop the wall we curse the other side,
> Villains! They have won the ball,
> A shout goes up as some brave chap
> Eludes the pack and throws for goal.

gave them *devil* and *chapel*.

'It has been staring us in the face for days,' said Pritpal. 'I kick myself that I didn't see it sooner.'

269

'But what does it add up to?' said Perry. '*Painting, knight, Flemish, devil* and *chapel*? What's the significance?'

'You also have to look at what the poem is supposedly about,' said Pritpal. 'The Wall Game. This clue is a game about a wall, or more precisely a *wall painting*.'

'So we're looking for a chapel with a Flemish wall painting with a knight and a devil in it, then, are we?' said Perry.

'Yes,' said Pritpal. 'And the poem is about Eton's famous game. Fairburn was an Eton pupil and master, and the letter was sent to an Eton boy. I concluded that the obvious place to start looking for this wall painting was in Eton itself, which, let's face it, has a very famous chapel. In fact it was one of the very first structures to have been built at the school. Now, I do not know much about College Chapel, but are there some wall paintings there?'

'I'll say,' said Perry, who had always been something of an art buff. 'They're rather famous. Very old, fifteenth century, been rather m-mucked about with over the years.'

'And are they Flemish?' asked Pritpal.

'There's no *ish* about it,' said Perry. 'They're totally Flem. They were slapped up by a crack team of artists the college shipped over from the Netherlands, probably didn't have any bods of our own who knew one end of a paintbrush from the other. They're not m-much to look at, rather dull and m-murky if the truth be told, but they're probably the m-most important pieces of art in the whole of Eton. I've been in to sketch them a couple of times with the Drawing School.'

'Do you think they'll let us in there today?' asked Pritpal.

'Don't see why not,' said Perry.

Pritpal stared out of the window. 'I just wish this damned train would hurry up,' he said.

James didn't want to wake up. He needed to sleep for much, much longer. Someone was roughly shaking him, though.

'Go away,' he grumbled. 'Leave me alone. I've only just nodded off.'

'Wakey, wakey. Up and at 'em!' It was Red's voice. James opened one eye. It was growing dark outside. Red was an indistinct black shadow in the unlit room.

'It's nearly three, mate,' said Red.

James forced himself up on to his elbows and blinked. His eyelids felt as if they were lined with sandpaper.

'Nearly three?' he said, trying to take in this information. 'I told your sister not to let me sleep too long.'

'You needed a proper kip, Jimmy-boy. You was knocking at death's door. In fact you was trying to kick it in.'

'But, Red, you don't understand –'

Red interrupted him. 'Keep your shirt on, Jimmy-boy. What were you gonna do? Where were you gonna go?'

'I've got to solve the rest of the clues,' said James sleepily. 'I have to find out where Fairburn is.' He swung his legs over the side of the bed and, as his bare feet touched the freezing linoleum, he winced. The room was cold as the grave.

He noticed he was wearing just his shirt and underpants. Somebody must have undressed him. He didn't ask who.

'By the sound of it, you been working on them clues for days,' said Red. 'Did you really think you was gonna solve them the state you're in? With the king of all hangovers?'

'I have to do something,' groaned James. 'You shouldn't have let me sleep so long.' He stopped himself and looked at Red. 'I'm sorry,' he said softly. 'I'm tired and fed up and my head hurts like hell.'

'Don't apologize, mate,' said Red, with a big grin. 'It's good to see you again.'

James stood up and brushed his hair back out of his face with his fingers. As usual a stray lock fell forward over one eye. His skin felt sore and his face and hands were spotted with tiny red marks from the potassium explosion.

A grubby-faced boy who looked like a smaller version of Red came in, a huge flat cap covering his flame-red hair. He was carrying James's jacket and trousers, which had been dried by a fire and pressed to remove the wrinkles.

'Your mum told me to bring these up,' he said to Red, then looked at James with a sad expression. 'She had to throw out your coat, though, mate, it was in tatters.'

'Thanks, Stanley,' said Red and he took the clothes and tossed them to James. 'James,' he said, 'this is me cousin, Stanley MacCarthy.'

'I'm gonna tell all me mates that James Bond slept in me bed,' said Stanley, staring at James with big, round, shining eyes.

'Your bed?' said James, pulling on the trousers. 'I'm sorry. I thought it was Red's bed.'

'It is,' said Red. 'I share it with Stanley. Top and tail, like a couple of sardines in a tin.'

James stood up.

'Is there a telephone somewhere I can use?' he said.

'There's one in the boozer,' said Red. 'It'll be shut right now, but Lou will open up if we knock loud enough.'

'I'll need to borrow some money for the call,' said James. 'But don't worry, when this is all over I can pay you back.'

'No problem, Jimmy-boy. You just do what you gotta do.'

The operator put James through to Perry's house in Regent's Park. James spoke to Braeburn, the butler, who told him that Perry had been expecting him to call. He explained that Perry had gone off somewhere with a friend but had asked for James to leave a contact number if he called. James left the number for the pub and then called the Eton Mission.

Pritpal wasn't there but he got hold of Tommy Chong who filled James in on events. Again James left the number for the pub.

He hung up.

The pub was closed for the afternoon and the landlord, Lou, was cleaning up after the lunchtime session, sweeping up broken glass and dirty sawdust.

Red and his sister Kelly had been listening to James's conversation.

'What you gonna do, then?' asked Red.

'There's nothing I can do except wait,' said James,

glancing at the clock. 'If Pritpal and Perry *are* on to another clue it might be the one we need to finally solve this puzzle and find out where Fairburn is, but time's slipping away. Today's Sunday, it's our last day. I just hope they come up with something, and come up with it fast.'

The Holy Poker was waiting for Perry and Pritpal beneath the vast, elaborately decorated organ that filled the space above the entrance to College Chapel.

Holy Poker was the nickname given to the chapel usher because of the silver-topped rod he carried as his staff of office during services. Most boys – these two included – had no idea what his real name was.

'You are interested in our wall paintings, I gather,' he intoned. He was a dry, stiff-backed man whose hair was as silver as the top of his staff.

'That's right,' said Pritpal, looking around the chapel.

It was a tall, narrow building, with elegant stone pillars supporting a vaulted wooden ceiling. Rows of carved, Gothic pews stood on either side and behind them on the walls were the famous paintings.

'They were painted some time between fourteen seventy-nine and fourteen eighty-eight,' said the Holy Poker. 'And then whitewashed over by the college barber in fifteen sixty, for which he was paid six shillings and eightpence.'

'Why would anyone want them painted over?' said Pritpal.

'It was the Reformation,' said the Holy Poker. 'Henry the Eighth had abolished Catholicism and converted the whole country to Protestantism. Any paintings showing fictitious miracles were banned.'

As he spoke, the Holy Poker slowly led the way down the aisle towards the altar and then turned and climbed some steps towards the paintings on the right-hand side. Just as Perry had warned, they looked slightly shabby and faded, like a blurry photograph of something that had once been bright and colourful.

'Later on, wooden panelling was fixed over the wall,' explained the Holy Poker. 'And the paintings were completely forgotten until eighteen forty-seven, when the panelling was removed. Although nobody seemed to have taken much interest in them at the time and the clerk of works was allowed to scrape off almost the entire upper row of pictures until he was stopped by one of the Fellows. It was still thought, however, that the images were unfit for Protestant eyes and they were covered over again. Now, at last, we can see them in all their glory, if glory is the right word. They have been restored, but years of neglect have left them rather forlorn.'

Pritpal studied the pictures on the wall, which showed various medieval scenes, but he could see no sign of a devil.

'The paintings here on the south side tell the story of a mythical empress,' said the Holy Poker. 'Those on the north side show various miracles performed by the Virgin Mary.'

'May I look?' said Pritpal.

'You may.'

Pritpal crossed the aisle and climbed the banked pews

towards the other wall. One of the first things he spotted was a man talking to a weird naked figure with horns whose face had been completely rubbed away over the years.

'Is this the devil?' he asked.

'It is,' said the Holy Poker.

'And who is that with him?' said Pritpal.

'Ah,' said the Holy Poker, 'that is a knight, Sir Amoras. It is an amusing story. Amoras tried to sell his wife to the devil, but was prevented by the Blessed Virgin. I'm sure he's not the only man in history who has wanted to sell his wife to the devil,' he added with a dry chuckle.

Now Pritpal could see that Sir Amoras was exchanging a contract, or perhaps money, with the horned figure.

He wondered how desperate someone would have to be to do a deal with Satan himself.

James had been sitting by the telephone for nearly three hours when it finally rang. Without waiting for Lou to answer it, he jumped up and snatched the receiver from the cradle.

'Hello?'

'James!' It was Perry. 'You're alive! I knew it. But where on earth are you?'

'I'm in a pub in the East End,' said James.

'Here we were worried stiff about you and all the time you're down the pub living the life of Riley,' said Perry.

James swiftly put him right on that count and told him everything that had happened since they'd split up last night.

In return, Perry told James about the wall painting in College Chapel.

276

'Amoras?' said James. 'I've heard that name before.'

'It was in Fairburn's second letter,' said Perry. 'You remember? The one in binary code. He said something about how he'd told Charnage the story of Sir Amoras and he'd found it amusing.'

'But it's no help at all,' said James wearily. 'What was Fairburn trying to tell us?'

'M-maybe he was trying to warn us,' said Perry, 'about a knight who'd done a deal with the devil. Sir John Charnage to be precise. And he was right. You've had a very lucky escape, James.'

'There must be more to it than that,' said James.

'Well, if there is, we're stumped,' said Perry.

'Where are you now?' James asked.

'We're at the station in Eton,' said Perry. 'The London train will be here in five m-minutes, Pritpal's got to get back to the m-mission. I'll come and m-meet you in the pub, see if we can't figure this thing out, eh?'

'OK.'

'Here's Pritpal,' said Perry. 'He wants a word.'

Pritpal came on the line.

'A parcel arrived for you this morning at the mission, James,' he said. 'What should we do with it?'

'Who's it from?' asked James.

'I do not know,' said Pritpal. 'It was hand delivered.'

'It may be a clue,' said James. 'When you get back, open it and see what's inside.'

'All right,' said Pritpal.

James put the phone down and slumped on to a stool at the bar. He felt like death. Dry and sick and exhausted.

No matter what he did he couldn't get warm and he shivered continuously. His head ached and everything seemed fuzzy and distant, as if in a dream. He had a crippling pain in his side and he knew it wasn't caused by being kicked. It was his poisoned liver. He prayed that it hadn't been permanently damaged.

He was miserable.

He had been hoping that this new clue might be the final missing piece of the jigsaw puzzle but it had only made matters more confused. It was a dead end, he had nowhere left to go.

'I've been thinking,' said Kelly Kelly.

'Oh, gawd save us,' said Red, rolling his eyes towards the ceiling.

'Shut yer gob, Red,' she snapped. 'And listen for once.'

'Why don't you keep your nose out of this?' said Red. 'This is between me and Jimmy-boy.'

'Look here, Red Kelly,' said the girl, glaring at her brother, 'I'm in this now, all right? I nearly killed the bloke, so now I'm going to help him. I'm gonna make it up to him, like. And I don't need any clever comments from you, because you never was the brightest one in the family.' She turned to James. 'What exactly are we looking for?' she said.

'A man,' said James.

'This Fairburn bloke?'

'Yes. Charnage has him somewhere.'

'And he's built some sort of machine?' said Kelly.

'Yes.'

'And this machine,' said Kelly, 'you said it was pretty big?'

278

'Peterson said in his letter that it would almost fill a room.'

'And they're building it for the Russians?'

'Yes.'

'So how are they going to get it out of the country?' said Kelly.

James grinned. 'I hadn't thought of that,' he said.

'You haven't thought of much, have you?' said Kelly.

'Leave it alone,' said Red. 'You know nothing about this, Kel. You're just showing off for Jimmy-boy.'

'You never did like me being cleverer than you, did you, Red?' said Kelly.

'Oh yeah? Well, if you're so clever, where's this machine, then?'

'It's on a ship, stupid,' said Kelly. 'Has to be.'

'You don't know that,' said Red.

'No,' said James. 'I think she's right. It fits. How else could they get it to Russia? It *has* to be on a ship, somewhere, or it's being loaded on to one. It'd be too big to move it any other way. And Charnage can't leave until it's ready. That's why he couldn't pull out sooner.'

James smiled and suddenly forgot all about his pain.

Thanks to this girl, they had a breakthrough.

At last they were getting somewhere.

The Pneumatic Railway

'The Paradice Club in the old Charnage chemical works is down near the West India Docks,' said Red. 'But if they're sailing to Russia they wouldn't leave from there. There's loads of docks in the docklands, and thousands of ships.'

'Is there someone you know who might be able to help us?' asked James.

'Most of the men round here work down the docks,' said Red and he checked the clock. 'It's nearly opening time. Me dad'll be first in, we can ask him.'

'If he's sober,' said Kelly. 'Knowing him he'll still be drunk from lunchtime. But you'll have to shout, James. He's half deaf from the Brunner Mond explosion.'

'From what?' said James.

'Brunner Mond,' said Red.

'What's Brunner Mond?' said James, his heart beating faster.

'It was a TNT factory,' said Red, 'in the war. They made explosives for the army. Tons of the stuff. And then one day, BOOM! The whole lot goes up. Seventy-two people killed, thousands of houses flattened. Biggest-ever explosion in this country. Everyone round here knows about it, but it was during the war when bad news was kept out of the papers.'

'And where was the factory?' said James.

'Silvertown,' said Red. 'By the Royal Docks.'

Before Red could say anything else, James threw his arms around him and crushed him in a bear hug.

'Oi, leave off,' said Red, pushing him away. 'What's got into you?'

'You've done it, Red,' said James. 'You've solved the last clue.'

'I have?'

'I thought it was nonsense. Last night when I was drunk I made the word Brunnermond from a clue, but I thought it was just meaningless gibberish, so I forgot all about it. But it's the answer. We have to get to the Royal Docks, that must be where the ship is.'

'Brunner Mond was by the King George the Fifth Dock,' said Red, 'but there's hundreds of ships down there. How will we know which one is Charnage's?'

'Ask Dad,' said Kelly, sourly.

Lou had unlocked the pub doors and a gaggle of men had marched in. Among them was a small, shrivelled man who looked old and worn out, but who James guessed was probably no more than thirty-five. He had a pale, creased face, no front teeth and the watery, unfocused eyes of a drunk. When he saw James he put up his hands in a sloppy boxing stance and took a couple of fake swings at him.

'There's your man,' he said and belched beery fumes into James's face. 'Let me get you a drink.'

'We don't have time, Dad,' Red shouted.

'There's always time for a drink,' said Red's father and he laughed.

'Shut up a minute and listen,' said Kelly. 'We need you to think.'

'Ah, you're a hard, mean, vicious woman,' said Mr Kelly. 'Just like your mam.'

He barged past Kelly and went to the bar where he noisily ordered a beer.

'He'll be in a better mood when he's had a pint,' said Red.

James went over to the bar. 'Mister Kelly,' he said loudly, 'I need your help.'

'Do you now?' said Mr Kelly, taking a pint off Lou and sipping it.

'I need to find a ship,' said James. 'It's at the George the Fifth Dock. It's due to sail tonight.'

'What's it called?' said Mr Kelly, taking another sip.

'I don't know. It may have a Russian name.'

Mr Kelly shook his head. 'You're whistling in the wind, son,' he said.

'Listen, you drunken old fool,' said Kelly, taking the beer glass from her father's hand and putting it down on the counter. 'You need to think.'

'Do you know how many ships there are down there, Kelly? There's Russian ships there, and Chinese and Eskimo ships for all I know. If you don't have a name, you don't have a hope.'

'*Callisto?*' said James. 'Is there a *Callisto*?'

The man shook his head.

'*Nemesis?*'

Again, no.

'*Amoras?*' said James. 'What about *Amoras?*'

'Sure, there's an *Amoras*, all right,' said old man Kelly. 'Used to be called the *Sapphire*. She's sailing on the tide, tonight.'

'When's that?' said Kelly.

'Eight o'clock.'

'Where's she sailing to?'

'And now just how in the hell am I supposed to know that?' said Mr Kelly. 'You ask too many questions, Kel, you talk too much. Just like your mam. Lord love her.'

Red glanced at a clock behind the bar and caught James's eye. 'It's twenty to seven,' he said. 'That don't give us long.'

'How far is it to the dock?'

'Five mile,' said Red. 'You could maybe make it on foot in an hour if you pushed it. There's no tubes run down that way, though, an' the buses and trams won't be hardly running on a Sunday.'

'It's too late, then,' said James bitterly. He slammed his hand against the wall. 'I was so close as well.'

'There is a way,' said Red, moving away from the bar towards the door.

'What is it?' said James, following. 'Do you have a motor car?'

'A motor car!' Red snorted with laughter. 'A bleeding motor car! Who do you think I am? The man who broke the bank at Monte Carlo? Nobody round here has a motor.'

'What then?'

'I'll show you. I wouldn't normally even think of it, but this is an emergency. Come on, we're going to pay the Bishop a visit.'

As he made a move to leave, his sister put a hand on his arm.

'You sure about this?' she said. 'He's not one of us.'

'Not one of us?' Red scoffed. 'This is James Bond, we owe him, sis.'

'But, Red —'

'Listen, sis, maybe I'm not as clever as you. I can't pretend I understand half of what's going on. But Charnage is a villain, I know that much, and this boy here is a hero. I know that much, too. If you don't know which side you're on, that's your look out, but I know which side I'm on.'

'Yeah, but, Red —'

'Shut it, Kel. I know what I'm doing.'

The air outside was heavy with soot and smoke from the countless coal fires in the area. It was also chilly and damp and James coughed painfully. In the dark, the crowded streets of east London were even more gloomy and threatening than they had been in the daylight. The guttering gas street lamps threw dim pools of yellow light and everywhere people lurked in the shadows, muttering to each other, waiting, watching, an endless number of them, huddled in black coats, their faces grey and blank.

Now and then there would be a cry from a back alley,

the sound of running feet. Once James heard glass smashing, but he didn't have time to be scared. He had to keep careering onward, because if he did stop he would have to think, and thinking would only show him how hopeless his situation was.

Ten minutes after leaving the pub they arrived at a large white church with a row of tall Greek columns across the front. Beggars and drunks sat on the wide steps waiting for salvation and two men were fighting in the graveyard at one side.

The three of them crossed the road, dodging round a horse and cart, and they ran inside, ignoring the raucous shouts of the men on the steps.

Inside, a service was in progress. The congregation was singing a hymn, a great organ lending a thunderous accompaniment. The interior was stark and bare and there was no heating. James could see the singers' breath coming out in frosty clouds.

Red put a finger to his lips, and, keeping to the shadows at the edge of the church, he walked briskly towards an opening in the wall beneath a row of tall arched windows, and then led the way down a flight of steps into the vaulted crypt.

The crypt was dark and deserted. James could just make out an altar at one end and a few tombs standing in the murky corners.

'I'm still not sure about this,' said Kelly, but Red ignored her. He went over to one of the tombs, which had a vaguely Egyptian look about it, with a pyramid on top supported by four spheres, one at each corner.

The name 'Charles Bishop' was carved into the stonework.

Red squeezed behind the tomb where there was a narrow gap. As James joined him he saw that there were two stone panels in the back of the tomb. Red put his fingers to one and tried to slide it sideways, grunting with the effort.

'Give us a hand, here,' he said and James helped him. The two of them managed to shift it and it slowly moved along a narrow groove with a grinding sound. Behind the panel was a dark space, and James could see that the tomb was hollow.

A foul, rotting, damp smell came out and James covered his nose and mouth. There was a small shelf fixed to the inside wall of the tomb, and from it Red took the stub of a candle and a box of matches. He lit the candle, which illuminated a staircase dropping steeply into darkness.

Red climbed through the gap and shuffled down the steps. Once James and Kelly were safely in behind him he told them to close the door and James managed to slide it shut with the help of two handles.

The steps led down some fifteen feet to what appeared to be a sewer. The stink was awful and James didn't like to look at the stuff floating by in the filthy water. They were in a narrow passage, separated from the main sewer by iron bars. Thick cables snaked along the ground and Red followed them, hunched over in the low passageway. They soon left the sewer behind and after a couple of minutes arrived at a rusted iron door that completely blocked the passage. There was a chipped and faded picture of a skull and crossbones painted on it and yellow lightning flashes.

Red removed a brick in the wall and took out a big home-made key from behind it. There was a clunk as he unlocked the door and then he carefully replaced the key in its hidey-hole.

The door opened easily and the three of them went through.

They were in a small chamber full of cables, which entered from all directions. There was the hum and buzz of electricity and the whole room seemed to be throbbing.

'Careful what you touch,' said Red, his voice suddenly loud in the cramped space. He closed the door and went over to a row of junction boxes along one wall. He removed the cover from one of them and James saw that there was a gap behind it where the box should have been.

'You first,' Red said to his sister and gave her the candle. She wriggled into the hole and soon disappeared. Red nodded to James and he went after her, crawling on his belly and feeling his way along the tunnel with his hands. He heard Red close the cover and his breath rasping as he followed them.

In a moment James saw a light ahead and he stuck his head out to see Kelly Kelly standing on a spiral staircase, waiting for him with the candle. They were about halfway up the stairs; at the top was a great door that had been closed up years ago. Huge planks were nailed across it.

Red popped out of the hole, retrieved the candle from his sister and started down the stairs. James counted thirty steps before they reached the bottom, where Red switched on a light.

James was amazed. They had come down into a decent-sized room crammed with a complicated series of dials and pressure gauges, levers and controls. It all looked ancient and unused, from another era. A railway track ran along one side, disappearing into a narrow tunnel, sealed round the edges with rubber.

It was like a miniature underground station. There was even a carriage waiting on a siding. But this was no ordinary tube train. The carriage was tiny, open at the top and shaped like a bullet.

'What is it?' said James. 'Where are we?'

'It's the pneumatic railway,' said Red. 'It was built last century.'

'But what's it for?'

'It was meant to carry mail,' said Red. 'They was gonna build them all over London apparently. Well, under London, I suppose. High-speed mail delivery, shunting letters and parcels from the big sorting office up at Euston. But it never worked properly and was never used. They closed it all down fifty year ago, and it was forgotten about. But about five years ago a lag by the name of Nesbitt stumbled across it. He was running around down here trying to escape from the rozzers.'

'Rozzers?'

'The cops, police. Locals have always used the sewers as hiding places and secret tunnels to get from one place to another without being seen. Well, old Nesbitt didn't know what it was exactly he'd found, but he thought it might be useful. It wasn't working then, of course, so he set about exploring the tunnels, crawling along until he'd mapped the whole system. He asked around and eventually worked out it was the remains of the old pneumatic railway. Very handy. And even more handy when he got the trains fixed again. A mate of his who was an engineer for the railways figured it all out, got it up and running. It used to run on steam, but he converted it to electric, nicking the power from all the cables that run down here. Had a whole team of blokes fixing it up. The gangs use it now, mostly for smuggling things, but sometimes for smuggling people. I got one of me uncles drunk one night and he told me all about it, all the codes and everything.'

As he spoke, Red was pressing switches and pulling levers, and he eventually slipped on a pair of headphones and listened intently.

'There's a big mail depot down at the Royal Docks,' said Kelly. 'For taking mail off the ships. The railway runs all the way there.'

'You mean we're going to travel on that thing?' said James.

'Yeah,' said Kelly Kelly and she grinned, her eyes twinkling mischievously.

'You up to this, Jimmy-boy?' asked Red, sniffing and scratching his tangle of copper hair.

'I think so,' said James.

'I don't know how you do it, mate,' said Red. 'If I'd drunk what you drunk last night I don't think I'd even be able to speak, let alone stand up. And look at you, walking around right as rain. I reckon you must be made of iron, or something.'

'I don't feel right as rain,' said James. 'I feel like something dead that's just crawled out of a specimen jar.'

'Well, you were certainly pickled.' Red laughed, then turned serious for a moment. 'Be careful,' he said, 'and look after me little sister.'

He winked at James, pressed a green button on the wall and spoke into a microphone.

'This is Cairo speaking,' he said. 'Cairo speaking . . . Anyone there . . .?' He paused, listening again. 'Osiris,' he said after a while.

'That's the password,' Kelly whispered.

Red was speaking again. 'Yes. I have a parcel for shipment to Alexandria . . . It's ready now . . . All right. I'll wait for your signal.'

Red took off the headphones and walked over to the siding.

'Give us a hand,' he said and James and Kelly helped him push the carriage on to the main track until its nose was in the tunnel mouth. It fitted snugly with no gap around it.

'How does it work?' said James.

'It's pneumatic,' said Red. 'There's a bloody great pump at the beginning and end of each section. They blow from one end and suck from the other. You shoot along like a pea in a peashooter. When you stop you'll be at the Royal Docks. Kel knows the way out. She'll go with you.'

'Aren't you coming?'

'Can't,' said Red. 'I need to stay here and work it. Now, hop in quick, the signal'll be coming through any minute. I'll follow when I can.'

There was the hum of big motors starting up. James could feel the ground shaking beneath his feet and vibrations running through the brickwork. There was a howling noise, like wind coming through the gap in a window. The air around them became suddenly chilly.

James climbed into the carriage, lying on his side with his legs slightly bent. Kelly climbed in next to him. It was very cramped and they lay crushed together face to face. Red shunted the carriage further forward so that it slid fully into the tunnel and they were plunged into darkness.

'This is cosy,' said Kelly and she laughed.

James could feel her breath on his face, tickling his nose, but he couldn't move his hand to scratch it. He was aware of her knees pressing into him and he could smell her hair.

'This morning I tried to kill you, and now look at us,' she said. 'Snug as two bedbugs.'

'At least it's warmer like this,' said James.

'Don't you go getting no ideas,' said Kelly.

James didn't say anything. The only idea he had was going to sleep.

'I've heard Red tell stories about you so many times,' said Kelly quietly, her voice sounding very close in the pitch dark. 'But I never imagined I'd end up like this with you . . .'

Before James could speak he felt a tremendous pressure as the air seemed to press in all around him. His ears hurt like mad and he wrenched a hand loose and pinched his nostrils shut. He blew into his nose until his eardrums popped and the next moment there was a rushing sound and the carriage shot forward along the track, taking his breath away.

Into the Lion's Jaws

It was impossible to tell how fast they were travelling, but it felt as if they were hurtling along, wildly out of control. There were no springs or suspension to cushion the tiny carriage and it rattled and banged and bounced about on the track, throwing James and Kelly against each other and shaking the teeth in their skulls. In the confined space the noise was deafening.

Luckily the journey didn't last long and was over almost as soon as it had started. Soon they felt the speed dropping and as they hit a pocket of air they slowed almost to a halt, then trundled gently forward. The next moment they were blinking as the carriage rolled slowly out of the tunnel into the light.

They sat up, stretching their backs and rubbing bruised hips and elbows.

They were in a room very much like the one they had just left, though slightly larger. There were no signs of life apart from an amber light that was blinking on one wall. Kelly ran over to it, straightening her skirt, then looked over the various buttons and dials before pressing one.

The roaring noise of the fans died away and the room became very still and silent.

'I've given them the all clear,' said Kelly. 'To let them know we arrived in one piece.'

'Only just,' said James. 'That train wasn't really designed to carry passengers, was it?'

'Oh, fussy, *aren't* you?' said Kelly. 'I suppose you're only used to travelling first class. I'm sorry I couldn't lay on any champagne and caviar for you. Honestly, I get him here in record quick time and all he does is moan.'

'Are we going to stand round here chatting for hours or are we going to get on?' said James.

'Follow me,' said Kelly. 'And no looking up me skirt.'

There was a sealed-off tunnel sloping upwards that led to the mail depot, but Kelly took James up a ventilation shaft. It had rough brick sides and ran at a shallow angle, so that climbing was fairly easy-going and in no time at all they were at the top, which was closed off by a metal grille. Kelly quickly loosened a bolt and pushed the grille open.

'Be quick,' she said and wriggled out, fast as a snake. James followed and she swung the grille back into place. They were outside, in a narrow passageway between two tall buildings. One end was blocked by a wall, and the other led out into a large yard.

'Stick close to me,' said Kelly. 'There's two night-watchmen with dogs. They usually stay over by the main gate, but they do patrol every now and then.'

So saying, she hauled herself up on to a low window ledge, forced the casement up and disappeared inside the building. James was quick to follow and he found himself in a vast transit shed, stretching into darkness in every direction, crammed with mountainous piles of boxes, barrels, crates and containers. James had never seen a room this large before. He felt tiny, dwarfed by the Alp-like stacks that towered over him. The only light was from the moon that shone through a long line of dirty windows in the roof.

'I know all the secret routes round here,' said Kelly, as she threaded her way between the boxes. 'The gangs use them to smuggle stuff out of the docks. For every ten crates that come through here, there'll be one opened by the boys and the stuff inside shared out.'

It was like a vast maze inside the warehouse, but Kelly knew exactly where she was going and after a few minutes they reached the other side, where she climbed up a tower of crates on to a gantry. James scaled the crates easily and followed her along the gantry, trying not to make any sound. Half a minute later Kelly stopped by one of the windows and slid it open.

'After you,' she said.

'Ladies first,' said James.

'I ain't no lady,' said Kelly.

'Don't I know it,' said James and he pushed past her through the window. He was outside again now and on the side of the warehouse roof. It was another chilly evening and he wished he had a coat of some sort. In fact, he wished he was back at Eton in front of his cosy little fire, eating sausages and playing cards with nothing more important to worry about than his Latin construe.

From up here he could see out over a second row of

warehouses southward to the city of ships known as the Royal Docks. Directly in front was the Royal Albert Dock and beyond it the George the Fifth Dock; to the west was the Royal Victoria Dock.

The Albert Dock was a massive, oblong stretch of enclosed water, nearly a mile long, connected to the Thames by wide canals and lined with warehouses and industrial buildings. There were cranes standing everywhere waiting to service the flotilla of ships that choked the water. A floating grain elevator sat idle on the water. In the morning the place would be teeming with men, loading and unloading cargo, but for now it was almost deserted. The only signs of life were some lightermen unloading a barge and a lorry driving slowly along the far side of the dock. Over to the west, near where the Albert joined the Victoria Dock, there were some bright lights, and the sound of working machinery drifted on the still night air.

'There's so many ships,' said James. 'I had no idea. Which one's the *Amoras*, do you suppose?'

'Don't ask me,' said Kelly. 'I got you here, didn't I? You're supposed to be the golden boy. Don't you think it's time you did something for yourself?'

'Don't be so hard on me, Kelly,' said James, wearily. 'I've been through a lot these last two days.'

'Yeah, I know,' said Kelly, a hint of kindness in her voice. 'I was only teasing you. What's the matter?' she said, moving off towards the edge of the roof. 'You got no sense of humour.'

'I did have one once,' said James, shuffling after her. 'But it hurts too much when I laugh.'

'I won't tell no more jokes, then,' said Kelly. 'If the little man can't take it.'

'That's all right,' said James. 'Your jokes aren't that funny.'

Kelly stopped and turned round. 'Watch it, James Bond, or I'll throw you off this roof.'

'I'd like to see you try.'

'Don't tempt me. I could be back home right now, instead of risking me neck up here with a swell who reckons he's the bee's bleeding knees.'

'I didn't ask for a hero's welcome,' said James. 'I was just trying to find Red.'

'Yeah, and it looks like you found more than you was looking for.' Kelly gave a dirty laugh and carried on.

When they reached the edge of the roof, Kelly lowered herself down on to the top of a covered over-roof conveyor that stretched across to another building like a bridge.

'Not scared of heights I hope,' she said, and dropped into a low crouch.

James joined her and they scurried along the conveyor, passing over yards, streets and lower buildings. When they got to the other side, Kelly slid down the sloping roof to a ladder that led down to a high wall. The wall was topped with glass, but it had been broken off and smoothed flat to make a clear channel down the middle that wouldn't be visible from the ground. The two of them ran along the wall then swung out on to a lamp post and slithered down to the pavement.

Kelly set off at a run towards the dock, James, like a faithful dog, at her heels.

'Keep up,' she said after a while, as they hurried between

two high warehouses. 'Red told me you was a champion runner, or something –'

'I *am* keeping up,' James interrupted. 'I just wish you could go a bit faster.'

'Oh, hark at him. Maybe you should enter the next Olympics if you really want to show off.'

'Well, if they had an event for talking,' said James, 'you'd certainly win gold.'

Soon they arrived at the water. From up on the roof the ships had looked big, from down here they were huge, reaching thirty or forty feet up into the sky.

'Left or right?' said Kelly.

'Not sure.'

'You want to do eeny-meeny-miney-mo?'

'That doesn't seem a very scientific approach.'

'What do you expect? I'm just an empty-headed girl who talks too much.'

'We'll go this way,' said James, heading to the right.

'Why?'

'Because I say so.'

'That doesn't seem like a very scientific approach, either.'

'All right. I saw some working lights from up on the roof. If they're getting the *Amoras* ready to sail, there'll be men around and activity. It's worth checking out. Come on.'

'Yes, your majesty.'

James shook his head and walked off, glad to be leading for a change instead of following. He just hoped his hunch was right. He could imagine how scathing Kelly would be if he was wrong.

The lights were much further away than they had looked and it was a long walk before they got near enough to be able to see what was going on.

A medium-sized cargo ship was being loaded. She looked to be about seven thousand tons and had twin funnels.

A dockside crane that ran on rails was lowering a cargo net full of crates towards the deck where a group of men were waiting. This part of the docks had been cordoned off with heavy chains and three men in dark overcoats stood guard.

James recognized one of them instantly. He pulled Kelly into the shadows beside the locomotive of a dockside railway.

'That's Charnage's butler,' he said. 'Deighton.'

'Is this it, then?' whispered Kelly. 'Can you see the name of the ship?'

'She's the *Amoras*, all right,' said James, picking out the freshly painted writing on the ship's hull.

'So what do we do now?' said Kelly. 'Stroll past the guards and up the gangplank? Rescue your Mister Fairburn and stroll off again?'

'Something like that,' said James.

'You don't have a clue what to do, do you?' said Kelly.

'If you'd shut up for one moment I might be able to think,' said James and he looked back the way they had come. 'We passed some rowing boats a little while ago,' he said. 'Maybe we could take one and get round to the other side of the *Amoras*.'

'You're serious, aren't you?' said Kelly, her eyes wide.

'You're going to try and get on the bloody ship.'

'Of course I am,' said James. 'I haven't come all this way just to wave goodbye to her as she sails off into the sunset.'

'And just what the bloody hell do you think you're going to do once you're on there?'

'I don't know,' said James, 'but if you've a better idea I'd love to hear it.'

Kelly thought for a while. 'Where's this boat of yours, then?'

They retraced their footsteps until they came to where a row of barges and rowing boats sat in the water.

James jumped down and clambered from one boat to another until he found one suitable, with two oars stowed in the bottom. Then he looked in all the barges until he found a length of coiled rope.

He returned to the rowing boat and readied it.

Kelly sat down awkwardly, facing him. 'Go careful, won't you?' she said, glancing nervously at the filthy water.

'Not so tough now, are we?' said James.

'I don't like the water.'

'You can't swim, can you?'

'No, of course I can't swim,' snapped Kelly. 'What would I need to be able to swim for? I'm not a fish, am I?'

James untied the rope and cast off, using an oar to push himself clear of the barges. Then he pulled out on to the open water and rowed along parallel to the dockside.

Their progress was hidden from Charnage's workmen by the other ships moored along here, but there was a nasty gap between the last ship and the *Amoras* in which they could be spotted. James slowed down and steered the rowing boat alongside the hulking cliff face of the last ship, a rusty steamer called the *Newhaven*, and edged forward until his prow was almost at the end.

He stowed the oars and moved into the prow, where he crouched down and pulled the boat along the hull of the *Newhaven* using his hands. When he could see round the bow he stopped and took a good look.

The stevedores on the wharf were busy with the crane, their attention focused upward. With the floodlights in their eyes there was a good chance they wouldn't notice a tiny rowing boat out on the dark water.

James reversed a few feet and readied the oars.

'Lie flat in the bottom,' he said and Kelly obeyed quickly without talking back to him.

'I'm going to scoot the boat out and hope we can glide across without being seen,' James went on. 'Hold your breath, keep quiet and don't move.'

Kelly nodded.

James filled his lungs then gave a hefty tug on the oars before yanking them out of the water and laying them in the bottom of the boat next to Kelly. In a moment, he too was lying down as they slipped silently across the still water.

James looked up. He could see the bulk of the *Newhaven* falling away, a patch of unbroken, starlit sky, and then the grey shape of the *Amoras* slid into view. There was a bump as they hit her hull and James sat up quickly.

He let out a long sigh of relief. They were round the back and hidden from the dockside. He doubted whether anybody had heard anything. What with the crane and shouts of the men, there was a lot of noise coming from the busy working party.

There was almost complete darkness in the shadow of the *Amoras*. James looked up at a row of portholes about fifteen feet above the waterline.

'Perfect,' he whispered.

'What's perfect?' said Kelly.

'There,' said James, pointing. 'An open porthole.'

'And us without a ladder,' said Kelly.

'We don't need a ladder.' James uncoiled the rope, tied one end to the seat, and then tied a loose loop in the other end. The porthole window was half-open. If he was lucky he could snag the rope on it and climb up.

'What you going to do, lasso it?' said Kelly. 'Who do you think you are? Billy the Kid?'

'Stop moaning and help,' said James. 'Sit in the middle of the boat and try to steady her while I throw this up.' He glanced at Kelly. Her face looked strained. She was frightened, but trying to hide it behind her cheek. He didn't blame her. He was frightened too. He'd three times only narrowly escaped death at the hands of Charnage's men. He was sticking his head back inside the lion's jaws now. He could smell its hot breath.

But what choice did he have?

As long as he kept moving he could stop the fear from taking hold.

He just had to hope that the lion's jaws didn't close around his neck.

He had no luck at all on his first two throws, both of

which missed the porthole completely. On his third attempt the loop hooked on, but, when he tugged it, it fell down back into the boat.

'Fourth time lucky,' he said and chucked the rope up. This time it fell neatly over the open window and rested on the sturdy iron hinge. He gave it a jerk and tested its strength.

'I think it'll hold,' he said.

Kelly was grinning now. 'You're a madman, you know?'

'Maybe. You stay here and look after the boat, I won't be long.'

James gripped the rope and put a foot against the side of the *Amoras*. It was awkward stepping off the boat as it bobbed about in the water but he managed to get both feet against the ship's hull and then walked up, hauling himself hand over hand, until he got to the porthole. He gripped the edge of the frame, the sharp metal cutting into his hands, and then bent his arms until his head was level with the opening.

He looked in. There was a tiny lavatory, painted a dull green. He hoisted himself up, slid on to his chest and kicked and wriggled until he was inside, though not before nearly falling head first into the lavatory bowl.

He looked back down at Kelly and to his dismay saw that she was struggling up the rope. In her heavy skirt, she had a much harder time of it than James and her face was set in a grim mask of fear and tension. Twice her feet slipped and she was left dangling, bumping against the side of the ship, but she was terrified of falling into the water and clung on like a limpet. Eventually she got near enough for James to reach out and grab hold of her, and with a grunt he pulled her inside. She threw her arms round him and hugged him tight. He could feel her whole body trembling.

'Don't ever make me do that again,' she said.

'I thought I told you to look after the boat.'

'You didn't think I was going to sit down there all by meself, did you? I told you I don't like the water.'

'Well, we *are* going to have to climb back down, you know?' said James.

'Yeah, I know.' Kelly was as green as the walls of the lavatory.

'Listen,' said James. 'I want you to wait in here.'

'In here?'

'Yes. Lock the door when I go out. And don't let anyone in. When I'm back I'll knock like this.' He demonstrated, giving two quick bursts of knocks. One-two-three, one-two-three. 'Then, and only then, you can open the door. When I get back, I want to find you and the rope and the boat still here. Got it?'

'I'd rather come with you.'

'I need you here,' said James. 'Don't let me down.'

He saw the old fight come back into her eyes. 'I won't ever let you down,' she said. 'I wouldn't ever let no one down.'

James smiled at her. 'I know,' he said.

For a moment they looked at each other in silence. Water dripped steadily into a cistern mounted on the wall, and they could hear the gurgling of the ancient plumbing system.

'This is romantic, isn't it?' said Kelly after a while. 'A bleeding khazi.'

James smiled at her. 'I'm glad you didn't kill me this morning,' he said.

'Yeah,' said Kelly. 'Me too.'

James went to the door, opened it a crack and peeped out into a long passageway. It was all quiet. He slipped out of the lavatory and heard Kelly turn the lock shut behind him.

From somewhere far off he could hear music from a badly tuned wireless set echoing down the lonely corridors of the *Amoras*. He took his bearings, making sure he would recognize this area later. Luckily there were markings on the wall and the passageways and doors were all numbered and labelled in the orderly way that a ship is organized. That would be a help, but he knew how easy it would be to get lost.

He padded along the passageway until he came to a companionway that led up and down. He went down and found a map of the ship mounted on the wall of the next level.

There were two holds, a smaller one to the bow and a larger one to the stern. Checking them would be as good a place as any to start his search. If Fairburn's machine *was* on board it would have to be in one of the holds. And if he could find the machine, then maybe he could find Fairburn.

He hurried through the ship, checking and double-checking any maps as he came across them. For the most part he saw no one, but twice he had to duck into empty

305

cabins to hide and he heard the clatter of feet and voices as crewmen went past. At last he found a bulkhead door marked FORWARD HOLD. He spun the handle, eased the door open and stepped through.

He was on a high metal walkway looking down into the hold. The roof was open to the sky and the crane was lowering in another full cargo net. A group of sailors stood below, calling to each other in a foreign language that James instantly recognized as Russian.

There was no sign of a machine, though, and James had to move fast. The ship would soon be ready to set sail and if he wasn't careful he'd end up heading for Russia across the North Sea with no hope of escape.

He went back out into the passageway and backtracked until he was at the lavatory. He gave the secret knock, and Kelly opened the door.

'Took your time, didn't you?' she said. 'Where is he, then?'

'I haven't found him yet,' said James. 'I was just making sure I could find my way back here and that you were all right.'

'Don't worry about me,' said Kelly. 'Just get a move on, will you?'

James nodded and ran off, making his way in the other direction, towards the stern of the ship. He quickly found a door almost identical to the one through which he had entered the forward hold. A sign next to it read AFT HOLD. AUTHORIZED PERSONNEL ONLY and a skull and crossbones, the universal symbol for danger, had been painted on to it.

Underneath the skull was the word N.E.M.E.S.I.S.

Well, it would take more than a skull and crossbones and a scary word to frighten James Bond off.

He opened the door and went through.

Another walkway. Another hold. But this one was different.

The roof was closed and, instead of being filled with cargo, the whole space was taken up by a giant, gleaming framework of brass and steel supported by cables and iron struts.

He had found it.

Fairburn's machine.

Nemesis.

Nemesis

It was vast. Bigger by far than he had ever imagined. Bright lights shone down on it from all sides so that it was picked out from the dark walls of the hold.

James could make no sense of it; it was studded with gauges, dials and levers. Bits of it were like the workings of a motor-car engine, other bits looked like brass bedsteads or huge sewing machines, and it made a whirling, clicking noise, like a thousand typewriters all working away at once. It was like looking into an ants' nest – all the intricate parts were constantly moving: rods, wheels, coils, cogs and gears, tiny pistons and seemingly endless strips of thin card, punched with holes, that snaked from huge rolls, then threaded their way through tirelessly chattering gates before returning to the bowels of the great machine.

It was similar to the machine in Charnage's office, but James could see now why Charnage had described that one as a mere toy. This was a colossus compared to it.

It was powered by a series of belts that must have been driven by the ship's engines and there was a tremendous heat coming off it, filling the space with humid air. The sudden contrast with the freezing night outside caused sweat to spring to James's forehead and his skin felt itchy under his shirt.

He shifted slightly to get a better view and saw a man sitting slumped at a table next to the device, his head sunk in his hands, a picture of weariness and despair. He was stripped to his vest and appeared to be staring at a series of rotors with numbers on them. In front of him on the tabletop were piles of notes and a large typewriter-style keyboard connected to the main machine by a tangle of coloured wires. James recognized the familiar untidy bush of hair, rising in a wave to one side. This had to be Fairburn. If only he would lift his head, James would know for sure. He couldn't call out, or go down to him, however, because two armed Russian sailors were watching over him.

A door opened and a group of four people appeared. They walked over to the stooped figure at the table and started a conversation. One of the group was Sir John Charnage; two were squat, bulky, stone-faced men in cheap suits who James had never seen before; and the fourth person was the mysterious woman he had last seen in Charnage's office.

The man at the table rose slowly and stiffly, then stretched and turned into the light. He was ten years older than in the photograph that James had taken from Peterson's room, but it was unmistakably him.

Alexis Fairburn, born Alexei Fyodorov.

The two stone-faced men led him away, followed by the sailors. Charnage and the woman stayed behind. They went over to the machine and studied one of the strips of card.

James made a quick decision and scooted along the walkway, keeping an eye on Fairburn and his escort as they went through a door at the end of the hold, heading towards the centre of the ship. James spotted a ladder fixed to the hull wall and slid down it. Then, after checking that it was all clear, he darted through the door after Fairburn and the others.

He couldn't see them, but could hear them up ahead. Five pairs of heavy footsteps on the steel floors of the passageway made quite a din.

James moved as fast as he dared, trying to make no sound of his own, keeping the escort party in range of his hearing, but well out of sight. Once, he thought he'd lost them, but realized they had simply gone up a run of steps to a higher deck and he was soon right behind them again. At last the footfalls stopped, and so did James. He flattened himself against a wall and listened. There were voices, then the sound of a door opening and closing. He waited. It was almost silent now. All he could hear were the ship's steam engines steadily turning over.

The walls and floors throbbed.

How long did he have?

However long it was, he feared it wouldn't be long enough. He couldn't afford to hang about here all night. He had to try and see where Fairburn and the others had gone. First of all he took his bearings. There were two main passageways, running along either side of the ship from fore to aft, and smaller passageways, running crossways, connected them.

James was in a main passageway, which meant that the

escort party had turned off into one of the smaller, linking corridors.

He crept forward and peered round the corner. One of the sailors was sitting on a stool outside a cabin door. As James watched, the door suddenly opened and voices spilt out. He ducked back and scuttled into an opening behind him. Presently he saw three people go past. The two stone-faced men and the second sailor. He heard their footsteps clattering away down the passage, where they paused for a moment. There was a brief conversation and then returning footsteps. James feared that he might have been detected, but it wasn't one of the men returning, it was the grey-haired woman. As she went round the corner to the cabin, the men walked off.

James let out his breath in a long sigh of relief and for the first time looked to see where he was hiding. He was in a galley, its heavily polished aluminium surfaces shining under bright lights. Neat rows of pots and pans hung from racks alongside a bewildering array of utensils. A skinny cat sat on a stove top, keeping warm. A mouser, probably, whose job it was to keep down the army of mice and rats on board ship. It eyed James snootily and blinked once.

James explored. Next to a row of sinks there was a cupboard for cleaning items, including a slops pail with a lid that fastened shut. There were lockers filled with dried goods, like beans and rice. There was an array of vast jars containing flour, oats, sugar and salt standing on a counter, and along one wall were two large storage rooms, one of which was refrigerated and packed with sides of meat hanging from hooks in the ceiling. The cold-storage room door was as thick as the door to a bank vault and had no handle on the inside.

James looked along the rack of utensils and picked out a large, shiny ladle, then he went back out into the corridor and crept along to the corner. He squatted down and eased the bowl of the ladle out into the opening until he could see the whole of the linking corridor reflected in its convex bowl.

There was the guard on his stool. He hadn't moved. The woman must still be inside the cabin.

James waited, keeping perfectly still. The minutes ticked away.

Come on.

Maybe she hadn't gone into the cabin after all. Maybe he should risk it.

No.

The sailor suddenly jumped up and stood to attention as the cabin door opened.

James scuttled back into the galley. In a moment the woman walked back the way she had come.

Now he had to work fast.

He fetched the slops bucket, put it down on a worktop next to the cooker and took off the lid.

He looked at the cat.

The cat looked at him.

'Here, puss,' he said. 'Nice puss. There's a good moggie. Time to say goodnight, now.'

He picked the cat up. She didn't look very happy about it, but didn't try to struggle. He stroked her gently.

'I don't want to do this,' he said. 'But I can't think of anything else . . . Sorry.'

As soon as the cat knew that she was about to be shoved into the bucket she tried to wriggle free, meowing loudly and lashing out with her claws. James held on tight and bundled her in, jamming on the lid and fastening it shut. There were scratches all over his hands, but he hardly noticed. He took the bucket over to the cold-storage room, sighed, and lobbed it in.

'Help!' he yelled at the top of his voice. 'Come quick! Help me! In here . . .'

Then he let out a long scream and hid behind the cooker.

The cat was going crazy, yelping and hissing and fighting to get out of the bucket, which rolled drunkenly about the floor, bashing into things and making a frightful racket.

Soon there was the sound of running footsteps and the sailor appeared. James could see his back as he cautiously approached the cold-storage room, gun at the ready. There was a moment of stillness before the cat went into a wild frenzy, hurling the bucket around the room. The sound of the poor creature trapped inside was weird and unrecognizable.

The sailor took one step into the freezer and James dashed out. He gave the man an almighty push, which sent him stumbling into a side of beef, and slammed the door shut, pulling down the big lever to lock it fast.

He heard some dull thuds coming from inside, and a muffled shout, but it was barely audible. Nobody else on board would be able to hear him.

He picked up the ladle and hurried round to the cabin door that the sailor had been guarding. There was no sound coming from the other side. He opened it.

The cabin was tiny and windowless, with one bunk bed and a small table.

Fairburn was sitting on the edge of the bunk, his head slumped in his hands again.

He didn't look up as James came in.

'What is it now?' he muttered.

'Mister Fairburn?' said James and now the man did look up. He had a quizzical look on his pale, unshaven face. He was very tired and his large nose and ears gave him a slightly comical look, but a fierce intelligence showed behind his bleary eyes.

'Who the devil are you?' he said.

'It doesn't matter,' said James. 'We've got to hurry. The *Amoras* is going to sail any minute now and we don't want to be on board when she does.'

'I don't understand,' said Fairburn. 'Are you from the police?'

'No,' said James. 'I'm from Eton.'

'Eton?'

'We got your letter. We solved the clues.'

'I don't understand.'

'Isn't it obvious?' said James. 'I'm here to rescue you.'

'But –'

'Oh, for goodness' sake,' said James, grabbing Fairburn and pulling him up off the bunk. 'Just follow me, will you? We can talk later. And put a coat on, if you have one, it's freezing out there.'

'Right, yes, right . . . of course,' said Fairburn as he grabbed a jacket and followed James out into the passageway.

'Where's the guard?' said Fairburn.

'He's cooling off,' said James. 'But, please, don't talk, just try to keep up.'

'Wait,' said Fairburn, and he darted back into the cabin, reappearing moments later with a handful of papers, which he stuffed into his pocket.

James hoped and prayed that he'd be able to find the way back to Kelly, and that she'd still be there when they arrived. They moved quickly, and James used the ladle to check around every corner they came to. There seemed to be only a skeleton crew on the *Amoras*, which had been built to carry both cargo and passengers. As Fairburn was the only passenger, this part of the ship was largely deserted and all hands were making ready for departure.

They only got lost once, but, by retracing their steps, James was able to get them back on the right track. He could tell that Fairburn was bursting to ask him questions, but he shushed him whenever he opened his mouth and made him understand that they must be as quiet as possible.

They were climbing a companionway to the next deck when they felt the ship lurch and begin to move.

'She's sailing,' said Fairburn.

'We still have time,' said James. 'If we hurry. They'll have to manoeuvre her out of the dock first.'

Before they could say any more they heard the sound of heavy boots and had to duck into a cabin.

Several men ran past.

They waited until it was quiet once more and carried on, the deck vibrating under their feet.

This was taking too long. They should be there by now. James was just beginning to think that he might be completely lost when he turned a corner and there was the lavatory door.

'This is it,' he said, knocking three times, and three times again.

There was a scrabbling and a rattle, the door opened a crack, and James was relieved to see Kelly's heart-shaped face appear. Her mouth was set grim but her brown eyes gave away a hint of nervousness.

'Bloody hell, you had me scared there,' she said as she opened the door and James and Fairburn squeezed past her into the lavatory.

'This him, then?' she went on, looking Fairburn up and down through narrowed eyes.

'Yes.'

'Don't look much, do he?'

'Shut up for once and let's get out of here,' said James. 'You go first, Kelly, then try to hold the boat steady. I'll come last, once I'm sure that Fairburn's safely down.'

'I'm not climbing out there,' said Fairburn as James helped Kelly on to the rope.

'You've got no choice,' said James. 'It's either that or sail to Russia.'

'I'm not an athletic man.'

'That's all right,' said James. 'I won't be scoring you for technique. Jump if you have to, but unless we get off this ship sharpish we're dead ducks.'

She didn't do it very gracefully, but Kelly made it down in one piece, sliding the last few feet into the rowing boat.

'I'm really not sure I can do it,' said Fairburn. 'I've no head for heights.'

'Please,' said James. 'Don't think about it, just do it.'

Fairburn saw the desperate look on James's face.

'All right.'

James helped Fairburn up to the porthole. He leant out and grabbed hold of the rope, then nervously squeezed through the narrow opening until he was outside, dangling and bumping against the hull.

James could hardly bear to watch as Fairburn slithered down the rope. He had only got halfway when he let go completely. He landed awkwardly, with his legs in the water, and badly winded himself. Luckily the sound of his splash was drowned out by the noise of the churning propellers and the diesel growl from the tugboats that were steering the *Amoras* out of the dock.

Kelly quickly hauled Fairburn aboard and looked up at James.

The *Amoras* was pulling the little rowing boat along, and they were gradually picking up speed. The rope, still tied to the seat, was stretched taut, but James was out of the porthole in a flash and shinned down without even thinking about it.

Fairburn was huddled in a heap, shivering with shock.

'He'll live,' said Kelly as she sat down and turned to James. 'So, now what?'

'We'll let the *Amoras* pull us along until we're out of

sight of the dockside, then we'll cut loose and try to get ashore on the other side,' said James.

Once they were in the middle of the dock, James took the knife out from his boot and hacked through the rope, whose knot had been pulled too tight to loosen by hand.

They bobbed in the wake of the *Amoras*, watching and waiting as she was pulled slowly away from them.

Kelly cackled. 'I wonder how far they'll get across the North Sea before they discover he's not aboard,' she said, but almost as soon as the words were out of her mouth they heard a siren and saw the tugs slow down.

'What's happening?' said Fairburn.

'She's stopping,' said James. 'It looks like luck's not running entirely our way tonight.'

Now the *Amoras*'s propellers went into a frothing reverse screw and soon she was still. Next lights came on and the whole ship was lit up like a Christmas tree. At the same time James noticed a commotion on the far side of the dock. Big floodlights were fired up and men with torches began to run in all directions, blowing whistles and shouting. Finally, a motor car jumped into life and raced along the dockside.

'I shouldn't have said nothing,' said Kelly quietly.

'I thought it had all been a bit too easy,' said James.

'What are we going to do?'

'Don't worry,' said James. 'I'll think of something.'

The Empress of the East

James thought quickly. They had to get off the open water before they were spotted, and they couldn't go back to the north side of the docks where the *Amoras* had been berthed, as it was swarming with Charnage's men.

A huge passenger ship was berthed on the south side, sitting serenely in the water like a vast floating hotel, its windows unlit.

'What ship is that?' said James. 'Do you know?'

'That's the *Empress of the East*,' said Kelly, following his gaze. 'She's not in use any more. They're going to take her up north to be broken up. They're stripping everything out of her.'

James pulled on the oars and steered towards the *Empress*. Soon they were swallowed up by her shadow and James carefully manoeuvred the rowing boat round the stern. There was just space enough between the great sloping hull of the ship and the dockside for them to fit and they floated into the gloom. The water slapped and echoed, and, as they nudged against her side, there was a deep, metallic boom.

'Now what?' said Fairburn. 'We can't stay here all night. It's freezing.'

'We might have to,' said James.

There were shouts and the sounds of vehicles and running feet in the far distance.

'We can't risk trying to get away through the docks,' said James. 'Charnage will have his men everywhere.'

'And there's the Russians,' said Fairburn wearily.

'The two who took you to your cabin?' said James.

'Yes,' said Fairburn. 'They are Menzhinsky's men – OGPU, Russian secret police. You do *not* want to tangle with them, Bond. They are cold-hearted killers. They came over here to assassinate a Foreign Office clerk called Ernest Oldham in September, and stayed on.'

'And who's the woman?' asked James. 'Is she one of them?'

'She's running the whole thing for Menzhinsky,' said Fairburn. 'Colonel Irina Sedova, but they call her Babushka, the Grandmother. She might look harmless but she's the worst of the lot.'

'We can't stay here,' said Kelly anxiously. 'We just can't.'

James looked up. 'Stay put and keep quiet,' he said. 'I'll go up top and see if I can't find out what's going on.'

'Be careful,' said Fairburn.

'I intend to,' said James.

There was a ladder fixed to the wharf. James grabbed hold of it and climbed up. As he neared the top he went slowly and cautiously until his head was above the lip and he could see along the dockside. He was well hidden here, beneath a platform and a gangplank that connected the *Empress* to the dockside.

There were men down at the far end. They appeared

to be searching the area with torches. So far, though, this part of the docks seemed quiet and deserted.

James took one last look around, then scrambled back down the ladder to the boat.

'All right,' he said. 'Here's what we're going to do. We're going to sneak on to the *Empress*, find somewhere safe to hide out for a few hours and, once we're sure the coast is clear, we'll make a run for it. And before you say anything, there's no time to argue, just follow me and, for God's sake, keep quiet.'

Without waiting for a response, he scurried up the ladder, and then crawled on to the dockside and checked the area. The wharf was fenced off and guarded by a hut next to a flimsy gate, where two nightwatchmen sat. Luckily they had their backs to the ship and were watching the excitement further along the dock.

The search party was still some way off, but it was getting nearer.

Kelly was next up. James signalled to her to keep low and she dropped on to her belly and crawled up alongside him. Soon Fairburn was with them, breathing heavily and shaking.

James glanced up the gangplank.

'Are you ready?' he said quietly.

'As I'll ever be,' said Fairburn.

'Come on, then.'

Keeping in a low crouch, they hurried up the gangplank and on to the ship. They found themselves on a narrow stretch of open-sided decking.

'We need to get inside as quickly as possible,' said

James as they ran along, keeping in the shadows. All the doors and windows they tried were fastened tight, however.

'We're not likely to find a key, are we?' said Fairburn. They had reached the end of the deck and were still out in the open.

'Oh, I don't know about that,' said James.

He had spotted a rolled-up hose next to a rusted bucket and a box labelled IN CASE OF FIRE.

He opened the lid of the box and took out a fire axe.

'There you are,' he said, grinning.

'What are you doing?' said Fairburn.

'It's a skeleton key,' said James. 'I think you'll find it'll open anything.'

'You can't just break in,' said Fairburn.

'Can't I?' James moved closer to Fairburn. 'The ship's about to be broken up for scrap. I don't think anyone's going to complain much about a broken window.'

So saying, James pulled off his jacket, folded it double, and got Kelly to hold it against a large square pane of glass.

The coat muffled his blows as he swung the axe. It took him several goes before the window, designed to keep out heavy Atlantic storms, at last gave way. There was a satisfying crack, then another, and finally the glass fell inwards and rattled on to the floor.

James cleared away the last few jagged pieces, put his jacket back on and climbed inside.

'I must say,' said Kelly, climbing in after him, 'a night out with you is certainly memorable.'

They found themselves in a fancy cocktail lounge with an ornate bar, murals on the walls, a plush carpet but no furniture.

Kelly whistled as she took it all in.

'I ain't ever seen nothing like this before,' she said. 'It's like a palace, or something. I can't believe they're going to smash the whole thing up. It don't seem right.'

'Why are they doing it?' said James. 'She's perfectly seaworthy.'

'They got bigger, faster ships now,' said Kelly. 'Everything's changing. They're building a new passenger ship up in Clydeside, the *Queen Mary*; she's going to be like nothing you've ever seen before.'

James rummaged around behind the bar and found some candles and a tray of matchbooks with the name of the ship on them.

'We can't risk lighting these here,' he said, handing out the candles. 'Someone outside might see. But we'll need them once we're down below. Now, let's find somewhere to hole up.'

'You know,' said Fairburn, 'this is all really rather exciting!'

'Well, let's just hope it doesn't get any *more* exciting,' said James. 'Right now all I want to do is eat and sleep.'

A quarter of an hour later they were standing outside a row of first-class cabins on a lower deck. The doors were secured shut, but James picked one and easily splintered the lock with his axe.

'Better put out the lights,' he said, before opening the

door, and as they blew out the candles they were thrown into cold, inky darkness.

As the door swung open it revealed a room lit by silver moonlight, and through the windows they could see the *Amoras*, waiting out in the middle of the docks, its lights blazing.

As their eyes adjusted, Kelly gasped.

'Look at this,' she said. 'It's not real.'

There was a small sitting room furnished with sofas and chairs, and from there a door led through to a separate bedroom and bathroom.

'I'm utterly shattered,' said Fairburn, testing the bed. 'Mind if I take this one?'

'Go ahead,' said James. 'I'll try to find some bedding.'

James eventually found some boxes in the steward's quarters along the corridor. They had been stapled shut, but he ripped one open to reveal a pile of moth-eaten blankets. He gave a couple to Fairburn and an armful to Kelly before going to smash open another cabin for her.

'Where you going to sleep?' she asked.

'Plenty of cabins to choose from,' said James. 'But I want to try and find some food first.'

'Do you think there'll be anything on board?' said Kelly.

'I don't know; everything's packed up, but it's worth trying.'

'I'm coming with you,' said Kelly.

'Fine,' said James. 'I could do with the company.'

They told Fairburn where they were going and set off to explore the *Empress*.

James felt like he was becoming an old hand at finding his way around ships and he set off with some confidence. The *Empress* was much larger than the *Amoras*, however, and in the candlelight it was quite confusing. It was a good half an hour before they found the galley, a huge, industrial affair, designed to cook meals for a thousand people at a time.

It had been stripped clean, though. The cupboards were bare, the cold-storage areas empty and mouldy. Some of the stoves had already been dismantled and taken away. They were just about to give up hope, when Kelly forced open a locker and found a pile of forgotten tin cans.

'Look at this,' she said. 'Pilchards, beans, tomatoes, peas, peaches, pear halves. We can have a right royal feast.'

James opened some cans with his knife and they set to, sitting on a worktop with their legs dangling over the edge. The food was cold and tasteless, but James didn't care. He couldn't remember when he had ever been so hungry. Or so thirsty. He drank the liquid from the fruit tins as greedily as if it had been mountain spring water.

'Just think of all the places this ship's been,' said Kelly. 'All the stories it could tell. I never been out of the East End.'

'Really?' said James, amazed.

'Yeah, really,' said Kelly. 'What would I want to go anywhere else for? I wouldn't know anyone.'

'You must have been somewhere,' said James.

'I been to Epping Forest a couple of times and last year we all went down to Southend,' said Kelly. 'But nowhere foreign. You ever been anywhere foreign? Any other countries? I know you went to Scotland that time with Red, but anywhere else?'

'I've been to Italy,' said James. 'Germany, Switzerland, France –'

'All right, there's no need to show off.'

'You *did* ask.' James laughed and jumped down off the worktop. 'Come on,' he said, wiping his mouth. 'Let's get to bed.'

'You think you can find your way back?'

'I hope so,' said James. 'I wouldn't want to lose Fairburn after we've been to all this trouble.'

As it was, five minutes after leaving the galley they were hopelessly lost.

'You don't know where you're going, do you?' said Kelly, as they tramped along a passageway deep in the freezing interior of the ship, their candles sending flickering shapes across the walls.

'I just need to get my bearings,' said James. 'I think we should have gone up instead of down at that last stairway.'

'And here I was thinking you knew what you was doing.'

'Your moaning's not helping much, Kelly.'

'I like to moan,' said Kelly. 'Don't worry about it none. I only have a go at people I like.'

'And what do you do to people you don't like?'

'You know the answer to that,' said Kelly.

'You kick them to death.'

'Something like that.'

'Well, I'm glad you're on my side,' said James.

'Me too. I never met anyone like you before,' said Kelly.

'Anyone posh. I don't get the chance much round our way. I thought all posh people were stuck-up snobs, but you're all right.'

They came to another stairway and ran up it. It led to a very grand part of the ship. Very different to the drab, dull passageways they had been walking along. A lot of the fittings had been removed, but there was still enough left to show what the ship had once been like. There were carved wooden banisters, carpeted floors, and glittery light fittings, like cascades of diamonds and crystals, falling from the ceiling.

James pushed open two double doors and they came into a ballroom. The windowless walls were covered in mirrors and gold leaf; there was ornate moulded plasterwork everywhere and a few elegant circular tables shoved into a corner. A low stage at one end was still set out with the chairs of the last orchestra to have played there.

Kelly looked around in wonder and laughed. Then she ran across the great wide-open expanse of the floor, skirts flying, arms outstretched, twirling round and round and whooping.

Her candle blew out and James came over to relight it.

'We should stay here forever, Jimmy,' she said. 'We could come and live here. I could be the queen and you could be a prince, or something. No, I should be an empress.'

'The Empress of the East End,' said James.

'Yeah, that's me!' She spun away across the dance floor again. 'Empress Kelly.'

'We should get back,' said James.

'Why? What's your hurry?' said Kelly. 'We're never

327

gonna get the chance to come somewhere like this again. At least I'm not. Maybe you will in France or Italy or some other fancy country. What have I got to look forward to, eh? You know what my life is like, Jimmy? No. Course you don't. I been looking after me younger brothers and sisters since I was seven. I quit school two year ago and now I work at the biscuit factory. I sleep four to a room, with me two sisters and me Auntie Ruby. The only place I ever seen as big as this before was in a dream.'

She searched around among the shadows and found an old gramophone. She wound it up and placed a record on it. James ran over.

'Kelly, I really don't think you should do that. Someone might hear it.'

'Who?' said Kelly. 'Who's going to hear anything outside this room? I'll only play it quiet.'

As band music came out of the speaker, she grabbed James by the hand.

'Come on,' she said. 'Let's dance. You *do* know how to dance, I suppose?'

'A little,' said James. 'My aunt taught me a few steps.'

'Well, teach me some then.'

James held on to Kelly and they clumsily stumbled around the dance floor, collapsing into laughter every couple of minutes. Slowly, though, they worked out a dance of sorts with their own steps until they were spinning and gliding across the room without thinking.

The two candles, which they had placed in the middle of the dance floor, threw their giant shadows on to the walls and ceiling.

'You dance divinely, your highness,' said Kelly in a mock posh voice she had picked up from the cinema. 'Especially for someone with a wooden leg.'

'Damn the war,' said James with a stiff upper lip, and Kelly smiled.

'You have a very pretty smile,' said James, in the same clipped tones. 'Especially for someone with wooden teeth.'

'Oi, less of your lip,' said Kelly. 'I'll give *you* wooden teeth.'

'Promises, promises,' said James.

The music stopped and there was the sound of clapping from the doorway. James and Kelly jumped, but it was only Fairburn.

'I couldn't sleep after all,' he explained. 'Too excited. I looked for you, but you'd gone. Then I heard music.'

'I told you,' said James to Kelly.

'Oh, I wouldn't worry,' said Fairburn. 'I was close by. I don't think it could be heard from far.'

'All the same . . .' said James, 'no more music.'

'You have me at a disadvantage,' said Fairburn, sitting down on the edge of the stage. 'You seem to know all about me, but I know nothing about you.'

'I'm a friend of Pritpal Nandra's,' said James. 'He's my messmate.'

'James Bond,' said Fairburn and his face broke into a lopsided smile. 'He was always talking about you.'

'It's because of him I'm here,' said James. 'He solved most of your clues.'

James and Kelly joined Fairburn on the stage. The dancing had warmed them up and their faces were glowing. James was almost starting to feel normal again.

'Good old Pritpal,' said Fairburn. 'He always was the cleverest in the Crossword Society. How is he? You must tell me everything.'

So, sitting there in the deserted ballroom, with the flickering candlelight playing over them, James began to tell Fairburn his story. While two hundred yards away across the water another story was being acted out on board another ship.

Babushka

Colonel Sedova, known by all as Babushka, the Grandmother, was standing in the hold of the *Amoras* looking up at the Nemesis machine. For several minutes she had been standing like this, turned away from the others, and she had said not a word.

Sir John Charnage looked at her broad back, looked at the grey jacket stretched tight across it. Below the jacket, her skirt and the thick stockings on her sturdy peasant legs were also grey. With her grey hair she might have been a statue carved out of rock.

It was hot down here. Charnage was sweating. He could feel a drop of moisture crawling down the small of his back. The only other people in the hold were the Smith brothers. Ludwig was picking his rotten brown teeth with a nail and Wolfgang was clutching his bandaged hand. He looked sick. His face was yellow and he shivered uncontrollably, occasionally letting out a small whimper. The man should really have been in hospital, but the ship's doctor, a fat Russian who smelt of cloves and cheap wine, had patched him up, crudely stitching his hand and closing the wounds where his fingers had been severed.

When they got to Russia, Wolfgang had been promised the best care in the country, but for now, he was needed here.

Babushka took a deep breath. Charnage saw her back expanding and the seams of her jacket stretching even more. Then at last she turned. Her flat, unremarkable peasant face showed no emotion.

'Without Fairburn,' she said, 'this machine is useless. It is a pile of junk.'

'We can get it to work, Colonel,' said Charnage, wiping sweat from his moustache. 'You have scientists, after all, mathematicians —'

'It could take years,' said Babushka dismissively. 'And it is not even finished.'

'I'm telling you,' said Charnage, 'if we don't sail tonight we can't sail until the next tide. Fairburn could even now be talking to the police. We need to get going.'

'I do not believe that Fairburn has left the docks,' said Babushka bluntly.

'How can you be sure?'

'I am sure. I have men at every exit. He is hiding here and we will find him.'

'Well, I'm glad one of us is certain, at least,' said Charnage. He was hot and tired and he needed a drink.

'I do not make mistakes,' said Babushka.

Charnage looked at the woman. He didn't like her, he never had. She had no sense of humour. She reminded him of a Polish nanny he'd had when he was a boy.

'We all make mistakes,' he said and laughed quietly.

'Some make more mistakes than others,' said Babushka

and she took the chair from by the worktable and sat down, folding her hands neatly in her lap.

'Don't look at me like that,' said Charnage. 'If it wasn't for me you wouldn't be here. None of this would be here.'

'Twice you had the boy, and twice you let him go.'

'I'll admit that the first time was my mistake,' said Charnage. 'I didn't know how resourceful the lad was.'

'And the second time?'

Charnage nodded at Ludwig and Wolfgang.

'You can blame these two clowns,' he said.

'A good officer never blames his men,' said Babushka.

'A good officer wouldn't necessarily be landed with these two idiots,' said Charnage.

Ludwig muttered something and Wolfgang swore under his breath. Charnage turned to them.

'Well?' he said. 'You think I'm being unfair? Come off it. All you had to do was drop a half-conscious boy into the Thames, and look what happened.' He waggled his fingers mockingly at Wolfgang.

'You are responsible,' said Babushka, calmly. 'That boy should have been dealt with properly. Your plan was not serious.'

'Oh, my plan was not serious, eh? I wonder what you would have done with him?'

'I would have strangled him with my bare hands,' said Babushka, and Charnage did not doubt her.

'He already knew too much,' Babushka went on. 'You should not have taken any more risks.'

'Well, you might have said something at the time.'

'You were in charge, John.'

'I got Fairburn here, didn't I, for God's sake?' Charnage shouted angrily. 'I got him to build this bloody thing for you. I did what you wanted. I did my job, I completed my side of the deal.'

'If your work is complete, then you are of no further use to us.'

'Now that's not the deal we made, and you know it,' said Charnage, jabbing a finger at the seated woman. 'I'm getting out of this godforsaken country and starting again in Russia, and don't think you're going to get away without paying me. I'll kick up such a stink.'

Babushka started to chuckle, softly and quietly, like a kindly grandmother chuckling over a baby. 'How little you seem to know of the world, John.'

'Oh spare me,' said Charnage and he slid his cigarette case out of his jacket pocket. He took out a cigarette, knocked the end of it to tamp down the tobacco, then lit it with a safety match. He threw the spent match on to the floor.

'If you're going to punish anyone, punish these two,' he said. 'They had several chances to do away with the boy and they botched it each time.'

'I wonder who they serve,' said Babushka. 'I wonder who they are loyal to.'

'We're loyal to whoever pays us,' said Ludwig. 'Our only boss is hard cash.'

'I wonder how you can show your loyalty,' said Babushka.

'They can show their loyalty by doing what I tell them,' said Charnage, blowing out a great cloud of smoke.

'Do you really think they are loyal to you?' said Babushka, raising her eyebrows quizzically.

'Listen, I've had enough of this,' said Charnage. 'It's getting boring. I've told you what I think we should do. Set sail now and get away from here. We'll figure out how Nemesis works somehow, but if we stay here any longer we're risking everything. We can always come back for Fairburn.'

Babushka turned her eyes on Wolfgang and Ludwig. Those eyes that had seen so much. That had watched countless men die. There was a message in her eyes. A message that Ludwig clearly understood.

Charnage didn't notice, he was busy wiping his face. He felt dizzy and his head ached. He hadn't slept at all last night and it was now nearly one in the morning.

'You were only ever a servant, John,' said Babushka. 'Perhaps you dreamt that you were something more, but you were simply a tool. What use would you be to us in Russia? A drunk. A gambler. A capitalist. You were a servant. And a wise servant serves the strongest master. Isn't that right, Ludwig?'

'Oh, to hell with the lot of you,' said Charnage. 'I'm going to bed.' He dropped his cigarette on to the floor and stamped it out.

There was a tiny *schink* sound and then Charnage grunted.

Ludwig had punched him in the back.

Charnage tried to turn round and say something but his muscles wouldn't obey him. He couldn't move. The trickle of sweat down his back had become a flood. Warm liquid soaked into his shirt.

He dropped to his knees, suddenly too weak to stand.

'What have you done?' he said flatly and, as Ludwig stepped into his field of vision, Charnage saw that he held one of his Apache guns in his hand, the brass knuckleduster curling around his long, white fingers.

But he hadn't hit him with the knuckleduster.

The blade was extended and slick with blood.

Ludwig plucked Charnage's handkerchief from his top pocket, wiped the blade clean and stuffed the handkerchief back.

'What have you done . . .?'

'Put him out of the way,' said Babushka. 'Then throw him over the side somewhere in the North Sea.'

Charnage looked at Babushka. He looked into her merciless black eyes. They were growing larger, filling first her face and then the entire hold of the ship, they were two bottomless black pools and he was falling into them.

'I told John that I wouldn't cooperate unless he allowed me to at least let people know that I was all right,' said Fairburn. 'He saw the sense in that. He didn't want anyone to come looking for me, after all. So he let me set one final crossword puzzle, which I sent to *The Times* with a brief letter telling them it would be my last. And he let me write a harmless letter to the Head Master and one to Pritpal. I knew John never did crosswords or puzzles of any kind so he wouldn't spot the hidden clues. However, the other day, while I was working on Nemesis, his men searched my cabin and found an early draft of the letter with some notes on it that I had foolishly failed to destroy, and he realized he had made a mistake.'

'Your clues were too subtle,' said James. 'We didn't realize until it was too late just how serious it was.'

'I never meant for you boys to try and find me by yourselves,' said Fairburn, shaking his head. 'I thought Pritpal would simply discuss it all with the Head Master who would alert the police.'

The three of them were still sitting on the stage in the ballroom on the *Empress of the East*. Kelly was very sleepy and her head kept nodding forward, but James was burning with excess energy and he felt slightly delirious.

'If the police *had* been involved,' he said, 'Charnage would still be stalling them and you'd be halfway to Russia.'

'You could be right,' said Fairburn sadly. 'John always was a troubled character, but I still find it hard to believe that he could do this to me. This whole affair is ghastly, quite ghastly.'

'How did it all begin?' said James.

'At Cambridge, I suppose,' said Fairburn. 'After the war. I was there with poor Ivar and John. John was a few years older than us; he had delayed going to university to go off and fight, but we were good friends. We had rooms next to each other in Trinity. Ivar and I were both reading mathematics, and John was reading chemistry. The only thing we fell out over was politics. Ivar and John were both interested in communism. For a young man with a brain, it seemed to be the future. Equality for all! Banish poverty! Take power away from the hands of the men with the money, overthrow all the stuffy old rules and

337

give the poor a chance. All fine ideals. But I knew it wasn't like that. I was living in England, but my mother and father were still there, in Russia. I heard about what was really going on. My father managed to smuggle letters out in secret to me. Then one day the letters stopped coming and I have never heard from him or my mother again.' Fairburn paused and rubbed his eyes.

'The revolution started with bloodshed,' he said. 'Lenin had the tsar and all his family shot. And it didn't end there. Terrible things were happening. People who supported Lenin's rivals were disappearing. People who questioned him were disappearing. The ideal of communism died, and Lenin became just another tyrant.'

'Could Peterson and Charnage not see that?' said James.

'I tried to show them the truth,' said Fairburn. 'But Ivar was a pure mathematician, he was always more at home with numbers than human beings. He was in love with the *idea* of communism and, like many, he refused to see what was really happening out there. For John it was something else. He felt guilty about his family's great wealth, and his father's factory where the workers died. And when he went to war he lost all faith in his country. He could never understand how any government could send its young men off to die like that. He was badly injured at Gallipoli, you know, which is why he limps. Lying in hospital, fending off the flies, he changed, and when he recovered, he wanted to change the world. Even then, though, he was a gambler and a drinker. We could see that it was going to destroy his life. After Trinity I lost touch with John, though Ivar and I remained firm friends. And then one day Ivar told me about a numbers machine he was building. It was to help in gambling, in predicting numbers and generating numbers. I don't understand gambling. I didn't really understand what the machine was for, but as a mathematical device it was intriguing.'

'I saw it,' said James. 'In Charnage's office.'

'Some Americans had been helping them design it,' said Fairburn. 'Gambling men from New York. In particular an accountant with an extraordinary mind for numbers. Abracadabra, or something.'

'Abbadabba?' said James.

'That's the man. Not my sort.'

'He's a gangster,' said James.

'The worlds of gambling and crime have always been closely linked,' said Fairburn.'John has no head for business, but he has a genius for picking the wrong people to deal with. The criminals have been bleeding him dry. When the communists came knocking at his door with offers of great wealth and a glorious future in Russia, he let them in. They had heard about his numbers machine, and they wanted one of their own.'

'Why?' said James.

'Not for gambling, that's for sure,' said Fairburn. 'But for codes and code breaking. That's what this has all been about, right from the very start. Intelligence is power, James. We Russians love secrecy. We love our spies, and the history of spying has been the history of trying to find out what the enemy is up to without them finding out what you are up to. Unless you have the latest secret codes you cannot win. No man has ever been able to invent a code that couldn't be broken, but a machine might just do it. A machine with a mind a million times cleverer than a man's. The Russians were willing to pay John a vast sum of money to build such a machine. On a much larger scale than the original one, of course.'

'But they needed you,' said James.

'Yes,' said Fairburn. 'Ivar tried, but failed. He couldn't build what the Russians wanted by himself. He asked me if I would help.'

'But you knew who Charnage was building it for, didn't you?' said James.

'Not at first, and when I found out, I would have nothing to do with it. By then John was in too deep, though. He knew that if he tried to back out the Russians would murder him, that is their way. So he kidnapped me and forced me to complete the work that Ivar had started. And now it's almost finished. The Numeric Evaluating Mathematical Engine and Serial Intelligence System. N.E.M.E.S.I.S.'

'Can they operate it without you?' asked James.

'No. At least not yet.' Fairburn pulled out the sheaf of papers that he had taken from his cabin on the *Amoras*. 'Every day they would ask me to write down instructions, and every day I stalled, because I knew that if I ever did manage to write down how to work Nemesis, then they would have no more use for me and they would snuff me out.'

'So the machine's useless now?' said James.

'For a while,' said Fairburn. 'In a year, two years, they

might figure it out, but it is very complex. You see, the scientists in Russia have all been killed. There are new ones being trained now, young men, but it will take time, and they are scared to think imaginatively, because imagination leads to questions, and the men in power do not like their people asking questions. Ask a question in Russia and the answer is always the same – prison or death.' Fairburn stood up. 'Come along, now. We must sleep. Who knows what tomorrow will bring?'

They woke Kelly and navigated the short way back to the first-class cabins.

Fairburn stared out at the *Amoras*, sitting at anchor in the middle of the dock.

'John knew what he had done,' said Fairburn. 'He knew the terrible mistake he had made dealing with Russians. In a way I feel sorry for him, I can almost forgive him. When a man is in a corner he will do anything to stay alive. That is why he renamed that ship. It was his little joke. His confession to God. Amoras, the knight who tried to do a deal with the devil.'

James said goodnight and took Kelly into her cabin.

'It's freezing in here,' she said, wriggling under the blankets. 'Stay with me, eh? We can keep each other warm.'

'I don't know . . .'

'I feel like as long as I'm with you, nothing bad's going to happen to me,' said Kelly.

'Don't say that,' said James. 'You're tempting fate. You say something like that and five minutes later there's a huge explosion and the whole world blows up in your face.'

'Please,' said Kelly. 'I don't want to think about the trouble we're in.'

'Don't tell me the fearless Kelly Kelly is scared.'

'Course I'm scared,' said Kelly. 'Who wouldn't be? And I'm not used to sleeping on me own, neither. I've never spent more than five minutes by meself. Come on, get under the blankets, James Bond . . . And no funny stuff, all right?'

James was too cold and too tired, and, he had to admit to himself, too scared, to argue, so he crawled on to the big double bed next to Kelly. They wrapped themselves in the blankets and they soon felt warm and drowsy.

'Tell me about your life,' said Kelly sleepily. 'I want to know all about you.'

James told her about his childhood, moving between Switzerland, England and Scotland. He told her about his parents dying in a climbing accident in France when he was eleven. He told her about his Aunt Charmian who he lived with in Kent, and his life at Eton.

He never usually talked about any of this. At school you had to appear to be tough, you didn't want to be called a sap or a mummy's boy, so you talked about other things, about motor cars and cricket, about wars and battles and who had punched who and why. Other boys could go home in the holidays. They could be children again and hug their mothers and talk any nonsense they liked, but not James.

He had no one.

Here in the dark of the cabin, though, he could tell this girl everything. It didn't matter that she was soon fast asleep and snoring. He carried on talking and looking at the lights of the *Amoras* through the windows and picturing Nemesis in her hold.

He had Fairburn, but the Russians had the machine.

This wouldn't be over until the machine was safely out of the way.

It was all or nothing.

He had to shoot the moon.

Wake Up or Die

James was awake. One moment he had been in a deep and dreamless sleep, and the next his eyes were open and staring at the ceiling.

He had heard something – a footstep – the unsleeping sentinel at the back of his brain had detected it and sent out a signal . . .

Wake up. Somebody's there. Danger.

He lay perfectly still, his ears straining for any sound, his eyes adjusting to the dim early-morning light in the cabin.

And then he heard it again. A clink, a thump and a shuffle.

There were people moving about on the ship.

He clamped a hand over Kelly's mouth and gently shook her awake. Her eyes snapped open in panic and she glared at him, ready to fight. He put a finger to his lips and held her still.

'There are people here,' he whispered in her ear. 'Keep quiet.'

Kelly nodded. He'd say one thing for her: she may know how to talk, but she also knew when to shut up.

He took his hand away and beckoned her to follow him.

They slid off the bed and crept next door into the living room, where James put his ear to the door. He could hear nothing. Then there was another footfall above them. James looked up and nodded at the ceiling.

'It sounds like they're on the next deck,' he whispered. 'We need to get Fairburn.'

He opened the door just enough to look out into the corridor. Nothing.

They darted out and in a moment were in Fairburn's suite.

He was asleep on his bed, tangled in blankets, looking old and tired. James repeated the process he had gone through with Kelly, silencing him before waking him. It took Fairburn longer to surface, not sure of where he was at first, his hair sticking up madly in all directions, but at last, still looking groggy and confused, he swung his legs off the bed and stood up.

'What time is it?' he said, checking his watch. 'Six o'clock.' He shivered and coughed. James shushed him again and glanced out of the window. The *Amoras* was still there, though the lights were out and she was slowly being swallowed by a fog that was rolling across the dock.

The three of them tiptoed out into the corridor, but they hadn't gone three paces when someone appeared around the corner.

It was one of Babushka's stone-faced secret policemen. He raised a pistol and shouted something in Russian.

James turned and saw the second Russian advancing from the other end of the corridor.

'Stay with me,' he yelled, ducking into the steward's quarters. He had spotted a door last night while he was searching for the blankets and he prayed to God that it would lead through to another corridor.

There were no windows in here, so it was very dark. He tried to remember the way through the maze of small rooms, but crashed into a bulkhead. As he staggered back, though, he bumped into a door and his hand fell on the familiar shape of a handle. He turned it and the door popped open.

'Through here,' he said.

The door did, indeed, lead into another corridor. There was a patch of brightness to the left where light was spilling down a stairwell.

'Run,' he shouted, dragging Kelly along beside him. There were shouts in Russian from behind and the sound of pounding feet. There was a shot and the whine of a bullet passing overhead. It hit a light fitting and ricocheted away, rattling and hissing.

'If they'd wanted to kill us, they would have,' Fairburn yelled. 'They want us alive.'

'They want *you* alive,' said James. 'I doubt they care very much about me and Kelly.'

'That's a cheery thought,' said Kelly as another shot rang out behind them.

James realized that their only advantage was being more familiar with the layout of the ship than their pursuers, but it was only a tiny advantage.

They leapt up the stairs to the next deck and James took them on a twisting, turning route through the ship.

'Can your machine be destroyed?' he yelled to Fairburn as they ran through the galley.

'Of course,' Fairburn shouted back. 'You'd simply have to take a sledgehammer to it, but it wouldn't be quick.'

They charged up a companionway and back into the public part of the *Empress*. They were just managing to keep ahead of the Russians, but as they raced into a dining room they saw two men.

One was a young Russian sailor. The other was Deighton, Charnage's thick-set butler.

'You again,' he grunted. 'Well, I'm ready for you this time, boy.' He flexed his meaty hands, formed them into fists and advanced slowly, almost casually, across the dining-room floor.

The sailor grinned and followed him, not in the least worried about a frail professor, a young boy and a girl.

That was his big mistake.

James grabbed a chair and knocked Deighton to the ground. Kelly quickly caught on and picked up another chair, smashing it over the sailor's head. He put up his arms to defend himself and there was a crack as his forearm snapped. He fell to his knees with a howl of pain.

He was out of the fight.

Kelly and James then bombarded Deighton with every chair they could pick up. He was strong. He almost got to his feet again, but James viciously kicked a table towards him and the edge of it struck him at the base of his skull and he went down for the last time.

The three of them then turned and ran, but, as they left the room, Kelly, who was first out, rushed straight into the arms of one of the Russians. He was as solid as a tractor and didn't move an inch as she careered into him. He held her easily.

And that was *his* big mistake.

Kelly erupted into a wild frenzy, kicking, biting, scratching and twisting crazily. The man let her go with an angry curse and pulled his pistol out of his pocket. James yanked Kelly back into the dining room and, as the Russian tried to follow, his pistol held out in front of him, James kicked the door in his face, crushing his wrist against the frame. He dropped the gun and retreated.

Fairburn snatched up the fallen weapon and fired wildly at the door, the bullets punching through the dark wood.

They didn't wait to see whether he had hit the Russian, and ran across to the other side of the room. The sailor with the broken arm made a feeble attempt to stop them, but backed away when Fairburn aimed the gun at him.

James had been worried about where the second Russian was and now, as he ran out on to the deck, he found out. The man had circled the ship and was waiting for them, his gun at the ready.

Fairburn let fly another clumsy barrage, the shots going in all directions except towards the Russian. It was enough, though, to make him throw himself behind a ventilation cowling and take cover.

James glanced over the side. They were on the deck above the gangplank.

'Quick,' he said, climbing over the rail, 'we're nearly there.'

He lowered himself a little way then dropped down on to the gangplank below. He landed with a thump and tumbled down the slope before coming to a halt tangled in the safety chains along the side.

Kelly was next, landing with such a crash that the gangplank swayed dangerously and James feared it might give way completely. It held fast, but as he looked up he saw the Russian grab Fairburn and try to haul him back over the railing on to the deck.

James had no way of getting back up there to help.

'Quick, Kelly,' he yelled, crouching down and making a stirrup out of his hands. Kelly put one foot into the stirrup and he boosted her up, almost throwing her into the air. She grabbed hold of the railing and scrambled up to the next deck.

The Russian was still leaning over, wrestling with Fairburn, who wasn't going to go without a fight. Kelly sank her teeth into the Russian's ear. He screamed and loosened his grip on Fairburn, who turned and grabbed hold of the man's jacket. There was a brief, fierce tussle and the next thing James knew the Russian was toppling over the railing. He struck the edge of the gangplank and spun down into the black water below.

James had no time to celebrate, however, because at that moment he was struck bodily and sent sprawling down the gangplank. Deighton had run down a deck and come barging out of the ship. James slithered on to the quayside and managed to get to his feet, ready to fight.

But to his dismay he saw that there were more sailors from the *Amoras* waiting on the wharf.

Kelly and Fairburn were manhandled off the ship. There was no point resisting, the game was up, and the three of them were herded into the centre of a ring of jeering men.

'Drop the gun,' said Deighton, and Fairburn let it fall to the ground. He looked sad and scared and done in.

'Sorry,' James said to him quietly. 'We almost made it.'

'Never mind,' said Fairburn. 'It was quite exhilarating, really, but the odds were always stacked against us.'

'That's the problem when you're trying to shoot the moon,' said James. 'If one bit of your plan goes wrong, you're sunk.'

Then he became aware of a noise. A hum of voices, and the sound of feet, like a herd of cows on the move. The men in the circle looked round questioningly. It was impossible to tell where the noise was coming from in the fog which now shrouded the docks, but it was definitely getting louder and nearer.

'What is it?' said Fairburn, blinking. 'What's going on?'

There was a crash and James looked round to see that the gate to the dock had been forced open.

An army of men was approaching. Tough dockers, many armed with clubs or cargo hooks. And at their head was Red, with Perry Mandeville at his side and some of the older girls from Kelly's gang, the Monstrous Regiment.

The army surged forward relentlessly and the knot of sailors around James was quickly overwhelmed. The dockers swarmed over them, clubs and hooks raining down, and the sailors were beaten to the ground. They didn't stand a chance. Sheer force of numbers swamped them. There were screams and yelps, dull thumps and the sounds of skulls cracking. There was a splash as someone was thrown into the water, then another and another. Soon James was at the centre of a huge brawl.

Someone grabbed him by the shoulder and he spun round, ready to fight. It was Red. He grinned at James.

'Can't leave you alone for a moment, can I?' he said. 'If you'd let anything happen to my little sister I'd have killed you.'

'I can look after meself, thank you very much,' said Kelly.

'Looks like we got here just in time,' said Perry. 'I was worried I m-might m-miss out on all the fun.'

'Bloody hell, Jimmy-boy,' said Red, 'I thought *you* was posh, this bloke takes the biscuit.'

'What are you doing here?' said James.

'I spent half of last night looking for you two down here,' said Red. 'Then I went back home to get help.'

'We m-met in the pub,' said Perry. 'I wanted to go to the police, but the Kellys aren't too keen on the law.'

James turned to Kelly. She was wide-eyed and breathless. 'I need your help,' he said. 'I want you to get Fairburn well away from here. We're not safe until he's out of the docks. Take him on the railway, it'll be quicker. Take him back to your house. Perry will go with you. I'll catch you up.'

'I want to stay with you,' said Kelly.

'Go,' said James. 'Get him to safety. I need to talk to Red for a moment. We'll be right behind you.'

'Come on,' said Perry, grabbing Kelly by the wrist. 'Once James Bond's m-mind's m-made up, there's no use in arguing.' He pulled her away through the tangle of fighting men and Fairburn followed, shouting his thanks back to James.

The battle was nearly over; just about the only one of Charnage's men still standing was Deighton, who was swinging a crate hook round his head and yelling obscenities.

A second later and he was down, felled by a blow from behind.

James stooped down to pick up the pistol that Fairburn had dropped.

'You're planning something stupid, aren't you?' said Red.

'Yes,' said James. 'I'm going to try and destroy the Nemesis machine.'

'I'm coming with you,' said Red.

'I'd be too worried about you,' said James.

'I owe you one,' said Red.

James understood.

'Follow me,' he said, then climbed over the edge of the wharf. He quickly made his way down the ladder to where the rowing boat still lay moored at the bottom. He looked up. There was no sign of Red. Maybe he'd changed his mind. But no, in a moment his familiar shock of orange hair appeared over the side of the wharf and he climbed on to the ladder, followed by two bruisers and a boy who looked not much older than James.

'Thought we might need some back-up,' Red explained as he clambered into the boat. 'This is me Uncle Ray, his mate Harry and me cousin, Billy Jones.'

Billy smiled at James. He was a good-looking lad with eyes as dark as his hair.

'Billy works on the ships,' said Red. 'He'll know his way around. The other two are for knocking heads together.'

Ray and Harry grinned at James. They looked like men who enjoyed a fight, and had only about eight teeth between them.

As they settled on to the benches a Russian sailor tried to climb aboard. James fended him off with an oar and they slipped out along the side of the *Empress* and into the open water.

'Hey, Jimmy-boy,' said Red, straining at the oars, 'you and my sis seem to be getting on all right.'

James grunted.

'She's always just been an annoying little sister to me.'

'Shut up and keep rowing,' said James.

The fog that now lay over the docks was thick and yellow, and, although the day was brightening, they could see little more than twenty feet in any direction. The *Amoras* was just a darker patch of grey in a blanket of nothingness.

As they watched, though, powerful fog lights came on and they heard the sound of her engines starting up.

'They're going to try and slip away in the fog,' said James.

'They're crazy,' said Red.

'I thought you already knew that,' said James.

'Do you really think we can stop them?'

'We can try.'

Out of the Fog

As they neared the *Amoras*, they could see that she was still roped to the two deserted tugboats, which were sitting at anchor. Water was foaming above the propellers at her stern and she was starting to move forward.

'The stupid berks are going to try and get her out under her own steam,' said Red. 'It'd be hard enough normally, but in this fog it'll be near-on impossible.'

'They're desperate,' said James.

'We can't stop her with this rowing boat,' said Red.

'We'll have to board her,' said James. 'Then try and put her out of action. Half the crew's back on the dockside, so there shouldn't be too much opposition.'

A gangplank had been lowered down the side of the *Amoras*, ready for the returning crewmen. James steered the rowing boat alongside and the five of them stepped off. The *Amoras* was steaming ahead slowly, straining the ropes that were still fastened to the tugboats.

James and the others clattered up out of the fog on to the deck, where a startled sailor was on lookout duty nursing a tin mug of hot tea. Ray and Harry made short work of him and, before he knew what was happening, they had knocked him cold. They then hid his body behind a lifeboat.

'Doesn't look like there's anyone else about,' said Red. 'They'll need every spare hand to get her under way.'

Both ends of the ship were completely invisible in the fog, and the air was cold and damp. A thin film of moisture covered James's face and his clothes felt heavy.

They crept along towards the bridge deck that jutted up like a tower amidships. The fog not only made seeing difficult, it muffled all sounds, so that there was an eerie stillness and silence, the noise of the ship's engines seemingly coming from far, far away.

They found an open door and went inside.

'The machine's this way,' said James, leading the others down into the ship. They passed the galley, which was once more deserted, and James remembered his adventures of last night with the cat in the bucket. It all seemed a lifetime ago.

They arrived at the door to the rear hold without seeing anyone else. James opened it and they went through on to the walkway.

The great machine was silent and still, its brass rods and gears gleaming under the lights. Down below two sailors stood guard, handguns in holsters on their belts. James had a quick whispered conversation with the others, then got ready.

As Ray and Harry went quietly down a ladder, James, Red and Billy Jones climbed over the rail and waited on the edge of the walkway, leaning out into space.

The sailors turned when they saw the two big men

walking towards them across the deck. They said something in Russian and their hands strayed towards their guns.

'Now!' said James and he jumped. Red and Billy followed. There was a brief exhilarating rush, followed by a bone-loosening crunch. The sailors were flattened. Ray and Harry dashed forward and finished them off. In a minute they were bound and gagged.

James walked over to Nemesis and looked up at it, filling the hold.

'Find some tools,' he said. 'Anything. We've got to smash it to pieces.'

He was about to say something else when he felt a hand grip his ankle. He stifled the urge to yell and looked down.

Sir John Charnage was lying on the deck beneath the machine, all colour drained from his skin. A puddle of blood had formed around him and there was a dark slick where he had pulled himself along. His eyes were wild and feverish and he was trying to speak. James bent down and put his ear to his mouth. He heard two words:

'Help me.'

James and Red dragged him out from under Nemesis and propped him against a bulkhead. Billy Jones found a bottle of water and gave it to Charnage, who drank greedily.

A little life seemed to come back to him, but blood was seeping steadily from his back.

'They turned on me,' he whispered hoarsely, shaking his head as if he still couldn't quite believe it. 'They blamed me.' He looked at James. 'Your fault.'

'No, your fault,' said James. 'You betrayed your friends and you were going to betray your country.'

'It was unforgivable what I did to Ivar and Alexis,' Charnage muttered, 'but, believe me, I had no choice.'

James snorted.

'As for my country . . .' Charnage tried to laugh but it was too painful. 'The country that sent me to Gallipoli . . . I care nothing for my country.'

'You betrayed everyone,' said James.

'You weren't there,' said Charnage. 'In Gallipoli. It was madness. The generals and the politicians didn't care a jot about the ordinary men. They were just numbers. Rule Britannia? Great Britain? A *great* lie. They told us the Turks were barely human, but they were just boys like us. My country betrayed *me*. I hate this country. I realize now, though, that the Russians are no better. The men who rule this world are nothing but a bunch of gangsters.'

'Who did this to you?' said James.

'She did,' said Charnage. 'Babushka. And those two sewer rats, the Smith brothers. But it wasn't well enough done. I survived a mortar blast in the war. It'll take more than this to kill John Charnage.' He grabbed James's arm, a wild look on his face. 'She's not having the Nemesis, though. No one is going to have it.'

'We'll destroy it,' said James. 'If you tell us how.'

'Get me down to the engine room,' gasped Charnage, trying to stand. 'If we put too much pressure on the boilers they might rupture. The explosion would send the *Amoras* and everything on it down to the bottom.'

James looked to Billy Jones.

'Can it be done?' he asked.

Billy looked worried, but he nodded his head.

'Don't use this unless you absolutely have to,' James said to Red, handing him one of the handguns they had captured from the sailors. 'You're in charge, but do as Charnage says. Take him to the engine room. Billy and the others will come with you. If anyone gets in your way, flatten them.'

'Where are you going?' said Red.

James untied the legs of the two trussed-up sailors. 'I've got to get them out of here,' he said. 'If they stay down here they'll drown.'

James took the other gun and prodded the two sailors. They were groggy and sheepish and had no desire to be shot, so they moved off willingly.

In a few minutes they were outside and James hurried them along the deck. The lookout they had dumped behind the lifeboat was just coming to. James marched his two captives over to him and indicated in dumb show that he should untie his comrades.

James looked at the three of them. They were tough-looking young men.

He hoped they were good swimmers.

He aimed his pistol at them and nodded towards the edge of the ship.

'Over you go, now,' he said.

They looked at him dubiously, but his meaning was clear.

'Now,' said James, and something in his expression told them that he was not to be argued with.

There were three splashes as they hit the water.

James was just about to go back and help the others when he heard footsteps and he ducked behind the lifeboat.

Two familiar figures loomed out of the fog. Ludwig and Wolfgang Smith. Ludwig's big, white skull face was almost glowing, and his mouth, with its rotten brown teeth, was a dark hole. He was carrying an axe in his bony fingers.

Wolfgang, who was carrying a lantern, looked as yellow as the fog and there wasn't a part of him that wasn't bandaged. James almost felt sorry for him.

Just then, the ship gave a sudden lurch forward as the tugboats' anchors were torn loose and James was thrown to the deck. There were deafening thuds as the tugs swung round and hit the *Amoras*'s hull, as they were both still attached to her by their towing ropes. James got to his feet and moved off after the two brothers.

He heard the sound of chopping and was soon able to see Ludwig in the forecastle, hacking at one of the towing ropes with his axe. Wolfgang stood there, shivering, the lantern held up in one hand, his other hand, the wounded one, thrust deep into his coat pocket.

The ship was picking up speed.

James crept closer for a better look, trying to see if there was any way of stopping Ludwig. With the tugboats cut free, there would be a greater chance of the *Amoras* escaping if Charnage's plan to sink it didn't work.

The first rope gave way and Ludwig crossed the deck to start on the second one. He took a couple of swings

360

and then there was a horrible crashing sound and the whole ship was jerked around in the water.

The helmsman, steering blind, had got too close to another ship and the trailing tugboat was jammed against it, the towing rope hopelessly tangled. The whole ship was creaking and groaning, the rope stretching, the engines pounding.

'Bloody idiots,' snarled Ludwig and he started shouting to them to stop and reverse the engines. Someone shouted back from the bridge.

'What is going on?'

'The tugboat's caught!' yelled Ludwig, turning round, and then his eyes went very wide.

James had been thrown over again and fallen badly. He was lying out in the open, half-stunned.

'It's the rat,' yelled Ludwig.

'Let me at him,' said Wolfgang.

'He's all yours,' said Ludwig and he passed the axe to his brother, who dropped the lantern and went into a hopping, gammy run.

James got groggily to his feet and bolted, stumbling along the deck, which was damp and slippery, sliding into things, like a man on ice in the dark. He glanced back. Wolfgang was gaining on him, moving surprisingly fast on his injured leg, the axe raised above his head. A look of pure hatred on his face.

A particularly dense patch of fog drifted across the ship. James could see nothing and, before he knew what was happening, he'd skidded and fallen for a third time. He was blind, disorientated. All he could hear was Wolfgang's approaching feet. He scrabbled around for some sort of weapon but could find nothing.

Then there was a huge twang and a crack followed by the sound of a giant whip slicing through the air. At the same time the *Amoras* gave another almighty lurch and shot forward in the water.

The other end of the remaining towrope had snapped, and now, released from the tremendous tension, it scythed back across the deck. If James hadn't fallen over it would have taken his head off.

Then he saw an extraordinary sight.

Where Wolfgang had been running towards him out of the fog, suddenly there was no body, only legs. They staggered and slumped to the deck and the next moment the axe came tumbling through the air and embedded itself half an inch away from where James was lying.

James shivered as a flood of nausea welled up from his guts. He swallowed hard and screwed his eyes tight to try and shut out the image of Wolfgang's mutilated body.

He opened his eyes and looked around.

There was no sign of the other brother. Maybe the cable had got him too. James didn't wait to find out. He ran towards the bridge deck. Freed of both tugs, the *Amoras* was making better progress. In fact she was steaming ahead recklessly fast.

Red and Charnage obviously hadn't made it. The engines were working all too well. James's only hope now was to get to the bridge and somehow put the ship out of action from there.

He passed someone running in the opposite direction

along the deck, but in the fog James was mistaken for another crewman and he carried on unchecked.

He almost missed the bridge deck, but at the last moment spotted white-painted steps going up into the fog. He climbed two decks and peered into the wheelhouse.

A sailor was at the wheel, straining to see anything ahead. The captain stood next to him, looking more than a little anxious. As James watched he wrenched the lever on the telegraph round to the SLOW position but it appeared to have no effect. If anything, the ship speeded up. The helmsman said something to the captain who yelled a torrent of angry Russian into the speaker tube that connected with the engine room.

He got no reply and ran out of the wheelhouse on the other side.

James opened the door and went in, yelling at the startled helmsman.

'Off! Get off! Abandon ship!'

The sailor stared at him, panicked, but unwilling to leave his post.

'Go!' James shouted. 'Get away.'

Suddenly there was a crash and James was showered with broken glass. Next moment a hand grabbed him by the collar and yanked him backwards.

Ludwig had punched through the window with his knuckleduster. He held James in the broken window frame, an arm clamped round his throat.

With a *schink*, Ludwig released the blade on his second Apache and put it up to James's eye.

He pressed his face next to James's. The smell of his rotting teeth was overpowering and James gagged.

'I'd love to make this slow,' he whispered into James's ear, his breath hot and damp. 'But I don't have time. So, say your prayers quickly, the Apache's going to give you a goodnight kiss.'

Before Ludwig could do anything, however, there was a terrific boom from the depths of the *Amoras* and she seemed to lift out of the water and then thump down again.

The boilers, thought James. *Red made it.*

Ludwig was thrown off balance and his grip on James weakened.

James slammed him with his elbow through the broken window. Moments later a second, even bigger, explosion rocked the ship and she tilted sideways, tipping Ludwig over the railing.

James rubbed his bruised neck and looked round. The helmsman had disappeared. The *Amoras* was going down. He cautiously peeked out of the broken window to see if there was any sign of Ludwig.

He was welcomed by a loud bang from below, and a bullet whistled past his head. He ducked back into the wheelhouse as another shot ripped through the fog, leaving a vapour trail. He crawled over to the far side, slithering on his belly through the broken glass, and out on to the deck. There was another shot and a bullet pinged off the railing next to him.

He jumped up, feeling another bullet pass him so closely it singed his cheek. It was too risky to go down, towards Ludwig, so he scrambled up on to the roof of the wheelhouse and lay flat.

The ship was out of control now, the steering mechanism taken out by the blasts in the engine room. It was wheeling across the water in a wide arc, carried along by its own momentum.

James kept still and hoped he hadn't been spotted, but his hopes were short-lived. There were three hard clangs as three bullet holes appeared between his legs. Ludwig was in the wheelhouse firing up at him through the roof.

James jumped to his feet and ran to the rear of the roof where there was a thick, wooden, radio mast with a ladder running up it.

There was nowhere else to go.

Another shot rang out as James began to scale the ladder. He looked down. Ludwig was climbing on to the roof. He fired wildly with both guns at James, who pressed himself against the mast.

Ludwig stood up and steadied himself on the tilting roof. He was going to take his time on this one.

James carried on climbing higher into the fog, hoping it would hide him.

Ludwig took aim. He could just see James moving up the ladder.

He pulled the trigger.

Nothing.

He raised his second gun. James was fast vanishing. The Apache was not designed for shooting at a distance.

He fired.

Nothing. And now he was out of bullets. Ten shots

was all he had. Even though each cylinder held six bullets, he always left one chamber empty on each gun, with the hammer resting in it, so as not to risk shooting himself when the weapons were in his coat.

James was nearly at the top of the mast. There were no more gunshots, but he knew it wasn't over. He heard the familiar *schink* again as Ludwig readied his bayonets.

Then Ludwig was climbing the mast, quickly and efficiently, the knuckleduster grips of his guns leaving his fingers free to hold on.

James climbed higher. The mast narrowed and the ladder ran out. From here on up there were just metal spars jutting out from each side of the mast and he had to go slowly or risk falling off.

Ludwig loomed out of the fog and James kicked out at his head, catching him a glancing blow on his right eyebrow. Ludwig cursed but held on tight.

James heard shouts and looked round. He had forgotten about everything else. His world had narrowed to this lone radio mast in a universe of fog, but reality was approaching fast. He was shocked to see that the *Amoras* was heading towards the dockside at a sharp angle. He could see a small tramp steamer unloading, a crane holding a full cargo net over its deck. Men were waving and yelling. A siren blared.

The *Amoras* was completely out of control. Nobody could stop her now. James held on for dear life as she powered into the rear of the tramp steamer, splintering the wooden hull. The next thing he knew the crane was coming straight for him. At the last moment he jumped and took hold of the thick rope mesh of the cargo net, clinging to it with hands and feet and teeth. With a terrible groaning and grinding noise the prow of the *Amoras* scraped along the dockside, slowly pushing the tramp steamer underwater.

James looked round for Ludwig but could see no sign of him. Maybe the impact had knocked him off the mast.

But then he saw him. He hadn't fallen. Like James he had jumped on to the cargo net and was even now coming around it like a great black spider.

James looked down. It was too high to jump, and too dangerous with the *Amoras* breaking up below.

Ludwig took a swipe at him and he had to let go with one hand or risk having it sliced off.

Before Ludwig could lunge again, though, the net became tangled in the *Amoras*'s own steam winch at the rear of the main deck. The cargo net twisted round, then there was a rip and a jerk and a mighty crack as the cable supporting it snapped and the whole thing dropped.

James and Ludwig hurtled down, and a second later the net crashed on to the *Amoras*'s rails and they were dumped into the water. Most of the cargo of tobacco crates spilt on to the deck, exploding in clouds of dried leaves. The net ended up hanging down the side of the *Amoras*'s hull, a few crates still held in its web.

As James hit the oily water he was momentarily stunned, but he soon came to his senses and knew that he had to get out fast. Stray ropes dangled down from the netting and he managed to grab hold of one as the *Amoras* drifted past. He hauled himself up until he was safely on the net, where he rested, shaking and panting.

He realized, though, that it wasn't over. He was in more danger now than before. The *Amoras* was still moving, her prow nosing along the wharf in a shower of dust and sparks, gouging out great lumps of stonework. Her stern still sticking out into the middle of the dock, but slewing across and inwards. Soon the whole ship would broadside the wharf.

With a shudder, James remembered what had happened to Wolfgang's hand, pinched between two boats. The *Amoras* was much bigger than them – seven thousand tons would crush more than just a hand. If he didn't get off the net fast he was going to be sandwiched between the hull and the wharf.

Before he could think what to do, he felt a sharp pain in his ankle.

He looked down.

It was Ludwig.

He, too, had climbed on to the net, his bayonets still fixed to his hands, and he had got James with the point of one blade.

Didn't the man ever give up? Couldn't he see that they were about to be killed?

The blade hadn't penetrated deeply, the angle had been too awkward for Ludwig, but the pain was intense and James felt warm blood soaking into his already sodden sock.

'Don't be a fool,' James shouted. 'We're going to get crushed!'

But Ludwig ignored him. He climbed quickly and jabbed again. This time James was ready for him, though, and he pulled his foot out of the way, rolling sideways. Ludwig grunted and stabbed at him once more. The blade missed and stuck fast into the side of one of the crates that was still caught in the net.

Ludwig swore and tried to wrench the Apache free, but it was jammed tight. James saw his opportunity and kicked out at him, smashing his heel into Ludwig's knuckles. Ludwig yelped and James kicked again. And again. Filled with an awful, bloody fury.

He carried on kicking, shattering Ludwig's joints so that he couldn't let go of the knife. His fingers were tangled in the knuckleduster grip. He had to use his other hand to hold on to the net, so he could do nothing to stop James.

James was plunged into darkness and he looked over at the dockside, which was swinging ever nearer, blocking out the light. He frantically pulled himself up the net, hand over hand, unable to go too quickly or he would risk getting his feet caught and becoming trapped like Ludwig.

The strip of grey sky above him was narrowing by the second.

He wasn't going to make it.

He could sense the dock swinging towards him. Sense the great, unstoppable weight of the ship.

He screamed. The scream of someone making a superhuman effort, and threw himself upward, willing his body to fly.

He had done it.

He was clear of the dockside. He looked down to check and saw Ludwig's giant skull head looking back up at him with a look of sheer, hopeless terror in his eyes, his rotten brown teeth bared in an animal howl.

James looked away at the last moment, as the hull finally pressed in against the dockside. There was the sound of splintering wood from the crates and, with a final crunch, Ludwig was suddenly silenced.

As the ship slammed against the dock, James was thrown off the side and he landed in a graceless heap on a pile of ropes, tobacco falling all around him through the fog.

There was another deep boom from the *Amoras* and she sank lower in the water.

All the dockers had cleared the area. They knew only too well the dangers of an exploding boiler. James got up quickly and ran away from the dockside himself, and as he rounded a warehouse building he heard a mighty double bang behind him and felt the air punch at him.

He carried on running, straight into Red Kelly.

'I thought you was a goner for sure,' said Red, 'but I should have known you'd pull through.'

'Did you all get off safely?' said James.

'Yep. It was a close thing, though. We got into the rowing boat about half a second before the second explosion.'

'And Charnage?'

Red shook his head. 'He's gone down with his bloody machine.'

A crowd was forming around them, and James wanted

to get away before too many questions were asked. As he was shouldering through the throng of dockers, however, he heard a shrill cry and looked round to see Kelly Kelly running towards them, her heart-shaped face twisted and anxious.

'Something's wrong,' said Red.

'What happened?' asked James as Kelly appeared.

'The woman,' she said breathlessly. 'The Grandmother, whatever her name is.'

'Colonel Sedova,' said James. 'What about her?'

'She must have followed us somehow. I've gone to the control room with a couple of the girls. We're getting the controls set up, and there she is with one of the men from the *Empress*. The one whose arm you shut in the door. She's got a gun, James. She knocked out your mate Perry, grabbed Fairburn and the rest of us have made a run for it.'

'Where's Babushka now?' said James.

'I don't know,' said Kelly. 'I don't know. I've hid meself and waited, but she never come out. I think she's still in there with Fairburn and Perry. The girls are keeping an eye on the place. But it don't look good, James. It don't look good at all . . .'

The Eyes of a Killer

Two members of Kelly's gang were waiting outside the transit shed. They hadn't seen Perry, Fairburn or Babushka come out.

The grille covering the ventilation shaft hung half-open. James pulled it back and crawled in. He went slowly and carefully, until he could see down into the control room, all the while expecting a shot to tear upward from below.

But when he got there, the room was empty.

'It's all clear,' he shouted and jumped down on to the stone floor.

Red and his sister were soon beside him.

'They must have got out, after all,' said Kelly.

'Not necessarily,' said James. 'Look at this.'

He pointed to a trail of blood, small scarlet drops leading into the tunnel mouth.

'She hasn't used the train,' said Red. 'She wouldn't know how, and, besides, there's no noise. The fans aren't working.'

'Can you walk in there?' said James, looking into the dark tunnel.

Red held him back. 'No, Jimmy-boy,' he said. 'You're not going in there after her. She's got a gun, for God's sake.'

'She's also got Fairburn,' said James. 'And maybe Perry, too. I have to go after them.'

Red thought for a moment. 'Here . . .' he said and opened a box on the wall. 'These should help.'

He took out two candle stubs, lit them and passed one to James.

James smiled at Kelly Kelly. 'My bright idea to keep you out of trouble didn't work too well, did it? We might as well stick together this time.'

'Less of the sweet talk,' said Red. 'Let's get on with it.'

James squeezed past the rubber flaps into the tunnel.

Red and his sister followed.

It was hard going, trying to step on the sleepers and not stumble over the gaps. They had to walk bent double, almost crawling, their heads and shoulders bumping against the low ceiling. It would be harder going for the Russian woman, particularly if she was dragging prisoners along with her, but could they catch her up? James listened for any noises in the tunnel ahead, and so far there was nothing but the sounds of their own harsh breathing.

He kept his eyes on the spots and splashes of blood that left a trail along the ground and after a little while he found a spent match. A little further along he found another one.

The Russians must be using them to see where they were going.

For twenty minutes they trudged on, the tunnel never

373

changing as they passed a dreary procession of grey bricks. They might as well have been walking around in circles for all that the scenery changed. Then at last the tunnel curved slightly and, as they rounded the corner, James saw something and stopped.

There was a dark shape up ahead. He pointed it out to the others and they stayed still, watching and waiting. Every muscle in James's body felt stiff and tense. For the first time he became aware of his damp clothes and the pain in his ankle where Ludwig had stabbed him. In fact there wasn't a part of him that didn't hurt in some way. His vision swam and blurred and he blinked to clear his mind.

The shape lay still. It hadn't moved at all since James had first spotted it. Eventually he risked approaching. As he got nearer he saw that it was Perry, sitting slumped against the wall, his eyes closed, a hand clamped to a bloody handkerchief at his head.

James shook him.

'Perry?'

Perry opened his eyes.

'James!' he said and tried to smile. 'Good to see you, old thing.'

'Thank God,' said James. 'I thought for a moment you were dead.'

'M-me?' said Perry. 'You're joking, aren't you? Never better. She m-made the m-mistake of hitting m-me in the head, anywhere else and I'd have felt something.' He laughed and winced, screwing his eyes shut.

'What happened?' said James. 'Where's Fairburn?'

'I came round in the control room,' said Perry. 'The

old woman was still there, with some other chap, looking a little the worse for wear. I thought it best to lie doggo and pretend to be out cold, watched them bring Fairburn in here, tried to follow, but I'm still feeling a bit faint, to tell you the truth, lost a fair few pints of blood, I reckon, did m–my best, though, eh?'

'You did well, Perry,' said James. 'You did very well.'

'Trouble is,' said Perry, 'I got this far and then didn't know which way to go.' He nodded to where a small access tunnel branched off to the right. 'They were too far ahead of m–me, I m–must have dozed off . . . Sorry.'

'We'll have to take a guess,' said James. 'It's pot luck, I'm afraid.'

'We'd better split up,' said Red. 'You take Perry and I'll take me sis.'

'OK,' said James.

'We'll carry on down the main track,' said Red.

'Any idea where this leads?' said James, shining his candle into the access tunnel.

'Nope,' said Red. 'There might be a way up to the street from down there, but it's more likely all blocked off.'

'Listen,' said James, 'when you get to the end, if you've seen no sight of them, try and get the fans started, at least that'll block the main tunnel and cut her off if she tries to double back here.'

'If you say so, skipper.'

'Why won't you ever let me come with you?' Kelly asked James, her heart-shaped face turned golden by the candlelight.

'This isn't a tea dance,' said James.

'But still —'

'We have to split up,' said James. 'And I'm responsible for Perry now. He's my friend.'

Kelly suddenly darted forward and kissed James. Red whistled.

'And here I was thinking you didn't like boys, sis!'

'Yeah, well, I've never met a real one before,' said Kelly. 'Come on, let's get those fans going.'

James watched the two of them scurry away up the tunnel.

'She'd be quite pretty if you scrubbed her up a bit,' said Perry.

'She's fine as she is,' said James. 'Just fine.'

'I think she m-might be sweet on you,' said Perry.

'Right now, that's the last thing on my mind,' said James. 'So, what do you say? Are you ready for this? Can you go on?'

'You bet I can,' said Perry. 'Lead on, M–MacDuff! I'll be right behind you.'

'Just be careful,' said James, putting a hand on Perry's arm. 'You're already pretty bashed about. You're lucky she only *hit* you with her gun and didn't shoot you. You saw at the museum what a mess a bullet can make of someone. Just bear that in mind and don't do anything reckless.'

'Don't worry,' said Perry with a shudder. 'I shall never forget those pictures.'

The access tunnel was even lower and narrower than the main tunnel, and this time James did have to get down

376

on to his hands and knees, holding the candle awkwardly out in front of him.

'By the way,' said Perry as they shuffled along, 'I almost forgot: that parcel that arrived for you yesterday at the m-mission, the one you told Pritpal to open.'

'What about it?'

'When I got back to London I telephoned the pub, you weren't there so I went on to Hackney Wick with Pritpal, just in case the parcel held any surprises.'

'And did it?'

'Not half.'

'So, who was it from, then?'

'A M-Mister Flegenheimer.'

'Mister Flegenheimer?' For a moment James's mind was blank, and then he remembered the Paradice Club, the American gangster, the roulette. He stopped.

'What was in it?' he said.

'It was brown paper,' said Perry, 'all tied up with string, and inside was three hundred pounds in five-pound notes. We'd none of us ever seen that m-much m-money before.'

James awkwardly turned round to face Perry. 'This has been the strangest weekend of my life,' he said.

'M-me too,' said Perry.

They had reached the end of the access tunnel where a series of rungs led up the side of a vertical shaft. James silenced Perry and listened. Still nothing. Babushka and the others must have gone the other way.

He hoped Red and his sister would be all right.

'What do you think?' said Perry.

'We'd best check,' said James.

Slowly he climbed the ladder. At the top the shaft came out into the corner of a large chamber filled with various pieces of ancient machinery. The room was partially lit by pale, wintry light spilling down from a circular vent in the ceiling. Beneath it was a large, wooden framework that had been built over an opening in the floor that presumably led back down to the tunnels.

There was a great black boiler against one wall, its chimney disappearing into the roof. It was rusted and evidently hadn't been used in years.

This was obviously once the engine room for the fans that ran the railway before it had been converted to electric power.

'You m-must tell me,' whispered Perry, sticking his head up into the chamber, 'what you're going to do with all that m-money? It'll certainly buy you a lot of sock!'

'I'm not spending it on grub,' whispered James. 'I'll tell you what I'm going to do with it —'

But he never finished the sentence. A muzzle flash flared briefly and a single shot split the air, terrifyingly loud. A spray of chippings and dust scoured James's face and he dropped the candle, which went out.

The only light in the chamber now was from the ceiling vent.

James crawled behind the boiler. Another shot sounded and he felt a bullet smack into the floor nearby. If he hadn't moved he would have been hit for sure. His ears were ringing, and each shot made him jump out of his skin.

'Boy?' It was a woman's voice. A Russian voice. Calm and even.

James didn't make the mistake of replying and offering up a target.

'Boy? I know you can hear me,' Babushka went on. 'We have Fairburn. We will shoot him if we have to. There is no way out from here. We are going back into the main tunnel. If you are clever, and I know that you are, you will not try to stop us.'

James felt a vibration in the floor and heard the hum of an engine starting up. Red must have reached the controls. At the same time an amber warning light started slowly flashing on the wall at the far end, lighting the chamber for a second then plunging it back into semi-darkness.

James saw the silhouette of Babushka near the wooden structure, and she obviously saw him, for she raised her gun.

James dived out of the way and rolled behind a thick oak beam. There was a bang and the beam splintered. The bullet had missed him by inches, but the force of it had dislodged a huge, jagged splinter of wood, as large as a kitchen knife, which smashed into James's shoulder. A searing jolt of pain passed through him, and when he put his hand up to his collarbone he felt the wood sticking out. He pulled it free and his shirt was instantly drenched with blood. But, worse, he was sure the bone was broken.

This wasn't good. This wasn't good at all.

He felt a breeze tug at his clothing and the next moment a howling gale was blowing through the chamber. Bits of leaves and debris were being sucked down the ventilation shaft in the ceiling and there was a deep whirring, throbbing, churning noise.

The wooden framework was evidently the housing for one of the fans that drove the railway.

Hoping that Babushka would be as distracted as he was, James jumped up and ran across the room to a new hiding place.

The noise of the fan and the buffeting wind were deafening, and with the flashing amber light and the pain in his shoulder James was becoming dazed and confused.

He sat down behind a brick support, closed his eyes and took a few deep breaths, trying to slow his heart rate and clear his mind. Then he leant out to find where Babushka was.

He could see nothing of her, but in an amber flash of warning light he saw the stone-faced OGPU man hiding in a corner, with one arm holding Fairburn, the hand over his mouth. His other hand hung uselessly at his side and was swollen and purple-looking.

The amber light flicked off and James rolled across the floor to a better vantage point. When the light came back on he was shocked to see Perry crawling across the floor, blood trickling down his face.

Where the hell was he going? What was he trying to do?

James wanted to call out to him to be careful, but he couldn't risk it, not without knowing where Babushka was.

There was a moment of darkness and then James saw her move quickly from behind a wall and grab Perry.

'I've got your friend, boy,' she roared above the noise of the fan. 'Now show yourself.'

The light went out. James didn't think. He acted.

He ran straight out from his hiding place and barged into Babushka before she knew what was happening. The three of them staggered back across the floor and collided with the wooden framework of the fan housing.

James got a glimpse of Perry, lying still on the ground before the light went out again.

He tried to stand up but Babushka grabbed him. She may have looked like a grandmother, but she was surprisingly strong. She lifted James up as easily as a doll, raised him above her shoulders and hurled him over the top of the wooden structure towards the fan. He landed heavily on a steel platform. He could feel the broken bones in his shoulder scraping against each other and he screamed.

As the pain surged through his body his brain shut down for a moment.

He fought his way back to consciousness through a fizzing, swirling cloud of sparkling bubbles, and struggled to his feet. The noise of the fan was worse than ever here and the wind rushed past in a spinning fury like a tornado.

He looked round. He was on the edge of a circular hole about fifteen feet wide and six feet deep. Halfway down a narrow wooden walkway spanned the gap and below it was the giant fan. He could see it spinning in the darkness, its vicious metal blades sucking the air down into its maw.

He turned back to see Babushka standing below, pointing a gun up at him. Her expression was relaxed, almost kindly, but her eyes told the truth. They were dead. And in her hand was the gun.

'You are very lucky,' she said.

James didn't feel lucky.

'I meant to throw you into the fan,' Babushka explained.

James realized that he should be back at school today.

He supposed he wouldn't ever be going back now.

That was a pleasant thought, at least.

No more school.

He felt sorry that he would miss Christmas, though. Sorry that he wouldn't be sitting by the fire with his Aunt Charmian in the little cottage in Kent. He'd miss all of it: the carol singing, the goose, the chocolates and nuts . . .

Babushka put her gun into her pocket and nodded towards the man holding Fairburn. She said something quickly that James didn't understand and the man smiled. He let go of Fairburn and chopped him on the side of the neck with the edge of his palm. He then flung him to one side, where he flopped lifelessly to the ground.

The Russian now climbed on to the platform and advanced on James, his good hand raised.

He was going to push James into the fan.

James had thought of all the colourful ways in which he might die.

Being chewed up by a fan was not on his list.

He got into a crouch, readying himself.

The man grunted and rushed at him.

At the last moment James flung himself backwards, hoping that he had judged it correctly.

He landed on the wooden walkway, flat on his back, and he cried out with the pain.

The big Russian found himself clutching at thin air. He teetered off-balance on the lip of the huge hole, his arms windmilling, his mouth open in a wide O of surprise.

As he toppled forward he made a grab for the walkway. He missed.

The fan sucked him down into its teeth.

James heard an awful slicing sound and a series of thumps. There was a metallic grating and a grinding of gears and the whine of overloaded machinery, and then vicious shards of broken metal exploded upward out of the hole.

Sparks sprayed out from a junction box on the wall, the amber light flickered, and with a bang the fan's engine shut down, the noise dying away like a last breath.

James looked up. Far above he could see an iron grille and blue sky beyond.

The fog had cleared and it looked like a beautiful, crisp winter's day.

There would be people up there, going about their business.

It was a Monday morning, the shops would be open. The streets of London would be busy with Christmas shoppers.

It was a normal day. They would have no idea what was going on down here, twenty feet beneath the pavement.

He patted his body to check that nothing more was broken, and his hand felt something in his pocket.

In the dead silence that followed the shut down, Babushka walked over to the wooden structure and climbed up on to the platform. She wasn't quite sure what she would see when she peered over the edge into the hole. The fan would have made quite a mess of the two bodies.

What she never expected to see was the boy, lying on his back above the broken fan, his arm outstretched, a pistol in his hand.

James had completely forgotten he had it, and now it was aimed squarely at Babushka's head.

She smiled. 'Stalemate,' she said.

'Looks like it,' said James.

'You won't shoot me, though. You're just a boy.'

'Won't I?' said James. 'You think I won't do it just because you're an old woman?'

'I am not so old.'

'And I am not so young,' said James.

Babushka smiled. 'You remind me of my own son,' she said. 'He is a strong, brave boy.'

'Don't lie to me,' said James. 'Don't try and get me on your side. You don't have a son.'

'You are right. They call me Babushka, the Grandmother, because all Russian boys are my children. All of her soldiers. Russia is a beautiful country, but she has seen so much sadness. You would like Russia . . .'

James realized what she was doing. She was trying to throw him off his guard. She had seen that he was weak and growing weaker by the minute. He could hardly hold the weight of the pistol. Already it was wavering.

'Shut up,' he said.

'You will not shoot me.'

James thought about it. Could he kill someone? He remembered the awful photographs at the Royal College of Surgeons, men with half their faces gone. *Could he do that to this woman?* It was a terrible thing, to take someone's life.

He felt very cold and alone.

He knew the answer.

Babushka knew the answer too. She could see it in his eyes. This boy was different.

'Will you let me go?' she said quietly. 'I know now that you could pull that trigger.' She paused. 'But you do not want to, do you? So, will you let me go? Just let me walk away from here. I ask you this as one soldier to another. You have what you wanted. You have Fairburn. The machine is gone.'

James's vision was dimming. He could hear his blood dripping down into the ruined fan.

Enough people had died today.

'Go,' he said hoarsely.

Babushka saluted him, slipped over the edge of the hole and climbed down past him through the ruined fan.

It was over at last.

James closed his eyes and slept. It could have been for a few seconds or it could have been for a few years, but when he opened his eyes again he was lying on the chamber floor with Kelly Kelly peering down at him.

There was concern in her deep brown eyes, but her wide mouth was smiling. She looked very beautiful.

'She knocked you about a bit, didn't she?' she said.

James nodded. 'I think my collarbone's broken.'

'I knew I shouldn't have let you go off without me,' said Kelly. 'You know you can't look after yourself.'

Perry's face appeared next to Kelly's.

'It's never a dull m–moment with you, eh, James?'

'Afraid not.'

'Sorry I couldn't help, banged my head again, luckily I've no brains to dislodge.'

Perry's voice was coming from far, far away. He was at the other end of a tunnel.

'Watch it. Stay awake, old chap,' said Perry. 'We need you conscious if we're going to get you out of here in one piece.'

'Sorry,' said James. 'I'll try.'

'Red's gone to get help,' said Perry. 'Some good strong lads.'

'I could certainly do with some help,' said James.

They got James to his feet. Then Perry went to check on Fairburn who was sitting up on the floor looking dazed and confused.

Kelly put her arm around James and he could feel the warmth of her body.

'Talk to me,' he said.

'I thought I talked too much.'

'Never,' said James. 'I love to hear you talk. It's the nicest sound in the world.'

'And what about m–me?' said Perry, bringing Fairburn over to them.

'Like the singing of a lark in springtime,' said James.

'Do I detect a hint of sarcasm?'

'At least you make me laugh,' said James and his vision dimmed.

Perry shook him. 'I say,' he said, propping him up so that he was supported between the two of them, 'you never finished telling m-me what you were going to do with all that m-money.'

'Well,' said James, 'the Bamford and Martin's gone to the big garage in the sky, but there's a lovely wreck behind a pub in Slough that needs some attention.'

'You sly dog,' snorted Perry. 'You're going to buy the Bentley!'

★ ★ ★

Twelve years later, at the close of the Second World War, Commander James Bond R.N.V.R. drove his lovingly restored $4\frac{1}{2}$ litre Bentley convertible to a secret location fifty miles north-west of London. Over the years he had made some modifications to the car and added an Amherst Villiers supercharger. She was big and powerful and painted battleship grey.

The secret location was known only as Station X and it was located at Bletchley Park. Station X was Britain's best-kept secret. It was here during the war that a brilliant team of scientists had worked night and day to break Nazi Germany's toughest military codes.

To do it they had built the world's first working semi-programmable computer.

Bond arrived to find the place being packed up and mothballed. Nobody was to know for a very long time what had gone on here. Even Bond himself had been told only what he needed to know – that he was to take a code breaker back to London for debriefing at the ministry headquarters, and that he was never to talk about it to anyone else.

As he entered the main hall of the big house at the centre of the Bletchley complex, he saw a man standing lost in thought, staring out of the window at the rain.

He was perfectly ordinary-looking, but something about him seemed familiar, and, when he turned and saw Bond, he too frowned in recognition.

'Don't I know you?' he said.

'Probably shouldn't say,' said Bond. 'This is all supposed to be very hush-hush.'

'I know,' said the man, and he raised his eyebrows, humour sparkling in his eyes. 'But I've never been very good at all that cloak-and-dagger stuff. Were you at Cambridge?'

'Afraid not,' said James, and then it struck him. The man was Alan Turing, the student he had met that day at Trinity all those years ago. The young man who had been working with Professor Peterson.

Before he could say anything, however, there was a shout from across the room.

'James? James Bond?'

Now James got his second surprise of the day. The man he was to take down to London was none other than Alexis Fairburn. His hair wilder, his nose and ears even bigger.

On the way back to town in the Bentley, Fairburn told James a little about Bletchley Park. There were many men like him there: mathematicians, code breakers, cipher experts, cryptologists.

'And crossword addicts?' Bond shouted over the noise of the Bentley's supercharged engine.

'Them too,' Fairburn yelled back. 'As a matter of fact, one of the tests for applicants at the beginning of the war was to complete a cryptic crossword.'

James laughed. 'Hell of a way to fight a war!' he said.

'In the future,' said Fairburn, 'wars are going to be fought more and more by men like me, and less and less by men like you.'

'Oh, they'll always need someone who can knock a few heads together,' said Bond and he turned and grinned at Fairburn.

'I'd love to talk,' said Fairburn, 'but I'm afraid I'm sworn to secrecy.'

'I'm just thinking out loud here, you understand,' said Bond, 'but my guess is that you've been working on something like the Nemesis machine.'

'My lips are sealed,' said Fairburn. 'But I'll tell you one thing. After my run-in with Charnage and the Russians I wanted nothing more to do with superbrains and thinking machines. I wanted to put all that stuff out of my mind for good, but the war effort, the evil of the Nazis . . . I wanted to help.'

'I expect they couldn't have done it without you.'

'Ah. Not me, I'm afraid,' said Fairburn. 'Alan Turing. He's the clever one. His ideas are way ahead of mine. Charnage kidnapped the wrong man. Do you know, I still to this day have no idea if my Nemesis machine would have worked. I sometimes dream about it. Being back there, in that hot and sweaty hold on the *Amoras*, my machine chattering away. They're the future, Bond, these machines. We've barely scraped the surface of what they could be used for.'

'Well, your secret's safe with me,' said Bond. 'I never did understand how your machine worked and exactly what it did. As you say, I'm just a foot soldier. I tend to solve problems with my fists, or with a gun, and I suppose I'm doomed to spend the rest of my life trying to sort out the problems that the clever people of this world make for the rest of us.'

DON'T MISS YOUNG BOND'S NEXT UNSTOPPABLE ADVENTURE . . .

HURRICANE GOLD

James Bond is staring death in the face. And he isn't about to blink.

As the sun blazes over the Caribbean island of Lágrimas Negras, its bloodthirsty ruler is watching and waiting. Criminals come here to hide, with blood on their hands and escape on their minds.

On the mainland, ex-flying ace Jack Stone leaves his son and daughter in the company of James Bond. But a gang of thieves lies in ambush – they want Stone's precious safe, and will kill for its contents.

A deadly chase through the Mexican jungle begins and on this terrifying trail of greed and betrayal, only danger is guaranteed . . .

Survival is not.

Read on for the chilling first chapter

HURRICANE GOLD

There were thirteen men around the table. By the end of the day, one of them would be dead.

Two huge fans in the ceiling turned slowly, stirring the hot, damp air. No breeze came in through the row of open windows that looked out towards the bright blue waters of the Caribbean. A big storm was coming and there was a tense atmosphere. It was the sort of day that gave you a headache.

The men looked like they would all much rather have been somewhere else. A few of them were used to the heat, but most were sweating and uncomfortable. They tugged at their collars, fanned their faces, and pulled sticky shirts away from damp skin.

The man at the head of the table, though, seemed cool and relaxed. He sat perfectly still, staring at the others in silence, a glass of chilled fino sherry standing untouched at his elbow. He was well dressed in the style of a Mexican aristocrat, with an embroidered velvet suit and a frilly cream cravat at his throat held in place with a pearl stud.

He had a flat nose in the middle of a dark brown face

that had the appearance of being carved out of old, hard wood. His thick mop of hair was pure white, as was his neat little Vandyke beard. He might have been forty, or he might have been eighty, it was impossible to tell. His eyes looked like they had lived a thousand years and seen all there was to see.

At last he spoke, in English with a strong Mexican accent.

'Gentlemen,' he said, 'we have a problem.'

'What sort of a problem, El Huracán?' asked a lean, handsome man with a mouth that was permanently set in a mocking smile. He was Robert King, a grifter from Chicago, who had married a wealthy widow, heiress to a diamond fortune, and pushed her from their yacht in the middle of the Atlantic. He had paid off the crew to keep their mouths shut and inherited all her wealth, but the skipper was a drunk and after one too many whiskies in a bar in Nantucket had blabbed the whole story.

The next day the police went looking for King.

King fled the country, but not before he had visited his ex-skipper in his cheap lodging house and quietly slit his throat with a razor.

He had come down here to hide out, his bags stuffed with banknotes and diamonds.

'It is easily solved,' said El Huracán. 'But it is, nevertheless, a serious problem.' He spoke quietly and sounded almost bored.

'How serious?' said King, taking a glass of cool water.

El Huracán stood up and walked to the nearest window, ignoring the question. He waited there, watching the distant waves breaking against the reef.

'Tell me,' he said at last, 'is it not beautiful here on this island?'

There were mumbled yeses from around the table accompanied by the weary nodding of heads.

'Is this not paradise?'

Again there were mumbled yeses.

El Huracán turned back from the window and looked round the tough faces of the men. 'So why would one of you wish to leave?'

There were a couple of grunts and mutterings, but nobody spoke up.

'Here on Lágrimas Negras we have the finest food,' said El Huracán, gesturing at the table, which was, indeed, piled high with dishes: thick steaks, chicken, grilled fish and lobster, sweet potatoes, rice, salad and tropical fruit.

'It is never cold. There is no disease. You never want for anything. Is that not true?'

'Very true, El Huracán . . .' said a fat, sunburnt man with yellow piggy eyes, his white shirt stained grey with sweat. His name was Dum–Dum White. He was a hold-up artist who had robbed a string of banks in the American Midwest with a tommy gun loaded with dumdum bullets. He had skipped south of the border when the rest of his gang had been killed in a shoot-out with FBI agents in Tucson.

'Here, you are all safe,' said El Huracán. 'You and the hundred or so other men and women who have come to my island.'

'That's right,' said Dum–Dum, who was melting in the heat.

'I know how you men hate authority.' The brown-skinned man chuckled. 'You live outside the law. But you accept that there must be a few rules.'

'Yes.'

'You *do* accept that?'

'Certainly. Without rules there'd be chaos,' said another American, Chunks Duhaine. Chunks was a hired killer who had got his nickname from the condition in which he always left his victims.

'You are all quite new here,' said El Huracán, sitting down and taking a sip of sherry. 'But by now you should have learnt my rules. What are they?'

'First rule – you're the boss,' said a man with a wide, almost oriental face and a thin moustache. 'What you say goes.'

This was Abrillo Chacon, a Chilean explosives expert who specialized in blowing banks open at night. In his last job, in Concepción, twelve policemen had been waiting for him, but Chacon had used so much explosives that the entire roof of the bank had fallen in, crushing them to death.

'Correct,' said El Huracán. 'Every gang must have a boss.'

'No problem. You're a swell boss. You run a fine set-up here,' said Chunks.

'Thank you,' said El Huracán. 'It is always so nice to know that one is appreciated.' He looked at the men, taking his time, enjoying their discomfort. 'What are the other rules?' he said eventually.

'All our moneys is kept in you bank,' said a skinny, pockmarked man. This was Aurelio de la Uz. One night Aurelio had followed a mafia gambler who had won a small fortune at a casino in Havana. He shot him through the back of the head, took his winnings and slipped away from Cuba a rich man.

'*Sí*,' said El Huracán, with a slight, elegant nod of his head. 'If you had not come here, you men would be dead or in jail, and your money would be scattered to the wind. Instead you are all alive and happy and your money is well looked after.'

'We ain't got no choice,' said Chunks Duhaine and he laughed mirthlessly.

'If you will forgive me saying,' said El Huracán, 'on an island inhabited entirely by criminals, there might be a danger that one's money was not safe. There are four bank robbers in this room alone. But no one will ever rob my bank, because if they did they would have a hundred of the most heartless killers in the world on their tail.'

'Damned right,' said Dum-Dum. 'Though I must admit that bank of yours sure is one hell of a challenge.'

There was laughter from around the table, and El Huracán joined in before raising a hand for silence.

'And what is the next rule?' he said.

'No communication with the outside world.' This was said by Eugene Hamilton, a small, quiet man wearing spectacles, who had stolen nearly a million dollars from an oil company. He seemed out of place here among these thugs. He looked more like an accountant than an armed robber. This was because he *was* an accountant.

'That is the most important rule of all, gentlemen,' said El Huracán. 'This is a unique place. An island where wanted men may hide out without fear of ever being captured. An island where their crimes do not matter. As long as you have the money to pay for it, you can live in paradise until the end of your days. But we do not want the outside world to know of our doings here. That is most important. So what is the *last* rule?'

'Once we are here we can never leave,' said Luis Chavez, a Mexican gangster.

'I wonder how many of you men would have come here if you had known about this last rule?' said El Huracán.

Once again nobody spoke out. El Huracán laughed.

'This place must remain a secret, a legend, a dream,' he said. 'But somebody in this room has been trying to send letters . . .'

El Huracán stood up and began slowly to circle the table, walking behind the seated men.

'Somebody here has tried to bribe one of my peons to take a message to the outside world. Somebody here wants to leave.'

El Huracán walked to the door and opened it. Two men walked in. They were Mexican Indians, rumoured to be from El Huracán's village deep in the rainforest of the Chiapas in southern Mexico. They were dressed in the same simple white clothing that would have been worn by their ancestors two hundred years ago, but there was nothing primitive about the weapons they were carrying, German MP28 sub-machine guns.

'What is this?' said Robert King.

'We do not want any unpleasantness,' said El Huracán. 'It might lead to indigestion after so lovely a meal.' He then said something softly to one of his men, who handed him a small glass bottle containing a clear liquid.

'What the hell's that?' said Chunks Duhaine. 'What's going on here?'

'It is an antidote,' said El Huracán. 'You see, when I heard about how one of you was planning to betray me, I thought I would solve the problem quickly. I have poisoned his food. Soon he will begin to feel the effects. He will feel hot and dizzy. His throat will grow tight. He will sweat uncontrollably and terrible cramps and spasms will grip his stomach. Then his blood vessels will begin slowly to rupture and he will bleed inside, dark patches will appear on his skin. Within a few minutes he will be dead. Unless, of course, I give him some of this antidote. I took this precaution simply because I knew the man would not voluntarily confess. But now, if he wants to live, he must come forward.'

El Huracán opened a wooden box and took out a syringe. He plunged the needle through the rubber stopper in the end of the bottle and extracted some of the liquid.

For a few moments nobody spoke. There was a terrible silence in the room. Then suddenly Robert King leapt to his feet, his handsome face distorted with fear. He was clutching his stomach and so much sweat was pouring off him it looked like he had just climbed out of a swimming pool.

'You damned snake,' he hissed. 'Give me that . . .'

'This?' said El Huracán innocently, holding up the bottle and the syringe. 'What for?'

'The antidote,' King gasped. 'Give me the antidote, you evil son of a –'

'Antidote?' said El Huracán as he stabbed the needle into a peach and pressed down on the plunger. 'What antidote?'

King looked on in horror. His breath was rasping in his throat as he held out a trembling finger towards the man standing calmly at the head of the table. 'You've murdered me, you swine . . .'

'I have done nothing of the sort, Mister King,' said El Huracán, taking a bite from the fruit. 'You have merely fallen for a cheap child's trick. There was no poison. It is only your own fear that makes you feel this way.'

There was a harsh snort of laughter from Dum-Dum, and Luis Chavez said something quickly in Spanish.

King looked round at the other men, trying to find a friendly face. Nobody would catch his eye.

'I haven't done anything,' he said.

'Then why on earth did you think you had been poisoned?' said El Huracán. 'Nobody else here jumped to their feet. Though I suspected all of you. That is why I invited you all for lunch. How gratifying to see that only one of you has been foolish.'

'I haven't done anything.'

'You have confessed, Mister King. That is all I required.' El Huracán nodded to his guards. 'Take him away,' he said, 'and prepare La Avenida de la Muerte so that I can show the others what happens to anyone who is disloyal.'

'What's an avenida de la muerte?' said Eugene Hamilton.

'An avenue of death,' said Luis Chavez, the Mexican gangster.

'It is my rat run,' said El Huracán with a grin.

BEFORE THE NAME BECAME A LEGEND.
BEFORE THE BOY BECAME THE MAN.

Meet Bond.
James Bond.

SILVERFIN

CHARLIE HIGSON

Death is
contagious

BLOOD FEVER

CHARLIE HIGSON

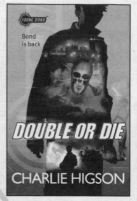

Bond
is back

DOUBLE OR DIE

CHARLIE HIGSON

Greed
is a deadly force

HURRICANE GOLD

CHARLIE HIGSON

For king and
country

BY ROYAL COMMAND

CHARLIE HIGSON

BRAVE THE DANGER WITH JAMES BOND.
youngbond.com

SEE  IN ACTION FOR THE FIRST TIME ...

An **EXCLUSIVE** extract from the

graphic novel

CHARLIE HIGSON & KEV WALKER

It's James Bond's first day at Eton, and already he's met his first enemy. It is the start of an adventure that will take him from the school playing fields to the remote shores of Loch Silverfin and a terrifying discovery that threatens to unleash a new breed of warfare ...

Look out for it in fantastic, full-blown colour!